KEEN EDGE OF VALOR

LIBRI VALORIS III

Edited by Chris Kennedy
& Rob Howell

D1547792

Chris Kennedy/New Mythology Press
1097 Waterlily Rd., Coinjock, NC, 27923
http://chriskennedypublishing.com/

Publisher's Note: This is a work of fiction. Names, characters, places, and incidents are a product of the author's imagination. Locales and public names are sometimes used for atmospheric purposes. Any resemblance to actual people, living or dead, or to businesses, companies, events, institutions, or locales is completely coincidental.

Cover Art and Design by Jake Caleb (https://www.jcalebdesign.com/)

The stories and articles contained herein have never been previously published. They are copyrighted as follows:

Keen Edge of Valor/Chris Kennedy and Rob Howell -- 1st ed.
ISBN

* * * * *

Get the **free** Four Horsemen prelude story **"Shattered Crucible"**

and discover other titles by Seventh Seal Press at:

chriskennedypublishing.com/

* * * * *

Get the free Eldros Legacy anthology **"Here There Be Giants"** at:

dl.bookfunnel.com/qabsr57lq3

* * * * *

Discover other titles by New Mythology Press at:

chriskennedypublishing.com/new-mythology-press/

* * * * *

Dedication

This anthology is about items of legend and myth.

Therefore, it's dedicated to those who create.
The smiths, weavers, jewelers, and tailors;
the brewers, carpenters, painters, and potters.

To all those who reach back into the past and
try to do things as they were once done.

For there is still magic in the doing.

* * * * *

Preface by Rob Howell

Three is a magic number. That's, of course, a great Schoolhouse Rock song, covered really well by Blind Melon, by the way. It's also the *Keen Edge of Valor*, book three in the Libri Valoris series of anthologies.

As usual, my list of acknowledgements starts with Chris Kennedy, who gave me the opportunities to create these anthologies in the first place. I can't thank him enough for all the trust he's given me. As I look at the stories that have already appeared in *When Valor Must Hold*, *Songs of Valor*, and those here, I can take pride that thanks to his support, we've created three excellent anthologies.

Obviously, this means we've had a bunch of great authors involved along the way. Three authors have appeared in all so far, Jon R. Osborne, Benjamin Tyler Smith, and D.J. Butler. I have grown to love the *Milesian Accords*, *Necrolopolis*, and the *Tales of Indrajit and Fix* almost as much as they do because I got to watch these series expand under my watch. And, if the response is any indication, I'm not the only one. They're great stories and I look forward to seeing more in all three universes.

There are other universes here. Casey Moores is just beginning his *Deathmage War* series; a combination of dragons, magic, machinery, and World War One. C.M. DeMott gave me a *House of Drimmett* story, which is a fun young adult series. Jamie Ibson's *Rebels of Westlocke* series makes its second appearance, having debuted in *Songs of Valor*. Mel Todd contributed a story in her *Small Magics* universe, which is focused on a combination private eye/pet whisperer. But, oh, what pets? And let's not forget the new fantasy universe from Mark Wandrey called the *Traveling Gods*. If you follow Mark's stuff already, you know how prolific he is and I'm very much excited to publish more in this series.

The *Eldros Legacy* makes an appearance, of course, as this shared universe continues to grow as well. In this case, it's another Hunter story from Sam Witt. Expect a Hunter novel at some point soon. Aaron Rosenberg's story here isn't in the Eldros Legacy, but his first *Eldros Legacy* novel, *Deadly Fortune*, is going to be published around the time of *Keen Edge of Valor*.

The biggest universe, of course, is another *Black Company* story by Glen Cook. I'm incredibly honored to get to work with him twice now as his *Black Company* and *Garrett, PI* series have long been favorites.

The best part of these anthologies, though, is the open call. Chris Hepler is new to me, but clearly an experienced, talented writer. You're going to love "The Torturer of Camelot." On the other end of the spectrum are Nathan Balyeat and J.A. Miller. I have the great honor to publish their first ever stories, "Fellblade" and "Furrows," respectively. DeMott's story, by the way, rounds out the four finalists for this year's FantaSci contest. At FantaSci, where *Keen Edge of Valor* will be released, I'll announce the winner. Last year's winner, by the way, was James Chandler.

Oh, wait, I was thanking people and I got distracted by getting to talk about the great stories in here. Joel Lyons and the crew at FantaSci entrusted their writing challenge to me, for which I'm greatly honored.

I've had a great developmental team coalesce around New Mythology Press, for which I'm very grateful. Jake Caleb has done all three covers for the *Libri Valoris*, and you can see why, what with the amazing art he's produced each time. Tiffany Reynolds was our editor this time, and she does a great job in record time.

With that, it's time for me to let you read these fourteen great stories in here, each with a keen edge and valorous deeds. Enjoy!

— Rob Howell

Table of Contents

* * * * *

The Silver Hand
by Jon R. Osborne
An Accords Universe Tale

"Your boyfriend is back," Meghan sing-songed as she leaned on the bar.

Grace set the two beers for Meghan's table on the tray. "Boyfriend?"

"That cute cop you've been seeing." Meghan flashed an impish smile. As if on cue, Luke Dahler rounded the corner. He adjusted his deputy hat as he spotted Grace. Meghan sighed. "I do appreciate a man in uniform."

Luke sidled onto a stool away from other patrons. Grace eyed the handful of customers at the bar—last thing she needed was someone complaining that she was socializing instead of fetching them another beer.

"What brings you in? A hard day chasing perps?" she asked. They'd only gone on a couple of dates, and again as many casual outings. She liked Luke, but didn't want to rush things, especially given her unusual side-gig fighting supernatural threats.

"I wish it was beer-thirty," Luke replied with a grin. "Unfortunately, I'm on department business. You got time to look at something? If not, I can wait until the end of your shift."

She glanced at the empty ticket printer. "What can I do for you?"

Luke held out his phone and lowered his voice. "What do you make of this?"

A video showed security camera footage for the entrance of an antiquated building flanked by bushy hedges. One of the bushes rustled, and a small form emerged from the night. The dim lighting washed the color from the picture. He stood about four feet tall, and wore simple garb, with a leather vest and a dark woolen cap. At first, Grace took the short, stocky man for a tomte or a brownie— diminutive helper-folk. As the figure turned dead, shark-like eyes toward the camera and flashed a wicked grin of serrated teeth, a chill ran down Grace's spine—redcap.

Three more redcaps joined the first, two taking watch, while the third produced a handful of slender metal tools. He prodded at the door's lock with one tool after another, shaking his head in agitation with each failure.

"Hurry! Get the door open," the first redcap snarled in Goidelc, an Irish-like patois used by supernatural folk.

"It's warded. My picks can't trip the tumblers by magic, and these confounded dunnie locks are too tiny for even nimble work," the other complained.

The door thumped, then opened. "What do y'all think you're doing?" A barking dog accompanied the demand.

"Maybe we should have knocked." The first redcap flashed a malevolent grin and drew a long, wicked knife from behind his back.

The other dropped his tools and brandished his own blade. "Knock knock, stab stab!"

"Y'all better step back before I sic Zeus on you." A rumbling growl punctuated the dog's barks.

"Move it, meat, or we'll carve both of you up!" the redcap ordered in English. He twirled his weapon.

Grace jumped at the gun shot, fumbling the phone. The nearest customer cast a curious glance but returned to the game on the television. In the video, the redcap staggered a step and brushed at his shoulder before cackling. Two more center-mass impacts had little effect. The dog lunged forward through the cloud of smoke from the discharged firearm, clamping its jaws on the redcap's knife arm, and driving the fae to the ground.

The rear guards spun toward the commotion, producing more knives. The gun *boomed* three more times. The redcap closest to the camera reeled back, clutching an eye, while one of the ones in the rear flinched twice.

A redcap jabbed at the dog, eliciting a yelp. A uniformed man stepped into view as he kicked the fae who'd stabbed the dog. The small fae stumbled out of the camera's field of view. With his free hand, the lockpicker slashed his blade at the new arrival.

"Sonuvabitch!"

Zeus leapt on the lockpicker, again seizing the arm wielding the weapon. The fourth redcap charged Zeus, his knife raised high. The man blocked the blade with his left arm. The redcap slashed at the limb, but the blade clattered off something solid beneath the guard's sleeve. The man planted his boot in the redcap's chest, sending the fae stumbling backward. Two gunshots tore holes in the small otherfolk's jacket, the impact driving him out of camera view.

The lockpicker struggled to free his arm from Zeus' grip until the guard turned and brained the fae with his pistol. The redcap fell limp and crumpled to the ground. A moment later, he faded from view, leaving the dog to snap at empty air.

"What the hell?" the guard muttered, barely loud enough for the audio to pick up.

"The bloody dunnie killed Colm!" one of the redcaps cried off camera in Goidelc.

The man snapped out of his stunned stupor. "Zeus! Heel!"

The dog growled into the night but backed toward the guard, favoring one of its hind legs. Aiming his weapon beyond the camera's field of view, the guard retreated into the building, urging the dog every step. Once the man disappeared through the door, the video ended.

Grace checked the patrons. One, a regular named Gus, nodded at his near empty glass. The others remained enraptured by the game. The printer spit out another order. "Let me catch up."

Luke nodded. He'd visited her a few times at work, and understood that her job, as cruddy as it might be, came before chatting with him—even about supernatural matters. It only took her a couple minutes to get Gus a refill and pour Meghan's order. When Meghan picked up the beers, she winked theatrically.

"You see why I need to consult an expert for this case," Luke said once Grace returned. "How much can you fill in for me?"

Grace kept her voice low. "Those were redcaps—otherfolk killers-for-hire with a fetish for knives."

"Could you make out what they were saying?" Luke asked.

Grace nodded. "Goidelc. I'm still learning, but I was able to piece together what they said." She gave Luke a quick rundown. "They're not conversationalists or academics."

Luke studied the frozen video. "When does your shift end?"

"In about half an hour. I spotted my relief, Kelsie, so I'm not getting stuck with a double," Grace replied.

"Feel like riding along? I'm going to see if I can get anything out of the guard they might have missed in the initial interview. I could buy dinner afterward," Luke suggested.

Grace took a quick mental stock of her homework. Troubleshooting supernatural problems had dug into her study time, but the compensation meant fewer shifts at Safari Jack's. "As long as we eat somewhere, we can order from the table."

Luke clapped a hand over his heart. "Ouch—still holding Grill Duke against me? They may be in an old fast-food place, but you have to admit, the fare made up for it. I still maintain they serve the best burgers in Central Illinois."

"I admit nothing." The burgers had been awesome, even if the plastic booths left over from the restaurant's previous incarnation were uncomfortable. "If I'm going to play subject-matter expert, I deserve seating with a pretense of upholstery and sit-down service."

"You drive a hard bargain. How about, once we talk to the guard, I take you to Brickhouse Grille?"

Grace smiled. "You have a deal, Deputy."

* * *

Grace eyed the limestone-columned building as they pulled into the tiny parking lot. "What is this place?"

"An old Masonic lodge," Luke replied. Only two other vehicles occupied the dozen spaces. "I'm not sure if it's a predecessor of the current one, or part of a splinter branch. My grandfather was a Mason, but he never talked about it."

"Safari Jack's is bigger than this place," Grace observed. "Other than being old, what's special about it?"

"I was hoping you could fill me in. The current owner, Ambrose Argus III, was less than forthcoming. He said it belonged to his grandfather, and nothing else."

"You understand I'm not a magical Geiger counter, right? I fight otherworld threats, but for the esoteric stuff, you need to consult with the Druid." Grace reached for her phone. "Want me to text him?"

"The last time I e-mailed him, it took five days to get an answer," Luke countered.

Grace tapped at her phone. "I sent him a message. I can tack on more once we interview this guard. The Druid usually gets back to me in a day. It depends on how long it takes for his girlfriend to prod him to check his phone."

Luke sighed. A year ago, his job as a Peoria County deputy bordered on boring. That was before Central Illinois became a hotbed for supernatural activity. "It would be easier if we could call him."

"That's for emergencies. Redcaps trying to burglarize an old landmark doesn't qualify."

Luke led the way to the door, which was illuminated by a single bright bulb. Dark, rusty stains mottled the concrete of the sidewalk before the door. Luke jabbed the doorbell. "You said redcaps are faerie assassins. Why would they stoop to breaking and entering?"

Grace shrugged. "Depends on what their boss offered. Plus, the Druid has zero tolerance for hits on the Dunwold—the mundane world—so their traditional work may have dried up."

A pair of *clunks* preceded the door cracking open. The security guard peered out, and an unseen dog sniffed behind him. "This isn't a public site."

Luke flashed his badge. "Deputy Luke Dahler. I'm here to follow up on the incident from yesterday."

The guard eyed Grace. Luke couldn't blame him. Even though she'd changed from her revealing work uniform of khaki shorts and a midriff-baring, tied khaki shirt, Grace's mixed heritage and athletic physique drew attention. "You always bring your girlfriend to work, Deputy?"

Grace scowled, but Luke cut off any retort. "Miss Ramirez is here as a subject-matter expert."

"We are sorely in need of expert advice," a cultured voice behind the guard intoned. "Gavin, please admit our visitors."

The guard swung the door open. A bit taller than Luke, and a decade older, the man exuded "eff around and find out." The German Shepherd at his side did nothing to alter that impression. The dog eyed Luke and Grace.

A middle-aged man in an expensive suit stood beyond the guard. He pushed up his glasses. "We've already given our statements to the police, Deputy. Do you have news?"

"Mr. Argus?" Luke waited for the man's nod. "I have some additional questions if you don't mind. Miss Ramirez's expertise may help us shed more light on the unusual nature of the incident."

"Please, come in," he said. "I'm Argus. This is Gavin Wirth, our security guard."

The guard closed and locked the door behind them. Luke spotted the metal prongs of a prosthetic sticking out of the guard's left sleeve. "You fought off the intruders last night?"

The guard glanced at Argus before replying. "Yes. I gave my statement last night—not that they believed me."

"I've watched the security video, Mr. Wirth. That's why I sought outside help," Luke stated. "We have a few follow up questions for you as well."

The guard shrugged. "I have nothing to hide."

"We can talk in the office," Argus said, beckoning for them to follow him down a wide marble hall suitable for the interior of a mausoleum. Wooden benches and small tables lined the walls. Doorways led into dark rooms on either side of the hall. Luke's boots echoed on the marble floor as he followed Argus into the office. Grace padded silently alongside him, scrutinizing the walls as though searching for something hidden.

"Please, have a seat." Argus gestured to an antique upholstered divan as he circled behind a huge walnut desk at least a century old. Bookshelves vied with old oil paintings for wall space, but a rug and thick velvet curtains over the lone window dampened the echo off the stone floor and walls. "I'm sorry to be a poor host, but we don't have any refreshments handy."

"That's fine, Mr. Argus." Luke pulled out a small notebook and a pencil.

"What is this place?" Grace asked, scanning along the edge of the ceiling.

Argus adjusted his glasses again. "It belonged to a splinter group of Masons. My grandfather's grandfather acquired it during the Great Depression, and the family has used it as something of a museum. I inherited it when my grandfather passed last year, and I haven't decided what to do with it yet. It's too small for a proper event venue, and too expensive for storage space."

"Do you have any idea what the intruders were after?" Luke asked.

"My grandfather possessed a number of unusual and esoteric heirlooms. I don't think any of them hold significant monetary value, but perhaps the men who accosted Gavin were misinformed."

"Did your grandfather dabble in the occult?" Grace asked. *Thank god they didn't serve us coffee—Luke would have sputtered it all over the vintage Persian rug.*

Argus leaned back and steepled his fingers. "An interesting question, Miss Ramirez."

Grace snorted. "I'll take that as a 'yes.' Why would someone hire redcaps to steal something from you—or rather, your grandfather? Please don't waste our time by playing dumb." *Yup, the coffee would have ended up all over the rug.*

"Fine, I won't play dumb, but I also won't pretend to know what's going on. Supernatural dwarves with knives tried to break in, and one vanished right in front of Gavin, leaving behind his weapon and tools—which are in police custody. While I might have chalked up such a tale to PTSD or some such, I watched the video, as well." Argus levelled his gaze at Grace. "You called them 'redcaps.' I suspect you know far more than I do, Miss Ramirez. I'm also beginning to suspect my grandfather wasn't as crazy as I thought."

"Why is that?" Luke tapped on the blank notebook page with his pencil.

"My namesake, Ambrose Argus I, was fascinated by mythology and legend. He swore this building was protected. If he hadn't also been a shrewd businessman, he very well could have bankrupted the family, between this place and frequent trips in search of additions to his collection."

"You mentioned this used to be a Masonic Temple. Was your grandfather a Mason?" Luke asked.

"Not the traditional Freemasons, but a splinter group. Technically, I'm a member as well—my grandfather paid for my father's membership, and mine—but I haven't attended any functions since I was twelve. As I understand it, the Enochian Masons have all but vanished. This place could easily accommodate their surviving membership."

"That explains it," Grace muttered. "How much do you want to bet these Enochian Masons performed magic? They probably warded this place when they built it."

"I thought magic was snuffed out until this year? How could someone have put a spell on this place a century ago?" Luke asked.

Grace shrugged. "I don't know all the details. I'm not even sure the Druid knows everything, and he's supposedly the expert. During the exile of the supernatural folk, the Avramites had power of their own, even if it was minimal. There was something in the Accords stating whatever magic the winners used on our world, the losers could access as well."

Argus watched the exchange intently. "I may have to revisit my grandfather's journals. He mentioned Avramites several times. I assumed they were another Masonic faction. What are redcaps—our would-be burglars?"

"They're fae who specialize in murder-for-hire. I guess they branched out into breaking-and-entering," Grace replied. "They wanted your guard out of the way. If he hadn't intervened, they might not have attacked—which, from what I know of redcaps, is unusual."

"Maybe they were afraid if they left a trail of bodies, the Druid would sic you on them?" Luke mentally bit his tongue—should he divulge so much in front of Argus? While the veil of secrecy around magic was an increasingly leaky sieve, Grace might not want people to know she acted as a supernatural enforcer.

Argus stood. "Let's take a look at my grandfather's collection. Maybe you can figure out what these redcaps sought."

In the hall, Gavin emerged from a door next to the entrance. Luke assumed it led to a cloakroom-turned-security office, based on the flickering light of monitors behind him. "Everything okay, Mr. Argus?"

"Yes, Gavin. Actually, Deputy Dahler and Miss Ramirez have answered more questions than me, but they've left me twice as many new ones." Argus led them into one of the side rooms and reached for a switch. A handful of incandescent bulbs flicked on; a few remained dark, leaving pools of shadows.

At first glance, the room appeared to house a small museum collection. Display cases lined the walls and formed an island in the middle of the marble-floored room. The closest case held the tattered remains of patinaed bronze armor and a corroded blade. Scraps of faded cloth were draped over a rack in the next one, with faded knotwork and the weird hashmark druidic script barely visible. A third held tableware, as though a time traveler had gone back and nicked it from centuries ago. A quick scan of the remaining glass cases showed nothing of any particular monetary value.

"What is this junk?" Grace mirrored Luke's thoughts.

Argus placed his hand on a case. "As I said, my ancestors traveled widely and bought historical artifacts. Except not from any history books I could trace. The armor and sword by the door supposedly belonged to Olhwch, the grandson of Culhwch. The only reference I found was that the grandfather was named after a character in a Welsh fairy tale."

"What if it was *the* Culhwch from the Welsh legend?" Grace suggested.

"That's ridiculous," Gavin said from the doorway.

"After your brawl with the seven dwarves' evil cousins last night, I thought you might be a little more open-minded," Grace rejoined.

"I know it's a lot to take in, but I've learned over the last couple months, there's a lot more to the world than what we learned in school," Luke said. "It sounds crazy, but magic is real, and a lot of myths and legends have a kernel of truth."

"Maybe they're after a relic or legendary artifact." Grace circled the room, peering in the assorted cases.

"How can you tell? It all looks like old junk to me." Luke followed her progress, watching for a magic lamp or an enchanted sword.

"We should call in the Druid," she said. "I'm out of my depth. He or his fiancée might recognize something. I've been focusing on things I might have to fight, not what could show up at a faerie flea market."

Argus adjusted his glasses. "Who is this 'Druid' you keep mentioning?"

"Is he like Gandalf or something?" Gavin added.

Grace stifled a laugh. "He's not some old wizard. Think of him as one part ambassador for the supernatural folk, one part adjudicator of magic on our world, and one part clergy for the old gods. Unfortunately, he's almost as new at his job as I am."

"Huh. They had prosthetics back in fairy tale times?" Gavin remarked. He tapped a case in one of the shadowed portions of the room. Luke peered through the dusty glass. A dull, tarnished metal forearm and hand rested on a faded red pillow.

"Go ahead and call this Druid. If nothing else, I'm curious to meet him. Maybe he can enlighten me on my grandfather's hobby," Argus stated.

"What I'd like to know is how those things took semi-jacketed hollow points without noticing," said Gavin. "I might as well have been shooting a BB gun at the bastards."

Luke nodded to Gavin's holstered pistol. "What are you packing?"

Gavin patted the holster. "Nothing fancy, just a 1911 .45 ACP.

"Too bad. I have a 9mm, otherwise I'd give you some of my elfshot," Luke said. "The supernaturals have magic protecting them from lead. You need steel, tungsten, silver, or another metal that isn't copper, tin, or lead."

* * *

The blackbird landed on the windowsill and tapped on the glass. Gabe sighed. He'd given the redcaps a burner phone, but they still insisted on messenger birds. Gabe slid open the window. "Good news, I hope?"

The blackbird whistled twice. "We tried breaking in, boss, but the dunnies had a warrior standing guard. He killed Colm. We had to retreat. We need more muscle. Subtle won't cut it."

Gabe drummed his fingers on the small table next to the chair. "Fine. I'll send someone to lend a hand. I want the item in question. If you fail me, no payment. Next time, use the phone I gave you."

Gabe paused and fished out some french fries from his lunch. The blackbird gobbled the cold fries. "Deliver my message."

It would take the messenger bird an hour to return to the redcaps. He considered his options. Using the redcaps had been risky enough, given their violent proclivities. If the First Druid caught wind, he'd come sniffing around, or send one of his accursed champions. Gabe rubbed the end of his truncated limb. He harbored no desire to run afoul of one of the dunnie warriors again.

Gabe tapped on his phone. "Tam? Yeah, I need to bring in a bruiser. What do we have in the area?"

"Depends on how messy you want to get. The boys have talked about trying to squeeze a fathach through a ford, but they're tough to control. My cousin knows a guy, Sudr Half-Giant, who bounces at the new club in south Joliet. He can pass for a dunnie with a big coat and dim light."

"Sounds perfect. I need him for a job in Peoria right away. What's his preferred currency?"

There was a moment of silence on the other end. Gabe hoped it wouldn't be something outrageous such as human flesh or dragon scales. "I know it sounds weird, but he's been hot for this big truck he saw on the television."

* * *

"We don't need help," Lot protested. "We catch the dunnie and his dog outside, and make with the stabbing."

Bain glared with his remaining eye. The dunnie guard had fired bullets ringed with steel. While they stung, there wasn't enough steel to do serious harm, except for the round that struck Bain in the eye. Even blood-magic couldn't mend it. "If we're getting messy, we might as well bring a hand to replace Colm. Besides, he was our doorman, so we need a bruiser. That door is the only part of the building not warded."

"Stupid dunnies. They broke their own wards by replacing the original door with a newfangled one." Cean grinned.

The phone buzzed. Bain picked up the infernal device and flipped it open. At least it didn't have one of those brain-rotting screens. "The boss is sending some guy named Half-Giant. Should be here by sundown."

"I heard of him!" Lot said. "He's part Fomor, part Jotunn, and has rune-magic tattoos."

Bain frowned. "Think he'll double-cross us and take the prize himself?"

"He's half Fomor, half Jotunn. I think that adds up to yes," Cean remarked. "So we double-cross him first!"

* * *

Mr. Argus slid a desk drawer shut as Gavin entered the office. "I'm about to leave for the evening, Gavin."

"Do you believe them?" Gavin asked. "I've seen some messed-up shit—I mean stuff—and the dead guy disappearing into thin air beats it all, but I still think all this talk of magic is far-fetched."

"It's safer to take them at face value and find out they were wrong rather than fail to prepare and discover the hard way they were telling the truth." He handed Gavin a blackened lump of metal. "Take these and have your friend melt them into bullets or buckshot."

"What are they?" Gavin turned the mass over in his hands. It consisted of smaller pieces, possibly coins, accreted together.

"A trove of silver coins my great-grandfather didn't judge worthy of work, let alone display. I suppose this lends some credence to the legends of using silver bullets on werewolves and vampires."

"If these fae folk and murder dwarves are real, do werewolves and vampires exist as well?" Gavin asked. Maybe he should swing by a church and see if he could get holy water.

Mr. Argus smiled. "I asked the same question as they were leaving. The young lady assured me they don't walk the world as depicted in pop culture. Some creatures have animalistic features, or drink blood, but they bear little resemblance to popular stories. Let's focus on our short, larcenous friends."

Gavin shoved the lump in his coat pocket. "Come on, Zeus."

The German Shepherd emerged from the security office. He still had a slight hitch in his step, but luckily the blade hadn't severed anything. A dozen stitches and a couple of weeks, and the dog would be right as rain.

The half hour drive across the river helped clear Gavin's head. He hadn't elaborated on the phone to his buddy Mitch, other than telling him he needed custom reloads for his sidearm. Better to answer any questions in person.

Gavin pulled into the gravel parking lot behind the Gun Bunker. Mitch dealt mostly in supplies and accessories, even though he had the licenses to deal in firearms. The door jingled as Gavin entered what resembled a military surplus flea market crammed into a 30' x 40' building.

Cindy, one of the clerks, looked up at the chime. "Hey, Gavin. Hello, Zeus." The other clerk, Harry, nodded. Cindy pointed to one of the doors at the rear of the cluttered showroom. "Mitch is back in the shop. He said to expect you."

As Gavin reached the door, Harry buzzed him through. The back room went from chaotic to claustrophobic. Gavin picked his way through to another door and rapped on it. After a moment, a bolt clunked aside.

"Hey, buddy, how are things?" Mitch asked, stepping aside to admit Gavin and Zeus.

"Pretty weird, to be honest." Gavin set the blackened metal lump on a workbench. As opposed to the rest of the building, Mitch kept his workshop orderly. "I need you to make silver bullets for my .45. Can you do it?"

Mitch poked at the tarnished mass of silver. "Do I want to know why? I've heard some weird shit over the past few months. You hunting werewolves?"

Gavin shook his head. "Supposedly werewolves aren't a thing, but... shit, you'd think I was crazy if I told you. Better you just make me the bullets."

"Two months ago, I'd say the sandbox got to you, or maybe you were tripping on something, but like I said, things have gotten weird." Mitch reached over to another bench and set down a 12-gauge round. "A buddy of mine in Metamora, another gun nut, has been making these for a handful of customers, including a couple of Feds."

"Shotgun ammo? What's so special about it?"

"Instead of buckshot, they're packed with tungsten carbide bearings. Even using factory seconds, they cost a pretty penny, but Zeke's buyers don't care," Mitch replied. "Tungsten carbide is denser than lead or silver, but it's harder. He makes bullets, also, but those are a pain because the metal is so tough."

Gavin frowned. "Won't they punch through a target? You'd lose stopping power."

"I don't care, as long as they're willing to pay." Mitch chuckled. "Silver is lighter and harder than lead, so you lose on both counts. Sure that's what you want?"

"Could you get me those tungsten bullets by tomorrow?" Gavin asked.

Mitch shook his head and gestured to a bench. "I don't have the gear to machine something as hard as tungsten carbide. I could knock out silver bullets tonight. Do you want the shotgun rounds? I have six."

"I have a 12-gauge, but I don't use it." Gavin tapped the hook of his prosthetic on the wooden surface of the workbench. "Hard to draw a bead with a longarm and one hand."

"How close you going to get to these not-werewolves?" Mitch asked. He hefted the lump of silver. "Give me half of this, and I'll toss them in with the bullets."

Mr. Argus hadn't told him how many bullets to get. "Sounds fair. I'll swing by tomorrow on my way to work."

* * *

"What do you think?" Luke asked as he parked the car in front of Grace's apartment building. The aroma of the pizza from the Brickhouse Pub made his stomach rumble.

"The rich dude played forthcoming, but he was still holding something back," Grace replied. "How much have you dug into him and the guard?"

"Argus didn't have anything interesting in his background, other than a couple of tax audits about a decade ago, and a messy divorce. Nothing smacked of secret occult fraternity squirreling away artifacts. The guard is a vet who lost his hand in Afghanistan ten years ago, had a couple drunk and disorderlies after leaving the Army, but he got his shit together and has had nothing since."

Grace pursed her lips. "Something seemed... off about him, but I can't put my finger on it. Let's take the pizza in before you climb into the back seat after it."

Grace's long-haired cat Taz greeted them at the door, protesting her half-empty food dish. The cat eyed Luke warily for a moment, then dismissed him as irrelevant to getting fed. She followed Grace into the kitchen, voicing her displeasure.

"Do you want a beer with your pizza?" Grace asked.

"Sure. I'm off duty." Luke had been in her apartment once before, but never at the end of an evening. Their relationship still hovered in the nebulous zone.

Once Grace fed her complaining cat, she fished a couple of beers out of the fridge. She handed one to Luke. The label read "Harter's Brewing—Kiss The Anvil Stout." "Knox put me onto this brand. Fair warning, it packs more punch than Guinness. More than two, and you'll have to spend the night here."

"Is that a warning, or an invitation?" Luke asked. Suddenly, the room warmed.

Grace turned away to hide her blush. "You're only getting two— tonight. Back to the case, what are we missing?"

"I suspect Argus knows what the redcaps were after, and it wasn't on display. Call it a hunch." Luke took a swig of the beer. The thick stout almost hid the burn of the high alcohol content. He checked the label—the stout was more than twice as potent as Guinness. "There's probably a basement with more stuff tucked away from prying eyes."

"The other large room was empty except for a table and stacks of chairs pushed against one wall," Grace remarked. Luke didn't know whether she merely had excellent night vision, or if seeing in the dark was a side benefit of her mantle as a supernatural champion. "There couldn't have been much else, given the size of the building, once you figure in the office, a bathroom, and a breakroom or kitchen."

"Since Argus isn't the one suspected of a crime, we lack leverage to press him on what he's hiding, if anything." Luke took another drink. More than two, and he wouldn't *want* to drive. "What now?"

Grace slid next to him on the couch. "We're stuck until the Druid takes a look at Argus' mini museum. He might suss out something we can't see. Might as well enjoy our beers—but only two."

* * *

"The dog is back." Cean glared through a pair of binoculars. "Accursed hound. It will sniff us out through our glamour."

"Don't worry about the dog," a deep voice grumbled from the back.

"You didn't get mauled by the beast," Bain snapped. His arm still hurt. He'd ordered his fellows to load up on the knives. While all the redcaps had their favorite weapons, extras would come in handy for throwing and as backups.

"Can't fight something you can't stab in the back from the shadows?" Sudr Half-Giant chuckled with a bass rumble. "How long do we have before the dunnie town guard arrives once we raise a ruckus?"

The rube hadn't even been on the Dunwold long enough to learn proper terms. "They're called *police*. Once someone sounds the alarm, we have five or ten minutes before the first arrive. Once they realize they're outclassed, it will quickly turn into a proper donnybrook."

"I'll deal with the dunnies; you find the prize," Sudr said, as though he was leading the caper. Bain couldn't wait to be rid of the hulking lout. "Joliet Gabe is paying me based on success, so don't foul up the job."

"Same goes for us, and we have a score to settle. There's a one-handed guard who killed Colm. We mean to avenge him with blood," Bain said.

"Buckets of blood!" Lot added.

Sudr grunted. "I don't care about your grudges. I want my truck."

"Hog piss! Two more dunnies showed up," Cean reported. "We shouldn't have waited for sunset."

"I hate the sun," Sudr countered. "The daystar burns me."

"Sure you aren't more troll than giant?" Lot muttered, earning a low grumble in reprise.

"Bicker and bollocks later," Bain barked, adjusting his eye-patch. Maybe a healer in Green Onion could heal him once they wrapped up this caper. "We want to be in and out. Remember, wards protect every other door and window."

"Even leaving the building?" Sudr asked.

"Hard to say, and I'll leave behind anyone who wanders off and gets stuck. Best not chance it."

Sudr shrugged and opened the side door of the van. The vehicle rose on its shocks as he climbed out. The large bruiser padded across the gravel parking lot with surprising stealth.

"We going to knock knock this time?" Cean whispered as they slunk through the shadows. Only a single light cast a pool of illumination on the lot and entrance of the building. They crept along the bushes to maintain the cover of darkness as long as possible.

Bain shook his head. "If it's locked, Sudr will knock for us. Remember, grab the prize first, stab second."

"We owe the dunnie for Colm," Lot protested, earning a cautioning glance from Sudr.

"We're redcaps, not filchers," Cean added.

"Noisy is what you are," Sudr grumbled. He stepped out of the shadows cast by the hedges and approached the solid metal door. He rolled up the sleeves of his coat, and runes etched into his skin flared with an amber light. He raised both fists over his head and slammed them into the door.

* * *

"Knox should be here in a few minutes," Grace said.

"Is he appearing in person this time?" Luke asked. Argus cocked his head. Luke didn't know how to explain the druid's ability to appear as a phantom. "It's a long story."

The dog growled toward the door. The security guard's hand slid to his holster. "You hear something, Zeus?"

Luke unsnapped his own holster. The door reverberated under a gonging blow. Strange white letters illuminated in sparking silver light along the door frame. The guard dashed for his office as a second blow blasted the metal door off its hinges. The door clipped the guard, bouncing him off the door frame before he stumbled into the office.

A huge man clad in a trench coat and fedora lurched through the doorway. His rolled-up sleeves exposed gleaming amber runes tattooed into his skin. His voice rumbled as if from the depths of a gravel pit. "Knock, knock."

Grace reached behind her back and drew a dull metal machete from thin air. "Who's there? Because you're about to get an ass-whooping."

The huge man cracked his knuckles. "You must be one of those champions the tricksters and filch-hobs have been wetting themselves over. You don't look all that impressive. I'd rather bed you than fight you."

Luke drew his 9mm pistol and leveled it at the intruder. Zeus growled and snapped, edging toward the open office door. A trio of short men in rust-red woolen caps emerged from behind the large rune-armed man. The one with an eyepatch barked orders in something that sounded Irish.

Ambrose Argus stepped forward and pulled a gold amulet from his suit jacket pocket. "I know why you're here, and you shan't have it! Get thee back, dwellers of the otherworld! In the name of Saint Andrew the Hermit, I abjure you!" He brandished the amulet, dangling it from a gold chain clenched in his fist.

All the invaders froze, staring at the amulet for a split second. Eyepatch broke the silence with a wicked laugh. "Pretty necklace."

"You're under arrest. Drop your weapons and get on the floor!" Luke yelled.

"You'll be the one on the floor." The huge man stepped forward.

"I warned you." Luke squeezed off two shots, both punching through the trench coat at center mass.

The huge man brushed at his chest. "Ow. That actually hurt, you Dunget. I'm going to smash you, free of charge."

"Forget about me?" Grace asked, stepping into his path. She lashed out with her machete; the blade drew sparks and blood as the huge man blocked it with his arm. Her opponent winced and swung a backhand at Grace's head. She danced back and flicked her weapon out as the limb passed.

"Oath!" the large man grunted. Another crimson line dripped blood down his arm.

"Druid-forged meteor iron." Grace twirled the machete into a ready position. "It's not too late for you to stand down."

Meanwhile, the redcaps fanned out into the adjacent rooms. Shattered glass tinkled off the marble floor in the display room. The guard emerged from the security office with a shotgun.

* * *

Gavin's ears rang, both from the hammer-blows on the metal door and slamming into the doorframe of the security office. He suspected the big guy would laugh off the silver bullets. Two pops from a 9mm echoed off the stone floors and paneled walls.

"Ow. That actually hurt, you Dunget! I'm going to smash you, free of charge!"

Yeah, the pistol, even a .45, wouldn't cut it. Shooting a 12-guage one-handed would suck, but if the intruder went down, Gavin could take a sprained wrist.

As Gavin stepped into the doorway, one of the redcaps dashed past. Zeus latched onto the dwarf's boot, sending him sprawling. The redcap twisted and slashed with a wicked knife, but Zeus flinched back out of reach.

The other two redcaps skittered into the display room and hammered at the cases with the pommels of their knives. Shattering glass raining onto the stone floor added to the cacophony.

The woman—Grace—fenced with the huge man. Gavin dismissed the shot at his back. Some of the pellets could miss his target and hit the people beyond. Then the brute grabbed a wooden bench and swung it one-handed. Grace twisted away, but the end of the bench clipped her, sending her flying.

Gavin leveled the shotgun, stepped in, and squeezed the trigger. *BOOM!* Half a dozen tungsten carbide pellets shredded the trench coat and elicited a roar. Gavin's target spun faster than he'd thought possible. Recoil had jerked the shotgun out of position, so all Gavin could do was block with his prosthetic.

"You'll pay for that!" the brute growled as he seized Gavin's artificial limb and squeezed. Cracking plastic and wrenching metal accompanied the huge man twisting his grip. One of the straps holding Gavin's artificial arm in place popped loose—failsafes in case the arm snagged on something. Gavin dropped the shotgun— he had no way to pump it. The gun clattered off the stone and skidded toward the display room.

"YARG!" Grace stabbed the brute, and he flung Gavin like a ragdoll, the remaining strap of his prosthetic tearing away in the process. Gavin twisted to try to catch himself as he slammed into the pair of redcaps, bowling the small fae heads over heels. Something metallic skittered across the marble floor.

One squirmed under Gavin, while the other—the one wearing an eyepatch—scrambled to his feet and drew a rusty knife. Gavin rolled aside before the fae under him found his own weapon. Broken glass poked him, but it beat getting stabbed. Instead of rushing Gavin, the upright redcap scanned the wreckage of the room—they'd quickly ransacked half a dozen cases and spilled the contents on the floor.

Gavin followed the redcap's gaze as he locked onto his quarry. The strange metal prosthetic lay against the base of a display a few feet from Gavin. The short man trundled forward, freezing when Gavin drew his pistol.

"Move aside, dunnie, and I won't carve you up," Eye-patch sneered. "I just want the prize."

"A good reason not to let you have it." Gavin kept his gun trained on the redcap. In the hall, the battle between the large man in the trench coat and the machete-wielding woman raged on. The cop yelled for her to get clear. Meanwhile, Zeus barked—presumably at the third redcap.

The other redcap groaned and rolled to his feet. "I want his liver for Colm."

"Give me the hand, dunnie." The redcap's lone eye flicked from Gavin to the metal limb. Behind him, his partner collected a dagger off the floor and scurried behind the cluster of display cases in the middle of the room.

* * *

The runes flared on the huge man's arms as he snatched another bench and wielded it like an over-sized baseball bat. Grace ducked the swing—she'd learned early on that supernatural strength only flexed the laws of physics. Blocking a 100-pound piece of furniture with her machete meant getting clobbered.

On the flip side, it made the brute slow to recover. Grace rolled from the duck and slashed with her weapon. The meteor-iron blade bit through the coat and his pants, drawing blood. That meant his coat didn't have a layer of armor magically folded into it like her hoodie. However, her blow didn't bite deep into his flesh. She could cleave a tree as thick as her arm with the machete, but it had only left a shallow cut.

Luke popped off a single shot while she ducked low, but caution sent the bullet high. Grace rolled away as the bench smashed into the marble floor, cracking the stone and splintering the wood. The big man lobbed the remains of the bench at Luke and Argus, knocking the men over.

Grace and the bruiser circled. Her weapon canceled his reach, but his resilience meant she couldn't count on landing a telling blow. He feinted and stepped in with a sweeping kick at her knee. Grace almost danced out of the way, but the glancing blow sent pain lancing through her leg. A few wary steps showed she could put her weight on it, as long as she didn't mind it hurting.

The bruiser grabbed another small table and threw it, but Grace twisted aside to let it shatter on the wall. She launched a volley of quick swings and stabs, aiming for his arms and hands. Once he yanked his limbs out of the way, she slashed at his side, slicing open the coat, but his counterpunch left Grace gasping for breath.

Another exchange left her opponent with two more cuts, but with every blow, the runes on his skin flashed. In return, he landed another bruising punch that might have cracked a rib. She tried to maneuver to expose him for Luke, but the bruiser didn't fall for it. He grabbed at her blade, willing to risk a cut to disarm her, but

Grace had no illusions regarding how she'd fare in an unarmed fight. She twirled the machete and left another gash on his arm for the attempt.

"Not bad." A smile split her opponent's craggy face. He squared up his arms, she spun her machete once, and they circled.

* * *

Even over the din in the hall, the crunch of broken glass gave the other redcap away. Gavin switched targets as the fae emerged around the display, charging forward. Gavin squeezed off a shot. As opposed to the previous encounter, this time, the bullet punched a bloody hole in the fae's chest. The redcap dropped his knife and toppled backward.

Eyepatch scurried for the antique prosthetic, but his boots skidded on the broken glass. Gavin fired as the redcap fell. The shot went high, spanging off a marble column flanking the doorway. As Eyepatch scrambled for his footing, Gavin swept the metal limb in with his stump. The murderous dwarf lunged before Gavin could aim, forcing him to roll aside. He winced at the sharp pain as the blade nicked him across the hip. Luckily, his belt and holster had blocked most of the shallow strike.

Gavin lashed out with his boot and was rewarded with a loud grunt and a blade clattering off the floor. He needed to get off the ground. The knife gave Eyepatch the advantage in close quarters. Gavin levered himself up, a task complicated by the pistol in one hand and trying to hold the metal arm the redcaps sought in the crook of his elbow with his stump.

The prosthetic slipped as he shifted to a kneeling position. He tried to catch it against his body with his stump. Pins and needles engulfed the end of his truncated arm, as though he'd shoved it into a catfish. Glass shards must have gotten snagged in the mix.

Eyepatch retrieved his knife and ducked behind cover, as Gavin aimed his pistol but held his fire. The redcap he'd shot had vanished. The tinkle of shifting glass told him Eyepatch hadn't gone for the doorway, but remained lurking behind the displays. Gavin took the momentary respite to stand, brushing glass from his shirt with his free hand.

He froze. The metal limb had attached itself to his flesh-and-blood stump. The fingers flexed—*and he felt them flex.* In his dumbfound gaping, he missed Eyepatch clambering over the displays in the middle. The redcap hurled a throwing knife. If Gavin hadn't flinched, the blade would have struck his chest. As it was, it impaled his right shoulder. His pistol slipped from his grip.

Eyepatch leapt from the display, knife raised high. Gavin's metal fingers balled into a fist, and he stepped into the punch. The impact jarred him, and black dust erupted from the patinaed metal of the ancient limb. The blow launched Eyepatch back the direction he came. His boots struck the edge of a display, sending the redcap into a tumble as he disappeared over the case.

Gavin yanked the throwing knife free and rounded the cases. As soon as he spotted Eyepatch, Gavin hurled the knife left-handed. The blade struck the redcap in the belly, and he doubled over from the impact.

"Stupid dunnie!" Eyepatch rasped as he straightened, holding the throwing knife. "Hardened bronze—it can't pierce my skin, but it will do a fine job on yours!"

Gavin cursed himself for not scooping up the pistol. Pain stabbed his shoulder every time he moved his right arm, but he'd only have needed one good shot to deal with the redcap. Gavin flexed the new hand again.

He steadied himself on the frame of a display case as his boots slipped on grating glass. The shotgun lay on the floor behind Eyepatch, who brandished the bronze weapon. The blade was half the length of the fighting blade the redcap had lost, but it was no less a threat.

Eyepatch flashed the blade in an arc, forcing Gavin to halt, then stabbed. Gavin's new hand moved of its own volition and snagged the knife mid-thrust. Eyepatch instinctively tried to pull his weapon back, giving Gavin the split second to drive his steel-toed combat boot into his opponent's crotch.

Eyepatch gasped an Irish-sounding expletive and hunched over. Gavin tore the weapon free of Eyepatch's grip and tossed it over his shoulder. Eyepatch straightened in time for Gavin to hammer his metal fist into the bridge of the fae's nose. Something crunched in Eyepatch's face, and he collapsed like a sack of wet cement.

Gavin grabbed the shotgun and stepped into the hall. The huge man's coat was in tatters, and he bled from a dozen cuts. Grace limped as they circled each other, while the cop held his pistol ready. The third redcap emerged from the darkened room on the other side of the hall, Zeus snapping at his heels.

Gavin pumped the shotgun, wincing at the pain from his right shoulder. "Zeus! Clear!"

The dog scampered back two yards. The redcap barely had time to register the new threat before Gavin pulled the trigger, firing left-handed. The fae vanished before his body hit the floor.

Gavin cocked the gun again and leveled it at the bruiser. "Okay, Big Guy. It's three on one, and I've already taken out three of you spooky-types. You really want to fuck around and find out?"

The large man's eyes narrowed in recognition. "You wear the hand."

"It attached itself to me, so I'm not partial to letting someone tear it off." Did the huge man understand guns well enough to know firing a shotgun into a melee endangered both combatants? "You want to stand down?"

"What's your name?" The large man didn't lower his fists, but maintained a defensive posture.

"Gavin."

"I bear you no ill, Gavin Silver-Hand. Looks like my job is over," the bruiser rumbled. He reached toward a coat pocket, causing both the deputy and Gavin to tense. He extracted a business card. "I'm Sudr Half-Giant. If you bear the hand, you might need my services. I'm not cheap, but I can hold my own with one of your dunnie champions."

When no one stepped forward to take the card, Sudr scanned the hall for an intact surface upon which to deposit the card, but the brawl had demolished what little furniture had lined the hall. Sudr lowered his other fist and stepped toward Gavin. Gavin drew the shotgun back and accepted the card, leaving a bloody fingerprint.

* * *

Sudr nodded to Grace. "Not bad."

"For a woman?" Grace challenged, still on guard. The rune-skinned man still stood within reach of the security guard.

"No, for a dunnie. My great-aunt was a Valkyrja. You're still green, but tough and fast." Sudr straightened the ragged remains of his coat. "See you around."

"Are we going to just let him go?" Luke asked. Sudr paused at the door and raised an eyebrow.

Mr. Argus cleared his throat from the doorway to the office. "If Mr. Sudr will leave in peace, I think it's for the best. I shan't press charges."

Grace wiped her machete and sheathed it in its extra-dimensional pocket. "Fine. I don't need to prove who's tougher."

Sudr disappeared through the doorway before anyone else voiced an opinion.

"What are we going to do about One-Eye?" Grace asked. While the giant warrior might have some sense of honor, she didn't presume the same of the murderous redcap.

A gust of wind preceded a new voice from the entrance. "I see I missed all the fun. Sorry, I got hung up in a traffic snarl at the 150 bridge."

Druid Knox stepped over the shattered remains of a side table. For all that he was the grand poohbah of magic on the mortal world, he looked ordinary, wearing a flannel shirt and blue jeans. Only the gleam from his off-colored eyes, one green and one blue, betrayed his supernatural status.

His fiancée, a purple-haired fae wearing a pink tracksuit, picked her way over the rubble. "I told you the big lad on the street came from here."

Knox nodded and surveyed the scene. "What happened? Did the big guy and this redcap trash the place?"

"Who are you?" the security guard asked.

"Liam Knox—First Druid, Druid of the Accords, yadda yadda." Knox offered his hand. The guard shifted his shotgun to his right hand and shook the druid's hand. Both men stared at their clasped hands. Knox released his grip and took a step back. "That's new. Grace—what do you know about this?"

Grace shrugged. "Gavin had a traditional prosthetic five minutes ago."

The fae woman uttered an oath in her musical accent. "It's the Hand of Nuada."

"A magical limb named after him?" Knox asked.

The purple-haired fae shook her head. "I mean the literal item. It went missing when King Nuada fell in battle, before the first challenge."

"Who is Nuada?" the guard asked. Grace was glad someone else could ask the question.

"He was king of the Tuatha Danaan following the Fomorian War and into the Milesian War," the fae replied, her eyes glowing purple. "He lost his kingship when a Fomor chopped off his hand. Once Dianecht and Goibhnu crafted a replacement, he liberated the Tuatha from the corrupt king who'd replaced him."

Luke whispered, "Did any of that make sense to you?"

Grace held her tongue.

"Pixel, does that mean Gavin is the new king of the Tuatha Danaan?" Knox asked.

The fae shook her head, bouncing her purple tresses. "It's not like Excalibur—possession doesn't infer kingship. However, it would be seen as a badge of prestige. A few fae lords would love to get a hold of it."

"That, um, belongs to me," Argus protested half-heartedly.

"Who are you?" Knox asked.

"Argus Ambrose the Third. My grandfather gathered this collection."

"Was your grandfather an Enochian Mason?" Knox asked.

"What does that have to do with anything?" Argus asked.

"You might want to find the original door. When you removed it, you compromised the wards protecting this place. The redcaps couldn't have crossed the threshold otherwise," Knox replied. "As for ownership of the Hand of Nuada, unless you think you can chop it off Gavin, or trust that a court of law will believe in magic limbs, I'd call it even for services rendered."

The redcap groaned. Knox conjured a bladed staff out of thin air almost as fast as Grace drew her meteor-iron machete. Zeus growled. The fae blinked its one eye open and squinted at the bevy of weapons pointed at him.

"Bollocks," One-Eye slurred.

"Who sent you?" Knox demanded.

One-Eye clutched his bloody, ruined nose. "Why should I tell you?"

"If you don't, I'll stick you in an iron box and bury you alive in a churchyard," the druid replied.

The redcap's single eye widened. "Joliet Gabe. He wanted the Hand."

"Tell him to quit mucking around on the Dunwold, and if I catch wind of you causing mischief, my threat regarding a box and a church stand." Knox gestured to the door with his staff. "Get out of here."

"Why'd you let him go?" Grace asked as the redcap scampered into the night.

"Shaking a tree starts with grabbing a low-hanging limb."

* * *

Gavin watched the short fae disappear through the door. He held up his metal hand, closing and opening a fist. Fae, kings, magic—his head swam. "What now?"

The druid shrugged. With a gesture, the staff he held vanished. "I sure wouldn't hop a wold-ford, walk up to the nearest holt, knock on the door, and announce yourself as king."

"Hop what and walk where?" Gavin asked.

"I know how you feel. This stuff makes my head hurt, and I'm on the sidelines," Deputy Dahler remarked.

"First, I'd make friends with Grace and Luke. We'll figure out a Supernatural 101 for you," Knox said.

"Maybe I could cover it with a glove and live an ordinary life?" Gavin stared at the silver-and-gray limb. The movement was so life-like, perhaps he could hide it.

"If I've learned anything, it's that once you step into the world of the supernatural, trouble will find you," Grace stated. "You can stick your head in the sand, but that just means you won't see trouble coming."

Gavin's gaze went to the business card Sudr had handed him. "Gavin Silver-Hand"—the epithet resonated. "I guess ordinary is over. Where do I start?"

* * * * *

Jon Osborne Bio

Jon R. Osborne is a journalism major and veteran gamemaster turned science fiction and fantasy author. The second book in Jon's The Milesian Accords modern fantasy trilogy, "*A Tempered Warrior*", was a 2018 Dragon Awards finalist for Best Fantasy Novel. Jon is also a core author in the military science fiction Four Horseman Universe, where he was first published in 2017.

Jon resides in Indianapolis, where he plays role-playing games, writes science fiction and fantasy, and lives the nerd life. You can find out more at jonrosborne.com and at:

facebook.com/jonrosborne.

* * * * *

The Torturer of Camelot
by Chris Hepler

I t was folly to try to capture a fugitive who had no fear of death, but after days of hunting, Vaughan had a grip on the old man at last. Struggle as the codger might, Vaughan was younger and stronger. They both went down in the mud of the road, twisting until Vaughan was on top. Even a fist to the jaw didn't stop him. With the weight of his body and chain armor pinning his quarry, it was easy for Vaughan's partner Roldan to snap on the manacles. Vaughan rose, thinking the scuffle was over, but his captive kicked at his groin, and when that landed poorly, he spat.

The spit shocked Vaughan more than the kick. The prisoner was bound—he knew his captors could show no mercy if they chose, yet he defied them anyway.

Vaughan couldn't let disrespect go unanswered, so he struck the man across the face, leaving a scarlet cut and a honeycomb-print across his skin from the mail of his gauntlet. The prisoner fell to one knee in the mud.

"Spit again and lose your teeth," Vaughan said. "By order of his majesty King Constantine of the Britons, you, Madoc of Caerleon, are to face justice in his court at Camelot."

Vaughan saw the man shake, and expected another blast of spittle, but the smile on his face gave it away. The man was chuckling.

"Justice," he said in the tone of a man who believed in none.

"That it is. Though it may be unfamiliar to you, you will feel its edge soon enough."

Roldan hoisted the captive to his feet. Vaughan retrieved his sword from where he'd lost it in the tussle and pricked Madoc's back with it to encourage him to march back to their cart.

Madoc didn't struggle as he was loaded, but cast an eye at Toff, the donkey hitched in front. "Are we both to ride on this? Or can you not afford a horse?"

"Not yet," Vaughan said. "Think of me as Sir Perceval, who rode upon an ass before he found the Grail."

Madoc waved off the legend. "His name was Peredur to those who knew him. He was a fool then, and giving him arms didn't improve him a whit. It took Galahad to find the Grail." He addressed himself to Roldan. "Have you heard the same lies as this one here? Children's stories from the half-wits across the sea?"

"Yoo ah aiah," Roldan said. Madoc paused, unsure of what he'd just heard.

"Roldan has no tongue," Vaughan said. "Mordred's men cut it from his mouth. As you can imagine, he's eager to see a man such as you on the block. What he said was, 'you're the liar.'"

Roldan nodded.

"Amazing," Madoc muttered. "He's heard me speak fifty words, and already he knows my full measure."

Vaughan walked behind the cart, sword flat on his shoulder, as Roldan led the donkey back toward the main way. Vaughan didn't relish entertaining Madoc, but the position let him keep the prisoner in his field of vision. "You were the usurper's torturer."

Madoc's eyes were oak-brown and unmoving. "What's your name?"

"Vaughan."

"And, Sir Vaughan, how many kings have you served?"

"Roldan and I are men-at-arms, not knights. The armor is from a kill."

"Ah, I begin to fathom your motive." Madoc's damnable smile crept back. "No shame in it. Many a poor sot has raised his station through skill at arms. But my question remains. How many kings?"

"I'm of an age where one will suffice. I serve Arthur's kinsman Constantine, who has ruled since Arthur's death."

"I served three, including Arthur."

"*Arthur* employed a torturer? Well, then, I'd better release you. I appear to have captured a jester by accident."

Madoc's smirk erased itself. "You fail to recall that Mordred ruled in Arthur's name while the man was over the sea at war. Then he returned and ousted his bastard from the town. He had to decide my fate... and my utility. I had information and, as you imply, he was a merciful sort."

"Ah, yes. Utility." Vaughan coughed and spat, briefly letting the cart get ahead of him as he checked to see if there was blood in the spittle. His jaw still ached where Madoc had landed his blow.

"What should I have done? Joined the march to the scaffold? I could serve a good man just as well or better than I served his bastard son."

"But not Constantine, apparently."

"When a king begins his rule, he's a dead man, unless he kills those who could bring him down."

Vaughan scoffed. "Ah, here it comes."

"What?"

"The bargaining," Vaughan said. "The claim you have some grand information on Constantine that you'll exchange for your freedom."

Madoc finally had fire in his words. "You think you're here for a noble reason? How did they word it to you? 'Mordred's torturer has blood on his hands, see his head in a basket?' Seals the gift up in a nice pie crust, it does."

"I'll do you a favor, old man. I'll hear your story. Got a long road ahead of us, and I enjoy a laugh."

Madoc's eyes narrowed. "No."

Even Roldan turned from where he was walking ahead of them.

"Why not?"

"Because those who claim the name of justice rarely hold the soul of it. You've heard the stories of knights, probably at your father's knee, but your finest deed seems to be that you killed one and took his armor."

"Ah," Vaughan replied, drawing out the sound. "So, it's not that you don't believe in justice, but that you don't believe in me."

"Why would I?"

"Because I'm neither as green as you assume, nor as dishonorable. I got the armor by force of arms in a fair contest."

"So you claim. Give me a reason to trust you, or silence is your answer."

"That will be well enough," Vaughan said, "I might not have laughed at your story anyway."

* * *

The road home was well-trod, and it wasn't difficult to find a tradesmen's campsite—a bit of ground with no grass, a ring of stones with a few logs that could be used as benches, and a pair of weeping beeches good for keeping rain off.

Vaughan indicated a stack of chopped wood under an old aspen tree. "We're in luck."

"Were it good luck, someone would have left an axe," Madoc said. "That much won't last the night."

Vaughan plucked a hatchet and a capped horn of out of the donkey's saddlebag. "Do you refuse half a loaf of bread when you're hungry for a full one?" Madoc gave nothing but a sullen glare while his captor freed the cap and sprinkled out dry kindling and a cylinder of jasper. In a few minutes, he had a pyramid of sticks smoldering with a decent flame.

"Sit. Warm yourself."

Madoc glared, but he felt the evening's chill as much as Vaughan. He came close and knelt. "You want something."

"If I were to deny that, you'd soon see I'm a liar."

Roldan piled branches nearby and moved in close as well. He retrieved the hatchet just as Madoc eyed it. "Ngo, goan eben hink aboup igh."

Vaughan fixed his gaze on Madoc. "I want Ron."

"Who?"

"Not who, what. There were three weapons gifted to Arthur by God. A sword, which lies with him in Avalon. A dagger, which Queen Guinevere took to her convent. And a spear, which the Welsh call Rhongomyniad, and the Britons, Ron. Arthur impaled Mordred with it before the traitor smote his head. You know where it is."

"Constantine must have been a mummer, then, for he sold you a story. Everyone knows Arthur's sword could cleave through armor, and the scabbard repelled wounds. What would he need a spear for?"

Vaughan didn't let up in his stare. "More reach when he was on horseback, I'd imagine." Madoc said nothing, his excuse transparent. "The point is, the king styles himself the successor, and the blessing of archbishop Mellitus would make his rule easier. Were Constantine to have God's holy spear, Mellitus might be…"

"Inclined?"

"I would say, 'marginally less intractable.'"

"And you think I have this spear where?"

"You know of Constantine capturing Mordred's sons, dragging them from the church they hid in?"

"He killed them."

"First, he had them tortured to find the spear they took from the battlefield. Would've found it out, too, had the man who broke them not scampered off into the shadows to gain it for himself. That man," Vaughan said, "would be you."

"You call me a liar and a thief, then."

Vaughan didn't rise to the bait. "I don't pretend to know your reasons. Your soul could be made of virgin snow, or perhaps you're the Devil's catamite. One would surprise me more than the other, but no matter. You get me the spear, and you walk free, but if your pride is so greatly offended that you keep your mouth shut, the outcome will be of your own making."

Madoc's glare had steel in it before. Now it had lost its glint, and Vaughan saw in it only a dead-eyed certainty. "What would it be, then?"

Vaughan shrugged. "Your move."

"I mean, what would it be? Chopping my fingers off with your precious hatchet? Burning me with branches from the fire? Don't dance around it."

"I would hope you'd see reason."

"And if I don't, you'll cluck your tongue as you pull my nails from my hands."

"Already you know my full measure," Vaughan shot back.

"Is it true, or isn't it?"

"I am not you, nor am I a person who thinks like you. If you prove intractable, I will take you to face justice in Camelot."

"Answer me this, then. Constantine still employs torturers?"

Vaughan's face stilled. "He may."

"He damn well does, and you know it. What good is it if you won't put me on the coals, but the moment I enter the donjon, his majesty stretches me on the rack? The salvation of your conscience won't count for much then."

"I favor persuasion—"

"Which will ease my pain how much when they sit me on a spike? Don't pretend you don't know, because I'll tell you. They put you on the spike so your weight drives it up through the arse. You die over days from the bleeding and the fevers. It reaches the heart faster if you wiggle, and there's not a man alive who doesn't thrash about in the end."

"It won't have to be that way if you tell me the truth."

"I buried it beneath a forest pine and forgot where it was."

Vaughan waited.

"No, wait, my brother has kept it safe in the rafters of his house. He's half a day's walk from here."

Vaughan stayed silent.

"No, I lied both times, it's in my tool shed. Go back and lay your eyes upon it right now." Madoc's face betrayed nothing. "Which one do you want to believe?"

Vaughan sensed a trap. "The last one can be verified most easily."

"Ah, so you want to believe it, not because you think it's true, but because it's *easier*."

"What do you want of me, to search every tree in the wood without skepticism?"

"No, I want you to recognize that men lie to save their hides, and their captors cannot satisfy their curiosity without enough blood and pain to break them down. Torturers know this. Constantine knows this. That is why, if you turn me over, your precious king will cut pieces off me until he's satisfied. And telling the truth from the beginning won't spare me a second of it."

"If you ask me, your comeuppance for doing the same is long overdue."

"Ah, you found an out. They always do. 'He deserves no less.' But comeuppance for what? Doing as Mordred asked so he wouldn't have *me* killed?"

"You had the choice to refuse and flee, did you not?"

"Is that what you would have done?"

"Of course."

"Why?"

"Because it's better than dishonoring oneself with foul practices."

"Then I suggest you find a pool of water and look at your reflection, for you are sending me to the fate you just condemned a breath ago. Because it's *easier*."

Vaughan said nothing, and for a moment it seemed as if Madoc had struck him. Then, with the rattle of a suit's worth of chain links, he sat upon the log that travelers before him had dragged to the fire pit. He stared into the middle distance.

He had little skill at rhetoric, and none at interrogation. But there were words that came back to him from Hadward, the older youth who'd first taught him the rudiments of the blade. An opponent who did nothing but attack, as Madoc was doing, was trying to hide his weakness.

Perhaps Madoc knew that, too, which was why the two of them lapsed into silence with no further insults. At last, Vaughan found what he thought was a flaw in the captive's story.

"Why conceal the spear from the king in the first place?"

Madoc, despite his scars and the gaze that made Vaughan think he was dead inside, didn't seem as confident now. "What do you care?"

Vaughan's brow was fully creased as he held on to the thought. "You're not a dullard. You decide when you've reckoned the odds. Surely Constantine would have rewarded you, had you turned it over. And it's not as if you could take it to a battle without it being recognized."

Madoc tried to betray nothing. "And?"

"And, it's a divine spear handed to a king. He who holds it can make all manner of claims to rulership, yet it doesn't seem as if you wanted it. More, you wanted it out of his majesty's hands."

"He shouldn't have the bloody thing."

Vaughan leaned forward. At last, he was getting somewhere. "Why not? God saw fit to make him king, didn't he?"

"God saw him sit on a chair. Mordred sat in that chair, too. Doesn't matter if you shit on a stack of gold, the smell is the same."

"But Arthur was different?"

"Of course he was. A maiden could walk naked from one end of Camelot to the other, and the worst she'd get was laughter. A knight could fight in a tourney without the crowd chanting for the dagger to end him just because he fell. We didn't feel afraid of one another all the damned time. But all the good Arthur did died with him."

"What if I could change that?"

The old man shook his head, and there was a hint of a smile on his lips.

"You think I can't?"

"I think you've got to have a dream," was all Madoc said.

"It is no dream. As a knight, I will have authority—"

"You will have no such thing. Lands and a title don't move hearts. Love and fear are the knight's stock in trade. There's no authority without them."

Vaughan's ire rose. "Lands and a title are the only thing I don't have. I have trained, I have fought three battles and never been defeated, I have listened to the lore of the wise. I have kept my mind and heart clear—"

"We've already proved you haven't. If you believe Constantine to be Arthur's equal, you're either stupid or greedy. And, I mean this in the most *insulting* manner, you're not stupid."

Vaughan punched Madoc in his smiling face.

The blow twisted Madoc around toward the fire. He went down too fast, and Vaughan instantly anticipated the counter. The bastard had gotten one hand free during the talk, and stood, swinging a stout stick topped with flame.

He had no time to enjoy his prize. Vaughan's shoulder slammed into him with all his weight, and an extra two stone's worth of armor besides. Madoc flew through the fire, all balance lost as his feet sought purchase, and tripped in the pile of burning sticks instead. His body landed in a spray of ash, branches, and embers.

Vaughan gave no quarter. He fell upon Madoc. Madoc got one good lash with the stick, but only clipped his assailant's helmet. Both of Vaughan's hands clamped down on Madoc's arm and pinned it to his chest before planting his forearm against his opponent's throat. Madoc's free arm, still in the manacle, flailed for the hatchet, but it was out of reach long before Roldan snatched it up and held Madoc's arm down.

Roldan raised the hatchet and looked to Vaughan as if to say, *he only needs one hand to sign a confession.*

Vaughan shook his head. "Get the rope." He leaned on his elbow, and Madoc spluttered. "He needs to be trussed."

Roldan handed him the hatchet, and Vaughan held its blade to Madoc's neck. Madoc stopped struggling. Roldan ran to the cart and returned with rope.

"It's too bad," Vaughan said. "Now the only conversation you'll have is with your successor, in the depths of a gaol."

Madoc said something just as Roldan slipped the rope across his mouth. Mangled words came out, but by that time, Vaughan was no longer listening.

Before morning, he cut wood for the next traveler, because a knight-to-be should know courtesy.

* * *

Five weeks later, a page led Vaughan down stone steps into the cold and darkness of the tower's cellar. The stone was unforgiving, but Vaughan was comfortable—he wore new shoes made of leather, and a twilled doublet made of the softest wool he'd ever felt, let alone worn. The gaol smelled of human waste. As he got closer, there was another scent—rushes, scattered across the floor in a vain attempt to make the stench tolerable. The page held a lantern, and Vaughan bore a second, staving off November's chill.

The lanterns brought little light, so Vaughan's first glimpse of the space beneath the hatch in the floor was only a dark pit. When his eyes adjusted, he saw a misshapen lump. It moved, allowing him to discern pale fingers and a burlap blanket. A face soon followed, covered in a mop of hair and beard. The figure shaded its eyes from the light.

"That's Madoc," the page said. The youth gestured. "Do you see that rope ladder there?"

"What of it?"

"Don't use it. And don't lean over the hatch. Stay well-balanced. He has a bucket down there he can throw. It's not likely to hit you, but it may spatter filth."

"I appreciate the warning."

"I'm to leave you two alone. The bench is there, if you grow tired. If you need the turnkey, he's at the top of the stairs."

"Leave your lantern."

"As you like." With that, the page skittered up the steps and vanished.

A croaking murmur came from Madoc.

"What did you say?" Vaughan said, wishing he had his dagger on him. They'd taken it and searched him so the prisoner couldn't snatch a weapon and hold him hostage.

It took a moment to discern the words, but Vaughan had practice at deciphering a pained voice. "I said, how'd you manage that? No visitor sees me alone."

Vaughan shone the lantern, trying to discern detail in the dank pit below him. The blanket concealed far too much for his liking. "It's a tale modestly long in the telling."

"Skip it, then. I don't have much time."

Vaughan couldn't help but imagine what other injuries were concealed in the dark. "Should I get you food?"

"You think I can keep anything down? This fever's got me vomiting from both ends." Madoc scratched his bushy upper lip. "You a knight now?"

"No," Vaughan confessed. "I was paid in coin and equipment. To be knighted, I'd have to have done a far greater—"

"Oh! Now I understand why you're here."

"Yes, I'm to persuade you."

"Typical monarch. When all else fails, he tries reason." Madoc coughed, a wet sound that ended in hacking. "Where's your tongueless man?"

"Spending coin."

"Whores?"

"I wouldn't know. I allow him his privacy."

"But you're here with me? What are you, some bastard who could never live up to expectations, now you've got to be a knight?"

"Just a tradesman's boy who understands defiance."

"Lower a lantern."

"Why?" Vaughan wondered if the old man could throw it in his condition.

"If I'm to talk, I don't want to do it in a pit as cold as a Viking's arse."

Mindful of the page's warning about the ladder, Vaughan found a platter and a rope he guessed was used to feed the prisoner. He set the page's lantern on it, and in moments, could see Madoc far better than before.

The light shone over two pieces of red meat, and it took Vaughan a moment to realize they were Madoc's legs. There was no hair nor skin left on them, only visible, seared muscle, as if they were chicken thighs peeled for a soup pot.

"Are you bleeding?"

"How the hell should I know? Everything's been dark and wet for days."

"What did they do to you?"

"They put me in the boot. First one leg, when they wanted me to talk, then the other because they wanted me to scream. Filled them with water. Put them up to boil." Vaughan's face must have betrayed him, because Madoc added, "Too much for your conscience?"

"I seem to recall you trying to stave my head in with a burning bough," Vaughan said. "The real question is whether we can broker a peace between us, but I don't think you'll grant me any answers. I know little of you, and I'm sure you're in a mood to resist so long as I'm his majesty's representative."

"As if that were as changeable as the wind, no doubt. No. He trusts you alone with me. I'm sure that didn't come easily."

Vaughan nodded. Madoc had lost little of his perceptiveness, even in a fever. "As you like. The fact remains that the turnkey is unlikely to hear your words. Unless there are others down in the darkness with you, we are alone."

"Then ask your questions and fail already."

Vaughan set his lantern down at the edge, and hunched forward, resting his chin on his fists. "Why resist?"

"Because bastards like you run the world, and it's a man's duty to keep them from getting everything they want on a platter."

"So, you're righteous. Do you pray?"

"Never met a one in my trade who didn't."

"In truth? I would have thought contempt for the Church would be a requirement."

"That's not the mindset. When you put the pain on and break a man down into a little boy, the first thing you want is a priest telling you you're not a complete shit for doing so."

"Have they brought you one for confession?"

"'Course they did. Didn't like what I had to say much. I said if the father forgave the man boiling my feet, he could fuck right off with forgiving me."

"The point is, you believe you have a soul. And Constantine—"

"—abuses his."

"Quite. But what does it concern you that he gains the power of the Rhongomyniad?"

"He'd kill a man with that lance, wouldn't he?"

Vaughan shrugged. "I suppose. In our meeting, he said he gives commands rather than charges in the vanguard."

"But if he had the opportunity, he'd end an enemy. I'd be contributing to his murderous ways. He's got plenty of weapons; he doesn't need Arthur's."

Vaughan peered into the orange glow below, contemplating. "You said 'Arthur's,' not 'mine.'"

"It isn't mine."

"Still, it's passing strange. When we first met, you didn't seem to have reverence for the man, nor his knights. Yet now, you face unimaginable pain for a stick with a blade on the end, just because it belonged to him." Vaughan shook his head. "No. I don't believe it for a moment."

Madoc went quiet long enough that Vaughan leaned over to try to discern if he'd died down in that foul pit.

"Your pardon," he said at last. "Was I supposed to care about your beliefs?"

Vaughan settled back. "They searched your home, you know. And yet here I am, because you hid the thing somewhere."

"If you're to threaten my family, you'll find I buried my wife before you were born. No children from the union, neither."

"Then who are you protecting?"

"If I were protecting someone, I'd be with them, wouldn't I? And I'd have kept the bloody spear."

Vaughan had to admit, the man had a point, but it was only one among many. "I'd like to hear your version of events."

"Why on earth would you want that?"

"With a fever, you may die, and to have no confessor is an ugly thing. No wife, no issue, no priest. Who wants to perish alone and forgotten?"

The man in the pit was quiet.

"Walk me through the time you saw the spear. Constantine's knights had killed Mordred's sons, who took the spear from the battlefield. Were you present at the church as torturer?"

"The young prick on the throne wanted me there in case we took them alive. I could get to work right there in the camp."

"And one of them had the spear. What did it look like?"

Madoc's voice seemed to croak less as he talked. "Nine feet. A footman's weapon. I thought the shaft was teak, at first. Dark red. But polished teak is smooth, and this was coarse, so it sat in your hand like a rock. Flexed rather than broke, but always returned to true. The tip was narrow, a leaf of silver as long as a forearm, with lines upon it like waves breaking in the surf. But not Damascus steel—these were gold, as if the sun were on the waves. A thing from another world, it was. And not a fleck of that traitor's blood on it, neither."

The contrast brought Vaughan back to the present. "It sounds as if it were a treasure. Did you return it?"

"T-to whom?"

Vaughan heard the quaver in Madoc's voice. It was tiny, but he was sure of it. What could possibly shake this man of iron?

"Did you return it from whence it came? As Bedwyr did?"

"I… I didn't spend much time with Bedwyr."

"Allow me to refresh your memory. Arthur, on his deathbed, handed his sword of many names to Sir Bedwyr, telling him to cast it into the lake at Avalon. At first, Bedwyr failed him. He couldn't part with such a magnificent blade, and hid it in the riverbank, telling Arthur he threw it into the water, and all he saw was the lake closing over the weapon. Arthur knew he was lying. Bedwyr returned, plucked up his courage, threw it, and the hand of the Lady of the Lake caught the mighty weapon's hilt, drawing it beneath the waves for the king's use in the next world. Is this tale familiar?"

Madoc was silent.

"So, I ask you. Did you return the spear to the lake?"

Again, there was nothing but the sound of the lantern's flame, billowing in its movements. Vaughan sensed he was near something vital, but if he pushed too hard, Madoc would die silent.

Vaughan asked softly, "Can the Lady of the Lake be killed by mortal men?"

"What?" Now there was real fear, as audible as a held note.

"I'm not a bookish man, but I do recall a sermon in which the priest asked if she was one of the angels. Archbishop Mellitus said she served the will of God, but her origin was as one of the Fair Folk, pushed from the civilized world to the wild places by the power of the Lord. And since iron is proof against the fay, it stands to reason that perhaps some archers with steel arrowheads—"

"Stop," came the voice from the pit. "You cannot be contemplating this."

"I see," Vaughan said. "You *were* protecting someone."

"What do you want?"

"For now, I just want someone in the know to tell me the full story, so I don't spend my days laboring in the dark. I've had enough of serving an ignorant king."

"Because he didn't give you your precious title?"

"Because he told me to cut your fingers off and leave them with you as your only food. I thought better of him, but..." He lapsed into silence.

Vaughan's lantern light flickered as the oil within guttered. He wasn't sure how long he'd been there. When Madoc spoke again, his voice was weaker. "I heard about Bedwyr," he admitted. "I went to the lake and hurled the lance as if it were a javelin. Had I more sense, I would have thrown it shaft-first. I saw the Lady's hand..." There, his voice broke. "She caught the blade, but her fingers bled, and from the water... she stood on the water like it was glass."

"Did she speak to you?"

"Couldn't tell you if she uttered a word, but I understood her all the same. I apologized for harming her, and I knew... I *knew* I couldn't tell anyone that I did so. Otherwise, there'd be men like Mordred... Constantine..." He swallowed. "You."

"You feel loyalty to the Lady, then."

"That's not the right word."

"It certainly seems to outweigh your duty to the kingdom."

"She has power."

"No doubt, if she made a sword that cleaves metal, a scabbard that prevents wounds—"

"No! Not powers, *power!*" Madoc's voice sounded strained, as if speaking were more of an effort now. "She gave Arthur the greatest sword in the world at a time when knights were killers and brawlers. He made Camelot to repay that trust. She has power, and unlike every other piece of shit grasping at land and crowns, she gives it away, asking only that her chosen build something with it."

"Did she ask something of you?"

"She didn't have to. She…" Madoc's voice hitched. "She gave me…"

There was a clatter from below, and Vaughan started, knowing something was wrong. The lantern light was smeared across the floor, a rivulet of flaming oil illuminating even less than could be seen before.

Vaughan called Madoc's name, but there was no answer. Amid black smoke, Vaughan thought he smelled burning straw, and guessed that both Madoc's blanket and bedding were alight. The pit's walls were stone, and the beams were stout, but fire wasn't something with which Vaughan would trifle. He ran up the steps and fetched the page and the turnkey, who lumbered down the staircase like a Flemish destrier, massive but sure-footed.

The three of them ringed the pit. The turnkey's wide palm held Vaughan back. "It may be a ruse."

"He's got no feet left," Vaughan retorted. "If he can't stand, he can't fight. I'll go down if you won't."

"On your own head be it." The turnkey withdrew the line from the smoking pit and disentangled the rope ladder to throw it down. Vaughan took a deep breath and descended.

The breath didn't last anywhere near long enough for him to reach bottom. He struggled with his eyes and lungs stinging, electing to leap off the last few rungs rather than carefully pick his way down. No surprise blow came—Madoc lay prone amidst the flames and smoke.

Vaughan shook him, receiving only a groan in response. He grabbed a bucket and hurled whatever liquid contents were in it onto the blaze, but the oil remained alight. Judging the fire too angry to beat out safely, he loaded Madoc across his back and hefted him, trying to keep him stable with one arm. He needed the other to climb the ladder.

It was painful, and hard-fought, but he reached the mouth of the pit, and the turnkey's giant hands plucked Madoc off him with a grunt of effort. Sweet air met Vaughan's nose. As the turnkey and the page handed off buckets of sand to douse the flames, Vaughan recovered enough to examine what was left of Madoc.

He smelled of urine and rot. Now that his legs were more visible, Vaughan could see the black and yellow patches of gangrene in addition to the red of the burns. As Vaughan brought the lantern near, he could see Madoc's eyes were wrong—the left pupil was huge and black, while the right one was a pinprick. He felt for the beat of the old man's heart.

"No, you don't, you old boar—"

He found none.

"—tell me what she gave you—"

He'd borne a body, nothing more.

"—tell me where it is—"

He shook Madoc by the shoulders, but got nothing for his trouble. By the time he felt like stopping, the page's hand was on his shoulder.

"Beg pardon, but I don't think you'll get answers from him like that."

Vaughan paused for breath. A stinking breath full of smoke and frustration. "I will seek my own. He hasn't defeated me yet."

* * *

The skiff they'd made was just large enough for one body, not two, and Vaughan gritted his teeth as he and Roldan dragged it through the marshland. He'd known he would be miserable when his boots crunched the frost on the ground, and this early in the morning, the water of the marsh that seeped into his footwear was no less frigid.

His doublet and shoes were gone. To soothe an enraged Constantine, he'd paid back every coin he'd been awarded, and fled the court before the king's whims changed. Roldan had stayed out of it, correctly guessing that if he said nothing, Constantine would forget about him.

It didn't matter. The two were here on a mission.

The lake didn't have a clean edge, it had reed-mace plants growing in thick profusion. Vaughan unbuckled his baldric and belt, leaving them with Roldan. He wouldn't have his diplomacy ruined by an implied threat.

He trod the reed-maces down instead of using the skiff to push them aside. That would have helped, no doubt, but Vaughan had no urge to use it as a rolling pin, nor a battering ram. As the water reached his waist, he grimaced, wanting to go no deeper into the lake. He braced his feet in the muck as well as he could and hauled the skiff past him.

Madoc's body was as clean and serene as he could make it. He'd had no embalming fluids, so he and the page had spent the night washing him and dressing him in one of Vaughan's old garments. There was a smell, but it had yet to become truly foul, and he'd covered it up by scattering pine needles across the bier. So it was that now, when he pushed the skiff into the lake, it was with little disgust.

For a moment, nothing happened. No birds called, nor frogs or crickets. The skiff drifted toward the center of the lake, into the morning fog, but came to a rest.

Vaughan exhaled, trying not to complain about freezing his nether region off. Instead, he concentrated on the fog coming from his mouth, then gave up and closed his eyes. He was unsure whether voicing a prayer would help or hurt. He couldn't say whether Madoc would be going to heaven or hell, or if being with Arthur in Avalon meant he would avoid both entirely, but he couldn't imagine anyone given to this lake suffering any kind of punishment.

When he opened his eyes again, Madoc's skiff was moving further out into the mist, despite there being no current. Vaughan's heart squeezed as if it were beating its last, for he knew he was in the presence of something he'd never seen before.

The depths of the water turned from ink to gold, swirling until the shimmering color floated right to the surface. It was hair—the endless auric strands of a being who had grown it out for more years than Vaughan could count. Her head broke the stillness of the lake, but she emerged silently until her eyes glared down at him. She was a tower—seven feet if she was an inch—and as Madoc had said, her bare feet stood on the water. A silken robe defended her modesty, appearing dry despite where it had been a moment before. In one bird-thin limb, she held the Rhongomyniad spear—in the other, a brilliant blade, its length and hilt made of some metal the color of emeralds, unknown to humans. It terminated in a sharp, triangular point that was currently aimed between his eyes.

You knew him, said a voice he understood, though the lady's lips spoke some tongue that was neither common to the Britons nor the Welsh.

Vaughan hesitated. Lying seemed like the best way to save his skin, yet he couldn't do it. "We were enemies. I cannot change that now."

Why are you here?

Vaughan stared into the depths of her pupils, as if he'd find the answer there, before averting his eyes. "He is dead because of me, and I wished to know..." He hesitated, and the words, once interrupted, did not come.

I see. You want his secrets.

"Yes. He said you gave him something. I thought at first it might have been the spear, but it clearly remains in your hands."

Do you wish this for yourself?

"I did… but no more. I want to know. I need not tell a soul. What did you give him?"

The Lady turned and indicated Madoc's skiff, now lost to the mist. *Dignity*, she said.

Vaughan's jaw quivered as he ground his teeth. He couldn't look at her more, not her eyes, not her pallid feet that reminded him of Madoc's bloodless flesh. "I tried to take that from him."

Why?

"I wanted to be a knight."

Why?

The answer he'd given Madoc was untrue, but he wasn't going to lie now. "Because I thought fighting was an easy way to wealth. And it would make me less afraid."

Then feel shame.

The words entered him, and he needed no ears to hear their echo. That was the true reason he was here. He owed Madoc a moment of his time. He didn't need land or a title. He'd just grasped for them, as surely as Constantine had grasped for the authority he couldn't command.

Water rolled down his face, and one warm droplet struck the surface of the lake. The chill of the water seeped into his bones, numbing his extremities. His breath came more raggedly as he shivered. "He bore pain because of me. Is there a penance I might do?"

You began that when you came to this lake.

"What else can I do?" he asked. "When a man has never had me at his mercy, but he can still make me suffer?"

You are the only one to keep his memory.

"I would tell his story so that his deed—his protection of this place—could inspire others. But I cannot, lest your secret no longer be safe."

Then you are sworn to me. Kneel.

Hating the pain of the freezing water as it rose to his neck, but hating his cowardice more, Vaughan knelt. The emerald blade tapped him on his left shoulder, then his right. Warmth spread from where it made contact, and he shuddered at the relief.

Say you will defend this place.

"I pledge my life and my honor for you," he said.

Then rise, Sir Vaughan, and let no pain draw words of Avalon from you.

Gratefully, he stood, feeling a deep joy and having no idea what to do with it, and held his hand over his heart as he bowed.

The Lady sank into the depths, receding as she went, until her billowing silk and swirling tresses vanished, along with Vaughan's last glimpse of the spear Ron. It was not for him to have, any more than he could have grasped the water itself.

He waded back to firmer ground, and the heat slowly left his body once more. He saw Roldan beyond the cattails, pacing back and forth to stay warm. They returned to the cart, where Vaughan could grab a dry woolen blanket and pour the lake water out of his boots.

Roldan pointed at his eyes: *See?*

"I sent Madoc's body to the lake. It is finished."

Roldan's eyebrows quirked. Another question. "Ba king?" he added, mangling a "the" but saying the last word clearly even without a tongue.

Vaughan hesitated. Roldan had always been good to him, yet he could still spill a secret, and Vaughan was now sworn.

"Let us not pretend. Madoc is gone, and with him, our chance. Constantine has no shortage of aspiring warriors eager to make names for themselves. We shall go elsewhere. Caerleon, perhaps.

Their harvest was good this year; we may find work." He didn't say whether it was as guards or laborers. Either would serve Vaughan's purpose.

Roldan mimed a spear.

"No," Vaughan replied. "What I found was different."

Roldan frowned. "What?"

"There are things I cannot say."

"Ooh ah shiling." *You are smiling.* It came out as an accusation.

"Yes. The old man defended his virtue to the last. I smile, for he may now take his place at the side of the man who gave him his honor."

"He wash a horsherer," Roldan said. *Torturer.*

Of course, Vaughan thought. He couldn't fault Roldan for refusing to forgive such a thing. But as Roldan turned to walk back to their cart, and the space between them grew, Vaughan fished for words. He needed to make his friend understand.

"No," he said at last. "He was more. Each of us is."

* * * * *

Chris Hepler Bio

Chris Hepler has recently shipped the Amazon Echo game *My Loft*, created the comic *Mythkillers*, and written the novel *Civil Blood: The Vampire Rights Case That Changed a Nation*. He has previously contributed to the universes of *Mass Effect*, *Star Wars: The Old Republic*, *Pirates of the Caribbean*, and *Shadowrun*. He dreads the day actual space marines, Jedi, pirates, and troll mercenaries will show up on his doorstep to tell him he doesn't know what he's talking about.

* * * * *

Wielding Authority
by Aaron Rosenberg

S unna stared at that naked blade where it lay across the arms of her father's empty throne, worrying about the future of her kingdom.

Behorde. The blade of legend. Forged by a god from the molten bones of a dragon in the fires of its own death—or so the stories went. Its very name meant "Authority," and whoever carried it wielded the ultimate authority, that of a weapon without equal. Its power was said to be such that its owner couldn't be harmed, couldn't even be touched, yet could strike down with ease those who would stand against him. The man to whom it had originally been given was considered one of the greatest rulers in history, an already gifted monarch who had used Behorde to expand his empire until it had spanned nearly half the globe. Not even such a sword could save him from the terrible storm that had sunk his fleet, however, and for many years, Behorde had been lost, fading from reality until it existed as the stuff of tales alone.

Then, a score of years ago, new stories had emerged. Accounts of a sword like no other, one that gifted its wielder with unmatched strength and speed, one that could carve through metal and even stone as easily as flesh.

It could only be Behorde, returned to the world.

The quest had begun, then, men from all over the world searching for the mythic blade, hoping to find it before anyone else did—for, so the stories went, thus far all its recent owners had been sailors and merchants, and even farmers or craftsmen. Men who perhaps knew how to defend themselves, but no more. Each of those men had been content merely to survive whatever strange dangers they'd faced, with little more ambition than that. In the grip of one born to combat, however, Behorde could once again be a maker of kings.

Many arduous journeys had occurred, and many battles, as each man fought against his would-be rivals, all of them desperate to reach the lost sword first and to claim it as their own. In the end, dozens had converged upon, of all places, an old mill. The miller's son had won the sword in a card game and brought it home to hang over the millstone, not knowing its true worth.

Both miller and son had been surprised to find a small army upon their doorstep, and even more so when the assembled warriors had begun to fight one another, the conflict spilling into the mill and reaching a fever pitch at the sight of Behorde displayed there on the far side, waiting for the victor to retrieve it.

Sunna's father Stigandr had not been the first to enter, nor even the largest and strongest, but he was the deadliest with a blade, and had cut his way across the wide room, dealing death to any who dared oppose him. At last, reaching the mill wheel, he'd brought his sword down in an enormous overhand arc and cleaved the last man before him nearly in two. He then abandoned the trusty blade there in the wreckage of his rival to leap past him and onto the massive stone wheel itself, where he reached up and tugged Behorde from the perch that had been fashioned there for it. With a resounding cry, Stigandr ripped the legendary blade from its sheath—the last time any had seen that humble housing—as he tossed the plain scabbard aside and gazed in wonder as golden runes formed along the naked steel, visible to his eyes alone:

Resisting power comes at a price

Laughing at the appropriateness of such a statement, Stigandr glared down at the men still rushing toward him, sidestepping their fallen comrades in their eagerness to pit their martial skill against his and contest with him for the prize he had already won.

"Fools!" he shouted to them. "I hold Behorde, and it thirsts for your blood! You could not hope to stand against me without it—how, now, will you fare when its strength has joined to my own? Lay down your arms and kneel, and I may yet spare you! Fail to do so, and I will cut you down like mewling calves!"

Some there were who listened, and cast aside their own weapons, falling to their knees and swearing fealty at the same time they begged for mercy. But many scorned the offer and continued their charge, convinced that, if nothing else, sheer strength of numbers might prevail, and one among them, at least, would live to wrest the ancient weapon from its current wielder.

The ancient mill was awash in blood that day, so the stories went, but in the end Stigandr emerged triumphant, Behorde held aloft in his gore-stained hand.

Thus the kingdom of Valernon had begun.

* * *

"And how stands your kingdom now?" Sunna murmured, the words little more than breath across her lips as she turned her gaze from the blade-barred throne to the long, golden casket beside it.

Stigandr lay there, heavily muscled arms crossed over his broad, gold-mailed chest, only a few skeins of silver glinting here and there among the thick beard laid in plaits radiating from his strong jaw like a shadowy sun. The hair, still equally dark and luxurious, had been braided along his temples. His stern face was composed in what was meant to be peaceful contemplation, but still looked much like a scowl, those heavy brows drawn in as if he might start upright at any second and glare at all those around him.

Yet all of it was a lie.

Not many knew that, of course. The senior members of the palace guard and a few of the oldest and most loyal servants: old Ulrich the steward, Lothar the royal physician, and of course Sunna herself. Only that small handful were aware that the arms and chest of the dead king's gilded chainmail had been padded with potatoes and carrots wrapped in cloth, that his beard and hair had been fashioned from tresses culled from Sunna's own head, that even his face had been filled out by stuffing wads of wool in his cheeks. It was Ulrich who had insisted, arguing that no one could see their mighty and powerful king, the great conqueror who had united all these lands and held them together by force of will and strength of arm all these years, laid low by something as common, as ignominious, as a mere illness.

Though there had been little to call "mere" about the plague that had brought Stigandr down. For all his years, he had still been vigorous, still capable of trouncing any three of his guards at once, still deadly enough to act as a deterrent to any who thought his advancing years might make him vulnerable—right up until the even deadlier disease had struck. Within days, his hair had begun to pale and break like dried wheat, his cheeks to hollow, his limbs to wither and shake. In under a week, he had seemed to age a dozen years, two dozen, three—he had transformed from warrior to dotard before their very eyes, even as his own grew filmed and dull. His mind had wandered as well, hazy visions of the past filling it and crowding out the present, until the fearsome Stigandr was left drooling and muttering to himself, reliving past glories, despite his limbs lacking enough strength to hold him upright.

The end had come quickly, his breathing growing more and more labored, his mind less and less clear. Lothar had done all he could, but none of his elixirs and poultices had slowed the disease's inexorable march in the slightest. It had almost been a relief when the king had rattled out his last breath, his trembling, wasted body relaxing at last.

But while his torments had ended, Sunna's had only just begun.

Even now, as she knelt here, her knees pressed against the hard marble of the first step leading to the low dais from which her father had ruled, she could feel the glares at her back, like so many daggers, sharp and pointed and often envenomed. The vast throne room was silent as a grave, no one daring to so much as breathe loudly at such a sorrowful occasion—yet she could hear the whispers, the jeers, as if they had been called out to echo across the long chamber. She knew what they were all saying, what they were all thinking. She had known most of her life, and heard it often enough from those without tact or sympathy.

From her own dearly departed father, most of all.

"Look at you!" he'd sneered at her often enough, eyeing her up and down. "Why couldn't you have taken after me, at least? If you had to be a girl, couldn't you at least have had some muscle on you?"

But other than his dark coloring, Sunna had inherited her looks and build from her mother instead, and Athala had been tall and slender, long, golden hair framing an oval face dominated by large, bright eyes. Stigandr had been drawn to her willowy grace and ethereal beauty—but would have preferred a brawnier child to emerge from their union. Particularly since Athala had taken ill and perished when Sunna had still been but a child, and her father had chosen not to remarry, thus ensuring that his daughter would remain his only legitimate and acknowledged child, and his presumed heir.

An heir who would soon find herself beleaguered, Sunna knew. Not at this moment, of course. Custom demanded that the dead king lay in state for three days, sundown to sunup, so all his loyal subjects might pay their respects. That time was sacred, and no one would dare breach it with something so crass as a play for the crown, not when such actions would bring them universal scorn and an accompanying resistance from every quarter. No, for three days, she would be left alone, and her father's throne would remain empty, his sword unclaimed.

At sunup on the fourth day, however, she would need to either step aside or take up Behorde herself—and to do the latter, she would first need to remove any obstacles in her path. Of which she expected many.

Still, while Sunna had not her father's brawn, she had certainly inherited his guile, and her mother's grace, along with a certain sharpness and strength of her own. Kneeling there, head bowed, hair still hanging in a thick braid down her back, even after sacrificing a third of its length to mask her father's final state, Sunna allowed herself a small, quick smile.

Yes, the first dawn after mourning will be an interesting time, to be sure. A good bit more interesting than many here might expect.

* * *

As it transpired, the interval before complications arose was far, far shorter than even Sunna had feared. She had only just departed the throne room, her knees, back, and shoulders aching from holding herself so still, so upright, for all those hours, when a throat cleared behind her.

Glancing over her shoulder, Sunna was too tired, too raw to entirely conceal the way she stiffened at the sight of the broad-shouldered young man making his way toward her down the corridor. His rich cloak and gold-trimmed velvet doublet caught the light of each torch he passed, but still didn't match the fiery tones of his long, wavy hair and neat, short beard.

Ancestors, give me strength, she thought, lifting her chin and assuming what she had been taught was a noble expression, which meant that she looked both bored and slightly annoyed, if what she'd seen when practicing in the mirror had been any indication.

She didn't speak, however. As she'd been told time and again throughout her youth, the one to move first surrendered the advantage, and this was as true in conversation as it was in combat. Instead, she held her tongue, fixing the approaching gentleman with a haughty gaze that spoke volumes, yet left the hallway silent save for his footsteps.

At last, upon reaching her, he swept into a shallow bow, though his gaze insolently remained upon her the entire time. "Milady," he declared, straightening and shifting his cloak to a handsomer angle, neither of which brought his own head higher than the bridge of her nose.

"Your Royal Highness," she corrected primly. "Graf."

He bristled slightly at both the reprimand and the use of his title, for while many might have been pleased to obtain such a rank, Sunna knew that for Odovacar Lanfrank, it was an embarrassment. He had often been heard declaring to any who might listen that, had his forebears possessed his own skills, charm, and drive, he would have been fürst or herzog by now, if not in fact könig. His tone and demeanor always made it abundantly clear that Odovacar meant to remedy that injustice as quickly as possible.

"I hope you will forgive my intrusion upon your grief," he stated, stroking his beard where it came to a sharp point in a vain attempt to disguise a weak chin, "yet there is a delicate matter concerning us both, and I felt it could not wait."

"Oh?" Sunna drew upon every bit of disdain her father, among others, had directed at her. "I cannot imagine how such a thing might exist."

Yet Odovacar was not to be dissuaded so easily. "It is the question of your inheritance," he persisted. "For surely, Prinzessin, you must know you won't be allowed to assume your father's throne."

At least this time, he addressed me correctly!

"Allowed?" She started to bristle, almost reaching out to strike him for his audacity, but then remembered her plan and allowed herself only to respond verbally. "I was unaware I required anyone's *permission* to possess that which is already mine."

Giving her what he no doubt thought a warm and engaging smile, but which came off as oily instead, Odovacar shrugged. "It is only yours if you can take it and hold it," he reminded her. "And that seems... unlikely." His smile widened. "Unless, of course, you have help."

She frowned as if only just getting his unsubtle hint. "And I take it you're offering such assistance?"

"I am indeed." This time his bow was far deeper, almost grandiose—if sadly offset by the leer framed between his whiskers.

"For, alone, you can never hope to hold the crown. Together, however, we would be unstoppable." He dared to reach for her hand. "Only marry me, and our claim will be unassailable, your heritage and my skill wedded in the perfect union."

Sunna could not stop herself from yanking her hand back, narrowly escaping his grasping fingers. "Marry you?" she replied sharply. "And, what, cede you my rule in the bargain? I think not." The smile she gave him in return was razor-edged. "You would bring little or nothing of value to such a match, my good Graf. No, I thank you for your kind offer, but I must decline."

"What?" Odovacar's eyes bulged slightly, and his face grew red, those same greasy fingers clenching quickly into fists. "You would dare refuse me, you—" His words died as a shadow detached from the wall just beyond Sunna and stepped forward, mail, conical helmet, and tapered spear tip gleaming as it entered the circle of light.

"Is there a problem, Your Royal Highness?" the royal guardsman asked, his eyes only upon Sunna, though she knew he was well aware of the greedy nobleman facing her.

"No," she replied after letting Odovacar sweat a moment. "The graf here was merely offering me his condolences. Is that not true, sir?" She gave him a bright smile, chuckling inside as his flush deepened.

"Yes, of course," he was forced to agree, especially since a second guard had just stepped out farther along the corridor, making it clear that Odovacar was outnumbered and vastly outmatched. "And now I must return to my estates. If you'll excuse me." He backed away even before she'd nodded her dismissal, face carefully blank, but eyes hot and angry as he turned and beat a hasty retreat.

"Thank you," Sunna said softly once he was gone. "I don't know that things would have resolved half as quickly, or as calmly, if you hadn't been here."

"Of course, Prinzessin," the guard replied with a crisp bow. "That is our job, after all." It was, and Badurad had been performing that duty since she'd been a little girl. He was now captain of the household guard, and his blond hair had begun to go white in places, but he was still powerful, and still deadly. And, though he'd never been kindly toward Sunna, he'd never actively disrespected her, either.

Which was more than she could say for some. Including a certain deluded young graf.

* * *

Orinda, of course, was pensive when Sunna related the incident to her—her lady's maid had not been present in the audience chamber, as only the nobility had been permitted to pay their respects this first day.

"Perhaps," the older woman stated carefully, well aware of the shaky ground upon which she trod, "you should've considered his offer, at least for a moment. Granted him the courtesy of that much respect."

Tucked carefully beneath the more innocuous statement was her true opinion, vividly clear after so many years together, that a union might indeed be the prudent course, and the only way to preserve any portion of Sunna's inheritance, not to mention her status and way of life.

But Sunna was having none of her maid's concern for circumspection. "Respect?" she retorted, dropping the heavy mourning robes onto a chest, and rounding on Orinda, who stood her ground in the face of the princess' wrath, as she had so many times over the years, when these private chambers had been the only place Sunna had been free to truly express herself. "Such as he showed me? Cornering me in a corridor, his words as slimy as his touch, trying to force himself upon me—I have little doubt, if Badurad had not been present, the oaf would have attempted to do so physically as well as verbally, presenting my bloodstained undergarments afterward as proof that we were now wed!"

Her companion gasped at the ugliness of both word and image, but Sunna would not be stopped. "There is no respect for such as him," she insisted, folding her arms across her regrettably slight chest, which was now constrained only by her thin linen shift. "There is only power, enough to keep him from making such a disgusting and demeaning attempt ever again."

"Then you still mean to go through with this nonsense?" Orinda's brow furrowed, but she only sighed and shook her head, knowing after all this time the futility of dissuading her mistress from following her own course. "I fail to see how you think this will end well."

"It will end how it will end," Sunna replied, trying to soften the bite in her words to make it clear it was still Odovacar she was angry with, and not Orinda, who'd raised her, educated her, and comforted her after her mother had passed. "But if it fails, at least I will know I did not give in willingly. I will force them to take what they want over my bleeding and broken body."

With that, she shrugged into the clothes already laid out upon her bed, and lifted her hair, a mute request for aid that her maid of course answered, the older woman's fingers still deft and sure as she fastened the ties across the back and down each side.

When she'd finished, Orinda stepped back and nodded once. "You are your father's daughter, and no question," she said, and whether she meant it as a compliment or a criticism, Sunna could not tell, but she chose to take it as the former, and as a sign that perhaps her mad scheme might yet succeed.

She left the maid standing there, staring after her, as she moved to the partially open door and then slipped through it, out into the hall.

But not back toward the audience chamber or the other public rooms of the palace. No, instead Sunna turned to the left, following the corridor around and deeper into the private areas, heading toward a space set near the back that she had come to know all too well. One that fools and knaves like Odovacar had no idea she would even consider approaching.

They would soon learn their mistake.

* * *

Kirsa frowned and tapped Sunna's arm with the wooden baton she held, and none too gently. "You are no chicken," the royal guard insisted, her words as harsh as her gaze. "Stop flapping your arms about like you mean to fly with them. Keep them tucked in tight. Every movement efficient, no more energy expended than needed. Again."

Blinking sweat from her eyes, Sunna scowled, but rose back into a half-crouch, glaring at the woman across from her, who returned her gaze with neither malice nor affection. They were not, and never would be friends, but in Kirsa at least, Sunna had found one of the handful who would treat her without prejudice, but also without coddling, and who would push her and test her without the deliberate intent to see her fail. As one of the few women in the palace guard, and the only one to ever achieve the level of sergeant, Kirsa knew all too well how infuriating it was to be treated as some fragile doll granted allowances merely because of her gender—as bad as being discounted for it and never given the chance to try.

That, at least, was one area where Sunna had to admit her father had been truly great. He'd taken each person on their own merits, regardless of age, gender, or birth. That was why Kirsa had risen so high, the king's recognition of her skills outweighing any prejudice she might have faced from her commanders. His treatment of Sunna hadn't been dismissive because she'd been born female, but only because of her slight build and apparent frailty.

If he could see her now, Sunna wondered, what might he think? Would he revise his opinion? Consider her not a weakness and a vulnerability, as he had so often over the years? Many times she'd longed to confront him, to show him, to force him to admit he'd been wrong. Each time she'd stopped, however, cold practicality outweighing her desire for validation and affection. Winning her father's respect would have been sweet, but in the end, keeping her true talents concealed was the wiser move. That meant her enemies would have no time to prepare, making them far easier to take on and topple than if she'd presented herself to her father, and he'd paraded her proudly before them.

She thought, were he still alive, Stigandr himself would have applauded such a choice. "Affection is a weakness," she could almost hear him saying, his voice deep and rough as it had been before the illness stole its strength and timbre. "It is a fleeting thing, and leaves behind only softness your enemy can exploit. Conceal such things deep within you, where they cannot see them, and thus cannot reach them. Show them only a hard shell, armor they cannot crack."

Very well, Father, Sunna thought grimly, readying herself once more. *Here is my armor. Let them try and crack it.* She set her feet, as Kirsa charged again, and concentrated on fending off the sergeant's swift and powerful attack. Kirsa never held back in these exercises. Sunna appreciated that. She knew the men she'd soon face wouldn't hold back, either.

Then again, neither would she.

* * *

The second day passed much as the first had, with Sunna spending it on her knees before her father's empty throne, head bowed in grief, but back straight with pride, heavy mourning robes stiff with gems and golden thread, dark hair unadorned and bound back in a simple braid. Behind her were those who had been allowed in to pay their respects—mostly lesser nobles and merchants today, men of substance who lacked the titles necessary to be admitted the day before.

Those came and went, some entering only long enough to kneel and duck their heads once, others lingering a few moments. But Sunna had entered before the sun's rays had touched the room through the high arched windows, having gulped only a cup of strong, hot tea, a small hard roll, and a pair of dried sausages beforehand for much-needed sustenance, and she had already been kneeling when the outer doors were opened.

And here she would remain, unmoving, until the sun had set, and the doors were closed once more. Such was tradition, and she would not let it be said, nor even hinted, that she had failed in her duties toward her father or her title.

Upon finally standing at the end of the day, massaging the feeling back into numb limbs before limping through the small door at the back of the dais and into the private hallway leading toward the royal family's chambers, Sunna found herself accosted yet again. This time, however, the figure was both more familiar and more dreaded than the oily Odovacar, for this was not someone she could simply brush off or count upon the palace guard to frighten away.

"We must speak, Prinzessin," Ulrich Eike insisted, planting himself firmly in her path, his stocky frame still sturdy after so many years at her father's side, even though he had long since traded shield and axe for a steward's robes and chain of office. "We must discuss the transition of power."

"There is nothing to discuss, Ulrich," Sunna told him sharply, hands going to her hips as she was forced to stop. "The day after tomorrow, I will assume my father's throne. That is all."

The steward's squared face flushed, his mouth set in a deep scowl. "You know that will not happen," he told her bluntly, for he'd never bothered to hide his disdain toward her, his attitude borrowed heavily from her father, as so much of his life had been. "They will never let you reach the dais, much less the sword." He gave her a strange look, almost one of affection. "Let me help you plan another course. One that will let you keep your life, and perhaps even your dignity."

Sunna could not help it—she laughed in his face, causing him to flush further. "How, by marrying one of those slavering beasts drooling over my father's crown? Would you have me accept Odovacar's empty offer, 'your heritage and my skill wedded into a perfect union?'" Her laughter died away at the look upon the aging steward's face. "You would! And not just as an example, but him specifically! You've spoken to him on the matter, perhaps even promised you'd convince me to change my mind. Gods above, is *everyone* plotting against me?"

"I am trying to *save* you!" Ulrich roared, hints of the old warrior emerging once more. "Do not let stupid pride cost you everything! Far better a long life as the wife of a king than a short and ugly death as a doomed princess!"

She was surprised to see genuine anguish in his gaze and stepped forward without even thinking about it, lifting one hand to cup her palm against his cheek. "Thank you," she murmured, "for wishing to help me survive."

Never would she have expected such a sentiment from her father's oldest and staunchest ally. But thoughts of Stigandr stiffened her own resolve, and she retreated a pace again, her hand once more lowering to her side. "But you do not know, you could not, what you ask. A life as a slave, a decoration, a plaything—no. That would be far, far worse than a quick and valiant death. My father would have agreed."

She favored the steward with a small, sad smile. "One of the few things he and I did agree upon. Thank you, Ulrich, for your devotion to him—and, it seems, to me. But do not despair. I am not so helpless as I might appear."

Then she slid past him, leaving him standing there, staring openmouthed, and continued toward her quarters. Orinda awaited with food, drink, and less weighty garments. And after her, Kirsa and that damnable room, a hell of Sunna's own choosing—and a chance to escape the fate Ulrich was so certain awaited her in two more nights and one final, dreadful dawn.

* * *

The third day began much as the other two had, with Sunna rising early and presenting herself before her father's casket well before the doors opened to admit the masses. And today it was truly the masses, for on this third day, one and all were allowed entry to honor their dead king, down to the lowliest peasant. Nobles could attend today if they wished, just as they could have the day before, but of course none of them would ever consider sharing the same space as the great unwashed. It was only Sunna and the commoners today.

Thus she was startled out of her half-reverie as footsteps echoed on the polished marble floor, approaching from the rear. None had dared breach the invisible wall betwixt her and them, not even the most powerful nobles, yet those same steps continued, crossing the assumed barrier, and proceeding to her very side. A shadow hovered there, then dropped down upon her like a striking hawk as the bold individual sank to their knees only a few paces to her right.

"Greetings, sister." The voice was deep and rich, if the words themselves were rough-hewn, and she glanced toward the speaker, shocked by the effrontery as much as the specific language. A man knelt there, smirking at her, and her eyes narrowed as she took in both his dark, heavy features and his garb, which was the crude chain and plain tabard of a common soldier.

"I do not know you, sir," she stated, keeping her own voice far softer than his, which had rung out across the room and elicited startled gasps from those assembled, but putting as much ice into it as she could, until each syllable chilled the air between them. "And I would thank you to remove yourself to a respectable distance once more, as all these others have."

"Do you not?" he replied, his volume still well above conversational. "Gumarich Boyce, at your service." The bow he executed showed that he'd never been taught the courtly graces, but his continued smirk made it clear that he also didn't care. "But previous acquaintance or not, you must admit we share a common parent."

Nor was he wholly wrong. The rugged features, the sharp, nearly hooked nose, the piercing eyes under a strong brow like the spread wings of a hawk, the dark hair that hinted at red within, all of it mounted atop a tall, broad-shouldered frame with long, thick arms, and equally powerful legs. Yes, if she were being wholly honest, she could acknowledge some truth to his statement.

It seemed Stigandr's blood *had* bred true, at least once.

Yet there were truths, and there were *truths*. "I do not know you, sir," she repeated, this time loud enough that the palace guards, who had held back, waiting to see how she wished them to respond to this strange intrusion, now bestirred themselves and stepped forward on either side. "I would again ask that you remove yourself and pay your respects as all my father's other loyal subjects are."

That brought a quick scowl to his face, like a thundercloud suddenly descending upon a previously sunny day. Yes, much like her father—*their* father, it appeared. "But I am *not* a loyal subject," this Gumarich argued, rising to his feet and looming over her so she was forced to crane her neck back to see his face. "I am the son of a king, and will be king myself."

And with that, he took a step forward, setting one heavy boot upon the first stair to the dais.

"No!" Sunna found herself on her feet as well, hand outstretched, though he had carefully placed himself just out of arm's reach. "You dare not! This time is *sacred!*"

He only shrugged, that smirk resurfacing. "What are rules to a king?" he asked with a short laugh, and his body tensed, clearly about to shift his balance so he could lift his other leg and advance farther along this presumptuous path he had set himself.

It was in that instant, as he was off balance, that Badurad struck. The guard commander leapt in, his spear flashing, the tip describing an arc well overhead as he swept the butt of the sturdy shaft up— catching Gumarich Boyce under his raised knee, and jerking his foot off the polished floor, sending him toppling backward with a low cry. The arrogant stranger was quick to react, twisting about and planting both feet solidly on the ground again, but by the time he'd straightened, Badurad's spear was an inch from his throat, and two other guards had theirs pricking either side of his neck.

"The time of mourning is sacred," Badurad stated, his own voice not as deep or powerful, but his words carrying clearly, nonetheless. "If you feel you have cause to pursue the throne, you may present yourself on the morrow, as will any other claimants. Until then, as you have already paid your respects, you will be escorted from here and may not return this day."

There was a moment, heavy with potential violence, as the man, in appearance so like the father Sunna remembered from her childhood, locked gazes with the guard captain and clearly weighed his chances. Then he allowed himself the smallest of nods, a motion constrained by the triple points framing his head. "Very well," he declared loudly. "I will return on the morrow." And as the guards pulled back enough to allow him freedom of movement once more, he turned toward Sunna. "Sister, until then."

He marched out, the whispers gathering behind him like rats following a trail of breadcrumbs, and Sunna scowled after him before she remembered where she was and carefully resumed the blank, calm face of deep mourning she'd worn the past two days and more.

* * *

She was still fuming hours later, after sunset, when she had retreated to her rooms. Finding no solace there, and not in the mood to face Kirsa and her physical abuse, Sunna instead took herself to the one place in all the castle she felt truly safe and loved: the kitchens.

"That man!" she raged once she was seated by the hearth, a mug of hot, spiced tea in her hand, a plate of her favorite cakes at her side. "How *dare* he!"

"Perhaps," Cyneric agreed from where he stirred the massive pot containing the evening's soup, "but then again, in his place, could you truly blame him? What other chance has he to rise from his current station?"

"It is not his, it is *mine!*" Sunna snapped, though not at the head cook himself, for she loved him dearly and would never take her anger out on him. "*I* am the one who has been raised to it, the one who has suffered for it, the one who must have it!" *Or else I die,* she continued but did not say aloud, for she knew how such a brutal reminder would hurt the kindly man before her.

"And I agree with you," he assured her now, setting his ladle aside to sit by her and pat her hand, the only person aside from Orinda ever permitted such a familiar gesture. "But, again, if you were him, what would you do besides stride in and try to take what you feel is yours?"

Seen from that perspective, Sunna admitted she could understand this Gumarich's actions. The problem, of course, being: "This complicates my own plans, though."

"Does it?" Cyneric asked. "How? Does it in some way alter what you'd intended?"

"No," she was forced to admit after a moment's thought, "but it adds one more combatant to the fray. And a powerful one, from what I've seen."

"Good," the cook replied. "Then perhaps he can remove some of the others from the mix, saving you the trouble."

Sunna had not considered that, and now she beamed at him, winning an answering smile in return. "That is true. But I will still have to kill him afterward."

"Must you?" A frown touched her companion's face. "Would not defeating him be enough?" She shook her head, but he touched her hand again. "If you kill him, he can never learn and grow and make amends for his mistakes," Cyneric reminded her. He glanced over to where a younger man was dicing vegetables for the soup. "Hadubert, remember when you first started here, how you argued with me over the carrots?"

The other man laughed, not glancing up from his work. "Yes, I asked you, 'Why cut them so fine when you are only adding them to soup anyway? Just toss them in whole, it will be quicker!'" He grinned and lifted his head just long enough to wink at Sunna. "Of course, I was only thinking about saving myself all that work!"

She couldn't help but giggle, something she wouldn't have allowed herself elsewhere. But this kitchen had been her refuge since her mother died, the one place she didn't have to be the princess and heir. The one place she didn't require her armor.

"And what happened then?" Cyneric prodded his assistant.

"We made the soup the way I suggested," Hadubert recalled with a grimace and a shudder, "and served it like that. It was awful! Whole carrots floating everywhere, most of them only half cooked! Even the other servants wouldn't touch it!"

"Correct." The head cook smiled at the memory, but his eyes were on Sunna. "Many would have fired Hadubert then and there for daring to refuse a direct order, for arguing, for ruining a meal."

"But you did not," Sunna said, though she had only the vaguest memory of the incident.

"I did not," he agreed. "I knew he'd learned his lesson. And look at him now! A finer dicer of carrots you will never see!" He studied her. "Death does not allow one to learn, and a good ruler should never throw away something—or someone—that can be saved."

"My father would never stay his hand," Sunna pointed out, though less out of disagreement than to hear his reply.

Nor was she disappointed, as Cyneric favored her with a warm, fond smile. "You are not your father, and while he was a strong ruler, had he your mind and your heart, he would have been a great one as well."

Then he patted her arm and rose to his feet once more to see to that night's meal. Sunna watched him work, allowing the familiar patter of the kitchen to ease her tension as she sipped at her tea, but her mind was awhirl with what he had said. There were pieces of a puzzle there, some quite old, and some brand new, and although they were still floating every which way, a part of her felt she was beginning to see how they could all fit together into a seamless whole.

* * *

The next morning dawned clear and bright, but Sunna was not in the throne room. No one was, the great gilt doors shut and barred, the vast hall as empty as the throne at its front. Instead, the nobles of the kingdom were gathered in the small private chapel affixed to one end of the castle.

Stigandr had never been a great believer in religious observance—despite wielding a blade that came from the gods themselves—yet he'd known better than to completely spurn the traditions and rituals of the past and of this land. Today marked only the third time the king of Valernon was within that consecrated space, the first being when he'd wed Athala, and the second when Sunna had been named and consecrated. Now he lay in his gold casket, there before the humble pulpit, and the lords and ladies who'd fawned upon him in life came to pay one last obeisance.

Standing at the front of the small chapel, her eyes fixed upon her father's visage before her, Sunna could feel the energy crackling from the assemblage. In the throne room, it had been subdued, muted by some small amount of grief, a great deal of tradition, and even more manners. Now, however, the waiting period was nearly at an end, and impatience and ambition were rising to the fore, like hungry wolves flexing their paws and working their slavering jaws as they circled a helpless fawn, moving in slowly for the kill.

Much like that proverbial deer, Sunna did not move, as if standing stock still might somehow render her invisible to these circling predators. There was little help for it, however, as the priest finished his short sermon, commending her father's life and deeds. The casket was closed and then lifted upon the shoulders of six brawny guards, who carried it out of the chapel to the tiny private cemetery behind it.

Only one grave stood here already, that of her mother, and beside that yawned an open pit, dug the night before. The casket was lowered into that dark space, and Sunna knelt at its side, a single long-stemmed white rose held in her cold fingers. She tossed it down, the flower landing perfectly near the top of the casket, right above her father's head. Then, rising to her feet, Sunna stepped back to let others add flowers of their own, or shovelfuls of dirt, or both, if they chose.

She wanted to run back to the throne room, to leap onto the dais and grab Behorde before any could try to stop her, but of course, she did not. That would've been improper, and she'd been raised better than that, raised to be a proper princess. Thus, she waited instead until the last man and woman in attendance had turned from the grave, and the workers had grabbed shovels of their own to fill in the rest and consign her father to his final resting place. Only then did Sunna make her way, with slow dignity, back into the castle.

The halls were lined with men—no other women here!—but the great doors were still shut, for none there had the authority to order them open. Only her. With a nod, Sunna did so, stopping only a dozen paces shy as the guardsmen to either side lifted the heavy bar and carried it to rest in the corner, while two others grabbed the sturdy rings on each half and tugged, the massive doors gliding open as silently as a spider's web rustling in the breeze.

That, however, was when all patience and propriety ended. Nobles shoved past, jostling one another in their eagerness to enter first, to race across the marble floor, to rush toward the prize awaiting the first man bold enough to take it. Pushes became shoves became punches, and then steel glittered as it was drawn, and mere fisticuffs became true battle as men slashed and stabbed, blood spraying across pillars, tapestries, and pews.

Sunna let the wave wash over and past her, so the combat had begun well beyond where she still stood. Now she entered the room at last, and for a moment she simply stood, just within the doorway, watching these nobles brawling like the worst drunken louts, killing one another with snarls and curses and crazed looks in their eyes. Already, a handful lay dead or dying upon the floor, and as yet, no one had covered more than half the distance to the throne. With a smile, Sunna strode forward, head up, eyes locked on the prize, neither flinching nor faltering as she walked through the melee as if it was a light summer rain, the breeze of blows barely ruffling her braid or her long robes.

She had crossed that halfway mark before a man lurched into her path, reeling from being turned aside by another, and, glancing up, saw her there. "You!" he sneered, and the sword in his hand rose until the point was aimed at her right eye. "At least I can make sure *you* never sully the throne with your womanish ways!"

Sunna faced him with a slow, sharp smile of her own. "Can you?" she asked softly, her hands going to the fastenings of her robe. "Are you so sure? And by womanish ways, did you mean *these?*" His eyes went involuntarily to her chest as she tugged the robe open—and then she twisted out of the heavy garment and hurled it over his head, blinding and constricting him both at once. His sword was trapped in the thick fabric as well, and another man—perhaps the same one he'd been fighting before, perhaps another who merely saw the opportunity—wasted no time, stabbing into the tangle once, again, a third time until the whole bloody mass toppled with a gurgle and lay twitching a time or two.

"Many thanks, my lady!" The victor laughed, turning to salute her with his sword—and then his own eyes widened as he took in the sight before him. That hesitation proved more than enough, as Sunna disarmed him and then delivered him a sharp rap to the temple, sending him to the ground right beside the man he had just killed.

Others turned now as well, and the fighting paused as they stared at the woman before them. Gone were the fine robes, the quiet manner, and the frail form. Before them stood a warrior, tall and slender, but her limbs taut with muscle, hardened leather and tight-knit chain wrapping her body, but allowing free movement, her hair tugged back in a long braid to leave her sight clear—and a pair of short, slim swords clasped in her hands.

This was what Sunna had been waiting for, training for, all this time. At last, she was done with the pose of the pale, feeble princess. At last, she stood revealed as her father's daughter in truth.

One lord—she knew him, an obstinate, arrogant lout who'd always leered at her behind her father's back—stomped toward her, his own heavy blade raised in one fleshy hand. "What game are you playing at, girl?" he demanded rudely, his face already red from his exertions, but the lack of cuts showing that he possessed at least some skill at arms. "Drop those toys now and stand aside while we determine which of us will bed you and take your father's throne."

In response, Sunna laughed. "None of you will touch me," she promised, her words carrying throughout the room. "Not with any part of you. And none of you will have that throne, either. For it is mine, by birth and by blood, and I will kill any man who stands in my way."

He sneered at her. "Fine. I don't need such a fragile bride, anyway!" His sword swung in a heavy arc toward her neck.

But Sunna's neck was no longer there. She dropped into a crouch beneath the ponderous sweep and stabbed forward with her own swords, the pair of them angled up. Their tips pierced his chest and met in his heart, and she yanked them down and free as she rose, dancing backward as the sword fell from his lifeless fingers an instant before he followed it to the floor.

"Anyone else wish to try their luck?" she declared, eyeing the lords who stood gaping at her and the death she'd just wrought. Many of them, shocked to their senses by the suddenness and unexpectedness of the bout, backed away, shaking their heads.

Good. Each one who yields is one less for me to face.

But one man forced his way to the front, and Sunna's heart sank a little, her stomach clenching as she took in his tall, broad, muscular form, his stern features, and his simple uniform.

"I have no desire to kill you, my sister," Gumarich Boyce announced, his own sword held almost idly in his hand. "Yet if I must defeat you to claim the crown, I will, even if it means your death." He lifted the blade, holding it straight and steady without effort. "Yield now, and I will spare your life."

Sunna snarled a wordless refusal, hefting her own weapons, and the battle was joined.

He was stronger than her, that much had been evident from the start. She was faster, though not by much. His blows were powerful, hammering at her defenses, but never so massive as to overbalance him and leave him vulnerable. She couldn't pierce his guard, his one blade fast enough to block her two, and large enough to shield him at all angles, yet she was quick enough that he couldn't reach her, either. She had the better training, but his reach and strength stole away that advantage, leaving her hard pressed. And she suspected his would prove the greater endurance, meaning in a drawn-out battle, he would ultimately prevail.

She'd have to find another way to gain the upper hand—which reminded her of a certain tale, and gave her an idea.

Slowly, Sunna gave way before her alleged half-brother, step by step. No one intervened, the rest of the room content to watch and wait, knowing whichever way this match ended, one of their strongest rivals would be dispatched. Gumarich himself was now drenched in sweat, his sword swings taking their toll even on his muscles. Sunna could feel the sweat dripping down her back as well, and along her forehead, but she blinked it away and continued parrying his blows, backpedaling as she did so. Then her right heel bumped up against something hard and unyielding.

The marble steps.

"Nowhere left to run, sister," Gumarich taunted, pressing his attack. He paused, however, frowning, when she smiled in return.

"No need," she answered as sweetly as she could. "I'm right where I want to be." She feinted high with both blades, forcing him to raise his sword to block—and then kicked him full in the stomach, driving him back a good three feet, and nearly toppling him.

Not that it mattered if he fell. All she'd needed was the space, enough room to turn—and leap onto the dais, where her father's throne waited for her.

And, more importantly at the moment, the naked sword straddling its arms, begging to be lifted.

Tossing her twin swords aside, Sunna reached out, her hand clamping down on the strangely scaled wrappings of the handle. Then she spun back, raising Behorde, its blade catching the sunlight as she held it high above her head.

A thrill raced through her, like when she had just beaten Kirsa in a bout, like when she'd been young and had run with her mother, laughing, through the courtyards. It sped down her arm, across her chest, into head and heart and legs, filling her with near giddiness from its power. This was what her father had felt when he had first held Behorde. No wonder he'd never wished to set it down again!

Gumarich had regained his footing and now glared up at her, but Sunna could see fear in his eyes as well.

"Think carefully upon your next move," she warned, her voice low but thrumming with excitement still as she brought her weapon into a proper ready position, held low in both hands, with the blade slanted upward and across her body. "We were well matched, you and I, but that was before I held the sword of legend. With its might added to my own skill, do you truly believe you can best me?"

He eyed her, his jaw set, and she thought he might still try for it, seeing that stubbornness she had grown up watching.

But then he sighed, lowering his eyes, and his sword drooped in his hands. "No," he admitted. "I yield." And he sank to his knees, proffering his blade before him in both hands. "I swear fealty to you, sister, and ask for mercy."

Mercy. Sunna's lips twitched at the word, for it had rarely been heard in this kingdom. The sword she held twitched as well, swinging outward as if it would leap across that gap and take Gumarich's head from his neck all on its own.

And perhaps I should follow the enchanted weapon's lead, she thought. He had fought against her, tried to take her life and her throne. That was treason, was it not? And the penalty for treason was death. She would be well within her rights to exact that penalty from him, from all of them.

The sunlight caught upon gold along the blade, drawing her eyes to the words etched there, words she had been told, but had never seen herself before now:

Resisting power comes at a price

Yes, she thought. Gumarich Boyce had resisted, and now he would pay the price. As would they all. That was lawful and good.

But was it *right*? Cyneric's words came to mind. Would killing these men, even if it was within her purview as queen, be the correct thing to do? Would it be the best use of her power? Would it in any way aid her kingdom?

Or was there another way? A better way? A way her father, for all his strengths, could never have seen?

The blade still rose in her hand, and Sunna knew, if she held onto it long enough, she would wind up using it. But what else could she do? There was nowhere to put it. There never had been, not since her father had first tossed its scabbard aside.

Odd that the sheath had never been found. Surely, they'd looked for it. Had someone made off with it? Had it fallen into the river behind the mill, to be washed out to sea?

Or was there another explanation? Words could be used in more than one way, and Sunna had spent her whole life twisting her father's orders and edicts to give herself enough room to breathe. She was an expert at finding hidden meanings. It was just another puzzle.

And in her head, those pieces finally came together.

Holding Behorde with one hand, Sunna raised her other, fingers splayed open. "Resisting power comes at a price," she whispered to no one but herself, "and that price must be blood. But only a tyrant indulges in the unnecessary use of their power, and a ruler—a true ruler—pays the price on their subjects' behalf."

And she pricked the ball of her thumb with the sword's tip.

A single drop of blood emerged, to flow down the length of the blade. It slid across the runes there, turning their gold red—and the letters flowed like ink under water, puddling, pooling, and reshaping until they had formed new words altogether, golden once more:

True power is worn with quiet dignity

At the same time her mind took in that statement, Sunna felt something encircling her waist, and a light but noticeable weight at her side. Glancing down, she saw that a wide, segmented belt had appeared there, its broad links hammered gold over supple leather. Hanging from it was a scabbard, covered in the same red-tinged charcoal scales as Behorde's handle.

With a smile, Sunna slid the blade home, and the battlelust that had risen within her upon wielding it faded, leaving her clearheaded and lighthearted.

"I accept your surrender, and your fealty, Gumarich Boyce," she stated in a powerful, majestic voice she hadn't known she possessed. "Arise and serve your queen faithfully and well, and be rewarded for your loyalty."

But even as her half-brother—for she somehow knew his claim to be true, without a doubt—stood once more, raising his sword in salute, another man shouldered through the crowd, his face blotchy with rage, and more crimson than his hair.

"NO!" Odovacar screamed, hefting the heavy dagger in his hand. "You will never rule! Die instead!" And the oily little graf flung the weapon at her chest with all his strength.

Whatever he lacked in sword skill, manners, or grace, the graf clearly possessed in throwing, for the dagger flew straight and true. There was no time to block it, no time to dodge, so Sunna stood still, refusing to flinch even in the face of her death. She was Stigandr's daughter, and if this was the end, she would meet it with her head held high.

She watched as the blade approached, its tip gleaming wickedly, her death clearly written along its edge—and then a golden light sprang up around her, a honeyed dome protecting her on all sides. The dagger did not merely bounce off the strange nimbus, but was hurled backward along the same path it had followed, spinning at the last second to bury the point deep in Odovacar's right eye. The graf barely had time to scream before he toppled, dead before his skull bounced against the marble with a dull thud.

If the throne room had been silent before, it was nearly sepulchral now, as no one moved even a muscle.

Then Sunna smiled, and it was as if a wave had broken, that strange dome shattering and spilling out across the entire room, all the anger, hatred, and rage washing away before the warmth and light.

For now, at last, the true power of Behorde stood revealed. Quiet dignity, indeed, it radiated from the slim young woman standing before them, one unafraid to use her authority—but also strong enough to rule without resorting to such measures unless needed.

Cyneric was right, Sunna thought as she gazed over the room at the row upon row of men who now lowered their swords and dropped to their knees. *I* will *be a great queen. Greater than my father ever was, kinder, but no less strong for all that.*

It was a new day in Valernon, and the future looked bright, indeed.

* * * * *

Aaron Rosenberg Bio

Aaron Rosenberg is the author of the best-selling DuckBob SF comedy series, the Relicant Chronicles epic fantasy series, the Dread Remora space-opera series, and, with David Niall Wilson, the O.C.L.T. occult thriller series. His tie-in work contains novels for *Star Trek*, *Warhammer*, *World of WarCraft*, *Stargate: Atlantis*, *Shadowrun*, and *Eureka*. He has written children's books (including the award-winning *Bandslam: The Junior Novel* and the #1 best-selling *42: The Jackie Robinson Story*), educational books, and roleplaying games (including the Origins Award-winning *Gamemastering Secrets*).

He is also an author in the new Eldros Legacy epic fantasy series, with his first novel in that setting, *Deadly Fortune*, coming out in May, 2022.

Aaron lives in New York. You can follow him online at gryphonrose.com, at facebook.com/gryphonrose, and on Twitter @gryphonrose.

* * * * *

Fellblade
by Nathan Balyeat

Davin slipped the overhand blow, his opponent's sword whistling past his helmet. He pressed inside his opponent's guard to deny him room to swing his sword, but failed to do so before his opponent stepped out of range. Again.

"Nicely done, Alaric," he said, panting. They were on the third minute of the practice duel, neither man having landed a blow with their wooden practice swords.

Alaric took a few breaths before responding, carefully keeping his distance. "You're still thinking like a soldier. You're holding back on your counters and trying to minimize risks as if you were on a battlefield and may have to defend from another direction at any time. Duels are different. You've got one man to worry about. If you'd used a downward block with the slip, you could have had a wide open strike."

"But that would have left me open to…"

"You're making my point for me."

"So more aggressive on the counters and ripostes? Even though it leaves me open to everyone else. That'll get me killed on the battlefield."

"You aren't Order of War, Dav. Your duties are bigger than that. Bigger than any of the orders. You can't just be one thing."

Davin stepped back, clearly disengaging. "War *is* coming, even if the high king isn't acknowledging it. You've seen the reports, too."

Alaric nodded. "I agree. What are the odds, if the old man goes to war, that you or your father will be anywhere near the front lines? You're more likely going to be back at the capital—"

"A glorified bodyguard," Davin spat. "The king is over a hundred years old. Outlived his children and grandchildren. All my father does anymore is sit in council meetings and follow the senile bat around. He does everything but change soiled undergarments."

"Milord."

Davin froze at the sudden formality from his friend.

"Milord, he's your sovereign, by the grace of the One True God. He rules through divine mandate, and he and he alone wields the powers that keep the Veil strong and the horrors from Beyond at bay."

Davin hung his head. "I'm not sure I believe anymore. The last Hellwar was hundreds of years ago. No one alive today has seen a miracle, and even the Order of Magic can't do anything more than fancy parlor tricks and keep the old works running. Where are the bolts of lightning? Walls of wind that turn aside skies blackened with arrows?"

"That's not why you don't believe, is it?"

"No."

"It's about the sword, isn't it? Your grandfather was never able to manifest its power. Neither could your father."

"And I don't know if it will work for me."

"It may be that it's just a sword. That it never had any power. It's not a thing that makes someone special. The measure of a man or woman is in how they conduct themselves. Do they fulfill their duty? Do they live a just life and make the world a better place? It's who they are, not what they are. Your ancestors were the best of us. Your father and grandfather are heroes and known as good, honorable men. You're a good man, Dav, and you're uniquely placed to do good for others, magic hereditary sword or not."

"It's just that without it, without an Order, I don't feel like I have a place. There's no heir for me to protect while my father serves High King Johannes. I… I feel useless."

"I don't know, you make a pretty good practice dummy." Alaric raised his sword to prompt Davin to take up his guard when the sound of a galloping horse approaching their campsite drew their attention.

"Lord Davin, a message for Lord Davin!"

Knights and soldiers in the camp pointed toward the pair of knights. Davin waved his sword and shouted a reply, "Here, messenger! Here!"

The messenger, a young woman wearing a green cloak embroidered with the black raven and silver crescent moon of the Order of Night, rode up. She stumbled as she dismounted her blown horse. "Milord Fellblade, a message for you." She reached into her satchel and pulled out a tightly folded letter, sealed with gold wax and impressed with the five crowns heraldry of the high king.

"You shouted for me, and then presented a letter for the Fellblade. Is the message for me or my father?"

"Milord Davin, you are the Fellblade now. Your father is dead."

He looked at the message in the hands of the exhausted young woman. "What happened?"

"I know not, only that your father is dead. That's all the exchange I had with the rider before me. This came straight from the capital via messenger, highest priority."

The messenger system of the Five Kingdoms maintained outposts along major highways and minor roads, and was used mostly for the routine transfer of communications. Normally a single courier would travel a hundred miles or so in a day, swapping horses a number of times along the route, until they passed their message to the next messenger in the chain.

This far on the road to Norfort, she would have been the sixth or seventh rider in the chain. There was no way she could have any personal knowledge of the message's origins.

"Thank you, ser—?"

"Ser Traithe, milord. Traithe Greenbriar."

"Ser Traithe, you and the other riders have my thanks."

She pressed the letter into his hand with both of hers, slipping a coin into his palm under the letter, and meeting his eyes with a meaningful look.

Davin gave a slight nod of acknowledgment.

"Alaric, could you escort the knight to the camp and have her horse taken care of? Ask my page to provide her with food and drink, and a place to rest."

Alaric bowed more deeply than he ever had before, the formality of it uncomfortable for Davin. "Yes, Milord Fellblade."

"Don't spread that around yet. Let me see what the letter says first."

* * *

Davin found a nearby boulder to sit on, suddenly exhausted, and opened the letter with trembling hands.

Ser Davin,

It is my burden to report the death of your father. He perished in a fire in the King's Tower on sixth day of Harvest. As is codified in law and in the longest traditions of the Five Kingdoms, you are formally recognized as the sole legitimate her to the titles and properties of the Fellblade, Champion of the Five Kingdoms. You are formally relieved of all other duties and obligations and are recalled to the capital with all possible haste.

In his High Majesty's Name,

Darius

* * *

"Well, Alaric, what do you think?"

Alaric tossed the letter on the table in Davin's tent. "I think that's as insulting as one can be without provoking a duel. I don't see any of the usual pleasantries that accompany even the most terrible news. There's no attempt to soften the news of your father's death, or even a token mention of your father's long service to the king. There's no mention of you assuming the *duties* of the Fellblade or reporting to the high king. And then there's the fact that snake Darius wrote the letter in the first place."

Alaric stood and began to pace. "It's an open secret he's been trying to pull more power into the hands of the Church for a long time. Your father and Warmaster Garrett, along with a handful of other high lords in their coalition, have been the primary opposition to his efforts. With Garrett up at Norfort, and your father dead..."

"The coalition might not survive."

"Leaving Darius in charge."

Davin muttered a profanity. "I need to leave as soon as possible to see what I can do to preserve the balance of power."

"I'm coming with you, Dav. We'll bring the whole battalion back with us in case there's something fishy going on. My knights and levies will support you."

"No. That would be too slow. My orders are clear, and I don't think we want to give Darius any more time than absolutely necessary to consolidate his position. I also want to reinforce Norfort, just in case. If Keleban's hordes are coming south again, like the rumors say, they'll be needed."

"I'll come with you, then, and leave Captain Harrison in charge of the troops. He's as reliable as they come."

"As much as I'd like that, I need you to personally carry our concerns to the king at Norfort. He needs to know what happened to my father and may have some additional insight. I can't trust anyone else here to do that."

Alaric sighed. "All right. I understand. You'll at least need an escort. Let me loan you some troops."

"I'll be fine. I was planning on taking Traithe. She knows how to travel fast and avoid trouble."

"Can you trust her?"

"I've got reasons to think her order is above suspicion. Especially at the messenger rank."

"What about your squires and page?"

"Take care of them for me. I'll enlist my father's team when I get back to Ger."

Alaric nodded. "When will you leave?"

"Before I got back to the tent, I ordered the horses and remounts prepared. I'll be ready to go shortly."

* * *

Davin was checking the contents of his travel bags in the now empty tent only to be startled by a voice behind him.

"You didn't mention the coin."

He spun and drew his dagger in a single motion. Traithe was standing well within striking distance. If she'd intended him harm, she could have put one or both of the short swords at her belt into him instead of speaking.

Only a little embarrassed to have been snuck up on, he replaced his dagger. "I didn't. I don't know that he needed to know."

The coins were a private code used by the Order of Night, and also by the Fellblade household. In this case, the gambling token from the Green Dragon Inn south of the capital meant he was requested to meet someone there. The denomination and other "wear" on the coin told him what time of day to arrive.

"Did the coin come with the letter?" he asked.

"Yes."

"Can I assume you overheard my conversation with Alaric?"

"Most of it. Enough. I'm not surprised, but capital machinations aren't my assignment, so I don't really have any insight for you, Milord Fellblade."

Davin shivered. It was going to take some time to get used to that. "Very well. Let's get going. We can fill each other in on what we know while on the road."

* * *

Davin's return journey to the capital city of Ger wasn't nearly as fast as the messenger relay that had brought him the news of his father's death. The first few days, they utilized horses and remounts they brought with them, stopping for the night at messenger stations and fortresses along the highways until they arrived at the town of Rockslide, where Davin commandeered a fast carriage transport company, writing a promissory note for reimbursement. While each mile passed slower than on a horse, the carriage companies maintained their own equivalent of stables and messengers, allowing them to travel day and night.

"Well, Traithe," Davin said quietly so as not to be overheard by the coachman as the carriage rattled down the stone paved highway, "what can you fill me in on? I can't believe you don't know more than you've let on."

The Order of Night were the scouts and skirmishers of the armies of the Five Kingdoms, in addition to their roles as official messengers. Their general lack of military structure, failure to use the heavier armors and weapons considered knightly and honorable, and perceived lack of discipline led most to dismiss them as anything more. Some, like Davin and his father before him, knew the Order of Night were the unofficial intelligence arm of the Five Kingdoms, reporting only to the high king, the Fellblade, and the mysterious head of their order. Davin had never been told who their leader was. His father had claimed not to know, either.

"Well, milord, you and Ser Alaric discussed much of what I can confirm. Keleban's armies have been mustering to the north, preparing for a fall and winter campaign." The insanity of engaging in a winter war in the north was one of the reasons given back at the capital for not taking the threat of imminent conflict more seriously. "Some of our agents who were watching Darius failed to report in recent months. He's been making himself very visible within and around the city, making personal donations to people and organizations of both high and low status. Despite his vocal opposition to calling a general muster from the kings and high lords, he's been quietly recruiting and training infantry and crossbowmen at Church holdings distant from the capital. They've been mustering them on lands held directly by the Church. The people love him right now, but the rank and file of the knightly orders are of very... mixed opinions."

"Is there anyone you think I can trust back in the city?"

"As I've said before, I don't have any real insight on the capital and its politics. You probably have more of an idea of who you can trust than I do."

"That's the problem. I don't. In retrospect, my father worked very hard over the past few years to make sure I was as busy as possible outside the city. He didn't have to work all that hard to encourage me. I've always preferred practicing for war to playing politics."

"I can sympathize, milord. There's not much in the way of politics you have to play as an official messenger. I like not having to worry about that."

"And when you were acting unofficially?"

"Politics is dirty business."

* * *

"What were you able to find out?" Davin asked Traithe.

The young woman looked defeated. "As at every other change of horse and drivers along the way, I haven't been able to connect with anyone I'd expect to. It might be that we haven't stopped long enough to make contact, but it doesn't feel right."

"It's the same on my end. The staff and patrons of the carriage stations seem to feel uneasy, even if they can't put a finger on it. There's some minor sadness at my father's passing, though there's a fair number of people who aren't even aware of it. As we get closer and closer to the capitol, I'd expect it to be common knowledge. Like you said, it doesn't feel right."

* * *

The carriage rattled to a halt at the gates to the Tower of the Fellblade late at night, well after the midnight bell. The squat, ugly tower was made of rough granite blocks. Its rugged and practical structure would have made an impressive citadel, towering above castle walls anywhere else. Here, it was almost insignificant compared to the other three towers of the Palace of the High King.

Davin looked out the window, expecting the usual night watchmen, only to see the assembled servants of the tower, his father's servants, arrayed to meet him. Byron, the steward, personally stepped forward to open the carriage door.

Davin motioned for Traithe to exit first. As he followed, Byron looked at him questioningly and made a meaningful glance at her back. He felt his face turn red at the implication and minutely shook his head.

"I've ordered the chambers of the Fellblade prepared for you, milord."

With a sigh, Davin replied, "I'm not ready for that quite yet. My old room will suffice for now." The carriage ride of the past few days over cobbled highways had been fast, but it had also been loud, and not particularly comfortable. A bed he was familiar with would help.

Byron stepped aside to confer with the staff as Traithe turned back to Davin. "Thank you for the room this evening. I'll depart in the morning."

"No. I want you to stay."

She looked meaningfully at him, almost in the same manner Byron had, but her glance had a distinctly unwelcome feel to it. "*Milord?*"

Davin flushed again. "What? No. I need someone I can trust right now, and that's you."

"While I appreciate your faith in me, you hardly know me. You don't know enough to trust me at all."

"I think I do. If you wanted me dead, you could have done it in my tent when we met, or at any number of occasions on the carriage ride. You've said yourself, you haven't been a part of the machinations in the city. You're young enough and of low enough rank, you're unlikely to be playing power politics, and you're Order of Night and a messenger. I can reasonably assume you're not bought and paid for by Darius, and that you're probably not a servant of one of the high lords."

"Those aren't the strongest of criteria *I* would use to decide whether to trust someone."

Davin sighed. "Alaric and most of the people I trust are at or on their way to Norfort. There's a handful of people I'm hoping we'll be able to find visiting the city, but I don't know of anyone in permanent residence who isn't tied into the agenda of factions that might have opposed my father. I need someone, Traithe, and you're all I have."

"So I'm the last potato in a starving man's cellar, am I?" Her smile as she said it let him know she wasn't offended.

"More like the goblet of wine I know isn't poisoned," he quipped. "You could still be sour and nearly undrinkable, but I'll survive the experience."

"Fair enough," she said with a laugh. "I'm in."

He turned toward Byron. "Please also have guest quarters prepared for Ser Traithe. She'll be staying with us a while."

* * *

"You look awful," Traithe noted as Davin stepped into the sitting room.

"Then I look how I feel. I didn't sleep at all. My father's death doesn't seem real. Byron said his funeral was a few days ago, so if I want to say my goodbyes, it'll be to a slab of rock in the family tomb complex."

"Well, if you want happiness, it's available in liquid form. Your steward makes a wonderful cup of coffee." She pointed to an ornate silver pot and a saucer on the small table next to her.

Davin made a face. "No, thank you. Never could stand the stuff."

"Your loss." She took a sip from her cup.

"I want you to come with me to my father's chambers and help me look around. You can bring the coffee with you if you want."

"Are we looking for something?"

"I don't know."

* * *

The Fellblade's chambers were immense, taking up the entire top floor of the tower. The floor plan was almost entirely open, with the vast space being bedroom, private dining, and museum all in one. Artifacts from before the Wars of Unification and each of the three Hellwars were hung on the walls, in cases, and positioned just so on display tables. Given prime real estate in the center of the room was the sword that gave Davin's family its name and reputation.

"Is that the Fellblade?" Traithe asked. "I've never seen black steel before. Other than the color of the steel, it's rather ordinary. I guess it just wasn't what I was expecting."

"What were you expecting?"

"I guess for it to be something fancier. Golden hilt or some ornate pattern welding. Maybe a jewel or two. Rubies maybe. The stories say it's supposed to shine with a brilliant blue light."

"Well, the stories seem to just be stories. No brilliance here."

The blade was of ordinary length for a sword intended to be wielded in one or two hands, though it was wider and thicker than what was carried by knights in the present day, and lacked the extreme narrowing at the tip used to thrust into gaps in the plate armor in modern use. It had a simple iron crossguard and pommel, with a worn sharkskin-wrapped hilt.

"It's supposed to be more than a thousand years old and used in hundreds of battles. There's not a nick or scratch on it and, according to family lore, never has been. It's supposed to have been brought by the first of the Fellblades from beyond the Veil." Davin walked in a slow circle around it, studying it as if it were a snake. "I've never seen my father draw it in anger. He never even practiced with it. It's been sitting here, or worn scabbarded on his waist when needed for a ceremony, my entire life."

Davin stepped up to the sword and reached for the hilt, but stopped short.

"What's the matter?"

"Would you think less of me if I told you I'm afraid it'll be just another piece of steel to me, like it was for my father and grandfather?"

"Everyone's afraid unless they're unhinged somehow. I'm afraid of centipedes. Absolutely terrified."

"I'd say you're unhinged to be afraid of a bug."

"Ever had one fall from the ceiling down your bodice?"

"I don't have a bodice."

"So you don't have a reason to be afraid of centipedes. Their bites are quite painful, I assure you."

Davin chuckled. "Well, I've never heard of the sword biting someone."

"Then the worst thing that'll happen is you'll have a new sword."

"Right." Davin closed his eyes and grabbed the hilt, raising the sword from its display stand. He opened his eyes to see just an ordinary sword.

"Well, you've got a shiny, black, new sword now." Traithe shrugged and took a sip of her coffee.

* * *

Hours later, Davin leaned back in his father's desk chair and stared at the ceiling. "There's nothing here. No notes for me, no codes, ciphers, or things out of place."

"I'm disappointed we didn't find any secret passages. I always heard this tower was full of secret doors and tunnels," Traithe remarked.

"Oh, it is. Just not on this floor or the roof."

"Really?"

"I used to play in them as a kid."

"Where do they lead?"

"Family secret, I'm afraid."

"You're just messing with me."

"Maybe, Traithe. Or I could be telling you the truth. The important part is that the stories of secret passages continue." Davin waved absently around the room. "Sometimes I think the entire family reputation is just stories. After all, it appears the fearsome Fellblade that made our reputation is just a story."

"So what do we do next?"

Davin reached into the pocket sewn into his pants and set the Green Dragon coin on the desk. "I guess we go drinking and gambling."

* * *

Davin and Traithe handed their mounts off to the stable hands and strode across the cobbled courtyard toward the ornate double doors leading to the entrance. The Green Dragon may have started as a mere tavern, but three hundred or so years, four major fires, and uncountable amounts of coin had transformed what was once a humble establishment on the south banks of the River Wyrd into the premiere entertainment destination of the Five Kingdoms. The entrance Davin had chosen was for the common room, another innocuous name for a large set of spaces given over to drinking and low stakes private gambling. A bored bouncer glanced at them as they approached and drawled, "Check yer swords, milords. No blades allowed."

Traithe started to reach for her twin blades when Davin tapped the heraldry on his otherwise unremarkable jacket. The simple white shield with a black sword could be mistaken at a distance for any of a number of minor houses. "She's with me."

The bouncer did a double take and stood from his stool quickly enough to knock it over. "Milord Fellblade, my apologies!" He made a poorly executed bow and hastily opened the door. "Please, enjoy yer stay. Iffin' there's anythin' I ken do fer ya, all ya has ta do is ask."

"Thank you—"

"My name is Mikel, milord."

"Thank you, Mikel. I will." Davin flipped him a large silver coin and stepped into a wall of smoke and sound. The common room was full of people busy with their own drink and raucous conversation. Four musicians with pipe and strings were barely audible over the din. Davin slid through the crowd, making a beeline for the long and crowded bar. Traithe followed closely in his wake.

He squeezed up to the bar, shouldering a couple of smaller men out of his way to do so. "Barkeep!" he shouted to a middle-aged woman pulling beers from a large wooden keg.

"Hold yer horses, ser, there's a line ahead of ya."

Davin slammed a heavy pouch down on the bar. "An hour of drinks on me!" Davin turned to the crowd. "An hour of drinks to honor Derek Fellblade! Drink to the honor of my late father!"

The patrons quieted to hear what was shouted. Davin called out again, "Anyone who wishes to honor my father can drink on me for the next hour!" He grabbed a mug sitting in front of a nearby patron and took a long drink. "To my father, the Fellblade!"

The room erupted in cheers and shouts of "Fellblade!" Davin made his way across the room to an unoccupied table behind silken ropes, where other high nobles and wealthy merchants were seated. His progress was slowed by individuals offering thanks for the free drinks, condolences for his loss, and congratulations on his ascension to the title of Fellblade himself. Once they were seated, Traithe turned and glared at him.

"What?" he asked.

"What are you doing? I thought we were here for a clandestine meeting with whomever sent the token," Traithe hissed.

"I beg your pardon. That was perfection."

"There's no way you can meet privately now. Everyone is watching you."

"That's the point. It was more or less impossible for me to go anywhere without people watching me when I was heir. Now? With what's going on? I guarantee, there's at least a half dozen people who will be paid to report everything I do here."

"I'm not sure I understand."

"The more people I speak with, the harder it'll be for anyone watching to figure out which conversations were the important ones. By dumping a bag of coins on the bar and giving the assembled patrons an excuse to come to me, I've pretty much guaranteed we'll meet lots of people tonight to muddy the waters for the watchers."

"Clever." Traithe sounded unconvinced. "Just out of curiosity, how much was in that pouch? I imagine there's at least a hundred people in here."

Davin shrugged. "I didn't count. Twenty or thirty crowns. It should be enough, even for the ones who drink the expensive stuff."

Traithe's mouth opened in astonishment. "That's the annual income of my family estates."

"The Fellblade family is rich. I believe there are three people with more wealth. The high king, of course. Darius. The merchant Gustavus."

"But that's an obscene display."

Davin nodded. "Also part of the point. I'm trying to make a spectacle, remember?"

"There's so much that could be done with that money—"

"And there is so much done with that money. There's easily a thousand times that given in charity and to employ people throughout the Five Kingdoms. Money is a weapon, just as much as my sword is. We've spent that coin to prevent the spending of blood.

Secure a few loans here, pay off some debts there, slip a little coin on the side from time to time to grease or seize wheels, and there's fewer reasons for lords to start feuds, fewer good families falling on hard times, and more bad houses unable to advance schemes detrimental to the peace of the realm."

"I suppose."

"Lots of people would abuse wealth, but my family just sees it as another tool to serve the high king."

A waiter arrived to take their drink order, and one of the house bouncers took up a place at the ropes to admit a growing line of people looking to talk to Davin.

The pair sat in silence for a moment as the waiter retreated.

"A thousand years of service, and your family has never turned their wealth and power to self-service, then?"

"Just the one."

"Well, besides him. What keeps your family so loyal and focused?"

"I have no idea what motivated my ancestors. I only know they've stood tall at the high king's right hand."

"Why are *you* so loyal?"

Davin turned and directed an intense stare at Traithe. "I'm not sure what else I'm supposed to do. Only that the Fellblades *must* stand with the high king, or the Five Kingdoms will fall." He sighed, and immediately the intensity left his face. "That's the family line. I'm not sure if I believe it, but I'll be damned if I'm going to let Darius ruin the realm on my watch. And now for the fun we came here for." Davin waved to the bouncer to let the first party through.

* * *

Several hours and dozens of groups of people later, Davin stifled a yawn. "I would have expected our contact to have shown up by now."

Traithe nodded in weary agreement. Her role had been mostly to sit at the table with Davin to listen and watch. Few seemed to take much notice of the low status noble in Davin's company, except to note her presence as a romantic accessory, making her uncomfortable. When the assumptions were accompanied by unsubtle innuendo, it made her angry. To Davin's credit, he did nothing to encourage people to believe they were any kind of a couple. To his *dis*credit, he had mostly ignored her presence as well.

"We'll give it another couple hours and then head back to the tower."

There seemed to be a few more groups waiting to see Davin casually milling outside the ropes, and he was about to wave another group in, when the room fell quiet for the second time that evening. A slim figure in a wide-sleeved jacket and billowing trousers of the finest silk floated across the room, lifting the rope and stepping lightly past the gaping bouncer.

Traithe gasped when she took in the pointed ears and catlike, violet eyes of the visitor. "An Elf."

The Elf bowed to Davin.

"Ambassador Merithoac, it's good to see you again."

"And you as well, Fellblade. Though you were much younger when we last met."

"My eighth birthday. Well do I remember it."

"I regret I cannot stay to share memories of your father, but I have been recalled to Elfhome with the greatest haste." He reached into his deep sleeve and pulled out a delicate crystal bottle filled with a deep turquoise liquid and a small, folded note on the green papyrus the Elves used instead of paper. "A gift from the King of Elfhome. Moonflower wine and a personal note." The ambassador handed Davin the wine and the note.

Davin unfolded the note and began to read it. Traithe looked over his shoulder. It was written in tight, Elvish script that completely covered the sheet of paper.

"My king wishes that you read it aloud so that all might know his thoughts."

Every eye and ear was turned to Davin's table.

"A moment, Ambassador. My Elvish is rusty." Davin read for long moments before standing and clearing his throat.

"To all who shall hear these words, know that I, Sulek Mar, king of Elfhome, guardian of the sacred forests, mourn the loss of Derek Fellblade, Champion of the Five Kingdoms. He was our friend and a true hero to the lands of Men and Elves. We do hereby extend our hand in friendship to Davin, his son and newest of the Fellblades, in the earnest belief that he will do honor to his family's legacy."

Davin's voice cracked at the last sentence, and Traithe looked up to see his eyes glistening with held back tears. He took a deep breath to compose himself. "Please convey my friendship to your king in the same spirit he intended. I thank him for his words."

"By your leave then, Fellblade. I must return to my king." Without waiting for a response, the Elf spun on his heel and departed through the still silent crowd.

Davin set the letter face down on the table in front of him and carefully pulled the cork from the bottle of moonflower wine. If there was a more valuable liquid in the Five Kingdoms, Traithe had never heard of it. He took a whiff of the contents before carefully passing the bottle to Traithe. She inhaled the delicate fragrance. It was indescribable. It smelled of summer and of sunlight, of citrus and of grapes. It was herbal and delicate, and she felt a sense of relaxed wellbeing flow through her from the scent.

"They say it tastes exactly like it smells and provides healing for those who need it. It's incredibly rare." He reached for the small, delicate bottle, and Traithe handed it back to him, only to watch it slip through his fingers and spill all over the table and the letter from the Elvish king.

Traithe gasped and reached for the bottle of precious liquid to rescue what she could of it. Davin snatched the letter out of the puddle of wine and shook it with a curse.

"Well, I saved a small glass worth. I'm sorry."

Davin shook his head. "It was my fault. I'm too tired and... and I think it's time to go." Davin smoothed the soaked papyrus on a dry part of the table, with the elegant runes facing upward. There were far fewer of them than there had been before the wine spilled on them. He stood and began his walk to the door, leaving the letter behind. Traithe quickly located the stopper and sealed the precious liquid within, tucked the bottle into her belt, and followed.

* * *

"You spilled the wine on purpose, didn't you?" Traithe turned to look at Davin, catching his grin as they rode beside each other in the moonlight. The roads weren't deserted, even at this hour, but they were far from any other traffic.

"Careful now, you're asking about state secrets."

"There were a lot more runes on the papyrus when you first read them than when we left. *And* you left the letter behind."

Davin said nothing.

"Does moonflower wine dissolve ink?"

"Some ink, not all, as you've observed. Now, whomever was watching us sees a very public visit with the only Elf in the Five Kingdoms to deliver a very public message with a very public note passed. Nothing at all secret happened. The trick with the ink, like the wine itself, isn't anything I thought I'd ever see, but my father told me about it. Nobody in their right mind will believe we spilled it on purpose."

Traithe sighed. "This goes against everything I've been taught about secret meetings."

"Goes against what almost everyone has been taught about secret meetings, which is the point."

"I saw your eyes get misty there with the letter. What else did it say?"

"You heard the sincere expression of friendship from the Elvish king. My father apparently was far closer than I'd known to the Elves. It doesn't translate well, but 'friendship,' as it was used, refers to friends who have sworn an oath, binding them closer than family, closer than blood. My father performed some sort of great service to Elfhome, and personally to the king." Davin's voice hardened. "It also said that Protector Kenna murdered my father and used the fire to both set the ambush and hide his deed."

"Protector Kenna, head of the Order of Kings?"

"The same."

"What do we do about that?"

"Tomorrow, I visit my father's tomb to pay my respects, and then we go see the king and hope he's lucid."

* * *

"I'm sorry," Kenna said. "You're not permitted to see His Majesty."

Davin was seething. "You don't have that authority. I am the Fellblade."

Kenna sneered. "The sword at your waist doesn't lend any weight to your insistence. My orders come from the king himself. *You* are not permitted to see him."

"Bollocks. He ordered no such thing."

"But I'm afraid he did," came a new voice.

Davin would recognize the cultured bass voice anywhere. "Darius," he hissed as he turned to see the high priest parade down the hallway to Johannes' chambers.

"I'm afraid the word of your father's passing was too much for the high king. He's outlived four Fellblades and can't bear to have any more in his service. I'm afraid," Darius paused dramatically, "your services are no longer required. You will, of course, be entitled to keep your lands, and even the tower here at the palace, but your role as champion now belongs to that of the Order of Kings, and specifically to Protector Kenna. It's convenient to have found you so I can deliver the king's writ in person."

Darius gestured to the scribe following him, and the scribe scuttled forward to hand Davin a rolled parchment with the gold and crown wax seal of the Five Kingdoms.

The instant Davin took the parchment, Kenna barked an order to other knights of his order nearby. "Please escort Ser Davin and his guest out of the King's Tower."

* * *

"That did not go well."

Davin ignored Traithe and stormed across the palace yards toward the Fellblade Tower. "We're going to see the high king tonight."

"How? There's no way past the Order of Kings without bloodshed."

Davin stopped abruptly and spun to face her, leaning down until his nose was inches from hers. "Secret. Passages."

* * *

"That was far less cobwebby and dank than I was expecting. Also, not as secret as I would have thought."

Davin had been in a foul mood all day, and Traithe's attempt at levity didn't raise so much as a grunt. There were a handful of concealed doors the pair had passed through, but most of their journey had been through quiet servant passages and storage rooms. Finally, Davin called a halt in a chamber deep under the King's Tower. In a maintenance room for the powered lifts maintained by the Order of Magic, Davin pulled a complex pattern of steam valves to open a narrow stairwell that spiraled tightly upward.

"Quickly. The door will only be open for a moment."

Traithe slipped into the narrow opening, with Davin on her heels, just quickly enough to avoid the stone wall closing with a hiss of steam behind them, leaving them in darkness. Before Traithe could ask about light, she heard a click, and small pools of magelight illuminated every third step upward.

"It's a long way up. Rest as you need to."

* * *

Both of them were perspiring by the time they reached the top of the stairs.

Davin said, "This is where we might get caught. This panel will open into the privy. There's no way to see if anyone is in there, but Johannes seldom uses this room anymore. Servants attend to his... needs."

"I knew he was old and had bad days, but—"

"He's *old*. Diapers and servants are all that protect that part of his dignity anymore." Davin took a deep breath and slid the panel open. "We're safe," he whispered and stepped carefully onto the tiled floor of the small room.

The high king's chambers were beyond a finely carved wooden door. There were numerous small openings in the carvings for them to peer through. Like the chambers of the Fellblade, the entire floor seemed to be given over to a single room. There was a single candle burning on a table next to a large, canopied bed, but no servants or guards in sight.

Quietly opening the door, Davin stepped onto thick carpeting and motioned for Traithe to follow.

Davin knelt at the high king's bedside. "My king, it is your Fellblade come to petition you. I am sorry if I'm waking you, but I believe your realm is at risk."

There was no movement or sound from the bed.

Davin stood, pushed aside the curtains, and stumbled backward with a curse.

"He's been murdered. Throat slit. We need to leave, or we'll be blamed. That won't go well." Another curse.

Traithe began to make her way back to the hidden stair when a cloaked figure armed with a wickedly-curved dagger unfolded from the shadows. She drew her swords and assumed a defensive stance.

The shadowy figure glided across the carpet without a sound and attacked. Traithe easily countered and made a clean thrust to the figure's throat, only to meet no resistance. Her surprise left her open to a guileless thrust into her side, and she staggered to the side in pain.

Davin grabbed his father's sword as he stepped forward with the intent of striking the attacker down with a single blow from the draw. As the blade left its scabbard, it lit the room with the brilliant blue glow shining from the blade. The blade felt good in his hand, the blow perfect and unstoppable. The shadowy attacker wasn't struck down, but instead dispersed into a cloud of vanishing shadow trailing in the wake of the blade. Its human shape and even its knife dissipated, leaving only a ragged black cloak on the ground.

"Traithe, are you all right?"

She shook her head, hissing in pain, sheathing her swords. "I don't know." She pulled her hand from the wound in her side. It was drenched in blood. "I don't think so."

Davin picked up the fallen cloak and shoved it to her side. "Hold that there as hard as you can. I'll get you to my physician. He'll stitch you up with discretion. Let me carry you."

* * *

By the time Davin reached the bottom of the stairwell, Traithe had lost consciousness, and the cloak she'd been holding against her side. She was barely breathing, and her pulse was weak and slowing. He set her down in the lift equipment room and removed cloth from her tunic for a bandage. As he cut the cloth, he saw a small crystal bottle at her belt, with a small amount of turquoise liquid left in it.

He'd already seen magic tonight. Doubt in its existence was no longer an option for him. Praying to the One True God, he unstoppered the bottle and poured it in her mouth. Almost immediately, her color returned, and she began to breathe more deeply. As he watched, the wound in her side clotted and then closed.

Her eyes opened, and she looked at him through heavy-lidded eyes, as though she was just waking up from a dream.

"I guess the sword works for you?"

Davin forced a laugh. "I guess so. Looks like moonflower wine heals wounds, too. I thought you were gone."

"Me, too. Thanks." She tried to sit up but couldn't. "I'm still pretty weak."

"You lost a lot of blood. Let me carry you some more. I think it's still a good idea to see my physician."

* * *

Traithe was still weak the next morning, and still in her bed in Fellblade Tower when she heard the unmistakable sound of heavy armor coming down the hallway. Remembering the events of the night before, she looked around for a weapon. When the door opened, it didn't bring danger, it brought Davin in the company of a number of young knights.

"Traithe. Good to see you awake. I'd like to introduce you to your new traveling companions."

"What have you done?" she asked.

"What I had to. Early this morning, they found the king dead. Darius summoned a council of high lords, representatives of the subordinate kings, and the heads of the orders or their deputies present in the capital. Apparently, Johannes left Darius the kingdom. I'm sure you're as surprised as I am."

Davin took a deep breath before continuing. "I crashed the council and called Protector Kenna out for the murder of my father. I accused Darius of forging the high king's will. One thing led to another, with me storming out, having made a formal challenge for a judicial duel against the Church's champion, which is, surprising no one, Protector Kenna."

He thumbed at a young man in a rusty chain coat. "Ser Wyll here also happened to have a message for me from Ser Alaric that really changes the game. That message also came with a list of others we can trust." He gestured to the others. "I don't know if I'm doing the right thing, or if I'll survive, but this feels right." He patted the hilt of the sword at his side. "And I've got the Fellblade."

* * *

The early moments of pre-dawn the following day found Davin, in full armor with the Fellblade at his side, waiting at the dueling grounds in the city center for Kenna and Darius to arrive. Byron had come from the tower to be present as his second, but he'd seen Traithe, Wyll, and the other knights off the night before. Davin felt the doubt in his gut growing along with the number of spectators who were arriving to witness the duel. The sword had awoken the other night, and he was confident, with the awakened blade, none could stand against him. If the sword didn't wake, he was up against one of the finest duelists in the Five Kingdoms.

At the last possible moment before the sun fully cleared the horizon, making Davin the winner by default, Kenna arrived in the company of a squad of knights from every order. Law, War, Kings,

Healing, Valor, Night, and even the rare Order of Magic were represented. Darius and an entourage of priests and scribes accompanied him. High lords of the realm stood behind Kenna. Davin and the Fellblade stood, by contrast, virtually alone.

Davin stepped to the center of the bare earth of the dueling circle and spoke to the gathered crowd, beginning the formal challenge to start the judicial duel. "I am Davin, the Fellblade of the Five Kingdoms. Like my father and grandfather, back through a thousand years, I serve the high king and stand as champion of the realm. I accuse High Priest Darius of treason against High King Johannes and party to regicide. I accuse Protector Kenna of murdering my father and hiding the crime by letting his body burn. Under the sight of Ger, the One True God, I invoke His justice. By the outcome of this duel will the truth be known. Darius and Kenna, will you acknowledge your crimes before Ger and these gathered witnesses?"

Protector Kenna stepped into the circle. "Your claims are false, Ser Davin. Your challenge of judicial duel is accepted. I will serve as both my own champion and as the champion of the Church. May Ger have mercy on your soul."

Davin made to draw the Fellblade, but was stopped by a shout from a young priest in Darius' retinue. "Hold! You are not permitted your own blade, Ser Davin. To ensure divine will is done and no trickery or forbidden magics are present, each combatant must use a sanctified blade from those provided by the Church. Each blade shall be cleansed in purified water before they are used." The scribe clapped his hands, and a cart with seven nearly identical blades was wheeled to the edge of the dueling circle.

Davin felt sick. He'd forgotten that the rules of a judicial duel were different from the rules of other duels. He didn't get to use his own sword. Filled with doubt, he stepped up to the cart, standing next to a smirking Ser Kenna.

"You'll be the eighth," he said quietly.

"Eighth what?

"Man I've killed in a formal duel."

"So?" Davin said, picking up a sword to inspect it.

"There are twenty more unmarked graves from less formal duels, too."

Davin did his best not to react. The lack of reaction seemed to irritate Kenna. "So?" he repeated.

"And then there's the new tomb occupant in your family graveyard. The fool never saw it coming."

He flushed with anger, despite willing himself not to react. "I already know you killed my father. That's why you're here."

Kenna chose his blade and handed it to a nearby priest for the ritual cleansing, then turned to whisper in Davin's ear, "No, I'm here to end you like I ended your father."

* * *

The sun was well into the sky by the time the swords had been ritually cleansed and returned to the duelists. Whatever enthusiasm and confidence Davin had once had had fled with the dawn. He looked over at Byron, standing alone with the Fellblade.

Kenna took up his blade, closed the visor on his helm, and stepped toward the middle of the circle. He raised his sword above his head and bellowed to the crowd, "Let this farce be finished! It's time to face me!" The crowd cheered at the prospect of action.

Davin dropped the visor on his helm and stepped forward, slipping by habit into low guard, keeping his distance, trying to gauge

Kenna's reach. Kenna started in high guard and circled both left and right, looking for a flaw in Davin's footwork, trying to cut the chord on the circle, and close to striking distance.

Kenna made the slightest twitch as if he was going to strike high, then lunged with a two-handed thrust toward Davin's face. Though his helm was immune to the thrust from a sword, there was always the possibility of a blade slipping through the eye slots, so Davin had to respect the threat. He parried high and stepped in to close the distance. Kenna was already flowing into a follow-on strike that would have cut into the less protected back of the legs of an opponent who attempted a riposte. Because Davin hadn't countered, the low blow rang harmlessly off Davin's armored thigh.

Ha! Alaric was wrong, Davin thought. *I can win this without my sword.* Counterattack and riposte against a master duelist like Kenna was a bad idea. Battlefield tactics Alaric had scolded him for were what was needed. They might not win every duel, but they would win *this* duel. That was all that mattered. If Davin could conserve energy, defend, and wear his opponent out, he could win. He *would* win.

After several more minutes of Kenna pressing and Davin's obstinate defense, it was obvious Kenna was getting tired and frustrated. His breathing became labored, and strikes were less frequent. He was having trouble keeping his guard up, and when he attacked, his combinations were less precise, and his blows were significantly weaker. One particularly poor attempt to get Davin out of position left Kenna wrong-footed and gave Davin enough of an opening to deliver a blow with the pommel of his sword that dented the temple of Kenna's helm.

Kenna staggered.

Davin decided that was his moment to press, and he came in with solid strikes high and low, forcing his weary opponent to counter and scramble backward to avoid being overpowered and knocked to the ground, where he'd be at a significant disadvantage.

With no warning, Kenna surged to attack as if he were as fresh as he was at the beginning of the battle. Once again, his attacks were precise, and now it was Davin who was caught wrong-footed, barely avoiding a half-sword thrust into his armpit.

Something's wrong here, he thought.

Practically running away to gain distance, Davin looked around the crowd. Behind the approaching Kenna, he could see Darius muttering, eyes closed. Shadows like those from the cloaked figure oozed from a purple tear in the air behind Darius, forming a writhing cloak around the high priest. Tendrils from the cloak crawled across the dirt, wrapping Kenna's limbs, strengthening him. Every breath saw those strands of shadow cover more and more of Kenna's form.

It was a tear in the Veil, the darkness from beyond answering the will of Darius.

Why does no one else see this?

With every heartbeat, Kenna grew stronger, and Davin's defense more desperate. The darkness deepened.

"No!" he shouted. "I will not allow this!" Throwing all thoughts of defense to the winds, he hammered at Kenna, concentrating on the thickest shadows. The tactics cost him a shallow cut on the back of his thigh, and a finger-crushing blow to his left gauntlet, but he continued his assault against the shadows.

Bit by bit, the shadows dissipated, and Kenna slowed. Beginning as a flicker almost too faint to see, Davin's sword began to shine with a blue light. With each blow, the darkness fled, and the sword glowed brighter. Soon enough, the crowd saw the light. Where there had been shouting and cheering, there was silence.

It's me! It's my heritage.

"I understand now," he yelled, slamming his sword at Kenna.

Kenna blocked it, but the blow's power sent him staggering.

"The Fellblade isn't a sword. It isn't a family name. It's not a position given by the hand of the king, and it cannot be taken away by anyone." Davin hammered at Kenna's defenses again.

Again, the blow drove the protector back.

"For a thousand years, the Fellblade was the weapon used to turn aside the tides of darkness from Beyond, and the shield to protect the Five Kingdoms."

With a final, overhand blow, Davin swung the brilliantly glowing sword. It cut effortlessly through Kenna's last, desperate block, through his helm, and halfway down the steel breastplate before stopping.

Davin withdrew his sword and stepped back, allowing Kenna's corpse to fall forward into the growing puddle of blood and gore.

The crowd remained silent as Davin lifted his visor and pointed his glowing sword at Darius and his retinue. "*I* am the Fellblade. I *am* the weapon against darkness. And you, Darius, servant of darkness, have lost."

* * * * *

Nathan Balyeat Bio

Nathan Balyeat is a United States Marine Corps veteran with a degree in history and a day job in project management. He's been forced into writing because the voices in his head won't let him be if he doesn't. Nathan currently resides in Michigan with three cats of unusual size, where he's working on more stories to share.

* * * * *

To the King
by Benjamin Tyler Smith
A Necrolopolis Story

"Cease this exorcism at once!" I slammed the butt of my bone shovel against the marble floor of the throne room's entryway. The cracking of tile resounded like a thunderclap and brought a startled hush to the crowded chamber.

The throne room was designed like an amphitheater, with steps leading down from the entryway, past rows of hardwood benches on either side, and to a floor that stretched out before a marble dais. A throne carved from what appeared to be a single piece of Ascian blackwood loomed over the center of the dais. That was where I'd expected my charge, Prince Lian, to be seated. With the recent death of his father, it was his to occupy. Or it had been, in any event. The heir to the throne of Quim had a condition that stood to keep him from his rightful inheritance—

He was undead, recently turned, according to my boss.

Instead of being seated, Prince Lian stood on the floor before the dais, recognizable both by his purple robes and his waxy pallor. The black aura around him only cemented his undead status, though no one in the room but me would be able to see that. A tight knot of nobles and knights surrounded him, swords drawn and leveled at an even larger group of soldiers. The soldiers arrayed against Lian were led by a gray-haired noble, who turned toward me and snarled, "Who in the Eighteen Hells are you?"

Next to the noble, a hooded cleric from the nearby cathedral to Vita, goddess of life, stood with her rod pointed at Lian. She looked in my direction, her mouth agape. "A necromancer!"

A murmur swept through those assembled, and more than one made warding gestures in my direction. Completely ineffective warding gestures, but if it made them feel better…

A pair of small, frostbitten hands clutched at my black robes. Edurne, an eleven-year-old shiver ghoul, peeked out from behind me, her ice-blue eyes surveying the scene before us. "Is this the kind of greeting you get often?" she whispered.

The poor girl had no idea. "Just follow my lead," I whispered back.

If the cleric's declaration of my profession had unnerved the gray-haired noble, he gave no sign. "What do you want, necromancer? Who let you in here?"

"This let me in here." I tapped the skull-shaped brooch pinned to the front of my robe as I descended the steps. "I am here under the orders of Lady Grimina, administrator of the city of Necrolopolis. She honors the agreement forged between her and the late King Aleix."

"What nonsense is—" the noble began.

"Be silent, Duke Corin!" Prince Lian snapped. For a youth of no more than sixteen years, he had a deep voice and a commanding air. Corin's jaw snapped shut with a click, but it was clear he wasn't happy.

Lian turned his brown-eyed gaze on me. "What agreement do you speak of, necromancer?"

Duke Corin's men parted to let us approach Prince Lian. The deeper into the room we ventured, the more the assembled people shivered, their breath coming out in a mist. "Sorry," Edurne murmured, her voice so quiet, I doubted anyone else heard her.

"The agreement was a simple one, Prince Lian," I explained, my voice raised to be heard over the muttered curses and chattering teeth. I removed a letter from my robe, unfolded it with one hand, and scanned its contents. "Should any member of Quim's royal family fall to the curse of undeath, that person will be granted safe passage and harbor in Necrolopolis. In return, no citizen of Quim will harm any undead who wish to peacefully cross through the land."

I stopped in front of Lian and made a show of looking around. "It seems like the entire agreement is at risk, wouldn't you say, Your Highness?"

Despite the gravity of the situation, Prince Lian smiled. "And you're here to rectify that, Mister—?"

"Adelvell, Your Highness." I returned the letter to its pocket. "And yes. I'm here to carry out Lady Grimina's will."

"Lady Grimina has no jurisdiction here, necromancer," Corin growled, "and neither do you."

"There's nowhere death lacks jurisdiction, my lord."

Lian grimaced. "True words, Mr. Adelvell."

I felt a pang of guilt. The recently risen didn't need to hear that. I removed the skull brooch from my robe and held it out to Prince Lian. "Prince Lian, do you seek the protection offered to you by the city of Necrolopolis and its patron god, Mortus?"

Lian tensed, and I feared royal pride would get in his way. His was a warrior's house, a powerful house that didn't typically need aid. Still, formalities had to be adhered to.

After a long moment, he touched the brooch with his fingertips. "I do. For myself, and all who would come with me."

"Then you shall have it." I pinned the brooch to my robe and turned. "Prince Lian is now under the protection of the city of Necrolopolis. He will come with me, and you will not stop us."

"And if we try to stop you anyway?" Corin demanded. "What can you do?"

"An attack against Lian, myself, or any with us is an attack against Mortus, god of death." I channeled necromantic power into my shovel. Black energy crackled along its white surface. "Know that it is a war you cannot win. My god has a long memory, and he always claims his due."

* * *

"That was quite the speech you gave back there, Mr. Adelvell!" Baron Sendoa shouted, his voice carrying over the clatter of hooves against cobblestones. "Quite bold, I daresay! However, there's just one question I have: why are we *running?*"

We rode in the middle of a column of horsemen at full gallop. The sun had set hours ago, and the city was largely asleep, but for the noise of our flight echoing through the cool spring air. I rode on a red chestnut named Aine, on loan from Mina. Edurne sat in front of me in the saddle, a blanket between her legs and Aine's body to keep the Vital from freezing at her touch. Baron Sendoa, cousin to Prince Lian, rode next to me, a baleful expression on his young face. "A fat lot of good your words have done us, *necromancer.*"

My cheeks burned with embarrassment, and I was grateful for the dim light of the street's aetherlamps. All right, so my speech was a little over-the-top, I admit. In my defense, it's a rare day I get to make declarations like that, and something had to be done to defuse the situation. I hadn't expected that damnable cleric of Vita to be aware of how impotent my magic is against the living. My black magic could cancel her white magic, and I could raise and command the dead, but that was about it. "She didn't have to point that out," I muttered. *Whatever happened to professional courtesy among magic wielders?*

Once Duke Corin's soldiers had realized my magic would be harmless against them, they became… rather angry. I knew that wasn't the sole reason they were chasing us out of the city, but it was certainly my main reason for staying ahead of them.

"We're blessed to have them on our side, Lord Sendoa," Knight-Lieutenant Ivonor said. He rode to my left, his visor raised so he could smile at Edurne. "We made it to the stables without bloodshed largely due to his assistant's efforts."

That was true enough. Edurne had created a thin coating of ice across the floor, turning the throne room into an ice skating rink like the fountain outside Necrolopolis Hall in winter. Corin and his men couldn't keep their footing, which had bought us time to escape.

Edurne ducked her head, clearly embarrassed by the praise. "Careful," I said to Ivonor. "Heap any more accolades on her, and she'll blush so hard she thaws."

"Well, isn't that grand?" Lord Sendoa grumbled. "We owe our lives and freedom to a little girl; an *undead* one, at that. How does that sit with your knightly honor, Ivonor?"

Ivonor's face reddened. "You strike low, cousin," he said, all pretense of respect gone. He snapped his visor shut and looked ahead. "Much too low," he added, his voice muffled behind steel.

"Right turn ahead!" one of the knights in the van shouted, and the order echoed down the line. Ivonor twisted in the saddle and bellowed, "Turn right and pick up the speed! We near the gatehouse!"

Ahead, the street we raced along ended in a T-shaped intersection with a wide avenue. Prince Lian and his vanguard were already disappearing around the corner to the right, followed by the next group of knights. We were next. "Hold on tight," I instructed Edurne.

She gripped the saddle's horn with her stiff, blackened fingers. "Ready, Mr. Adelvell!"

Sendoa, Ivonor, and I rounded the corner without slowing our mounts. I leaned into the turn, but let Aine handle the rest. The chestnut's powerful hooves clacked against the cobbles without losing her footing, and then we were off in a straight line again. Ivonor's destrier almost clipped an ale cart on the side of the street. As the cart's owner shouted and cursed at us, the horse sidled over close enough for Aine to nip at his tail. Ivonor noticed and pulled his mount toward the sidewalk again. "She's a spirited one, Mr. Adelvell!" he called.

"As spirited as my boss!" I called back. "Don't tell Mina I said that," I muttered to Edurne.

Edurne giggled and started to say something. Her words were drowned out by the screeching of iron-banded wheels against stone. I risked a look over my shoulder as a carriage careened around the corner and sideswiped the same ale cart from before. The proprietor's curses turned to a frightened cry as he dove out of the way of his now tumbling cart. Neither the carriage nor its team of four horses suffered any harm, and soon they were back up to speed. Carriages didn't usually travel at full gallop, but there were extenuating circumstances tonight.

The rearguard slid around the corner. One of the knights shouted, "The paladins are after us!"

I frowned. Paladins? I wasn't aware the local church of Vita had any paladins in its employ. It seemed too small and too far removed from any lands plagued by aggressive undead for there to be a garrison here.

"Open the gate!" one of the knights in the van shouted, his voice booming like thunder. "Open the gate in the name of the prince!"

The city's eastern gatehouse loomed before us, its massive doors barred shut for the night. It looked very similar to the western gatehouse I'd entered the city through. We'd have to get back on the road to Necrolopolis once we were beyond the walls.

The guards on the roof rushed over to our side of the wall to see what the ruckus was about. One shouted down into one of the tall, narrow windows directly below him. The doors groaned as they slowly opened.

Prince Lian and his vanguard were about sixty feet ahead of me, and they showed no signs of slowing. I feared the gate wouldn't open in time, and the knights flanking him must have thought so, too. They fell into a single-file formation behind him, each of them continuing to shout, "The prince approaches! Open the gate! The prince approaches!"

At last, the gates opened wide enough to let Lian and his knights pass. I swear, their boots must have brushed the worn wood on either side as they galloped through.

Ivonor raised his visor once more and bellowed, "Close the gate once the carriage is through! Assassins pursue the prince!"

Calls of "Assassins!" and "Protect the prince!" rose from the gate guards. More than half set aside the spears they would use against thieves and smugglers found atop the wall and took up crossbows instead.

By the time we reached the gatehouse, both sets of doors had been thrown wide.

"Long live the prince!" the gate's sergeant yelled, his voice ragged. "Come back to us a king!"

Any response was lost in the deafening thunder of our horses' hooves in the enclosed gatehouse. I gritted my teeth against the noise and was grateful it only lasted a few seconds. Then we were clear of the city and galloping along the cobblestone highway, headed east. The carriage and rearguard soon followed, and the gate began to close.

Aine slowed a bit, but Ivonor and Lord Sendoa raced ahead. I moved us far to the left to allow more knights by. Aine was good and dependable, but she wasn't as powerfully-built as the destriers favored by Lian's men-at-arms. We soon shared the road with the carriage and its team of powerful-but-tired horses.

Behind us, the gates slowly closed. Angry shouts echoed from the street and the gatehouse roof, and something whistled through the air. The whistling ended with a thunk. An arrow had embedded itself in the back of the carriage.

"Bastards took a shot at us!" a member of the rearguard cursed.

The gates closed with a deep boom, eliminating the possibility of more arrows headed our way. Relief flooded through me.

Edurne sagged against me, and a giggle escaped her lips. "That was more excitement than I signed up for, Mr. Adelvell."

I loosened my white-knuckled grip on the reins and patted her head. "You and me both, Edurne. You and me both."

A knight in the rearguard pulled his horse alongside the carriage long enough to wrench the arrow free. "Bloody elves. Can't they stay out of our affairs?"

A chill ran down my spine, and I shivered. Edurne looked up at me. "Not you," I said with another reassuring pat. As she looked forward again, I frowned. If the paladins chasing us were elves rather than human, that meant things were a lot worse than I'd initially feared.

We couldn't get back on the road to Necrolopolis soon enough.

* * *

We stopped to rest the horses a half-hour later, after we'd turned off the main highway onto a forest road. A narrow pathway branched off the road and ended at a small lakeside lodge. As we turned down the dirt path, Lord Sendoa spoke up, his voice cracking like a whip. "We cannot stop! If we tarry, Duke Tyrrell or those paladins will be on us!"

"If we don't rest the horses now," Prince Lian called, "we'll never be up for the rest of the journey. Patience, dear cousin."

While I could respect Sendoa's desire to push onward—especially considering how angry Corin and his men were at me—Prince Lian was correct. Aine needed to catch her breath, as did the carriage team. It was a long road back to Necrolopolis, and not one we would complete if we rode our horses into the ground.

We dismounted when we reached the lake, and Edurne and I walked Aine for several minutes to cool off. Knights and nobles handed the reins of their horses off to squires for them to do the same, while they gathered outside the lodge for a strategy meeting. The carriage driver halted the carriage next to the lodge, but not before he turned the vehicle around until it faced the path back to the road. Prince Lian sat astride his horse and surveyed the scene until the carriage came to a complete halt. Then he dismounted and bounded up into the carriage with an energy that belied his undead status.

I'd only seen one person enter the carriage back at the castle stable: a woman carrying a wrapped bundle. Her name was Ofelia, and she'd been dressed too plainly to be one of the nobles of the court, but her clothing had been far too rich for that of a simple servant. Did the prince have a mistress? If so, she would have been in danger if we'd left her behind.

Once Aine had cooled off, I handed the lead rope to Edurne and pointed to the lake. "She's bound to be thirsty."

While Edurne helped Aine drink her fill, I snacked on the last of the preserved rations Mad Molly had packed for me back in Necrolopolis. Though a ghostly tavernkeeper now, she'd spent her mortal days as a pirate, from ship's cook to queen. She knew how to make hardtack and raisin cakes taste good. I couldn't wait to get back to the city, so I could wash the road dust away with her famous red apple ale.

Edurne's frostbitten hands weren't very nimble, so I helped her tie Aine to a nearby tree, close to the line set up for the knights' horses. Together, we got Aine some oats and grain to mix in with the grass at her feet.

"Mr. Adelvell," Edurne whispered. She inclined her head in the direction of the lodge.

Prince Lian had exited the carriage, and now he approached us. Gone was the purple robe he'd worn in the throne room. He'd thrown that off in our flight to the stables, revealing a traveler's tunic and rider's trousers. In addition to that, he now wore a mail shirt and had a sword hanging from his belt.

He was flanked by Captain Marcel and another knight, both of whom had ridden with him in the van. They stopped a few yards away from us as Lian continued forward. As he drew closer, something drew my eye to his sword. The hilt was unadorned, and the scabbard was as plain as what a footman would carry into battle. Part of Lian's necromantic aura swirled around it, indicating a close attachment to him. A family heirloom, perhaps? "Mr. Adelvell, I would speak with you."

I tucked my hands into the sleeves of my robe and turned to face him. "How can I be of assistance, Your Highness?"

"About what you said in the throne room..."

I winced. "Highness, I apologize for my performance there. You see—"

"Think nothing of it." A small smile played at the corners of Lian's pale lips. "Father always said bravado had its place, even if it couldn't be backed by deed. Besides, it was backed by deed in this case."

He dropped to a knee and took Edurne's blackened hand. "Were it not for you, little one, I would have fallen today. For the sake of my cause, you have my eternal gratitude." His smile turned into a rakish grin. "Given our respective natures, those words mean more now than they normally would, wouldn't you say?"

Edurne's pale cheeks flushed a shade of blue as deep as her lips. "It was nothing," she stammered. After a moment, her eyes widened and she added, "Your Highness!" in a squeak.

If Lian took offense at Edurne's clumsy efforts at formality, he gave no sign. "I believe your master said your name is Edurne? Where do you hail from?"

"Ikatz village."

"I know the place! On the border between Quim and Kolbik? Your village is a disputed territory. Father—" Lian's voice faltered. He swallowed and continued, "Father knew it belonged to us, though we couldn't prove it. My family has long sought Ikatz for its coal production."

"No better coal in the entire continent!" Edurne put her hands on her hips and stuck out her chest. Then she slumped her shoulders and looked embarrassed. "I don't know what a continent is, but that's what Papa always said."

"And is your papa well?"

Edurne bit her lip, and a thin line of frost formed around the rims of her eyes. She nodded, but said nothing.

My heart ached. She hadn't been gone from Ikatz even a full season at that point, and the wounds were too fresh. Even though she'd saved the whole village from a monster of their own creation, they'd rejected her because she'd become undead in the process. Sometimes not even love could overcome hate. "Prince Lian," I said after an awkward silence, "you wished to speak with me about something?"

Lian looked at me, his expression worried. He knew what he'd asked had troubled Edurne, and he knew I was deflecting for her sake. He gave Edurne's hand a gentle squeeze and said, "We'll talk more later, little one." He stood and turned toward me again. "It's about our destination, Mr. Adelvell. I have a boon to ask of you."

I had a sinking suspicion this "boon" didn't involve helping him find the choicest accommodations in the city. "If it's within my authority to grant."

"We cannot go to your city yet. I understand Father's agreement with you and Lady Grimina." He placed a hand on his chest over a heart that no longer beat. "More than ever, I understand it. Necrolopolis is my new home, but not yet. There is something I must do, and my honor demands I see it through to the end."

"And what is that?"

"Before he was murdered, Father laid out his plan of succession. It was a formality, but something that needed to be done following my older brother's death in a hunting accident six months ago." Lian chuckled, though there was no humor in it. "Given what's happened, I somehow doubt it was an accident, but no matter. It was the last thing Father and I spoke of before..." He trailed off, and the hand that had been at his chest drifted up to his left ear. The inside of the ear was stained black.

If Pyria were here, I could have asked her about the poison used. She'd been a trained herbalist in life. My upbringing in a family of life mages had afforded me some knowledge of herbs, but not an exhaustive one. Whatever it was, it had to be nasty, if all it took was a little in the ear.

Lian noticed my gaze and dropped his hand back to his side. "We were both murdered the same night. I don't know who carried out the deed, nor who ordered it. Something must have been in our wine. I retired early, and woke as you see me now. Cousin Sendoa, my chambermaid, and the court's doctor were with me." He smirked. "They were quite surprised when I roused. I take it they'd come to inform me of Father's passing, only to find me deceased, as well."

"That was about two weeks ago, right?" Mina's father Mortus, the god of death, always knew the instant someone returned as undead. The instant he sensed Lian's return, I'd been summoned to Mina's office with instructions to ride for Quim with all speed. "All speed" had turned out to be quite a bit longer than I'd liked, due to snowmelt turning many roads into muddy mires. It would've been a fast trip on Ezella Airslicer's gyrocopter, but she was indisposed at present.

If Lian was surprised by my knowledge, he gave no sign. "Fifteen days ago. No one outside of a select few members of the court knew of my condition, but we couldn't keep Father's death a secret."

Nor could he keep his own death a secret, it seemed. "Did Duke Corin know the truth?"

Lian grimaced. "Heavens, no. His house has been at odds with ours for generations. He'd be one of the last nobles told, even if he's one of the most powerful ones in our kingdom."

That was… ominous. It meant someone in Lian's inner circle had betrayed him, whether wittingly or unwittingly. My thoughts immediately went to the dour Lord Sendoa, but it could as easily be Knight-Lieutenant Ivonor, or even Captain Marcel, standing a few yards behind Lian. I resisted the urge to look his way, but I couldn't keep a deep sense of unease from settling in me.

"I need your patience, Mr. Adelvell, and your aid. Help me in the coronation ceremony, and I will fulfill my kingdom's end of the bargain with Lady Grimina."

That was something that had bothered me since my arrival. Why was Prince Lian still "prince?" Shouldn't he have been crowned in the hours following his father's death? There was certainly the issue of his undead status to consider, but since they'd been keeping that a secret…

Lian must have noticed my confusion. "There's a tradition among my people. The new ruler can only be crowned on the battlefield our kingdom was forged on. Quim's Stand, a half-day's ride east of Neru. Only there, among the bones of the dead, and with the banner of the first king in hand, can the coronation take place.

There's a ritual involved, where we honor the oath of loyalty the fallen made to King Quim by reenacting Quim's rallying cry that ultimately won the day."

I remembered the wrapped bundle the lady in the carriage had been so protective of. If it was an ancient relic, it would make sense they'd transport it as carefully as possible rather than stuffing it in Lian's saddlebag.

Thoughts of the carriage reminded me of the arrow shot by one of the knights chasing us. "Highness, why would the elves send paladins after you?" I could understand the cleric under orders of Duke Corin, but Quim wasn't near elfin lands.

"That's troubling to me, as well." Lian crossed his arms. "We do have an elf ambassador at court, but he's gone, and his entire office shut down for some festival of theirs. How could his kind have found out so quickly?"

"Never underestimate the fae's ability to gather information," a feminine voice said from the open air.

Everyone jumped, including me. "Idrefe," I growled. "A little warning would be nice."

The ghostly form of a robed elf appeared before us. Lian took an involuntary step back. To their credit, Captain Marcel and his knight stepped forward after a brief hesitation, hands on sword hilts.

"Stay your hands, brave warriors," Idrefe said. "They would do no good against me, and I am not here to fight." She bowed slightly. "Greetings, Prince Lian. I am Idrefe, Maester of the Eleventh Circle. I am—was—an exorcist. Currently I am in the employ of young Adelvell, here, the end result of a favor I asked of him."

Idrefe had needed my assistance in eradicating the demon that had killed her and most of her companions and followers. Circumstances had led to us forming an impromptu contract so we could combine our powers. She'd intended to be exorcised once the deed was done, but my orders hadn't changed: Mina wanted her back in Necrolopolis, and to Necrolopolis we went. Idrefe was getting used to it, I think.

What I wasn't getting used to was her appearing whenever she felt like it.

Lian shook his head. "Now I've seen everything. I thought your kind couldn't become undead."

"We are as susceptible to the curse as any mortal. We are just very aggressive in our handling of it."

"You mean you do a good job of purging your ranks," I added. How many innocents had she sent into oblivion? I'd never asked, though I was sure the number was rather high.

Idrefe glanced at me. "It is true we are a bit... zealous in our duties, but we are also beholden to the politics of the court." She paced back and forth, her sandaled feet never touching the ground. "I do not know why exorcists and paladins would be dispatched to deal with a member of a human kingdom's royalty, not unless we were expressly invited by someone in authority."

Lian stroked his hairless chin, seemingly lost in thought.

Idrefe turned her attention to Edurne, who stared openmouthed at the elf ghost. "I thought I felt the connection of a new familiar of Adelvell's. Are you well, Edurne?"

"You're really pretty." Edurne's cheeks flushed blue again, and she stammered, "I mean, for a ghost. An elf. I mean, an elf ghost."

Idrefe's laughter was like the tinkling of silver bells. "I look forward to working with you, child. Do let me know if this one—" she jabbed a finger in my direction "—gives you problems. He and I may have a contract, but I have the strength to send more than enough life magic into him to make his day less than pleasant."

My stomach soured at the thought. Life and death magic, though they shared a common root, did not mix well. Having grown up in a family of famous life mages, I could work some white magic spells, though the casting left me ill. Having Idrefe infusing me with life magic was not my preferred way to spend the rest of the evening.

Before I could say anything, Idrefe whirled on her ghostly heel. "Adelvell, your barrier!"

Without thinking, I tapped into my necromantic power and erected a spirit barrier around Idrefe, Lian, Edurne, and myself. An instant later, a bolt of white energy shot from the distant tree line. It would have struck Lian square in the back, but it exploded against the barrier in a brilliant flash. I squinted against the light as Edurne screamed and dropped to her knees. Captain Marcel ran forward and placed himself between Lian and the trees the magical attack had come from. "Assassin!" he roared, his voice booming through the lakeside clearing. "Protect the prince!"

Someone screamed, and then horses were stampeding through the clearing. Riderless horses. "Bloody hell," Lord Sendoa shouted, "someone's cut the horse picket!"

A few squires ran after the horses, while others charged into the tree line near the picket, swords flashing in the moonlight. More bolts of white magic crashed against my spirit shield. The shield warped and crackled, but it held. I felt the reverberations in my soul and poured more power into the shield, my teeth clenched. Whoever was shooting at us was powerful. If it was the cleric from the throne room, she had my respect.

Captain Marcel continued to shout for his men to rally to him and Lian. Edurne clung to my robe, and I pulled her close in case we had to jump out of the way of a frightened horse. Aine was still tied to her tree a few feet away, ears back as she munched on the last of the oats we'd given her. She'd seen enough magical displays in her time in Necrolopolis to not be phased by this little exchange.

"The carriage!" Prince Lian yelled. He pushed past Captain Marcel and pointed, his finger almost touching the inside surface of the spirit barrier surrounding us. "They have the carriage!"

Three warriors in the same gleaming armor as those chasing us out of the city had clambered onto the carriage. One kicked the driver out of his seat and took up the reins, a second sat next to him in the seat, while the third crouched on the roof. The new driver snapped the reins, and the team of horses jumped to obey. Unlike Aine, they hadn't been trained to deal with explosions of magical energy and the sight of their own kind panicked and running, so they broke into a gallop right from the start, eager to be away from the chaos.

"Now, isn't that strange?" Idrefe murmured, her voice almost lost in the noise.

"Stop them!" Lian shouted. "Someone, stop them!"

Edurne tugged on my sleeve and pointed at Aine. "Mr. Adelvell, we have to help! That lady's in danger!"

Along with Lian's aspirations, if what he'd told me was true. He needed the banner the woman was carrying in order to be crowned king. I didn't want to risk my life against a squad of elf paladins over a scrap of moldy cloth, but Edurne was right. There was no telling what they'd do to the woman inside. I quickly untied Aine, mounted, and pulled Edurne into the saddle. "Keep the prince covered!" I said to Captain Marcel and Lord Sendoa. "The cleric's magic cannot harm you, but it will hurt him."

As I wheeled Aine around to face the path to the road, Lian shouted, "Bring her back, necromancer! Bring back Alaia!"

Alaia? I had been told the woman's name was Ofelia. My theory about her being Lian's mistress further solidified in my mind. Alaia must be her real name, and in his flustered state, he'd reverted to using it. Whoever she was, she was in grave danger, and Edurne and I were the only ones capable of helping her.

I pressed my heels into Aine's flanks. She bolted, eager to run after her brief rest. We galloped past a handful of squires who were still trying to get their knights' mounts under control. As things stood, we wouldn't have reinforcements for a while. I reached back and felt the handle of my bone shovel. I was glad I hadn't removed it from its saddle loop. I'd likely need it before the night was done, either as a magical focus, or as a melee weapon.

Aine galloped down the path. I hunched in the saddle to avoid low-hanging branches, and urged Edurne to do the same. Ahead of us, the carriage bounced and tilted wildly in its headlong flight. Its boxy form shattered branches to its left and right. Shouts and curses drifted back to us, likely from the paladins riding in the front seat. The third paladin had pressed himself flat on the roof, and his legs swayed left and right, depending on which way the carriage bounced. I prayed it wouldn't flip, even as I prayed that Aine wouldn't catch a hoof in a hole or trip against a root. Horses have better night vision than even the undead, but I didn't know how well their vision worked at full gallop.

The path abruptly ended at the point where it joined the main road. With a shout, whoever was driving the carriage yanked the reins hard to the left. The team of horses screamed and rushed to obey, and the carriage made such a hard turn that its wheels locked. The carriage slid along the hard-packed road, carving a rut in its surface, and kicking up a cloud of dust visible in the moonlight. The carriage leaned precariously to the right and almost pitched over into a ditch, but it righted itself, and the horses continued their flight down the road, back toward Neru.

I slowed Aine enough to safely make the turn onto the main road, then urged her into a gallop once more. As much as I hated flying, I really wished Ezella could have accompanied me this time. Her gyrocopter would have come in handy right about now.

As spirited as Aine was, the panic-stricken team of horses pulling the carriage seemed to have boundless energy. In the short amount of time it took me to slow and turn, they'd gained considerable ground. *Mortus, I hope we can catch up in time.*

Idrefe appeared, her long blonde hair and robes billowing in the wind as she floated alongside me. "About those paladins—"

"I'm a little busy right now, Idrefe." I pointed. "Unless you can help me catch the carriage, we'll talk later."

"What do you expect me to do? I'm a ghost."

"Uh, you know, ghost things." I floundered for an answer. "Just spook them or something."

Idrefe bristled. "I am not some simple house spirit that gets its undead jollies by frightening children. I am a maester of the—"

"The Eleventh Circle, the most famous demon hunter in all the elfin lands, touted by the queen herself, so on, so forth. I get it, Idrefe. You're important, but none of that matters now. What matters is we stop that carriage before those exemplary members of your race do something horrible to the woman inside it."

Idrefe grumbled in her native tongue as she glared at me. Even her complaints had a musical quality to them. Then she smiled. "Watch a maester at work, young Adelvell." With that, she vanished.

My focus returned to the carriage. For a long moment, nothing happened. It still raced ahead, its team of horses seemingly tireless.

We were gaining ground, but I wondered which would flag first: Aine or the carriage team?

Curses and shouts drifted back to us, and I saw the carriage slow before coming to a stop in the middle of the road. As we closed the gap, I could hear the crack of the whip from the desperate driver. Still, the horses wouldn't budge. What was going on?

The curses of the paladins turned into frightened screams. The two in front jumped to the ground and disappeared into the woods. The third hopped down and made as if to follow his companions, but he turned back to the carriage. He reached into a pouch at his belt with one hand and drew his sword with the other, holding the blade close to the hilt in a reverse-grip. A flame suddenly ignited in his hand, and I frowned. A lantern? A torch?

He struck the carriage door window with the pommel of his sword. Glass shattered, and the woman inside screamed. He stepped a few feet away and pulled back the arm holding the flame. Fear shot through me like a bolt of the cleric's white magic. It was an incendiary potion! The flame I'd seen was an oil-soaked wick inserted into the bottle, ignited by a piece of spinning flint affixed to the top.

I spurred Aine on, intent on running the murderous elf down. I knew I wouldn't make it in time. "Edurne!"

Edurne thrust her hands forward. Shards of razor-sharp ice formed at her fingertips hovered in front of us. "Please work!" she whispered as she launched them at the paladin.

The shards didn't strike him as I thought they would, and most sailed past his armored form. I opened my mouth to tell her to try again, but then I noticed the flaming wick had tumbled to the ground. One of her shards had sliced through it, rendering the potion bomb inert.

The paladin tried to light it again, but it was too late. Aine reared up, her powerful forelegs kicking wildly. She bowled the elf over onto the ground. I dismounted and started to bind the stunned elf's hands. His helmet had come off when he was knocked to the ground. I studied his face in the gloom, and pale moonlight fell on his ears. "He's a human!" I muttered.

"I tried to tell you that." Idrefe appeared next to me, arms crossed. "They may be dressed in the armor of my kind, but they are all human."

"Why?"

"Deniability?" Idrefe shrugged. "Easier to lay the blame for their prince's untimely end on overzealous elfin exorcists than risk the wrath of loyal retainers."

A high-pitched wail rose from inside the carriage. Edurne hopped off Aine's back and bounded up the carriage's two steps and peered in through the door's window. "Miss Ofelia, are you all right?"

She doesn't sound all right. I finished tying the fake paladin's hands and feet, then stood. I paused as I reached for the door, my head cocked to the side. Wait, that wasn't the sound of a woman crying.

The rhythmic thumping of approaching riders tore my attention away from the carriage. I pulled my shovel free of its saddle loop and turned in the direction of the noise. A dozen men rode toward us from the direction of the lakeside lodge. Lian and Captain Marcel rode in the van, with Lord Sendoa and Knight-Lieutenant Ivonor at their flanks.

"How did they get here so fast?" I asked. When we'd left, most of their horses were in headlong flight, and the knights were locked in a skirmish.

"I calmed the horses the same way I did the carriage team." Idrefe smiled. "I have always been good with Vitals. That is why you and I get along so well."

"Be nice."

"Is she all right?" Lian shouted as he reined in. He jumped from the saddle and ran for the carriage. "Is Alaia all right?"

Edurne opened the carriage door and stepped back to the ground as Ofelia—or Alaia?—exited. The wrapped bundle I'd seen with her squirmed and writhed in her arms. A tiny foot appeared, followed by a face.

Lian helped her down the last step. "Oh, thank Vita, Ofelia. I feared I'd never see you or Alaia again."

"As did I, my prince." Ofelia's beautiful face sported a bruise above her right eye, and her left cheek had a small cut, likely from the shattered window. She turned toward Edurne and me and ducked her head. "Thank you both."

"It would seem my debt to you both only grows deeper, Mr. Adelvell." Lian grinned, then waved a hand toward the baby. "Allow me to present Princess Alaia, daughter of my late brother, and the last living direct descendant of my family line."

I blinked. "Your brother's daughter?"

"You mean you're not a couple?" Edurne asked, her ice-blue eyes flitting from Lian to Ofelia.

Ofelia blushed, and Lian grew even paler. They looked at each other, then away.

Idrefe chuckled. "Ah, humans."

"I am Princess Alaia's wet nurse," Ofelia said, her tone level, even though her cheeks were as red as Aine's coat. She made shushing noises and rocked Alaia, who eventually quieted. "I've tended to the babe since she was born."

By the look of things, the baby wasn't the only one who received Ofelia's "tending." I tucked my hands into the sleeves of my robe. "What is Princess Alaia's role in this, Prince Lian?"

"Survival." Lian's expression turned grim. "My bloodline is being wiped out. Corin and his treacherous henchmen succeeded in killing Father and me, and likely my brother, too. If they can kill Alaia, the line of succession will be in question, and our nation will descend into civil war." He clenched both hands into fists. "That must not happen. Alaia must be crowned before it is too late."

"Wait, you intend to crown *her* as the next ruler?" I asked.

"Who else?" Lian touched a hand to his chest. "The people won't accept an undead king, nor should they. It goes against the natural order. Father's will was for our line to carry on. And it will, through her." He reached out and ran his fingers through Alaia's hair. She studied him for a long moment, her large blue eyes the picture of seriousness. Then she giggled, her lips cracking open into a big, toothless grin.

"She has such a beautiful smile," Ofelia said, her voice catching in her throat. Tears glistened in her eyes.

Lian placed his other hand on Ofelia's shoulder. "We'll keep her safe. I promise you." To me he said, "We knew it was risky to take her with us, but it would've been far too dangerous to leave her alone in the castle. Besides, she needs to be at the ceremony in order for it to be considered legitimate."

That explained the need for the carriage. "What about the banner?" I asked. "Don't you need that for the ceremony to work?"

"Trusted men are retrieving it from the reliquary as we speak," Lian said.

"They should already have it, cousin," Lord Sendoa said. "They will meet us at the coronation site."

"Which, incidentally, is back up the road we've been traveling down," Ivonor said. "Two hours or so by horse."

Of course. I suppressed a sigh. That explained why we were going this way in the first place.

The bound man groaned and stirred. I pointed. "Highness, we've got another issue to deal with. Those paladins chasing us aren't elves. They're men in disguise."

"Gods," the man croaked. "Your horse broke my ribs."

Sendoa's head snapped up, his expression fierce. "I know that voice." He pushed past me and rolled the bound man over with his boot. That elicited more moans and groans. "Pol? What in the Eighteen Hells are you doing here?"

"Who is this man?" Lian demanded.

"One of my retainers." A vein stood out in Sendoa's neck as he shook his head. "At least, I thought he was. It seems he's working for the enemy. Isn't that right?"

He kicked Pol in the side. Pol screamed. Edurne flinched and shied away. I gently pushed her behind me. "Lord Sendoa, that's enough! He's wounded and needs a healer."

"He needs a rope around his neck," Sendoa retorted. "Ivonor!"

Ivonor grinned. "With pleasure, cousin." He turned back to his horse.

"Do your worst," Pol spat. Blood trickled out of the corner of his mouth as he glared up at Sendoa. "When Duke Corin is crowned king, none of you will be long for the gibbet."

Lian smiled. "Would hanging even have an effect on me?"

"Don't let them break your neck," I said. "That's no way to spend the seventy or so years you'll be in Necrolopolis." The wait list to be seen by Mortus in his courthouse was rather long.

"You'll be done in by that cleric before the dawn, monster," Pol said.

Captain Marcel strode forward and struck the man across the face with the back of his gauntlet. "That's Prince Lian, you treacherous dog!"

"Captain Marcel, peace," Lian said, his tone level. As Captain Marcel stepped back, Lian dropped into a crouch and stared into Pol's eyes. "Let the man enjoy his last few breaths as a mortal. After all, if he doesn't talk—"

"I won't!"

"*If* he doesn't talk, he'll get the rope cousin Sendoa claims he's sorely in need of." Lian's smile turned wicked. "And he better hope his neck doesn't get broken in the process. I hear that's no way to spend the next seventy or so years. Isn't that right, Mr. Necromancer?"

Mina could make me wish I was dead if I ever went along with a threat like this, but a bit of bluffing never hurt in a negotiation. I channeled power into my hands until black energy danced along my fingertips. "Try to preserve the neck if you can. Paralyzed thralls aren't very useful, and I have too many severed heads to talk to as it is."

That last part was true. The Bony Barrows was littered with ossuaries, and even what was known as a "skull rack" from a culture that practiced human sacrifice. Many in the ossuaries and all on the skull rack were nothing more than heads lacking both body and flesh. What they lacked in the fleshly realm they more than made up for in the spoken word. For people who didn't go anywhere, they certainly had a lot to say.

Ivonor returned with the rope. He cast a wary eye my way, but went along with it. "We'll hang him from that tree over there. If we haul him up rather than drop him, there's less chance of his neck breaking."

"Woah, woah, woah!" Pol exclaimed before descending into a coughing fit. He clutched at his chest with his bound hands. "Mercy," he gasped. "Anything but becoming undead."

"It's not so bad, Mr. Traitor." Edurne stepped forward, knelt, and patted his arm. "There's lots of people to meet, and Mad Molly is—"

"G-g-g-gods!" Pol's teeth chattered worse than the occupants of the aforementioned skull rack. "How can you be so c-c-c-cold?"

"She'll visit you every day once you're interred in the city," I promised.

"Who knew hell could be so cold?" Sendoa murmured.

"That's enough, child," Lian said. "I think the point has been made."

Edurne looked hurt, but when she turned away, she flashed a brief smile in my direction. To hide my own smile, I said, "We might as well get started. The sooner he's enthralled, the sooner we can get the information out of him."

"I'll talk, I'll talk!" Pol tried to sit up, but he grimaced and dropped his head back to the dirt. "Please. Mercy."

"What does Corin have planned?" Lian demanded, all pretense at niceties gone.

"He plans to crown one of the late king's cousins, a boy few know of due to his… condition."

Lian and Sendoa frowned, and Ivonor shook his head. "I know whom he speaks of," Ivonor said. "Ronaen, son of Viscount Sohan. Something's not right in the poor lad's head, and hasn't been since birth. He'd be useless on the throne."

"Except as a puppet for a 'benevolent' regent." Sendoa's frown deepened. "Couldn't he have done the same with Alaia? She's a baby."

"A baby who will grow into a woman of sound mind and body," Lian said. "There's no guarantee she and those loyal to her won't cast off Corin's regency once they're able to." He looked down at Pol. "When does he plan to hold the coronation?"

"At dawn."

Everyone froze. For a time, the only noise was Alaia babbling away in Ofelia's arms several yards away. Finally, Ivonor asked, "Does that mean he has the banner?"

"What happened to the men I sent, Pol?" Sendoa demanded. "You knew where they were bound, and who was going."

Pol swallowed hard. "Dead, but not by my hand. Corin's men killed them."

Sendoa rattled off a string of oaths so foul, I covered Edurne's ears. Ivonor looked grim as he said, "He must have the banner. Considering that cleric was with him, he must also have the Church's blessing."

"Last question before we ride," Lian said. "Pol, do you know who murdered Father and me?" He laid a hand on his sword hilt. "Was it you?"

Pol's eyes widened, and he raised his bound hands, palms open. "No! Gods, no. It wasn't me!"

"Of course. How silly of me. Murdering men—even men in their beds—would be too much for a disguised baby-killer like you."

Anger flashed across Pol's face, but fear soon replaced it as Lian drew his sword. The blade was as plain as the hilt and scabbard, but its edge appeared razor sharp. "Do you know who did? Last chance."

"I don't know!" Pol doubled-up from a coughing fit. When it subsided, he continued in a strained voice, "None of the duke's spies know who the others are. That's how he operates."

Idrefe floated over Pol, and he shivered as her spectral feet passed through his flesh. "I sense no falsehood in the man. You can trust he's telling the truth, at least on this."

Lian sighed. "Very well. That's a mystery that will need to be solved another day. Captain Marcel, have the healers tend to Pol, then leave him with the rest of the wounded. If he tries to escape or any attempt to rescue him, he's to be executed immediately. Otherwise, he awaits the pleasure of Queen Alaia and her regent."

He started to sheathe his sword, and something caught my eye. "Prince Lian, may I see that sword up close?"

"Interested in it?" Lian's smile returned as he held it out. "Behold, the Sword of the First King." The smile turned bashful. "Not very fancy for an ancient relic, is it?"

"It appears perfectly serviceable." I leaned in to examine the weapon without taking it in hand. Swords weren't really my thing. Besides, my shovel's edge was sharper than steel. Sky whales had teeth strong enough to chew the stone off mountaintops. If I was being honest, I didn't care about the weapon. I cared about the necromantic aura surrounding it. While part of that energy pulsed in time with the glow wreathing Lian, black threads of pure death magic flowed from the sword's hilt and disappeared into the distance. I couldn't count the number of individual strands, but they all traveled in the same general direction.

I noticed Idrefe had floated closer so she could study the necromantic aura, too. She turned her head toward Lian. "Your Highness, where is the coronation site in relation to us?"

Lian looked around, then pointed. "Quim's Stand is about a league to the southwest."

The same direction the black magic flowed. "You said it was originally a battlefield, correct?"

"A very bloody battlefield, yes." Lian squinted at the blade, but he couldn't see what we could. "While a few nobles were brought back to family tombs and crypts, most of the dead were buried in a mound, right on the site of the First King's triumphant last stand."

"And it is there that the coronation takes place?" Idrefe asked.

"Yes. As part of the ceremony, the one to be crowned—or a guardian, in our case—stands in the center of the mound, holds the banner aloft, and reenacts the First King's rallying cry. Those in assembly respond, and that's it." Lian sheathed his sword. "It's a simple enough ceremony and could be held anywhere, but for tradition."

Possibly for other reasons, if those strands of black energy meant what I thought they did. "Let's hurry there," I said, "before Duke Corin catches up to us."

"He's already on the way," Pol muttered. "He took the road to Livia in order to approach Quim's Stand from the northeast."

"Likely to avoid any troops we may have already had stationed along the main road," Sendoa said. "He's cunning, that one."

"May it be his undoing," Ivonor added.

"Do you have a plan, Mr. Adelvell?" Prince Lian asked. "Without the banner, we cannot complete the ceremony."

"Oh, I've got some ideas," I said. "Follow my lead when we get there, Your Highness, and we'll see your niece crowned. On my honor as a representative of Necrolopolis."

* * *

I dove to the ground as a volley of arrows sailed overhead. I tried to scramble to my feet, but tripped over the butt of my own shovel, and went down again, striking my face in the grassy mound at the center of Quim's Stand.

The burial site was huge, more like a grass-covered hill than the small mound I'd envisioned. Based on what I could see in the moonlight, a fair number of crypts, or a good-sized mausoleum tenement could fill up this area, maybe two. How many people had died here? *If things go badly, there'll be a few more of us buried here before long!*

"Loose!" someone shouted from the tree line.

Edurne threw herself in front of me, icy mist swirling around her fingertips. "Please work!" she shouted, and the mist coalesced into a thick shield of solid ice. Arrows zipped past us in either direction, while others struck Edurne's shield. The arrows either deflected off to the side or bounced back and fell to the ground, leaving scratches and cracks in the shield's otherwise smooth surface. "Are you all right, Mr. Adelvell?" she asked.

I needed to sit her down and come up with some actual spell names. It wasn't necessary to speak at all when casting a spell, though many mages used them as a focus. If she was going to continue down this path, she needed more than "Please work!" I pulled myself into a crouch and nodded my thanks. "Let's go!"

The two of us ran behind Prince Lian, Sendoa, Ivonor, and a handful of knights who had all dismounted in order to climb the burial mound at the center of the field. More knights ran behind us, shields up to deflect arrows heading our way. We'd left half the force back on the road to guard our horses and protect Ofelia and Princess Alaia. I'd been told reinforcements could arrive from Neru with the dawn, but that was assuming they'd be loyal to a prince they now had to know was undead.

Sendoa looked over his shoulder and caught sight of me. "What happened to this plan of yours, Mr. Adelvell?" he shouted. "So far it seems to be shaking out the way the last one did."

"*My* plan included more horses and less enemy arrows, my lord!" I called back. "I didn't realize it was bad form to ride horses onto an old battlefield!"

Sendoa barked a laugh as an arrow embedded itself in his shield. "I'm starting to like this necromancer, my prince!"

We crested the hill, and Duke Corin came into view. He stood at the burial mound's center, holding what I could only assume was the banner of the first king. A priest of Vita and the cleric from before were with him, along with Ronaen, the troubled boy they would crown. He looked to be no more than about five or six, and he played in the grass at Corin's feet.

A group of Corin's men-at-arms charged at us without hesitation. Lian and his men also didn't hesitate, even though we were outnumbered. The prince, his nobles, and his knights threw themselves into the fray with wild abandon, each engaging two or three opponents at once. "For Quim!" they yelled.

"Kill them all!" Corin shouted, and his men roared their approval.

The female cleric aimed her rod at Lian. The ball at the end began to glow with white light. I tapped into my power and sent a bolt of necromantic energy sailing her way. Our spells struck one another in an explosion of black and white magic.

A trio of men-at-arms ran around Lian and his knights and charged at me.

Edurne dropped to a crouch and placed her hands in the grass. "Please work!" she yelled, and a sheet of ice rapidly spread out from her fingers, covering several yards in front of us. The first man-at-arms stepped on the ice, and his boots went out from under him. He landed face-first, and the second man-at-arms tripped and went flying over his comrade. The third attempted to dodge, but by then, Edurne's icy field had spread past the fallen soldiers and reached his feet, too. He landed on the others, and Edurne quickly bound them in frozen chains.

She swayed back and forth as if lightheaded, and I felt her energy draining out. I channeled more of my power into her, restoring her vitality. "Good work, but be careful," I said. "You need to be more efficient with your magic usage, or you'll thaw out if I'm not around to assist you."

Idrefe materialized next to me, her expression grim. "Bad tidings, Adelvell. After I finished scaring off the archers, I reached the road Corin had come from. Reinforcements are at the bottom of the mound, and they carry his banner."

I was wondering why the hidden archers had fallen silent. "Finally having some fun as a ghost, I take it?"

"Oh, just lovely. Maybe you can join me in the fun if your plan fails."

"Let's make sure that doesn't happen, then." I looked east and saw the sun beginning to peek over the horizon. Dawn was almost here, and with it, all of the prerequisites for the First King's last stand would be met: the time of day, the level of desperation, the will of the men to fight for their ruler, and the presence of the true relic that bound everything together.

All that was left was for me to do my part. "Idrefe, keep that cleric busy."

Idrefe arched an eyebrow. "By doing 'ghost things?'"

"Sit her down for tea and a discussion on different exorcist techniques, if you like." I planted the butt of my shovel in the grass and focused my power into it. I pushed that energy down into the earth beneath my feet, until I felt it touch the ends of the necromantic threads that flowed from Lian's sword. Whatever those threads were tied to waited below. I took one last moment to study the banner Duke Corin held. No aura surrounded it, nor were there any necromantic threads.

Mortus, please work, I thought in echo of Edurne's spellcasting phrase. "Prince Lian!" I shouted. "When you are ready!"

The cleric attempted to shoot another spell at Lian, but Idrefe appeared next to her, causing the woman to nearly jump out of her skin. Lian struck down one of his three opponents, then locked blades with the second. The third tried to stab Lian in his exposed flank, but Sendoa tackled the man. Lian took the opportunity to hold his sword aloft and yell, "To the king! Rally to the king!"

Sendoa and Captain Marcel took up the call, as did the rest of the knights. Over it all came Corin's scornful laugh. He held the banner aloft. "Fools! You cannot claim that monster as king, not without this! You'll meet your end here, Lian! You and your whole cursed line!"

The threads pulsed. I concentrated and poured as much magic as I could into them. *Awaken! It's time to rise!*

The ground trembled, then shook wildly. Corin's laughter was drowned out by surprised cries as men stumbled and fell. The ground opened up in dozens of places, and dirty skeletons clad in rusty armor climbed out of the holes, their eye sockets glowing a variety of colors: green, blue, purple, red, yellow. Teeth chattering, they repeated the same call as before. "To the king! Rally to the king!"

Surprised cries turned into frightened screams, both from Corin's men and Lian's knights. The skeletons charged, each wielding a sword that, while filthy, somehow still held an edge to it after all these centuries. Corin's men-at-arms tried to mount a defense against this ambush, but they were quickly overpowered by close to a hundred undead warriors. "To the king!" the skeletons shouted in their unearthly voices. "Rally to the king!"

The priest grabbed little Ronaen and shielded him with his body as the skeletons surged toward Duke Corin, who still held the First King's banner. "Give it back!" the skeletons shrieked. "Give it back!"

Corin disappeared beneath a clattering pile of bones, his screams abruptly cut off.

In the end, it didn't take much bloodshed for the fight to leave Corin's men, even the company of fresh troops who'd just reached the top of the hill. With their traitorous leader dead, they quickly threw down their arms and begged Prince Lian and his newfound allies for mercy. Lian's men—his *living* men—gathered up the discarded weapons as the company of undead soldiers kept the prisoners under a burning, unblinking gaze. Lord Sendoa walked the perimeter with a couple of knights, keeping one wary eye on Corin's men, and a warier eye on the skeletons.

Four skeletons presented themselves to Prince Lian. Though they were as filthy as the rest, what was left of their armor and tabards appeared to be of finer make than the rest. "I am Captain Itzal," the leader said, "and these are my officers." He quickly named them.

Captain Marcel stared at Itzal, mouth agape. "That name... are you my ancestor?"

Itzal looked Captain Marcel up and down, his neck bones clicking and popping with the effort. "You look like my brother does—or did." He shook his head. "How much time has passed since our slumber began?"

"Close to four hundred years," Lian said. "I am Prince Lian, direct descendent of Quim, the first king and your liege lord."

"Ah, so it was worth it!" Itzal spun on his heel and slammed a bony fist against his breastplate. "Did you hear that, men? Our side won! The kingdom won!"

Cheers erupted from the skeletons, and the celebration was soon echoed by Lian's knights. I couldn't help but smile. I didn't have many joys in my job in Necrolopolis, but the sight of the undead witnessing the fruits of their labors—or deaths, as was the case here—was something to behold.

"Are you to be our new king, then, Prince Lian?" Itzal asked as he turned around. "We honored our oath, to be loyal to King Quim's line even in death."

"If only it could be so, but I must soon retire from this place." Lian inclined his head in my direction. "An agreement between gentlemen must be honored."

"But you share our state," Itzal objected. He looked around, his sockets blazing with blue light. "Would a living king have use for soldiers like us?"

I grimaced. That was the problem with the undead in most societies, even those neighboring Necrolopolis. They never really fit in, and fear from the living played a huge role in that.

Idrefe hovered nearby, a pensive frown marring her normally placid expression. "We could bring them back with us," she said.

"You are welcome to do that," Lian offered, "to come with us to Necrolopolis, a safe haven for the undead. My treasury will pay the interment fee for all of you." He held up a hand. "Before you decide, please meet the one who will be the next ruler."

It took several minutes for the remaining knights to return with Ofelia and Alaia. In the meantime, it came to my attention that the cleric woman had vanished into the night with some of Duke Corin's men, leaving behind the priest and the boy Ronaen. The priest claimed not to know who the cleric was, even though they'd been dressed in the robes of the same order. Idrefe cleared him of any falsehood, which left us with a mystery on our hands. Who was the cleric, and what was her real motive for being involved in this strange plot?

Well, that was a mystery for another day and another person who wasn't me. Now that I'd fulfilled my end of the bargain, all that was left was to get Lian to Necrolopolis. Along with possibly a hundred skeletons.

I was going to need to come up with a good excuse for *that*.

Idrefe had also spoken with Ronaen. While he did have some sort of speech problem, he was very much aware of his surroundings. Surprisingly, he showed no fear toward Idrefe, but he did have some apprehension regarding the skeletons. Given how disheveled they all looked, who could blame him?

When Ofelia arrived with a sleepy Alaia, the baby princess had been wrapped in a woolen blanket to guard her against the chill. Ofelia looked nervous at the sight of so many skeleton warriors standing in the dawn light. She stopped near Lian, who brushed a loose strand of hair away from her face. He bent to stroke Alaia's chin. The baby looked up at him with her big eyes, and a laugh escaped her lips.

"Captain Itzal, may I present Princess Alaia, Quim's next ruler."

Itzal peered down at Alaia, who stared right back into his skeletal face. "She looks like King Quim when he was a babe!" he exclaimed.

The other officers crowded around, each wanting to see. Alaia turned her head this way and that, her lower lip sucked into her mouth as she studied them. Then she grinned and giggled.

"She smiles just like him, too!" Itzal said, his voice rising a few octaves.

"Ah, there he goes again," one of the officer skeletons said. "Captain Itzal's got a soft spot for children."

"He's showin' his age, too!" another added. "King Quim was an old man when I joined the military!"

"Hey, now!" the first officer growled. "He was the age I was when I died!"

"Like I said—"

By this point, all the skeletons were laughing and carrying on as they likely had in life. Alaia laughed along with them, as did Lian and the others.

"Isn't this nice, Mr. Adelvell?" Edurne asked. Frosty tears had formed around her blue eyes, giving them a glow in the morning sun. Despite the tears, she smiled. "Living and unliving getting along. It doesn't just happen in Necrolopolis."

My mood soured, but I tried not to show it. If only this was the kind of acceptance she had gotten in her village. "It'll be a long and hard road for them," I cautioned. "Not everyone will accept them."

"No, I suppose not." She chewed her blue lower lip for a moment, but the smile soon returned. "But it's a start, wouldn't you agree?"

Ronaen slowly approached, and Idrefe explained that he wanted to see Alaia. Lian knelt and introduced himself, then scooped up his newfound cousin and let him get a good look at Alaia.

Both children studied one another, neither saying a word. Finally, Alaia held out her tiny hand, and Ronaen gently took it. Alaia grinned, and so did Ronaen. Captain Itzal let out an "Aww," which brought another round of good-natured mocking from his men.

I smiled. "I suppose it is a start."

After a few moments, Lord Sendoa returned to Lian's side, his expression grim. The two held a hushed conversation, and Lian's face fell. They pulled away from the gathering and approached us. "Mr. Adelvell," Lian said, his voice pained. "We need to talk."

My heart sank. I could already see where this was going. "Your Highness, you know—"

"I know." He raised a hand to forestall me. "I know I can't stay in the kingdom, but neither can I go with you. Not yet."

"And why is that?"

"According to the captain of Corin's guard, the *good* duke wasn't the mastermind of this plot." His lips twisted at the words. "I know he wasn't blameless, but it would seem he had someone whispering in his ear, someone you've clashed with more than once this night."

"The *cleric?*" That was surprising. I didn't think any who wielded white magic were capable of assassination and subterfuge.

"So he says. He could be trying to protect the reputation of his fallen liege, or he could be mistaken. Either way, there's a greater conspiracy afoot."

"We also don't know who poisoned you or your father, Highness." Sendoa glared at the prisoners. "Though I intend to find out, and soon."

"As things stand, Alaia is at risk. That means Quim is at risk." Lian spread his hands in a helpless gesture. "I can't leave things as they are, not with my honor intact. You must understand, Mr. Adelvell."

I did understand, as much as I hated to admit it. I tucked my hands into the sleeves of my robe. "What would you have me do?"

"Allow me to remain behind for a time. A month, or maybe a season. Time enough to flush out the traitors and truly secure Alaia's position."

Mina would be furious, but wasn't my ultimate duty to help the undead achieve the goals and desires that kept them bound to this mortal coil? "It's going to be difficult for you," I warned. "For you, and for Itzal and his men. Without me to protect you, that cleric could exorcise all of you."

"That's what we're here for," Sendoa said. "We'll be his shield against her magic, as we were in the woods."

"We each have our duty," Lian said. "Mine is here, as yours is in Necrolopolis. Hurry home, and let Lady Grimina know we won't be far behind."

Idrefe materialized next to me. "For what it is worth, Adelvell, I think this is the best outcome." She cast a sidelong look my way, her lips quirked. "Now, whether Mina feels the same way or not is a different tale altogether."

I grimaced. "Mina's going to be angry, and you know it."

"She will accept it as the compromise it is." Idrefe cocked her head to the side. "As to how she will punish you, that is—"

"A different tale altogether, yes. I get it, Idrefe."

Edurne looked up at Prince Lian. "Will you be all right, Your Highness?"

Lian knelt and took Idrefe's hand. "I won't let anything happen to me, little one. Honor keeps me here for the moment, but that same honor binds me to the oath I made to Mr. Adelvell. I *will* come to Necrolopolis when it is time. That I promise you.

"To bind us to this oath, take this." He removed a sheathed dagger from his belt and handed it to her, hilt first. "My father gifted me this dagger on my naming day. It's one of my most prized possessions. Hold onto it, and return it to me when I enter the gates of Necrolopolis."

Edurne studied the dagger with wide eyes. "I'll guard it with my life." She hesitated, then smiled. "Such as it is, anyway."

Lian returned the smile. "It's a promise, then. And I'll reward you for what you've done for Alaia, and for the kingdom." He turned his head to say something to Sendoa.

Before he could, Edurne leaned forward and kissed him on the cheek. Her cheeks then flushed bright blue, and she ducked behind me, the sheathed dagger pressed against her chest with both hands.

Captain Itzal walked over then, his bony face somehow aglow. "Pray forgive me. I couldn't help but overhear much of the conversation." He saluted Lian and Sendoa, then looked at me. "I will honor Prince Lian's oath, as well. My men will stay with him here as long as he must, and then we shall either return to our rest on this spot, or accompany him to Necrolopolis."

"That is *another* thing you are going to have to explain to Mina, Adelvell." Idrefe pointed at Itzal. "She does not look too kindly on people raising the dead."

"They were already undead!" I snapped. "All I did was wake them up."

"Pray that Mina feels the same way."

Lian looked from Idrefe to me. "Lady Grimina sounds like an intimidating woman."

"You have no idea," I muttered.

Itzal crossed his bony arms. "She sounds like my wife when I was home from campaign. If I accidentally woke our children in the middle of the night, there was hell to pay." He paused for a long moment, then added, "And then I'd suggest to the king that we invade another neighbor of ours."

Everyone laughed, including me. "If we're suddenly back here in a few weeks, you'll know what happened." I looked at Edurne. "Don't tell Mina I said that."

Edurne giggled.

* * * * *

Benjamin Tyler Smith Bio

Benjamin spends his days creating maps for cemeteries and his evenings herding the undead and battling aliens. He's a writer of fantasy and science fiction, with two novels published in Blood Moon Press' Fallen World universe, and numerous short stories in anthologies, magazines, and floating about the internet. Many of these short stories are set in his Necrolopolis universe, a dark fantasy world where a necromancer protagonist must keep the peace in a city of the undead. He's currently writing the first set of novels in that universe, as well as working on projects in the shared universes of his fellow travelers of the writing path.

He lives in an area of rural Pennsylvania with more cows than humans as neighbors, ruled over by a benevolent Calico Countess and her feline knight, the Earl of Grey. Helping him maintain this noble estate is a saint of a wife and a beautiful baby girl who absorbs way too much of his productive time.

Follow him at BenjaminTylerSmith.com and join his mailing list for free short stories!

* * * * *

The Lost Cloud
by Casey Moores
A Deathmage War Story

"You see that, Celeve? I told you I could find it." Taylor, her gray-haired human pilot, snapped his head back at her to flash a smug, condescending smile. Even through his goggles, his conceit was obvious. With one hand, he held the airship's yoke. With the other, he raised the new pendant he wore on a necklace and kissed it. His words came out as steam in the cold, thin air. "You didn't believe me."

The marble-skinned, haute elf captain would normally have responded with customary banter and sarcasm. After all, they wouldn't even be up there if Celeve hadn't believed in him, at least a little. She had, of course, had her doubts. In the end, based on the sheer magnitude of the riches involved, Taylor had convinced her it was worth a try.

But she didn't respond because the sight of their discovery stole her breath.

A castle stretched out across the entire cloud. As she took it all in, she decided *castle* was not the right word. It wasn't some high-walled defensive structure with turrets and a drawbridge, or even one of the modern star-shaped designs. It was shaped more like an old wooden sailing ship, only flipped so that its hull pointed upward. It was carved out of what seemed to be a single piece of stone, creating a long, oval dome of light gray. Bright silver lines streamed down the sides. Windows, few and far between, were chiseled out of its sides, and rarer still were the handful of balconies near the top. Though their airship, the *Chien Salé*, was well above the structure, it was those windows and balconies that let her know how immense it must be.

The sight of the fabled Lost City of Brighthope made her light-headed.

"'Scuse me, love," Dewar said. The half-deep elf took a long, strained breath and gasped. "Mind thickening the air back up? It's a bit thin at the moment. Bad enough it's freezing up here."

In the excitement of having found the structure, she'd stopped concentrating on her magic. Though it wasn't the highest altitude they'd ever reached, it was high enough to necessitate she spend a little of her energy increasing the density of the air around them. The crew wasn't acclimated to such thin air. The cold was worse than usual, as well, and everyone but Brutus and Jaughn were bundled up in layers, wearing fur-lined caps and goggles.

Celeve shot her lover a wink and said, "Sorry, Dew." She drew her hands together and tightened the air around their airship. As her crew took long, welcome breaths, Celeve returned her attention to the ship's approach. They were dropping so fast that the pilot's pendant floated up into the air, as if yearning for their destination.

"Careful there, *mon capitaine*," Taylor said. "I'm trying to bring *Chien Salé* down gently. You mess up my buoyancy, and we could drop like a stone. I know you gotta keep everyone conscious, but—"

"Speak for yourself, oxygen hog," said Brutus, their grumpy little fairy. He fluttered up next to the pilot and sat on the man's shoulder. "I'll be fine, even if you crash the thing. In fact, that just means I get to keep whatever riches are down there to myself. So, by all means, drop it in."

Taylor reached up and swatted the fairy away. As he did so, the airship drooped down to the right. He grabbed the controls with both hands again and righted the ship.

"Good luck carrying it, you little butterfly," Taylor said.

"No one's going to die, and I don't need a lecture," Celeve said. "I'll take care of the crew, you just put the ship down in one piece, and don't tell your captain how to do her job."

"Tell me again why it didn't work out between you two?" Dewar asked with a snicker.

"Lasted well enough for decades, thank you very much, neophyte," Taylor responded.

The pendant flew up again, enough for her to really look at it for the first time. It was graced by a thin-faced nobleman, with a furrowed brow and a simple crown. A coin, she decided, though she'd never seen another like it.

She lost sight of the coin as her hair floated up around her face. They were falling out of the sky.

"*Mon Dieu*, Taylor, you're bringing us down too quickly," she said. "Why are you in such a hurry? You just said you'd bring us down gently."

Dreucht and Goshe, the short, squat half-dwarf twins, checked their tethers and bounded around the deck, grabbing loose objects and shoving them under the netting. Brutus fluttered around trying to help them, but only caught the really tiny objects. Jaughn, currently appearing as a much larger version of Brutus, lay against the railing on the far side. Jaughn's head lolled around, and she feared the shifter might soon empty its stomach. Although Jaughn had been with them for years, it still hadn't found its air legs.

"Just excited, I guess. Look… it's still another couple thousand feet down. I'll cut the descent before we get there. Air'll be thicker down there, too, enough that you can help me out as I make my approach."

The closer they got, the larger the domed structure appeared. Celeve floated forward to get a better look. Her view disappeared in a flash of white for a few uncomfortable seconds as they went through a cloud. Taylor was racing to get there as if it might disappear. Considering it was rumored to be a magical city that floated in and out of reality, he might have good reason.

As they approached, she found the bright silver lines were actually long, thin, silver statues of drakes that clung to the sides of the flipped hull. There were more windows than it had seemed from further up, and what she'd thought were windows were great docking bays. What she'd thought were balconies were expansive terraces. She should have known from the title that the Lost City of Brighthope would be far more than a few buildings atop a cloud.

"How has this place never been found before?" Dewar asked.

"From below, it's just a big cloud," Taylor said. With an absent hand, he tucked the pendant into his shirt. "One among many, as it creates its own pressure system, which maintains a collection of clouds around it. At least, that's the theory."

"So now the old dog has been learning about weather?" Celeve asked.

"Almost no one flies high enough to see it from above," Taylor said. "As you noted, the air's too thin, and it's too cold. Finally, even if someone were to fly this high, it's a big sky; they'd have to be looking for it to find it."

"So, how'd you know where to find it?" Dewar asked.

"Old, dogged determination." Taylor shot Celeve another smug smile and scratched his neck.

"Have you figured out where you're landing yet?" she asked.

Taylor shrugged and gestured toward the great openings. "I think we'll fit in any of those. I'm going to circle around a couple times, first, just to check for signs of life."

* * *

"That one. I'm taking it in." Taylor banked the airship right to turn toward his intended docking bay.

"No, that one's too small," Celeve replied. "Why don't we go lower? They're bigger down there. Or one of the terraces, even." Celeve deflated the balloon envelope slightly to lower the airship.

"The bays will be easier to defend, if need be, and all the good stuff is always at the top. We've only got so much time, and we should try to get the biggest score before we gotta go. We'll find wherever the royals lived and score some quick riches. Then we finance a bigger trip to come loot the place proper."

"It won't do us any good if we crash and die."

They'd circled twice without finding any traces of activity. Feeling confident enough to try boarding it, they just needed to agree on where. Taylor tilted the airship up and fought for altitude while Celeve encouraged him to go lower by cutting lift.

She decided no one would benefit from a fight over the controls. At best, they would just argue some more. At worst, they would counteract each other enough to smack into the stone sides and tumble ten thousand feet to their deaths. At which point Brutus, as he'd joked, would inherit the entire find. Once he found and convinced another ship to look for it.

Celeve re-inflated the envelope to give him time to stabilize before they docked.

"Finally, someone sees reason," Taylor said.

"No, I figured you were going to kill us all just to be stubborn."

"Totally false. Brutus would live, so I wouldn't kill us all. Jaughn might make it, too."

The airship rose up slightly as Taylor worked to get the base of *Chien Salé* lined up just above the lip of the docking bay. As the walls loomed large, Celeve tensed.

"I told you, it's not big enough; the envelope's going to scrape at the top, rip open and collapse!" Celeve shouted.

"Deflate it on my count. I'll buck us up at the last second."

"You've gone mad in your old age."

As they shot toward the bay, she wracked her mind for a way to deter him without crashing. She found no solution. With their speed and vector, they were committed.

"Three... Two... One!"

Celeve clenched her fingers tight and released a breath. The envelope of the airship collapsed. At that moment, Taylor jerked the controls back, and the airship responded. The front of the ship's belly cleared the entrance to the docking bay by a few feet.

The middle did not. It crunched against the stone lip and slammed the ship down. They slid forward on momentum and bucked again a second later, paired with a loud *cracking* noise.

"Told you we'd fit," Taylor said as they stopped.

Celeve couldn't bring herself to look back at the tail of the ship.

"Dreucht, Goshe... how do we look?"

The half-dwarf twins clambered over the railing and stomped back to the aft end of the ship. Dreucht, the serious one, looked up and down at it and rubbed his chin. Goshe, the artistic one, kept walking back to the lip of the bay.

"Well, the rudder's gone," Dreucht said.

"And by gone, we mean, *look out below*," Goshe said.

Celeve smacked Taylor with the back of her hand.

"Moron."

"I got us in, didn't I? And we'll get out just fine, don't worry."

He gave a big, toothy grin, retrieved his pendant, and rubbed it for luck.

"I'd hate to see what they were like when they were knockin' boots," Dewar said as he dusted himself off.

"Is that because you fear they fought even worse, or because you're Celeve's new plaything and the thought of her with him disgusts you?" Jaughn asked.

"Yes."

* * *

The docking bay was a large, arched tunnel that extended inward a hundred feet. There were openings on the left and right side along the back of the tunnel, and a double door in the middle of the back wall.

"Dreucht, Goshe, stay here and see if you can fashion something to make a rudder. Scavenge what you can from wherever. Anything you can do to get us to the ground safely."

Goshe stepped forward. "Captain, it might be best if I tag along to search for a good part while Dreucht stays here to prep our girl to receive it."

"If one of you comes along, both of you come along," Celeve replied, "so arm up. We'll all head in together. First sign of something you can use, you both head back and get *Chien Salé* fixed up, understood?"

They nodded and rushed about to grab their knives and pistols.

Jaughn puffed up until it'd become a small ogre and donned a leather harness fitted to that form. It placed its seven-barreled volley gun over its back, and then placed a pair of large dragoon pistols in opposing chest holsters. Finally, it grabbed a hefty iron pickaxe.

Dewar buckled a rapier onto his left side and checked the load on a carbine rifle that was attached by a leather sling. He tapped the sides of each boot to confirm his knives were still firmly in place.

Taylor lazily cradled a shotgun in his right arm and strolled toward the left opening.

"Taylor, wait!" Celeve shouted.

"This one's clear, just an empty storage room or something," Taylor called back as he peered inside.

While Celeve loaded her revolver, Taylor crossed the bay to the other side.

"This one's empty, too. Guess we're heading through the double doors."

Dreucht, carrying an axe, stomped toward the second room Taylor had looked into.

"Did they have wood shelving?" Taylor didn't answer, and the half-dwarf continued until he could see inside. "Darn. Stone shelves. Excellent craftsmanship, though."

Celeve waved her hand and knocked Taylor over with a gust of wind before he could open the double doors.

"Everyone ready?" she asked. She received head nods all around, except for Taylor, who cursed up a storm. "Brutus, check the door."

The tiny fairy zipped up to the large wooden double door and flitted along the seams, peering through intently.

"Hey, twin dwarf guys," Dewar said as he cocked his head to the side, "couldn't you fashion a rudder out of the door there?"

"They could," Taylor said, before either twin could answer, "but that door is the only reason a tornado isn't tearing through the bay here. You'll feel it in a second when we open up. A single gust won't be that big a deal... but, left unattended, our big girl would float around in here until she fell back out. Then we'd be permanent residents."

"Speak for yourself, I keep telling you," Brutus said. He drifted back from the doors. "It looks clear, no traps as I can tell, and no one's standing on the other side."

"The ship's secure?" Celeve asked the twins. They nodded. She checked to ensure her scimitar was sheathed to her right and holstered the revolver on her left.

"Jaughn," Celeve said.

The ogre nodded and sheathed its pickaxe. It retrieved its volley gun, reached out, and grasped one of the large iron rings. In one fluid motion, it jerked the door open and swung the gun out—just in case Brutus was wrong. The crew of *Chien Salé* trusted one another, but they never abandoned caution.

As predicted, a great gust tore through their ranks. It settled quickly. Smaller torrents swirled about as they hurried through and closed the doors.

An open area spread out from the door, stretching a hundred feet before ending in a stone railing. The group warily stepped out through the doors and discovered the promenade stretched to their left and right as far as they could see. Across the way from the railing was another terrace, a mirror reflection of the side they were on. Standing at the railing, Celeve looked down a dozen similar levels to a lower area, filled with the rotted remains of what must have once been a forested park. The structure had seemed massive from the outside, but it looked even larger from within.

Rows of broken-down carts of varying shapes and sizes spread along the terrace, paralleling the railing. Most seemed empty, but Dewar and Brutus set out in search of goodies.

Skeletons lay peppered about in various manners. Some were curled up, as if they'd just laid down and ceased living. Others had clearly died in combat of some kind, with cracked skulls or arrows laying loose in their rib cages. *Skeleton* was not quite the right word, as most still had leathery skin stretched over their bones, as if they'd dried out instead of rotting. Most were adorned in traces of tattered cloth and worn-down leather.

"It's strange," Jaughn said. In its chosen form, its voice was low and dull. Jaughn spoke so rarely that, when it did, all listened. "There's no sign any of them have been chewed on by scavengers. And it doesn't look like there was a great battle for anything, it just… looks like they randomly died in this place or that for one reason or another."

"Yeah," Taylor said. "Shit… you don't think they were animated at some point, do you?"

The entire group froze and threw him dirty looks. *Animated* implied a deathmage. Everyone, in every nation and every continent, knew the stories of the great deathmages of the past and how they'd nearly plunged the entire world into darkness.

"Bite your damn tongue!" Brutus shouted as he returned to the group. Jaughn spat to its left and dragged its right foot around in a circle three times.

"It's always a damn human what goes tempting fate like that," Goshe said.

"Taylor, knock that off," Celeve ordered. "And the rest of you, don't discount the possibility he's right. Vigilance."

"Vigilance," the others muttered in response. The word seemed to do its job and bucked them up a little. Backs got straighter, weapons were clenched tighter, and their eyes scanned about with greater intent.

"Did you guys find anything?" Celeve asked Brutus and Dewar.

"Not really," Dewar said. "Just some coins. Got a sun on one side, and some silly looking king or something on the other."

Brutus sneered. "Nothing worthwhile. Everything's broke or rotted away, but it mostly looks like it was picked clean already. We sure we're the first ones here?"

"Not in the slightest. For all we know, dozens of groups might have swept through here, but I doubt it," Taylor said. "I'd like to think word would've gotten around if it had been found. These days, even if it'd been found in the Eastern Kingdoms, news would've reached the Isles. Whoever found it would have come back... hell, the place might've been repopulated by now if that were the case."

Head nods and shrugs indicated a general agreement in the group from all but Dewar. He carried a scowl that suggested skepticism.

"All right, Taylor, this is your find," she said, "where do think we should go?"

After cradling the shotgun, he grabbed at his necklace and stretched it out in front of him. In all the years they'd been together—as crew members, as lovers, through all of it—she didn't remember him being so enamored of a trinket.

Holding tight to the pendant, he pointed up and to their left. Far off in that direction, she could see a wide double staircase leading up to some sort of temple at the pinnacle of the giant oval dome.

"Like I said. Royals always got the riches, and they always live as high up as they can. Better to look down on the little people."

"Then I suppose we should go up."

The group set off. Celeve got a chill as they started out. It wasn't from the cold air, as she was bundled up and adjusted to it. In such a wide open space, it was impossible to shake the feeling that someone or *something* was watching them.

* * *

The twins hugged the wall they'd emerged from. Brutus checked the doors for them, and Jaughn stayed close. The first room was full of dried-out refuse, but the second, better sealed and better preserved, housed an elegant suite. It had some worthwhile artwork and baubles, but the group agreed to continue searching for a more lucrative score. The twins picked a large oak table as the replacement rudder. Stronger than their diminutive nature would suggest, they lifted it easily and left the party to repair *Chien Salé*.

Celeve estimated it was half a mile to the great stairway. After the twins left, they stopped checking the doors. It seemed more prudent to find the big score, if there was one, and to return for everything else later on.

Dewar stopped for a moment and hunched over with a hand on a knee.

"Whew, that's quite a trek at this altitude. Air's thicker than it was when we were looking, but it's still a bit thin. Quick break before we hit the stairs, my love?"

"Worn out already, are you?" Taylor asked with a smirk. Somehow, the old pilot was full of energy, so jittery he looked as if he might leap up the steps four at a time. "I thought Celeve's newest pet would have more stamina."

"The old man's got a point, Dewey," Celeve said.

Taylor, sporting a big, stupid smile, charged up the stairs like a man possessed. Brutus flittered up alongside him. Jaughn, expressionless and quiet as ever, followed closely. Though she felt herself a little short on breath as well, she did her best not to show it, and kept up as gracefully as she could. Dewar cursed, took a deep breath, and continued up after them.

The wide, white marble stairs curved upward until they met an identical set that rose up from the other side. The two sides merged and drove straight up to another great terrace. This terrace was dotted with equally spaced husks of trees, ringed by the gnarled remains of bushes. Celeve imagined they might have once billowed with gorgeous, colorful blooms, with rings of flowers at their base.

She felt a collective unease among the group, and they rushed through the area to the great opening on the far side.

Large oak doors had fallen outward from a great archway. The rusted remains of hinges lined either side. The party walked over to the doors and into the tunnel beyond. The tunnel itself was well lit by a series of openings cut into the ceiling. The casual breeze that had harried them increased to proper gusts as they entered.

Inside, the walls were lined with various suits of armor. Brutus flitted up to one and peered inside. He flinched away with a look of repugnance.

"Dried up skeletons inside these ones as well."

Taylor shuddered, and Dewar tensed up. Their pace remained hurried all the way to other end. There, a set of double doors had survived. Brutus flew up to check them.

He bounded back with an enormous grin.

"Shiny!"

"Any signs of life?" Celeve asked. At the question, the smile faded, and his gaze swept back to the hall of occupied armor.

"No, Captain. Didn't see anything moving, but I think we found our score."

She would have thought there'd be more cheer in the group at the news, but there was none.

"Jaughn."

The shifter marched forward, volley gun in one hand, and pickaxe in the other. This time, it hooked the pick into the iron ring and jerked it back. Taylor and Dewar stood on its flanks, ready to start shooting.

A brilliant light blinded them as the door opened. As her eyes adjusted, she found all four of the others hurrying into the room. They kept their weapons ready, but otherwise succumbed to the sight.

Treasure lined the sides of the long, columned room. Piles of gold and gems of every color had been pushed back against the walls. Racks of well cared for jewelry surrounded each column.

"Gods, it looks like a dragon's hoard," Jaughn muttered. The others remembered themselves and glanced about with suspicion.

Taylor's necklace lifted up and stretched out in front of him. All at once, the thin chain snapped, and the coin shot across the room. Taylor watched it with curiosity, but made no move to stop it. Celeve gasped, and Taylor turned to say something, but a new voice echoed through the room and stole their attention.

"No dragons here, I assure you," someone shouted from the far end.

Guns snapped toward the voice. Celeve put a hand to the handle of her pistol, but didn't draw it.

"Just me for now. Don't be afraid, I can't imagine there's anything I could do to such a mighty group." It was a pained, labored voice, the voice of a tired old man.

The others scanned around and gave each other fleeting glances. Celeve moved cautiously along to get a look at the speaker. Taylor went forward with more confidence, and the others followed. Jaughn maintained the greatest awareness of the tunnel behind them.

As she approached, she discovered two rows of seats that paralleled the columns and stretched in her direction. Each was filled with another sunken-fleshed skeleton. These had the remnants of much finer dress—strips of silk or satin, fine jewelry—and all wore a crown of some kind. The very last one, sitting at the far end, wasn't hunched over as all the others were. He was the best preserved of the group. His chin was raised, and he wore a simple crown.

Upon closer inspection, the crown was adorned with a single object—the pendant from Taylor's necklace. The old man cocked his head to the side and motioned with a dry, leathery hand for her to continue toward him. His skin rippled and pulsed, thickening as it did. In seedy underground bars, she'd seen deathmages reanimate the dead. That was nothing like this.

"Can we presume you're the lord here?" Celeve asked.

Taylor, she noted, relaxed completely as he drew close to the man.

"Lord of Eternity, Lord of Emptiness, Lord of Nothing," the man replied. It was distracted speech, as if he were talking to himself. "Lord of the Dead, Lord of Lost Souls."

Dewar kept his carbine trained on the old man, though his gaze flickered back and forth to Celeve. She guessed he was awaiting her command to shoot and be done with him. Odds were he wouldn't wait long before settling the matter, with or without her permission.

The old man was all that stood between them and the great score they'd found.

"What happened here?" Taylor asked. His tone was casual and curious.

"Same as happens to all great empires. They became great, they became powerful, and then they became lazy. They became weak. Civilizations rise under the strength and minds of the great, and they crumble under the bickering of inauspicious fools. Brighthope, even high up here in its lofty kingdom, couldn't escape the infiltration of darkness. Darkness seeped into the cracks, subtle as a cool breeze. Before anyone knew it, the darkness had taken control."

"How did you defeat it?" Jaughn asked, though its gaze remained on the tunnel.

The old man sat up and smiled. Life seemed to grow within him.

"Oh, I didn't defeat it. I *am* it. I won, you see, but those crafty bastards stranded me here."

The revelation smacked into Celeve like a dagger to the heart.

"Brutus! Fly to the twins, tell them to—"

The man snapped his fingers. The simple sound boomed outward in a wave. When it reached Brutus, the poor fairy burst apart into sparks, which fell to the floor and faded in seconds. Celeve stared, mouth agape.

"Never much cared for their kind," the old man said. "Not much will fit inside those insects. The rest of you, on the other hand, will make a fine addition, and I understand you've brought me the means to escape this dismal rock."

"Shoot him!" Celeve ordered. She drew in her power and held it, ready to slam the man back if need be.

Taylor swung his shotgun to point at Dewar. Jaughn had been staring at the embers of Brutus, but now it looked at the betrayal with confusion. The volley gun hung useless at its side.

"Hold your fire, loverboy," Taylor said, with the most triumphant sneer she'd seen on his face since the first time they'd made love, decades prior. "No reason for us to lose our lives. This nice gentleman simply wants off... and he's willing to pay for it with the entire city."

"How do you know that?" Celeve asked.

"Oh, he's been sending messages out for centuries." Taylor shot a quick glance at their host and shrugged. "Millennia, maybe. Hell, I don't know. Anyway, one of them found its way to me. That coin of mine."

Taylor drove a finger toward the coin that now rested inside the old man's crown.

"I'm not mincing words when I say *it* found *me*," he said. He licked his lower lip and his smile widened. "It spoke to me. Promised life eternal to the one who rescued him."

"Life eternal, Taylor? Is that what it took to buy your loyalty?"

He made the slightest of gestures toward the treasure with his shotgun, careful to leave it trained on the half-deep elf. "That, and an eternity's worth of treasure. But, yes, it's the eternal life that sealed the deal for me. You haute elves wouldn't understand. You don't feel mortality the way the rest of us do. You live thousands of years, long enough to take a human male as a lover for decades... and then cast him aside when his hair starts to gray."

"Is that what you're doing, getting revenge on me?" Celeve asked. "It was *you* I lost interest in. *You,* specifically, I fell out of love with. Your age had nothing to do with it."

His face twisted a little, but then he visibly calmed himself. "You're lying. I know you still love me, you just can't bear to see me grow old and die, so you've pushed me away. But don't you see? I've found a way for us to be together. Always!"

Dewar, to her surprise, relaxed as well and lowered his rifle.

"Is this true?" he asked the old man. "Are you truly willing to give us all this, and immortality, if we'll just free you from this cloud? Return you to the surface?"

"Of course," the old man said. "Look at me. I've lived here long enough to see the continents shift. I've watched as great civilizations rose and fell down on the surface. I've no idea how long I've spent here, but I know I'll never die. And I will extend that power to you, as well as all of this," he said, waving his hand in a wide arc, "if you'll free me from this floating prison, that I might partake in the world once again."

Dewar smiled, relaxed his carbine entirely, and made a slight bow.

"Sounds good to me."

The air escaped Celeve's lungs, and she became dizzy. Brutus was dead, killed by the man two of her crew had abandoned her to join. By his own admission, and proven by his callous execution of the fairy, he was an evil man. To release him upon the world below could bring unimaginable devastation. It would very well extinguish all life down there, as it had up here. Yet, two out of the three crew members present were siding with the evil man.

She looked to Jaughn, whose tortured face told her it would be of no use. The soft-hearted shifter would never fire on their friends, betrayal or no. She was alone.

Though she had great confidence in her magic, she had no confidence she could kill either of them, much less the old man, before they shot her. If she died, the airship would be there for the taking.

Celeve didn't believe she could make her men see reason, but it was the only option she had.

"William Dewar, Maximillian Taylor, I implore you, you must see this man, this *evil* for—"

Bang!

In the blink of an eye, Dewar had swung his carbine back up and shot Taylor in the heart. The half-deep elf ratcheted the carbine's lever and shot the old man in the chest. He worked the lever again and retuned his aim to Taylor. A wry smile emerged on Dewar's face, and he winked at Celeve.

"Man's evil, right, my love? Couldn't let that get to the surface. Besides, now all this is ours, anyway. I might not live as long as you, but I'll live plenty long enough."

A part of her wanted to run forward and kiss him. Unfortunately, another of her crew had been shot. She rushed to Taylor and caught him as he fell. He looked up at her with sad eyes. The light inside them was fading. Deep emotions from decades past welled up to the surface.

"Dammit, Max, why'd you have to do that?"

She cradled his head in one arm, while the other hovered over the wound in his chest.

"I'm sorry, okay? I'm sorry! You were right, and I'm sorry. I thought if I moved on, if I showed you that I'd moved on, that maybe it would hurt less when I lost you, as I knew someday I would. But I *do* still love you, I do! Please, Max, don't go!"

The light went out. His eyes closed. A sob escaped her lips.

"Um, hello?" Dewar said. "I thought I just saved us all and won us the big score. What in the hells, Celeve?"

He frowned and cocked his head. As she'd run to Taylor, he'd trained his carbine back on the motionless old man. Jaughn continued to stare, as if it had lost all capacity to think.

"You heard the woman," Taylor said. "She doesn't want me to go."

His eyes popped open with a strange intensity. Strength returned to him, and he rose to his feet, almost as if levitating. He bucked Celeve away, raised his shotgun, and blasted Dewar in the face.

* * *

Shocked, Celeve found her legs lacked strength. Dewar, face shredded into bone and blood, stumbled and fell backward. Her mind seized while trying to process that Dewar was dead and Taylor wasn't.

Unable to control herself, she looked at the resurrected pilot. He smiled, but it wasn't his characteristic smirk. The grin stretched from ear to ear, more like a lunatic or a psychopath's. Taylor rolled his head around and scanned his body as if seeing it for the first time.

"As puppets go, it's not the worst. A bit older than I was hoping for, milord, but I'll take it."

"Could be much worse, fiend," the man on the throne said. Both spoke in a casual manner, indifferent to the recent violence. The man swept his hands toward the fleshy skeletons in the chairs. "Look about you. You could be in one of those. Though, while I'm on the subject…"

The old man bounced both of his hands around the air and wiggled his fingers in some strange dance. The noble skeletons twitched haphazardly. They seemed to inflate as some malevolent presence grew inside them.

"You're a deathmage!" Celeve gasped. She felt the blood drain from her cheeks. A chill flushed through her body.

The old man seemed offended at her remark. "Do I look like a charlatan to you? A third rate trickster? Shall I shoot cards out of my sleeves? A *deathmage?* Pah!"

The rows of reanimated corpses rose, one by one, from their chairs and tried out their legs.

The old man returned his attention to Taylor, or Taylor's body.

"What are you waiting for? Shoot the snooty little elf tart!"

Celeve took a few uncertain steps back. She was too overcome with fear to run, though her mind screamed at her to do so. In slow motion, she saw the shotgun's muzzle raise in her direction.

In a blur, Jaughn lifted her off her feet and sprinted away. It tucked her under its right arm and bounded past, through the gauntlet of noble skeletons. She heard the bark of the shotgun, and Jaughn shuddered, but didn't slow its pace in the slightest. She regained enough of her senses to see the door coming.

Wiggling her hands free, she collected enough wind to blast the doors apart. As they moved through them, she reversed the vortices and pushed them shut.

Jaughn halted so abruptly, it half-dropped her. The shifter set her down and swung the volley gun up. Celeve discovered armored skeletons blocked their path. Jaughn fired.

The great *boom* of the volley gun was deafening. It was also less effective than expected. It knocked the mass of armored undead back, but they collected themselves before Jaughn and Celeve could rush through them. The shapeshifter used the volley gun as a club against one, smashing it against the wall. It deftly drew its pickaxe with the other hand and cracked it through the helmet of another one.

One skeleton drove a spear into Jaughn with a squishy *crunch*. Jaughn seemed unaffected and clubbed its assailant, which broke into pieces.

Celeve clapped her hands and conjured a massive gust to knock the armored undead against the walls. That created an opening, and she sprinted to get clear of the tunnel. Jaughn followed closely, continuing to swing the volley gun and pickaxe at anything that got close.

As they passed the flattened doors, she lamented that her magic couldn't raise them and make another barrier. Fortunately, they seemed to have outpaced the armored ones. At the top of the great staircase, she looked out over the terrace they had to traverse to get back to *Chien Salé*. She caught the movement of a single skeleton slowly rising up.

She and Jaughn leapt down the steps two, three at a time. After every other jump, she caught sight of another skeleton or two jerking itself upright. Next to her, Jaughn was fumbling cartridges out of a pouch and stuffing them into the breech of the volley gun. It dropped every other cartridge, but eventually reloaded.

By the time they'd reached the terrace, dozens of skeletons converged on them in a widespread rabble. Some stumbled, a few staggered, but a good many ran toward them.

Celeve and Jaughn ran as best they could toward the thinnest populated areas. She drew her revolver and her scimitar. Jaughn put the volley gun over its back and drew one of the large pistols. The two of them sliced, clubbed, shot, and chopped every step of the way back to the docking bay. Whenever there was a tight collection, she swept them aside with a gust, and they continued on.

Few of the skeletons were actually armed, so it was mostly a matter of keeping them at arm's length and pushing past. The shots from her revolver only served to knock them back a few steps, not to kill them, but it was enough to get by. Jaughn emptied both pistols, but didn't use the volley gun, presumably saving it for a dire situation.

Several times she heard the whizz of a bullet fly past them.

By the time they reached the doors to the docking bay, Celeve's lungs and muscles burned, and her revolver was empty. She holstered the revolver and waved a hand to blow the doors open.

* * *

"Goshe, Dreucht! By the gods, please tell me we're fixed!"

She and Jaughn rushed inside. With one more wave of her hands, wind flung the doors shut again. They wouldn't hold long, but she could only hope they'd hold long enough.

"Fixed and ready," Goshe said. His tone, hollow and dull, troubled her. She spun to find the half-dwarf standing in front of the airship, aiming his pistol at her. He had the same creepy smile Taylor had when he'd risen.

Boom! went the volley gun, blasting Goshe—or whoever it was—past the airship and out of the bay. Dreucht jumped out from the rigging of the ship and charged at Celeve with his long knife. Jaughn flung its pickaxe across the room. It cracked into Dreucht's chest and carried him a few yards through the air.

"Quick, get aboard, I'll fly us out!"

Jaughn ran to Dreucht, collected the pickaxe, and gave the undead half-dwarf another hard *crack* for good measure.

Celeve ran to where the dwarves had chained the ship down, and she worked to unhook it. As she loosened the final chain, the doors burst open. A great rush of wind tore through the tall, wide docking bay. The airship lifted for a moment and settled.

"This has all been very fun," the old man's voice sent ice down her spine, "but let's be honest. You'll never get that ship out of here before we can swarm onto it. It's over, elf woman. But you don't have to die. You can join us."

The old man strode in with the demeanor of a god. Inside his crown, Taylor's pendant now carried a deep, sinister smile. A gray, sunken-faced Taylor flanked the old man on one side. On the other, she recognized the clothing and stature of Dewar, but his face was a pulpy, distorted mess.

The gusts settled a bit, but vortices still danced all around.

"I know what you're—"

"No, you don't. You think I'm some monster who'll bring destruction. Why can't you see I'm not the problem? I'm the solution to all the chaos and misery in the world. I'll bring peace to the world below."

"No... you'll create a graveyard and call it—"

"Shoot her."

Both the flanking minions raised their guns and jerked the triggers. Both clicked without firing. With a mix of disdain and incredulity, the old man looked at the walking corpses.

"Do either of you know how to reload these crazy contraptions?"

The possessed bodies of her dead lovers shrugged in response.

Celeve looked over at her airship. The carriage was the size of a small yacht, but made of a much lighter and thinner wood. Overhead was the great envelope that allowed it to sail through the sky. At the bow was the pilot's seat, with a wheel and several pulleys. Taylor had occupied the seat for so long, she couldn't even conjure the image of his predecessor. A very short area under the deck had just enough space for each of the crew to maintain a bedroll and keep their few possessions. At the aft end, she had a comfortable little cabin all to herself.

However, she'd seldom stayed in the cabin by herself. Over the decades she'd captained *Chien Salé*, she'd had many suitors. Two of whom stood before her, deformed and possessed. For all she could tell, the men who'd lived inside those bodies were gone.

The ship had been her life since she'd come of age, left her estate, and struck out on her own. The members of her crew had come and gone, much like her lovers, but the ship had been the constant in her entire adult life. It was home.

She collected the air into a great ball in front of her and blasted *Chien Salé* out the opening. On its own, it would pitch over and drop to the ground like a rock. After a ten thousand foot drop, it would shatter into a million pieces.

"Damned elf harlot! Grab her, you worthless idiots! Kill her!"

A tall figure swept her up in its arms and bounded toward the opening, a mass of undead tight on their heels. Jaughn, now a skinny gargoyle, leapt out and unfurled newly-formed wings.

"Hold me tight!" Jaughn shouted over the loud, whistling wind.

It wasn't a straight drop outside—it was the curve of a dome. Though frantically beating its wings, Jaughn remained mere feet from the stone face. Even when the curve steepened, their distance from it didn't increase much. Celeve realized that, carrying her as Jaughn was, the shifter couldn't create enough lift to truly fly. They weren't even gliding too well.

She generated a few gusts to push them away from the wall. Everything went white for a few long seconds as they cleared the bottom of the Lost City of Brighthope and passed through the clouds below.

"Relax!" she shouted. "Save your strength!"

Celeve twisted until she could see Jaughn's face. As they left the clouds, the shifter's eyes darted about in fear. She ascertained it was trying to work out where and how to land in a manner that wouldn't kill them both. Perhaps it was looking for water. She looked down and found none. They angled toward a wide open field. It was better than being impaled on branches in a forest, or smashed against rocks on a mountainside.

Having spent her life aboard an airship, Celeve had never had a fear of heights. Now, however, seeing the ground scream toward them, a debilitating fear overcame her.

"Any ideas, Captain?" Jaughn's question snapped her back to herself.

The shifter could easily have left her and made its own escape. Jaughn had remained in this form to save her. It'd done nothing *but* save her for the last hour. The least she could do was return the favor. She dug into her mind for something she could do. After pushing her hysteria aside, the answer was obvious.

"Jaughn, when I say so, open your wings wide and hold them, okay?"

"Yes, Captain."

"I'm not the captain of anything anymore."

"You'll always be the captain."

Deciding against arguing the point, she returned her attention to the field below. If she did it too early, they would run out of air, and drop anyway. If she did it too late—well, it would be too late.

The ground rushed toward them. Her nerves shouted to just *do* it already, but she held on. When she thought they were seconds from dying, she called out.

"Open your wings and hold them open!"

She summoned all her power to conjure the densest cushion of air she could muster. Their descent came to a near halt... twenty feet above the ground. They continued to glide forward and down as long as they could.

Then they dropped. Just before impact, Jaughn gave a few great beats of its wings and lifted her up. As Jaughn smacked the ground, she heard a great *crack*.

Celeve bounced hard against the ground. Bruised, but not broken. She rolled over and pushed herself up as quickly as she could. Jaughn, still in gargoyle form, lay face down, motionless.

"Jaughn! Jaughn, are you all right?"

The shifter groaned in great pain. When it rose up, Celeve found it'd shortened its arms to stubs.

"Thank the gods you're alive. You really must stop saving me like this."

"It's my main job, didn't you know?" Jaughn smiled and revealed a mouth full of broken, bloody teeth. It rolled its lips around and reformed its gums.

"Can you just shift and make it all better?"

"Somewhat. I'll live, if that's what you're asking. It's gonna hurt a bit more than I'm used to for a while."

"Well, I'm sorry to hear that, but I'm glad you're alive. And thank you. I know you could've just left me or let me go."

"No. I couldn't have done that."

She smiled and cupped Jaughn's face in her hands. After a tender moment, her gaze went upward.

"There's nothing to worry about up there," Jaughn said. "You destroyed *Chien Salé*. He's trapped again."

"For the time being," Celeve replied. "But he's been revived, thanks to Taylor, that fool."

Who did it all to be with me.

With a deep sigh and her eyes clenched shut, she forced the pain and regret aside. Then she looked to the sky once more.

"Taylor said that... *thing* had been sending out messages for centuries. There's no telling how many more of those coins there could be, or maybe other things, too. There are more airships than ever, these days... and better aircraft now, besides. It won't be long before someone else finds him. He'll make his way down, sooner or later. When he does, it'll be the end of us all."

* * * * *

Casey Moores Bio

Casey Moores was a USAF Rescue/Special Ops C-130 pilot for over 17 years—airdropping, air refueling, and flying into tiny, blacked-out dirt airstrips in bad places using night vision goggles. He's been to those places and done those things with those people. Now he lives a quieter life, translating those experiences into fiction.

He has written in the Four Horsemen universe, with stories in numerous anthologies, several novels about Bull and his black ops rescue company, and much more to come. In the near future, he will be expanding in the Salvage System and Fallen World universes as well.

Casey has also joined the JTF-13 series with *Witch Hunt*, a story about monster hunting marines in the Civil War.

Finally, he has several stories out in his Deathmage War fantasy series, one of which—"A Quaint Pastime"—was a finalist in the FantaSci fantasy story contest.

A Colorado native and Air Force Academy graduate, he's now semi-retired in New Mexico.

* * * * *

Furrows
by J.A. Miller

oft bones crunching, tender skin splitting, warm blood flowing...

Rek patted the muzzle of the big bay horse. He frowned and ran his fingers through a mottled patch of gray hair below the horse's eye. The horse flipped his head up and down with a measure of enthusiasm. The horse's nickering reverberated under Rek's calloused hand.

"When did this happen, King, old boy?" Rek muttered.

The horse snorted and stamped his front hoof. Rek did a little hop backward, out of the way. "All right, all right." He ran his fingers through his own unruly mane as he walked behind the horse. He had more than a few gray hairs in his own, and his beard was more white than black these days.

...the sons of the forest, crushed, broken, split open...

Rek bent down, his broad back creaking audibly. He grasped the beam of the heavy plow and dragged it up behind King. The horse nodded his head up and down, snorting.

The old horse wanted to work. If he was honest with himself, Rek was ready to break new ground himself. He gripped the heavy beam—ornate with carvings almost too worn to make out—and raised it up, fastening the chain to the long wooden tugs affixed to King's harness. He grabbed the leather leads, even though he never really used them. King needed no guidance, and the big bay horse wouldn't heed Rek's leads, anyway.

...the sun bakes the bodies as we sit under the poplar trees...

Rek walked behind King, guiding the handles of the plow as the horse leaned into the work. His forearms, as thick as the beam of the plow, rippled with tendons and veins as he gripped the plow handles. The curved blade of the plowshare carved through the rocky soil, earth spilling from the gash, folding over in a satisfying wave. The soil here was a rich, fertile black, but embedded with stones dug up and deposited by the nearby river. The gleaming steel plowshare split through rocks with hardly a jolt, pulverizing stones as large as a suckling pig, revealing clean rows of black underearth.

...dancing through their shields, under their spears, making widows and orphans with every swing...

The late autumn breeze chilled Rek's back as the sweat evaporated. He shivered. King did likewise, the harness and hardware clattering. He focused on the rhythms of the work, the *flump flump flump flump* of King's hooves thudding into the dirt, the babbling of the river, the *ching shwep ching shwep* of the swinging chains affixed to the beam, the steady sound of the earth unfolding under the sharp plowshare.

...separating arms from body, like lost lovers torn apart by a fool king's war...

Rek yanked the plow around at the end of the row, repositioning it facing back the way they'd come. "Come on, King." As King stepped back into a new row, and the plow sliced into the earth, Rek let himself melt back into the rhythms, and the Voice was lost as Rek let the sounds envelop him.

* * *

"Hullo, there!"

Rek clicked his tongue, and King stopped. Rek turned his face toward the afternoon sun and squinted. Coming down the river road, a buckboard wagon clattered among the loose river rock. Rek patted King on the back and unfastened the harness from the plow beam. King swished his tail, annoyed at the wooden shafts still fastened against his flank, inhibiting his movement slightly. He gave Rek a side eye as he sauntered off the plowed field, picking at some thistles.

Rek walked toward the road as the buckboard came closer.

"Hullo, neighbor!"

Rek waved at the approaching figures. The wagon pulled up along the field; the two mangy mules pulling it looked eager for a rest.

"Afternoon, Pikson." His nearest neighbor sat in the front seat. His two young sons, Jas and Jor, sat in the back, keeping hold of a rowdy pig.

...king's sons taste sweetest, leaving kingdoms in ruins, the daughters of the elves, warrior poets, their blood tastes like...

"Winter crop, eh? A bit late, isn't it?" Pikson asked.

"Maybe, but I have the land, and I could use some onions and some carrots."

Pikson just nodded.

Jas, a bright-eyed adolescent with burned-on freckles, stood up, letting go of the pig he was helping his brother keep under control. "Pa said you were crazy for settling this land here. Nobody can grow anything in these rocks, right Pa?" He dropped to his knees as the pig wriggled free from his brother's arms, enveloping it in a tight bearhug.

Pikson flashed a scowl at his boy, then a sheepish grin at Rek.

Rek just nodded. "Your daddy's smart. I *am* a fool. But King's strong and likes to plow, and it's not as rocky as you'd think." The rows gleaming with shards of gravel from the pulverized stones said otherwise.

Pikson seemed relieved that Rek wasn't upset at his hasty judgement of the old farmer.

Jas looked at the big red horse swishing his tail, eying a clump of greens. "King's a weird name for a horse."

"Well… I didn't name him. It's just, he used to be a king, so that's what I call him." Rek scratched his head. "I suppose I could call him Your Majesty."

The boys laughed as the pig squealed between them.

"Well, the wife keeps telling me to send you an invite, but we haven't seen you much this year… or last, really." Pikson threw his thumb up, gesturing over his shoulder. "We'll be fixin' this porker for the Lady of the Star Feast. If you don't have something else planned—" He looked over the austere farmhouse and barn. The trappings of an old bachelor hermit's abode. "—we'd be pleased to have you."

…*kingslayer, bloodletter, bonecrusher, veinripper, dragonbreaker, godender…*

Rek blinked twice, listened to two squirrels chattering over the last of the walnuts. He listened to the pig grunting with frustration as it was held captive.

"I'm not really a follower of the Lady."

"Oh, that don't matter. The Lady don't have anything but love for those who are strangers to her."

The warm words actually stopped the Voice for just a moment.

Rek hadn't had a meal with anyone other than King since… he couldn't remember how long it had been.

"The feast... that's three nights from now?" Rek brushed his hand through his hair, his bicep bulging, and he realized he was going to be pretty sore from the day's work.

"Yessir. Bring a bottle of spirits if you have it, but we'll provide the food. We'll have plenty." Pikson seemed genuinely enthused and satisfied that Rek was accepting his invitation. "Well... we better get this porker home before my fools of sons let her jump loose." His fond gaze over his shoulder said he didn't mean the cutting words. The boys just gripped the pig tighter, eliciting a *humph* from the constricted animal.

"Three nights... safe journey home." Rek raised a hand in half-salute.

Pikson nodded. "And may the Lady bless your labors." He slapped the reins over the mules' backs, and the buckboard clattered down the southeastern road.

...the priests of Dalo Ve'essen wailed their empty curses as we laid waste to their temple, the abbess trying to call down fire to consume us with her last breath...

Rek sighed and stretched his neck to one side. He was fine as long as he kept moving, but standing still, the soreness was setting in. It had been nice to hear a human voice.

* * *

Since he'd been forced to break from work, Rek decided to toss a few things into a pot. He started a fire in the sooty stove. A skinned and gutted rabbit from the salt larder, some yellow-skinned potatoes, and a head of garlic all went into the stew. He reached up to a high shelf and pulled down three small tins. He opened them and inhaled the rich aroma.

His log house was sparsely furnished. A bed, two chairs, a small table, a chest. He lived modestly, but he was liberal with his spices. He'd memorized when the spice merchants would be in the town thirty-odd miles down into the valley, and those days were the only ones he ventured away from his farm. Not even spending the night, riding all night back to his farm. Being away for longer... was... impossible.

...the fires of Forellia snuffed, just as the life of every flamewielder was snuffed in a single day's warring...

He pinched spices between his fingers and thumb—oregano, rosemary, thyme—sprinkling them into the stew as it started to simmer, leaving it to cook as he ventured back outside. He let his belly grumble as he returned to the plow. The slight hunger pangs from a missed lunch were a nice distraction from the Voice.

"Come on, King, back to it... Your Majesty." King whinnied, stamped his front feet, and shook his mane, looking downright regal, except for the dirty feet and fetlocks.

* * *

...I remember salty blood, milky marrow, spiced with the shards of brass breastplates cracked open...

Rek and King continued to plow the field. Steady, cutting the earth to the end of the row, hefting the plow around, pulling it back down the next row.

...crying, wailing, death moans of a horde of...

Back and forth, back and forth, up and down the field, as the soundscape changed from midday songbirds lamenting the end of autumn to the croaking and creaking of the late day insects and the rustles and flappings of the creatures who feasted on them.

... twelve horsed knights slain at the foot of the Great Mountain...

Both Rek and King plodded on as their old bodies started to succumb to weariness. Both seemed determined not to be the one to call it a day as the sun crested below the horizon.

...the twin giants, Gorlon and Rexxon, heads slashed from their bodies, necks like oak trees split against a tornado wind...

Rek looked over their work. Most farmers could plow an acre of good ground in a day with a strong horse. He estimated they'd done nearly twice that. A sense of satisfaction washed over him.

"What do you think, old friend?"

King hesitated for a long moment, breathing heavily, then leaned into the harness, starting a new row.

"All right, I surrender!" He laughed at the horse's stubbornness. He could tell the horse was as sore and weary as he was. He turned the plow onto its side and clicked his tongue to urge King to drag it back to the barn. "Come on. Let's get some food."

* * *

...to this day, no grass grows where I spilled the blood of the Retchlen, a barren field of...

Rek drew solace from the end-of-day ritual—taking King's harness off, giving him a rubdown, gathering the old boy a bucket of oats, and filling his trough with river water. He dragged the plow into the barn. The polished steel blade was always clean, but the wooden shafts and leather straps always needed the dirt knocked off them.

Before he went in to enjoy his rabbit stew, he scooped another bucket of grain and scattered it across the freshly plowed field. It would be nice to attract some wild goats. They provided good fertilizer. As he let the last grains fall to the ground through his fingers, he heard a faint sound in the distance. A sound he hadn't heard in a long time. It grew louder. Horse hooves, but many. He frowned. King sniffed into the wind to the northwest. Up the river road. The horse walked over beside him, grunting.

...knights, priests, ladies, lords—dead... hunters, thieves, pillagers— slain... demons, angels, spirits—destroyed...

A ridge of hair raised on King's neck and shoulders. He stamped his feet quickly, moving sideways into Rek, knocking him off-balance.

"Easy, old boy." Rek's knee nearly betrayed him, locking up as he was pushed to one side. Pain shot up to his hip. He grabbed the trough and managed to stay on his feet. He straightened up, lightly slapping the horse's flank. "Just more neighbors. Settle down."

As the sound of hooves rumbled closer, he doubted his own words.

A strange array of lights glowed from up the winding road, shining an odd green in the darkening twilight. A dozen or so spherical lights, spinning in random arcs and circles.

"Mages..." He frowned. *What's a magic user doing traveling through these hills, far from any real civilization?*

* * *

The leader of the horsemen wore a headdress made from a horse's head. It was inlayed with studded iron spikes throughout the horse hide. All Rek could think about was what the man's horse thought about his rider's adornment.

The man had painted dark pools around his eyes, and a great sword was strapped across his back. He was made up to look as frightening as he could be. The scars across his neck were certainly ghastly.

Behind him, a smaller man with a goat skull on a staff was waving his hands and muttering. When he stopped, the green orbs floating around the group faded, one by one. A single green orb remained as the man twirled his fingers. The green light illuminated the leader.

"Who else lives here?" the man snarled at Rek, his horse prancing and snorting for breath. All of the horses looked to have been ridden too hard.

"Just me."

The man eyed Rek up and down, then did the same to King. Rek saw that King had adopted an unsightly slouch, looking swaybacked. The big bay's head hung low. He looked a decade older. *Smart horse.*

…slice throats… dash brains… crunch ribs…

The scarred man seemed unimpressed with both of them.

He swung down from his horse and made a signal to his men, his hand over his head waving in a circle. The two dozen riders unhorsed. "See what he has."

They all had painted faces. Rek counted twenty-five. Some had leather hoods stained to look like blood. He saw some had bones— finger bones?—in chains around their necks or pinned to leather vests.

They dispersed throughout his property. Some burst into the barn, rummaging through his tools and farm equipment. He heard some wood cracking. He remained stoic, doing his best to appear unthreatening and compliant.

…I can hear the blood in their veins…

A whoop went up from the house as someone discovered the stew. The leader made a shout, claiming first rights to any food. He pulled the great sword from his back and let the tip drag in the dirt as he strode toward Rek.

"You don't have a problem with us spending the night... do you?"

Rek stood silent for a moment. "Of course. Whatever you need, you're welcome to."

The man sneered and led his horse to the trough. The weary horse lowered his head and drank deep, snorting.

"Whatever feed you have, bring it out. Our horses are hungry, and so are we. And if you're hiding any little treasures..."

...their... th-their heartbeats... their skin stretching over joints...

Rek had trouble hearing what the man was saying. Eventually he shook his head. "Just some spices, a few family trinkets."

The man raised his great sword with one hand and pointed it at Rek's throat. "Horses... grain... now!"

Rek found himself adopting the same kind of posture King had exhibited, hunched shoulders, lowered head. The limp was all too real. His knee throbbed. He dragged two heavy bags of feed from inside the barn and dropped them outside. A raider split the bags with the point of a wicked-looking spear, and a few younger-looking ones—barely more than boys—gathered the reins of all the horses and led them to the spilled grain.

Inside the barn, crashing. As Rek looked in through the barn doors, tools, rope, barrels came smashing down onto the hay-strewn floor. Three raiders were pushing each other around as they fought over anything of value. One put a hatchet into his belt, another scooped up some carefully tanned leather straps.

"Lookee hear, Sorru!" A voice from the loft echoed through the barn just before a heavy oak chest was heaved over the side. Rek flinched as it shattered open, smashed on the heavy steel anvil below.

The leader—Sorru?—strode inside. "Eh? What's this?" He kicked apart the chest, spilling the contents. Reaching down, he sifted through the contents strewn at his feet. A bit of red fabric, a leather journal. He thumbed through it before tossing it over his shoulder.

...scoop out his life from his skulllll...

Rek shifted from his left leg to his right.

Sorru picked up a tarnished brass medallion, emblazoned with a shaggy dog's head. He raised an eye and held it up to Rek. "What did I say about hidden treasures, old man?"

Rek shrugged ever so slightly. "Family trinket; it's just brass. I'd rather you not take it, it's worthless to you, but if you must..."

Sorru paused, squinting at the big man, then snorted a laugh before tossing it aside. It landed in the hay-strewn dirt of the barn floor. He picked through the mess and recovered a handful of small coins amid the rubble. He found a dagger which, when unsheathed, revealed a broken blade. Sorru threw it back in the heap of junk. He ran his hand over the cold steel anvil.

"You a farmer or a smith?" He looked Rek up and down.

"I was a smith's apprentice for a while, but I hadn't much skill at it."

"You have silver laying around, too? Believe me... if we find anything worth more than a copper..." He put his arm over his shoulder, bicep flexed as he rested his palm on the pommel of his great sword.

"I can't think of anything else, just the plow, if you want to haul it off."

...three blows to strike down the Knight of the Glen... two to lop off the head of the Great Griffon... one to fell the Giant Centipede of...

"...And my horse, King, but I doubt he'd be able to keep up with your charger."

Sorru seemed wary and just a little perplexed by Rek. He looked at the old horse, back drooping, head dragging, splotches of gray mottling his red coat. King managed to cough and snort at the same time, a long tendril of drool hanging from his half-open mouth.

"I have some turnips and dried meat and a little cheese in the house cellar; you're welcome to whatever you need."

Sorru's eyes glinted as he strode out of the barn. He added an extra air of malice to his voice as he called over his shoulder to Rek, "Generous of you. I'll need a bed for the night. You can sleep out here with *your* charger."

He paused, tapping his fingers on his thigh, then strode back to Rek. He stared at the old farmer, almost daring him to do something. His men shifted, and Rek knew the look, a pack of wild dogs waiting for a wrong move, the signal to rush in and tear apart their prey. Their leader stooped down, deliberately leaving himself exposed, vulnerable.

He stood back up, the dog's head medallion in his hand. He spit on it, rubbed it against his jerkin, a casual show of polishing it. He locked eyes with Rek—

...the first taste of human blood after being locked away so long in the dark... do you remember? The sycophantic sheriff, too young to be afraid of what came out of the hole in the ground, too proud to run.

—and put the medallion in his pocket. Rek kept his head lowered, but his eyes up.

...first they tried to fight us, to throw me back into the Abyss, do you remember? And then they started to scream and run. How many years now, locked away again, in a different prison, not as dark, but just as cruel as the Hole...

Sorru expected at least a flinch as he stole the man's family heirloom, but Rek didn't move.

...let me loose... smith boy... let me free... let me taste blood again...

Eventually, Rek had to shift from one leg to the other, pain showing in his face as he tried to unlock his frozen knee.

coward... cur... smith boy... weakest of the worms.

"Old farmer," Sorru said, as if coming to some sort of conclusion, "don't worry about us. We're easy guests; we'll take care of ourselves. Good night." He tapped his forehead in a mock salute and headed to the house.

And the Voice was silent.

* * *

Rek sat in the hay, his back against the stall wall. King stood, restless, facing the closed stall door. Three men sat out in the barn, playing some sort of gambling game, loudly arguing over the rules and why they hadn't gotten to eat any of the stew as they ate his cheese and dried meat.

Rek's own stomach gurgled and knotted. He regretted not eating a midday meal. He turned his head over his shoulder, King looked back at him, and Rek could see the concern in his face, and something else.

"No. They'll take what they want and leave, and we'll both continue on as we've done." Rek tried to get comfortable, but his body ached, and the ground was hard and cold. "I can't believe I make you sleep out here. It's miserable."

King whinnied, stamped his feet as he slowly shuffled toward the back of the stall, and lowered his legs under himself, laying down beside the big man. Rek looked over at the horse, eyes bright with appreciation.

"We've had a long day. I'm going to sleep like a baby."

But he wouldn't. It was too quiet. The men outside the stall door spoke of their plans, meeting their boss—apparently Sorru was just a lieutenant—down river. They were all wanted men, but there were enough of them that the law in this small, backwoods duchy would be afraid to touch them. They spoke of grand plans of driving out the duke and earls and claiming the entire duchy as their own.

Rek shook his head. Grand ambitions for a bunch of thieves.

He could hear the larger group up at the house singing, fighting. Things crashed, bottles shattered—his wine, no doubt—someone started yelling, and then the singing started up again.

And Rek couldn't sleep because it was too quiet.

Eventually everyone, including King, fell asleep. Someone sleeping in the barn snored the horrible roar only a professional drunkard can manage. The wind picked up and whistled through the cracks in the barn. The bare limbs of the trees scraped and rattled together.

Rek closed his eyes and tried to listen to all of them, but couldn't sleep, because, for the first time, since he was a boy, it was silent.

* * *

"You lied again, old farmer."

The raiders were gathering their horses, loading them with sacks of food. It looked like they were taking everything they hadn't eaten the night before. Rek was past the point of hunger pangs and just felt hollow in his belly.

One of the raiders kicked the back of Rek's knee. He grunted as his legs buckled. He tried to catch his hand on the plow, but his grip failed. His right shoulder rocked with pain as he fell to his hands and knees in the dirt.

"Aaah." He panted. "I didn't lie." He looked up at Sorru.

All of the raiders looked hungover, bedraggled, except Sorru. And the mage... the mage had a different look in his eye, a wild casting about of his gaze, as if seeing wraiths flying around that no one else could see.

Rek had seen that look before in a self-taught wizard. The wizard had found an old tome and had possessed the unfortunate ability to read it. She'd managed to work out the basic rules of magic-wielding, mastered a handful of spells, but lacked the regimented training required to control the mana rewriting her mind. This man had the same look. Even the staff looked too meticulously crafted. He'd probably stolen it, or found it on a dead wizard, and decided to give magic a try.

Someone behind Rek planted a boot in his side. Rek grunted and faltered but didn't keel over.

"This is definitely worth more than a few coppers." Sorru held an unstrung bow across his shoulders, wrists draped over the inward curves of the weapon. Beautifully carved, ivory-white, with a red tassel fastened to one end.

Rek grimaced in pain, and at his own stupidity. He'd forgotten about the old bow hanging over his bed.

"Please... it's just an old bow." For the first time since they'd come to his farm, his voice crackled with emotion.

Behind him, he heard one of the raiders unsheathe a sword. His fingers clenched into fists. Muscles tightened.

"We told you, old man." The voice from behind crowed. "You lie… you die…"

"You've taken all my food. Without the bow, I'll starve."

A dozen voices laughed. A horse reared up, his rider cursing.

It was all so quiet.

He could hear the man behind him swinging the blade in circles, an ominous *whoosh whoosh*.

"Hold on a minute." Sorru held up a hand, and the *whooshing* stopped. He grabbed the bow off his shoulder and held it out with one hand, letting an end rest on Rek's shoulder, as if in a bizarre knighting ceremony.

"You were a wonderful host. I had a delicious meal and a warm bed." He tapped Rek on the back lightly, punctuating his sentences. "I think we'll be back to visit again, and I most definitely wouldn't want our host to starve." He looked at the bow. It was definitely old, though beautifully made, clearly an ornamental piece now. He let go of the end of the bow, and it clattered off Rek's shoulders to fall to the dirt. Sorru swung up into his saddle and gestured a swirling motion over his head. The raiders whooped and whistled as they galloped off, leaving Rek in the dirt.

Rek clutched the bow with one hand and a clod of fresh-plowed dirt with the other. His knee throbbed, but the freshly-turned soil made his fall less painful than it could have been. King clomped over and nuzzled his side.

"Ouch. Didn't you see him kick me there?"

He grabbed King's mane and used the horse to help him get to his feet. He caught his breath, leaning on the horse, surveying the damage. "King, old boy. I'm hungry."

* * *

Silence.

They'd left no food whatsoever. His tin of spices had been spilled onto the floor. He carefully swept up what he could, picking out dirt and debris. The spice tins were the first thing he returned to their proper place inside the ransacked house. The stew pot had been licked clean. The salt larder was empty, the cellar bare.

Food was a more pressing concern than fixing the mess they'd left. He could feel the weakness setting in from more than a full day of fasting.

He thought of riding to Pikson's farmstead, but that was the direction the marauders had gone. He had no inclination they'd let him go if he ran across them on the road. He did worry about the Piksons... but their farm was miles off the road. It was unlikely the riders would turn off onto that one narrow trail. Besides, he didn't have the strength to walk that far, and he didn't have a saddle for King. No, he had to get through the next few days until he could make a proper journey into town.

The barn was the same, everything of value gone or broken. Except the plow. Rek sifted through the mess until he found a knotted bundle of twine. Half an hour later, he had it unknotted, and a portion of it twisted into a suitable bowstring.

Rek watched King plucking at grass growing alongside the barn. "We'll have to get you grain for when the snow comes." He had no money... no one in town knew him well enough to extend credit. "We'll have to do it like the old days."

King stopped eating, a tuft of grass sticking out of his lips as he turned to stare at Rek.

"Not *those* old days." Rek spread a bundle of straw out in his lap and started weaving them together. "I mean before the farm, when we tried hunting."

He hadn't been much good at hunting. Being silent and stealthy wasn't his forte. Farming required less creeping and more strength and stamina.

His fingers remembered the weaving patterns of his youth, and an hour later, he had large cone shapes of woven straw. He took off his boots and waded into the shallow river, found a suitable eddy, and sank the traps with large rocks. A couple trout would work for now... but he tried not to think of a long winter without the stores he'd laid up for himself and King.

Silence.

At first, King had tried to follow him. "I'll be fine, and I'm quieter than you in the woods." The big old horse had finally acquiesced, returning to his grazing.

Rek's mind was a tumultuous hurricane. He wasn't used to his thoughts careening about against each other. The thought of King starving this winter. The eyes of the crazed mage as the marauders rode off. The last time he'd eaten a meal in the company of friends. All while trying to silently follow the game trails that crisscrossed along the riverside. The rustle of a pair of does did little to focus his mind.

He moved as close as he could. The bow was true, but he wasn't as sure of his makeshift bowstring and the hastily carved arrow. The thought of one of the does limping off with an arrow in her side made Rek wince.

The wind was in his favor, and he still had the discipline to creep silently closer, ignoring the burning pain in his joints as he crouched beneath low-hanging pine branches.

Thwam. His arrow found its mark. The doe took a dozen steps, then fell, while her companion bounded off into the brush.

She was dead by the time he made it over to her. He sat for a moment, looking into her staring black eyes. He'd always hated killing deer. They were beautiful creatures.

"I'm sorry."

He tried to listen as the birds resumed the calls that had been so rudely interrupted by the life-and-death ordeal that had just occurred. Instead, he heard the gentle *clop clop cop* of King's hooves.

"I stand corrected, old boy." Rek unstrung the bow. "You're much quieter than I thought." Rek smiled at the old horse, who looked at him as if to say, *You really expected to carry this thing out of here without me?*

Silence.

After dropping the venison carcass outside the barn, he returned to the river, dunking his head in and drinking deeply. He told his stomach that water would suffice for now. His body pretended to go along with the ruse.

There were no fish in the traps, and he realized his weaving wasn't as artful as he'd thought. The traps wouldn't hold up for long, even in the lazy current of the river.

The deer carcass hung from a rafter in the barn. Rek rummaged around and found the broken dagger in the mess. It was still perfectly sharp, and Rek managed to skin and dress the deer without too much trouble. He built a little fire in the middle of the barn floor and covered the venison and fire with a blanket, leaving gaps at the bottom for air to feed the flames. King snorted and coughed.

"I know, I know. But I don't have it in me to make a smokehouse. I'm sorry. You can sleep in the house tonight if you want."

But King stamped off, shaking his head against the acrid smoke slowly filling the barn. *Silence.*

* * *

He woke with a start. Something had brushed his face. It took him a moment to gather his wits enough to realize where he was and to notice King lying beside him again, like a loyal hound dog. Morning sunbeams illuminated the barn. What had brushed his face was the sleeping horse's tail, whisking back and forth.

The fire was out. Rek groaned as he stood up and built a new fire. He was tempted to cut off a slab and eat it half-raw, but it hadn't cooked at all. He was numb to the hunger at this point. What was a few hours more?

He drank a hearty breakfast of river water. Nothing in the fish traps.

Silence.

Cleaning up the barn wouldn't get him any food, but he felt he had to start. Then he went to check his traps. To his delight, two small trout struggled to escape the straw prison. He dispatched them with a rock and gutted them with the broken dagger. He was so hungry, he just laid them at the edge of the fire, skin turning black in the hot coals. The smell of venison finally starting to cook and the burning fish skin made him salivate.

He didn't hear the horse hooves until King neighed a deliberate alarm. He was just about to dig into the trout when the first horses rode across his field.

He clutched the broken blade.

There were more this time. King kept up his racket, even rearing up as one of the raiders approached. The rider's horse started and stumbled at the big horse's aggression, spilling the rider.

"King!" Rek shouted.

Sorru dismounted before his horse even came to a stop, hopping to the ground and trotting up to the barn door.

"Farmer! That smells so good! I knew I made the right choice with you."

Across the yard, Rek heard the familiar sound of boots on wood floor as the men flooded back into his house.

"You took everything; why are you here?" Rek realized he was still gripping the broken dagger.

Sorru noticed it, too. He made a point to look at it, then at Rek, ignoring the half-weapon in the big man's hand. "Let's just say, I missed your cooking." Sorru knelt down and gingerly picked up one of the trout. "Owww—hot!" He pulled his sleeve over his hand to keep from being burned as he picked at the flaky fish.

Silence.

A big man, taller than Rek, walked into the barn. His face was painted red, and he wore a bear headdress. He was shirtless, his chest and shoulders scarred with brands of various patterns.

"This is the farmer?" He addressed Sorru.

"Yes, sir." Sorru's voice changed, and his deference assured Rek that this was the group's true leader. But there was also a bit of steel in Sorru's voice, and Rek thought the leader might have a challenger in his near future.

"Come." The leader eyed the dagger in Rek's hand. "And leave that here." He turned to walk toward the house.

Rek was a statue for several heartbeats. Then Sorru reached over his shoulder to grip the handle of his great sword. Rek dropped the dagger in the dirt and followed the bear shape to the house.

A group of raiders stood beside their horses outside. They were working on freeing bundles tied behind the saddles. Rek realized the bundles were people. When one of the people raised their head, his blood ran cold. Jor was barely conscious, hogtied and strapped to the back of the horse. Another small figure, the boy's brother. He couldn't see whether Pikson and his wife or their daughter were among the kidnapped.

"Come." The leader strode past the group.

Rek couldn't hear anything. It was so quiet. *Silence.* He couldn't think straight, so he followed the bear head inside.

"Aaaaarrrr!" A small man lay on Rek's kitchen table. He was clutching his abdomen. Dark crimson stained his shirt and hands.

"If you can save my brother, I'll make you a rich man."

Five or six raiders milled around inside the house. They looked weary this time. Rek noticed other superficial injuries on a couple of them.

"I'm not a doctor."

The man grabbed Rek's bicep like a clamp and pulled him close to the table. "You farmers always have remedies, some poultices to fight infections. I know your breed."

"You don't know," Rek said, too softly to be heard over the injured man's wailing.

Rek stepped up and pulled the man's hands away from his gut. The man fought him, so two raiders grabbed his shoulders. Rek pried his hands away from the bloody wound. A broken arrow shaft protruded from a black wound a few inches to the right and above the man's navel.

Rek let the man's hands go, and the man immediately curled his arms over the wound like a dying spider.

"Your brother's already dead. It's through his liver."

Silence.

The leader paced, then turned to one of his men at the back of the room. The underling handed him a spear. The silver shaft glinted as the sun's last light shone through the open door. The bear-headed man strode past Rek with a purpose. Rek found himself staggering after the man. The image of the boys strapped to the horses...

Four people were on their knees outside. The two boys, and a man and woman. The man and woman wore the livery of the duke's Keepers of Peace.

The bear head swung his spear overhead in a wide arc. It slashed across the man's torso, cutting him from neck to sternum. He fell without a cry. The boys and the woman cried out in fear, stifled by their gags.

Wiping the tip of the spear on the fallen man's coat, the leader turned to Rek. "Well, it's been a long day. Bring me whatever it is you're cooking out there in the barn." He handed the spear to his underling and strode back inside.

Raiders half-carried, half-shoved the woman and the two boys into the house. The boy's eyes pleaded with Rek as they were dragged past him.

Two men were holding ropes tied around King's neck, trying to pull him down as he reared and bucked at them.

Most of the marauders crowded into the house or sat on the porch. A handful milled around the barn.

Rek listened to it all as he stood in the midst of the cacophony of horses and men. Still, it felt silent. Then he heard his own heartbeat. As the last thread of sunlight faded, he stood outside his home and listened carefully. It was slow, steady, even... *babump badump*.

He strode to the barn, the smell of cooked fish and gamy venison wafting out as he came to the door. Three men were at the venison roast. One was trying to cut slices off with an unwieldly, rusted scimitar. The other two were cursing him for his clumsiness. Rek ignored them, heading straight for the plow. He raised a booted foot and kicked hard at the handle. *Crack!*

"Hey!" One of the raiders, a droopy-mustachioed man carrying an ugly mace, stepped toward Rek. "What are you doing there?"

Rek ignored him. He wrenched at the handle, breaking it free from the plowshare.

"I'm talking to you, farmer. You should be getting some food for the boss." The man came closer.

Rek started on the other handle, ignoring both the man and the searing pains in his shoulder, his knee, his back.

...smith boy... is that you?

The man rapped the mace on a barn support timber. "Farmer... you're gonna die if you don't listen up."

The third man, portly and wielding a chipped short sword, joined his fellow. Rek continued to kick at the plow handle.

"Old man—" The mustachioed man grabbed Rek by the shoulder. "You deaf, old man or just—"

Rek reached behind him, grabbed the man by the back of the neck, and slammed him face-first into the plow handle, cracking the wood loose. He threw the man onto the ground, where he lay gaping like a stunned fish.

...yesss... it is you, smith boy... free me...

Rek wrenched the handle and flung it aside. He started on the chains affixed to the beam.

The portly man roared and swung his short sword at Rek, catching him across the back as Rek barely managed to lunge away from a lethal slash.

...releeeaaassse meee... smiiittttthhh boooyyyy...

The man working on the venison dashed forward to join the fray. Rek reached for the short chains and yanked, pulling at the bolts. He broke one free and swung it at the fat sword-wielder. It caught around the man's wrist, and Rek yanked hard, pulling the man toward him. He let the man's sword arm go past him, clamping down on it with his own arm, and twisting his body. The man screamed as his arm snapped. The sword clattered to the ground.

Rek swung the chain just as the scimitar man reached him. The man dodged aside, catching Rek with a nasty slash across his forearm.

...I want to taste blood... it's been so long...

The man was quick, darting in and out. His sword found flesh again and again. The fat man with the broken arm went for his sword on the ground. Rek kicked it under the plow.

Rek dodged a swing, then roared in pain as the fat man buried a dagger in his upper back. He staggered forward, the blade still in his back. He fell across the plow, clutching at the dagger. The men whooped as they moved in, jackals on a wounded beast. Rek pulled the blade free and dropped it to the floor. His bloody hands quivered as he steadied himself on the plow beam.

...yes... blood... your blood... smith boy...

Rek gripped the heavy wooden beam. The shaking stopped. He felt the familiar icy relief flood through his body.

...take me up again... as in the legends...

"I'm gonna split you open, old man!" They moved in on him.

He wheeled around, and the plow, swinging up, sliced through bones as it caught the scimitar man square in the chest, splitting him open.

Rek let out a heavy breath, exhaling a cloud of frost. He felt the cold slow the bleeding from his wounds.

He hefted the plow in both hands. With the handles and chains ripped free, it looked like a massive, misshapen axe. The fat man fumbled backward.

...it is time to feast... I hunger... feed me, smith boy... feed me souls...

Rek's face curled into a snarling thundercloud. And the man ran.

* * *

The bandit leader watched the light fade from his brother's eyes just as one of his men burst into the house.

"He's... he's killing them!"

The leader turned. "Who's killing who?"

The man frantically pointed outside. "The farmer! He's got some giant axe, and he's killing everyone."

Sorru frowned. "Impossible. Like I told you, he's just a farmer. He was a coward last time we were here."

The leader clicked his fingers and waved them outside. "Take care of this, Sorru."

"Of course." Sorru ducked outside.

And into a bloodbath.

He couldn't understand what he was seeing at first. Bodies—and parts of bodies—strewn across the moonlit field. Five, six, seven?

The old farm horse reared up, flinging the men trying to restrain him with ropes as if they were dolls.

And there, in the midst of a dozen of his men, the farmer swung a giant axe like it was a simple staff. He feinted, blocked, parried, then delivered mighty blows that sent men flying, splintered swords, and separated limbs from torsos.

"Impossible." He hissed as he unslung his great sword.

* * *

...Seven, eight, nine...

Rek fell into the familiar motions. As his fingers remembered the weaving of straw, his arms, shoulders, everything remembered the dance of death.

...crunchy little spine...

Only this was even more familiar, more like an old friend come to visit after years away.

...nine, ten, eleven...

Like that old friend had left during a friendly conversation. When they returned, just continuing the same talk, as if the years hadn't transpired.

...souls trapped from heaven...

He was older and a little slower, though. One raider managed to take a chunk out of his back with a flail. A painful weapon, but useless against a giant, razor-sharp axe. Another had nearly severed his hamstring with a long sword.

But he knew this dance too well, and his dance partner knew it even better than he did.

...how many bad men can I have today...?

"As many as are foolish enough to stay and fight."

...I hope they're all fools...

And then Sorru was in the melee. Rek felt the ice in his veins as he faced the man. Rek swatted aside another attacker, pummeling another into the ground with a single swing. Sorru looked both eager and afraid.

"Come on, farmer!"

...oooohh... you want this one... you want him to hurt...

"No," Rek denied it.

"Whatever devilry this is, ends now!" Sorru shrieked.

A splash of greenish fire struck the plowshare, knocking Rek backward two steps.

Is that... mage... mage blood...?

The crazed magic user stood off to the side, chanting a sing-song melody, and swinging his goat-head staff overhead. He let fly another green firebolt. Rek swatted it away, but felt the heat singe his face.

Sorru took the opening to lunge forward. Rek barely managed to deflect the blade, and it cut him deeply along his right side. But instead of pulling backward like most injured opponents, Rek stepped forward into the strike. He grabbed Sorru by the horsehead he wore and yanked him forward, slamming Sorru's face against the flat of the plowshare. His face smacked off the ice cold steel, and he stumbled backward, falling to the ground.

Rek turned on the magic user.

...come here... little mage...

The mage froze, mid-chant. "Wha... no... I know that voice." The man wheezed.

...you've heard it in your dreams...

The man nodded, head bobbing violently. Rek couldn't believe it. The man could hear the Voice?

Without thinking, Rek struck down two, three, four of the raiders as he made his way toward the mage.

...come... I'll take you to your source...

The man clutched his hands and shook his head, tears welling up. "No-no-no! Not down... won't go under, please, no!"

Rek found himself staggering toward the man, a careening reaper, lacking control of his own movements. The man dropped to his knees, sobbing now.

Swhunk!

A crossbow bolt struck Rek between his shoulder blades, sending him to the ground. He pulled the plow axe under him to get back to his feet. He was inches from the mage. He ignored the pain.

"You can hear it?"

The man nodded, face dripping with tears.

"And you know where it came from?"

The nodding became more emphatic.

"Tell me. Where did the blade come from?"

...end him... now... feed me his soul...

The man sniffled and sobbed. "F-from m-m-my dreams."

Rek slumped a little. He spoke softly. "Run, little mage. Run."

The man broke from his sobbing and crawled backward until he could manage to get back to his feet. Then he took off, crossing the river and disappearing into the night.

Swhunk!

This time, Rek wheeled around and deflected the crossbow bolt.

"Who are you?" The bear-headed figure stood across the field from Rek.

Rek looked around and realized everyone else had either fled, or lay dead in his field. The leader dropped the crossbow and hefted his silver spear. It shone with an unnatural light, more than just the reflection of the moon.

...sssiiissterr?... is that you?...

"Sister?" Rek furrowed his brow.

"You've broken my whole army. I had forty men when I came here."

"You came here! I didn't ask for this!" Rek bellowed across the field.

The leader continued forward, picking his way over corpses and dropped weapons. "I go where I want and take what I want."

...I have been trapped... sister... deformed... debased...

"Not without your army of—Gaaaah!" Rek had barely seen the man draw back his arm. In a flash, the spear was across the field and through his midsection, nailing Rek to the ground.

The man flicked his wrist, and the spear ripped from Rek's body and flew back into the man's hands.

"I don't need an army." He continued picking his way across the battlefield toward Rek.

...what, sister?... I'm sorry... my bonded is worthy... we are one...

"What... who are you talking to?" Rek asked the Voice. His own voice was ragged as he choked on his own blood.

"Delirious? Already? Was it your liver?" The man chuckled.

...my sister... shining bright as I shine dark...

"The spear..."

...yes...

"Yes. It is quite something, isn't it? I killed a great general. Cut his throat while he slept. And now..." He reared back with the spear, twenty feet away from Rek now.

Rek let the cold take over. The ice filled his veins. As the spear hurtled toward him at such a fierce speed, he raised the plow up just as quickly. The curved blade of the plowshare deflected the spear. It went careening across the field.

Rek staggered to his feet, clutching the plow's heavy beam with both hands, the carvings now stained completely with blood. The symbols burnished bright in the moonlight.

"Does it speak to you?"

"What? What are you talking about?" He flicked his wrist, recalling his weapon.

"Your spear... does it speak to you? Does it haunt your every moment?" Rek stepped forward. "Is it burned into your being? Does it cry out for blood?"

...sister... I am sorry... but we can help you...

The man saw, then, saw the dark energy in Rek's plow.

"Do you even know her name?" Rek asked.

The man put his spearpoint toward Rek.

"This is Mori'vin, the Shadow of the Moon, the Soul Snare, and a hundred more names." Rek continued to step forward, nearing striking range for the man with the spear. "And I know them all. It speaks to me—always. It taught me the art of death when I was just a boy."

The man with the bear headdress faltered back a single step as Rek approached. "It's... it's just a plow."

Rek hefted the big wooden plow shaft in both hands. His arms rippled with muscles. "It is now. I was tired of fighting and killing men like you. But I'm bonded to this blade. I can't be rid of it, no more than I can rid myself of a lung. So I pounded the blade of the axe into a plowshare."

The man visibly steeled himself. "You'll lose. You've warped it into a farming implement."

...sister... we will help... you return to your light...

Rek shook his head. "I earned this blade, and it is me. My darkest side." He breathed out a thick cloud of frost. "You should run."

The man sneered. "You're just an old farmer!" He lunged forward.

Rek whipped the axe upward. Just inches away from his face, the edge of the plow axe caught the point of the spear and shattered it. The swing continued, splitting the shaft of the spear, then up, splitting the man's chin, up between his bear head ears.

...goodbye... sister...

* * *

It was days before King and Rek managed to burn all the bodies. Rek's wounds were severe, and he moved slower than ever.

And the entire time, the plow was incessant.

...smith boy... the taste of death was so sweet... when can I have more...

It promised him they would only heap vengeance upon the wicked. It promised to topple despots again. It promised to free the oppressed.

Rek threw the last of the broken weapons and the last torn pieces of leather armor onto the bonfire.

...to the east... we've never been to the eastern edge... sea serpents... pirates... so much opportunity for death and legend...

Rek leaned the axe against the wall of the barn while it went on and on.

...we were as glorious as ever... the spray of blood... the screams of the dying... it was the most brilliant return...

He took two long, curved saplings and started carving them down.

...to ride into battle again... A'Barek of the Stormspire and his axe, Mori'vin Moonshadow... a thousand songs more will be written...

He sanded the saplings and polished them smooth.

...when do we ride?... today?... what... what are you doing?...

Rek propped the axe on a stump and put one of the newly carved handles beside it.

...NoooooOOOO!...

He bolted the wood to the plowshare.

...curse you... A'baaaarreeekkkk...

And then he did the same to the other side.

...I should have let my sister send us both back to the Darkness...

Rek hitched the plow up to King, who snorted over his shoulder at Rek. He stamped his feet at the edge of the trampled rows.

"I know." Rek firmly took hold of the plow handles. "Gittup, Your Majesty, we have furrows to plow."

* * * * *

J.A. Miller Bio

J.A. Miller was born in Minnesota, raised in Illinois and Pennsylvania, and now lives outside of Atlanta with his wife, two cats, and a stubby-legged dog. Somewhere in between, he spent some time in the Army, serving in the fabled 101st Airborne Division. He spent a couple trips overseas, and then used Uncle Sam's help to get a degree in journalism and creative writing. Now he edits books and tries to write them. "Furrows" is his first published fantasy story.

* * * * *

Good Intentions by Jamie Ibson

A Rebels of Westlocke Story

As the fists rained down upon him, and boots battered his ribs, Flint began to worry that maybe, just maybe, the hal'far Garda might truly kill him this time. A hardened leather toe caught him in the belly, and he doubled up as he violently retched his guts out onto the cobbles of Downtown Westlocke. The squad's Overseer grabbed him by the hair and dragged him to his knees.

"Where is it?" the half-elven thug hissed. "The *tryllestav*, boy! The focus! Which one of you townies has it?"

Flint coughed and spat out a bloody tooth. "I don't got no staff. Magic's a death sentence, milord!"

Unusually, this particular Garda squad numbered six. The extra hal'far was dressed differently, but the staff he carried marked him as a magic user just the same. Most Garda wore trousers, jerkins, and cavalier hats marked with feathers that denoted their rank and position. Most wore flintlock pistols on one hip and a rapier on the other, but not this one. This extra one wore teal robes the color of the sea, and his cloak and mantle were drawn up to conceal his face in shadows.

The staff he carried, though? Flint feared he knew what it was. The four-foot length of cypress was wrapped in sealskin, with an opaque blue gemstone the size of a child's fist at the top. He was an *Examiner*, armed with a potent water focus that would let him channel mind magic. He could feel the Examiner's intrusive presence, probing and crawling through his thoughts like a cockroach might climb over one's legs at night.

"Truth," the Examiner said simply, and turned away. "Find another."

Enraged, the Overseer threw Flint back to the cobbles and stalked away. One of the brutes put one last boot to Flint's ribs, and he felt a sickening *crack*. They left him there in the street, bloodied and broken, and went in search of other victims. Unconsciousness came to claim him, and Flint welcomed it.

* * *

He awoke with a scream.

"Hush, Flint," Kiara Maximus snapped. She knelt with his head in her lap, having lifted him into a seated position, and she wiped his face with a damp scrap of linen. "That bloody mindbender has been all through Downtown twice now. Da's got his hands full healing those who were injured during their little pogrom. I've got no stretcher; you'll have to walk."

Flint tried to get his legs under him, but couldn't, not with the broken rib in his side. Instead, he rolled out of Kiara's lap onto his hands and knees, got his feet under him, and staggered to his feet with her help. "I can—ugh—walk," he groaned. "They were in a particularly foul mood."

"S'no wonder." Kiara got under Flint's shoulder, on his uninjured side, as a crutch. "We kicked a bloody hornet's nest, didn't we?"

"We?" Flint tried to laugh, but the pain in his side turned it into a gasp. "I was but an unwitting participant, dragged into this mess against my will by the same arseholes what just tuned me up."

"And here I thought you bravely staying behind to cover our retreat was a vain attempt at heroism," Kiara snarked back, but there was humor in her voice. "So much for that, Sir Songbird."

"Ouch. Thus demonstrating it's not just the Garda who are merciless," Flint whined, but he smiled, too. He stopped to catch his breath.

Helping rescue Kiara's father from the Stormford gaol was the least Flint could do, after he'd been the one to put Felix there. Coerced, admittedly, but considering they'd killed Mutt out of spite after all, he should never have given in to their demands.

After two hands of days hiding, running, and sneaking from house to hovel to hole, they'd thought the streets were safe-ish.

They were wrong. The Garda had left a host of battered innocents in their wake, beaten to a pulp in their search for the perpetrators. The half-elven guards marked the ones they'd "examined" with their fists; fresh bruises and split lips indicated they'd been seen to already.

They reached the base of the Blackwood switchback, which separated Downtown from Central Park and the rest of Midtown. "If I'm to hike this damnable cliff, I'm gonna need a moment to catch me breath."

Sweat dotted his forehead, and his hair grew matted as he made the ascent. Two weeks ago, he'd wondered how they'd ever hollowed out these "cavehomes" from the cliff face. Now he knew. Nero and Wen, another shadow knight Flint hadn't known previously, were both armed with magical foci attuned to earth and stone. They'd worked feverishly, shaping solid rock as though it was putty or clay, opening up a void *behind* one of the cavehomes, and hid the entrance behind an armoire. In time, and with practice, Flint's force wand could be used for that purpose, too, but he was far too inexperienced for that kind of wizardry now.

"Evening, Shara," Flint said as he passed through the older woman's foyer. "How's Duncan?"

"He'll live," she replied. Shara was old enough to have grandkids, and she looked up from her knitting. A baby sock, Flint guessed. "Gods'n Demons, boy, have you been working on that illusive magic like Nero asked? Or did you lose a scrap with an ogre?"

"I was *examined* this afternoon. Seems they're not done just yet. Think they broke something."

Shara jumped to her feet and slid the wardrobe that concealed their hideaway aside. "I'll put a kettle on."

Flint nodded his thanks and followed Kiara through the passageway into her father's new clinic. He placed his hands on the walls of the passage and followed them as they curved left, then right into inky blackness, until his face found the heavy curtain that hid the well-lit interior. He stepped through.

"Lookin' good, boyo," Nero said as Flint emerged. "You've been practicing? Very convincing."

Kiara chuckled at his comment. "Not an illusion, Nero. They laid the boots into him down by Dad's old place."

"Oh."

"I'll admit, I'm curious how you evaded the mindbender?" Kiara asked. "I wouldn't have thought you could deceive his magick. That was a neat trick."

"I just didn't answer the questions he asked," Flint said. "He wanted to know where the *tryllestav* is, which I presume is a fancy name for a focus. I told him I didn't have one, which was true." He nodded his head at a small, plain jewelry box in the corner of the clinic, where his wand and amulet were hidden away. "If I'd been carrying them, I'd be dead."

"We'll just have to be sure we don't get caught tonight." Kiara gave her father a peck on the cheek. "Can we get him sorted, Da? We've got work to do."

"Busy at the moment," Felix said. He applied a poultice to an urchin's battered leg, and the boy hissed in pain. "If he's not bleeding out nor unconscious, he's third in line. Biggest issue?"

"Busted me ribs, I think," Flint replied. He pulled up his jerkin and hissed in pain. His entire left side had already turned an angry purple, and he bled from a few minor scratches and abrasions he hadn't even noticed.

Felix finished bandaging the urchin's leg and fixed his eyes on his daughter. "That's not nothing. Does it have to be tonight?"

Kiara chewed her lip for a moment. "I can try," she offered. "If I screw it up, Nero can re-break it, and you can fix it properly."

"Beg pardon," Flint said cautiously, "Nero can *what?*"

"I'm not done my schooling," Kiara said defensively, "but it should be fine. There's a slim chance I could heal your ribs wrong. That would be *bad.*"

"Yes, I'd guessed!" Flint retorted, but then he quenched his temper as quickly as it had risen. The two hands of wounded on the other side of this room were, in one shape or form, here because of him. If Felix were to exhaust himself treating his ribs, the rest would suffer more.

He still didn't have a good read on Kiara. She was fiery like her hair, impatient, and suffered no fools gladly. He suspected she still put him in that latter category. Her inner fire manifested itself in her passion for undermining the hal'far at every turn. Until this last admission of apprehension, she'd always projected an aura of supreme confidence.

"I've never heard you admit a weakness, Red," Flint mocked. "It must be serious."

"First time for everything, Songbird," she replied. "Unless you really do object?"

"Just give me something to bite down on first. And make sure you heal me throat, too; wouldn't do to lose my singing voice."

* * *

With a leather bit in his mouth, Flint braced his arms against the wall of the cave in as comfortable a position as he could manage. To his left, Kiara peeled off one of her red, elbow-length calfskin gloves and tucked it through her belt. She retrieved her blade from the same plain box that held Flint's foci and steeled herself. "Ready?"

"Rr-eee"—" was the closest Flint could manage with the leather in place. In one quick motion, Kiara ran the edge of the knife across the back of her forearm, leaving a weeping red line behind. She hissed, then returned the knife to its place. Daubing her fingers into the blood, she kneeled next to him and traced the blood over his mottled injury.

It built in waves of pressure, like holding his hand over an evertorch. The pressure changed to heat, passing warm to uncomfortable to hot to painful. He let out his first whimper.

"You're doing great," Kiara murmured.

Inside, liquid pain singed his fingers, the abrasions, the cuts, the pressure at the back of his head where he'd been knocked to the ground in the first place. Each injury heated up, itched, creeped, and crawled as his skin and muscles, sinew and nerves rebuilt themselves.

His bloodied wounds grew scabs, healed over, and were replaced by intact skin in mere seconds. Flint ground his teeth and growled. He couldn't take much more of this.

"Almost ready," Kiara said. She was sweating openly now, and her normally blue eyes had taken on a strange, ethereal golden glow.

Then the heat coalesced. It flowed down his neck, between his shoulder-blades, and out along his broken ribs to engulf them. It seeped down into the fractures in his bones, and with a burst of molten fire, wrenched them back into place. Flint screamed against the bit in his mouth, panted, and screamed some more.

Then the pain faded, leaving just a memory of the all-too-intimate scorching he'd just suffered. He let out another whimper and collapsed onto his cot. *All the pain of months of healing, compressed into one second.*

He lay there for a moment, then patted himself down all over. The cuts were healed. Purple bruising faded away to yellow; he poked the ribs and felt nothing.

Felix joined him at the cot and ran his fingers over Flint's ribcage. "Nice and clean. Well done, Kiara."

When Flint sat up, Kiara was rinsing her face in one of the wash basins. She'd used a touch of her magic to close the wound on her arm, but that was all she could manage. Something about using the blood to power the magic meant the magic couldn't heal it properly. The skin around the cut was red and angry, and would stay that way for a long time. She pulled the calfskin glove back on and hid the injury away.

When Flint stood, he found he felt better than he had in weeks, maybe months. He stretched, touched his toes, did a few side-bends, and it was like the injury hadn't happened at all. Kiara nodded approvingly. "Thank you," he said. "Thank you *very* much."

"Grab your gear," she told him. "We're going hunting."

* * *

With his force wand tucked under a bracer beneath his sleeve, and his water amulet under his jerkin's neckline, Flint followed Kiara out onto the Blackwood switchback, and back Downtown. "I thought we were scouting Midtown tonight?"

"We are," Kiara said, "but it wouldn't hurt to give the patrols something to busy themselves with first. Remember the day we first met?"

"You can't be serious," Flint said. "They've been on the warpath since we freed your father, and you want to take out *another* patrol?"

"Yes. Nero says it's time to push back. So, we're going to push back, hard. They should be scared every time they visit Downtown. And to add more spice to the mix, there's a Dog Squad on patrol tonight, collecting mutts again."

She led the way through the warrens silently. Every few houses, she knocked, exchanged a few words with the occupant, and moved on. Flint followed her, watching their backs, his eyes in constant motion. As she spoke to another of the Downtowners, Flint heard a dog yelp from nearby and tapped Kiara on the shoulder. "They're near."

"Find them," she whispered.

Nero had had him drilling every day on the kinds of magic that could be most easily channeled through the water focus. Elemental water was essential for magic of the mind: illusions and divination, mostly. That was one reason so many reflective pools were used for scrying, he'd said. Nero hadn't exactly explained what scrying was, but the point was that Flint could use water magic to see beyond his own senses and cloud the senses of others. Flint closed his eyes and willed his ears to *listen*.

At first, the noises of Downtown threatened to overwhelm him. Fires crackled, and soup pots bubbled. An infant cried. Half a block down, a young couple was enjoying a rendezvous, gasping with ecstasy, trying to keep their voices low, but failing. For a moment, Kiara's face came unbidden into his mind's eye, and it jolted him out of his trance. There was no doubt Kiara was intelligent, fierce, and beautiful, but she was utterly disinterested in romance. No, she was focused like a sunbeam through a ground lens, and whoever came under her gaze was more likely to get burned. He shook the thought away and dropped back into his trance.

As Flint identified all the sounds of the block, he filed them away and paid them no more mind, until he heard the dog snarl. Then a meaty thump, and the snarl became a whimper and a whine. The Garda soldier berated it in elven, and low voices followed.

"That way. No more than a hundred paces," he said, pointing. "Across from Hangman's Row."

"Perfect," Kiara said. They discussed the ruse they'd use to get close. She asked, "Ready?"

"Lead on, Red."

Kiara rounded a corner and cut through a narrow alley between a pair of rough-hewn shanties that were more post than wall. As she entered the alley, she staggered, giggled, and half-fell into Flint's arms.

I don't think I'll ever get used to her playing the drunken tramp, Flint thought, but he leaned right back into her, laughing as well. They'd emerged right on top of the Dog Squad patrol, barely a dozen paces away. "So, then I says, that's not *his* boat!" Flint chortled as though delivering the punchline to a joke. Kiara squealed in laughter, turned her back to the squad, and pulled Flint with her.

"Oi!" the squad's Overseer barked. There were five of them, with three dogs on braided leads looped around their necks. There was a sixth, a human as well, with his cloak hitched up as a hood.

No matter. Kiara ignored the Overseer's warning and collided with one of the squad as she backed into the bunch of them. As she did, Flint *pushed* with his mind and willed the dampness on the cobbles to freeze. It worked, and to the squaddie's surprise, his feet went out from under him.

"Oh!" Kiara gasped. "I'm so sorry!" She released Flint's hand, reached down to pull the squaddie to his feet, and as he rose, she buried the dagger concealed in her other hand in the man's chest.

The man gasped and fell back as Kiara spun to bury her blade into another squaddie's throat.

With a flick of his wrist, Flint let his force wand slip from his sleeve into his hand, and manifested a translucent club topped with spikes. He swung it two-handed into the Overseer's head, where the spike punctured the half-elf's unprotected temple and brained him.

The other squaddies were slow to react, and of course their hands went to their pistols first. Kiara was ready for that and had abandoned the knife for her fire wand. Before the barrels cleared leather, she willed tiny sparks into the pistol's flashpans, discharging the flintlocks with a roar into the cobblestones. One squaddie shouted in pain and fell, missing a fist-sized chunk of his calf where his pistol had blown it apart.

Flint reversed the swing of his club and smashed another of the Garda troops, as Kiara manifested a fiery sabre of her own.

She advanced on the only half-elf still standing. He drew his rapier in time, retreated two steps, and dropped into a well-practiced fencer's crouch. Kiara didn't give him time to center himself and slashed her flameblade as she approached.

Flint repeated his previous trick and froze the ground under the half-elf's feet. His boots shot out from under him, he hit the ground with a thud, Kiara pounced, and she ran him through.

The one with the wounded leg—the only one still breathing—moaned in pain. Flint shifted his spiked club into a simple forceblade and cut his throat. He released the captured dogs from their leads and turned his attention to the human who cowered under a shanty awning.

"It's all right, mate," Flint said. "They won't be bothering you no more."

"Gods'n Demons, izzat you, Flint?" the man stammered. "What—how—oh, oh no—"

Flint knew that voice. He threw the man's cloak back. "*Kaeso?*"

"Aye," the man replied. "It's not—it's not what it looked like, I swear, I swear to the Raven!"

Behind him, Kiara finished searching the Overseer for his magical foci, now unbonded, since his soul had fled. "Got it! Got *two!*" Kiara held aloft her new treasures. "Grab an ankle, let's go!"

"Wait," Flint commanded. The tone of his voice drew Kiara up short.

"What? Why?"

"Hushed midnight meetings with the Garda, Kaeso?" With barely restrained fury, Flint hauled the man out into the alley and threw him down with the cooling bodies. "Chitchatting with the same squaddies you sicced on me not two weeks ago? Empty your pouch."

"No, Flint, you've got it wrong, I—"

"*Empty. Your. Pouch.*"

With a whimper, Kaeso turned his leather belt pouch out. A smaller velvet pouch fell onto the cobbles. It *clinked* from the coin inside.

"Turncoat!" Flint snarled.

"Flint!" Kiara snapped. "What is this about?"

"He's the one what sold me out to the Dog Squad. Me *and* Mutt."

"I didn't have a choice!" Kaeso blurted, then his eyes widened as Kiara took a sharp breath in.

"Why?" Flint demanded. He grabbed the cowering man by the tunic and dragged him upright. "What do they want with the dogs? What are they worth, that the Garda would *pay* you? In *coin?"*

"Overseer Gunnar, he said they—they *harvest* them."

"You'd best start making sense. We don't hold with turncoats," Kiara said.

"There's a device. A relic. Something from before. Proper Alfar magic, they said. They said it can imbue a gemstone with an animal's soul or something, to fuel the magic within. Eventually the gemstone runs out, and they need more."

"So they slaughter another animal for magical fuel?"

"Exactly!" Kaeso said. "Carnelians for evertorches, and the flowstones are lapis lazuli. Those are the ones we see down here. Above Midtown, though, the Alfar use all kinds of magic for all kinds of things. Malachite to boost farmer's crops, rocky quicksilver at the smithies! I don't know anything else!"

"Where, *exactly*, did they say this device was?"

"They didn't! They just wanted to know where to find dogs—full grown, healthy ones! They didn't tell me anything else!"

"Useless," Flint spat. "You got Mutt killed, ye bastard, and more people besides. Time to balance the scales." He grabbed a handful of tunic and dragged Kaeso toward the gallows of Hangman's Row.

* * *

"That is *not* what we discussed," Nero snarled as he entered the clinic behind Shara's cavehome. It was after noon the following day. Flint sat up, bleary-eyed, and threw the covers back. Kiara was already up and helping her father with the injured. "You were going to make them *disappear.*"

"We improvised," Kiara retorted.

"What happened?" Felix interrupted. "I was asleep when they came in last night."

Nero rolled his eyes heavenward and threw his hands in the air. "Someone danced his last down on Hangman's Row overnight. No one knows how or when he got there, nor can anyone explain the five Garda bodies piled up below the platform in front of him, nor does anyone know why, in front of the newcomer, they found a bag of shiny new hawks and gyrs."

"Aye, and the ravens will feed well for a few days, what of it?" Kiara snapped. "Flint, get your arse out of bed and tell them."

"Yes, Flint, tell us. And you'd best start making sense," Felix said, arms crossed.

Flint repeated the story of how Kaeso had sent Flint directly into the Dog Squad's path, how that had precipitated Felix's capture, and then the night's encounter. "All this?" He waved his hands toward the door. "Started when he walked me into their trap."

"That doesn't make any sense," Nero said. "Dogs don't have souls. A soul is what gives us our intelligence, our reason, our sense of self. Dogs and other animals have spirits, which isn't the same thing at all."

Kiara said, "To be fair, I rather doubt they discussed the finer points of magical theory with their snitch while he sold out his fellow townies."

"True." Felix's eyes had softened as Flint related how the Garda had coerced him into giving up the location of Felix's home, and how they'd killed Mutt just to spite him. "Could be some form of blood magic, not too different from what we do."

Kiara gasped in shock, but Felix held up a finger to silence her objection. "Not morally the same, of course. But magic isn't a moral creature. Magic doesn't care about right or wrong. It just is. A focus is the conduit by which we channel our soul's energy into the real world. What if they have a device to channel an animal's spirit, or animus, into the real world? Into a stone already predisposed to some elemental effect?"

Nero considered the healer's words and shrugged. "This is beyond my ken. Maybe check in with Mother Corvaria at the Respitoreum. She taught me the basics when I was just a boy." Flint and Kiara rose to leave, and Nero held up a finger. "We can't undo what's been done. I agree, this Kaeso had earned a bad end, but it's the public who suffers when we send a message. This last fortnight's shown us that's true. Next time, the Garda bodies disappear into the bay for the sharks, and leave the rest to me."

* * *

Flint hadn't been into the Respitoreum since he was a child. He'd had his arm wrenched from its socket by an older boy who wanted Flint's scrap of bacon and crusty bread. The boy'd come away from the encounter with bruised testicles, and Missus Decarius had dragged both of them to the sister's tender care. He rotated his shoulder in its socket, remembering the phantom of the pain, and he smiled. "Amazing."

"What's that?" Kiara asked.

"I was just remembering the last, first, only time I've been here. Seems your healing worked for more than just my ribs. For the first time I can remember, my shoulder doesn't ache. First time I met Ceres, for that matter."

The Respitoreum was even larger than Flint remembered. Columns four times the size of a man supported the roof on all sides. They gleamed with polished white marble, save where some stonemage had fused green marble tracery and "leaves" to give the illusion of ivy climbing their height. Within the columns, stacked blocks of more white marble formed the inner walls, save where they'd left gaps for air flow, or added intricate stained-glass windows. In front, a trio of warm pools bubbled and burbled from an unseen hot spring.

The Sisters of Mercy were easily identified by the plain, brown linen robes they wore, hooded with a coif, and belted at the waist. One of the sisters helped a twisted, hunchbacked grandmother into the pool, where the heat and her natural buoyancy left the elderly matron smiling dreamily.

The sister saw them coming, and her face lit with a broad grin. "Kiara! How are you? It's been so long!"

"Viridia!" Kiara squealed and ran ahead to embrace the woman. She was pretty, with warm green eyes, and wisps of chestnut hair that had escaped from beneath her headdress. She looked to be a few years older than Kiara. Flint waited a few paces back until the women had exchanged their pleasantries. "Flint, this is Sister Viridia, the closest I've ever come to having a sister by blood. Vi, this is Flint."

"Pleased to meet you," Flint said, and Viridia bowed.

"What brings you all the way to Midtown?" Vi asked.

"Flint and I, we have a favor to beg," Kiara said. "It shouldn't take long, and we know how valuable her time is, but we humbly request an audience with Mother Corvaria." Kiara leaned in. "It concerns *magic*."

Vi blinked. "Oh. Oh no, you haven't gotten mixed up in—"

"Ask me no questions, and I'll tell you no lies," Kiara said seriously, and Vi's eyes flashed in shock. "It could be a matter of life and death, truly. We know full well the sisters are forbidden from using life magic to aid your patients. This is not that. At least, not directly. We could think of no one else to bring our question to but the Raveness herself."

"Wait here, please," Viridia said, and retreated into the temple.

"The Raveness? Mother Corvaria?" Flint asked. "I'm so lost. Same person, right?"

"Yes. The Respitoreum has three Mothers, and the Matronia, who is—well, they say first among equals. When one of the sisters assumes a leadership role, she assumes the name as well. Mother Eostre oversees pregnancies, childbirth, midwifery, and such. Her symbol is the hare. Mother Chironea governs the largest group of sisters, who study medicine, convalescence, and healing; that's who I studied under. Her symbol is the horse. Last, Mother Corvaria, the Raveness, is concerned with the end of things. Her sisters handle palliative care, funeral rites, and the crematorium. Ravens, because they inevitably follow death wherever he goes." Kiara gestured to the matron reclining in the hot spring, submerged with her head back, water up to her cheeks, and ecstasy writ on her aged, wrinkled face. "Viridia must be under her tutelage."

Vi returned with Mother Corvaria at her side. Of all the membership present, she was the only one who wore a black robe. She appeared middle aged, but Flint detected a weariness, a hollowness behind her eyes that made her appear older. Her smile was brittle, as if saying the wrong thing could irreparably destroy it, gone forever. He suspected caring for the elderly and the departed in Westlocke had wrought its own damage on her soul.

"Kiara, it is well you've returned, although Vi tells me you have a question, and a troubling one?"

"It is, Mother," Kiara admitted. "May we speak inside? It should only take a moment."

Corvaria nodded and stood aside to welcome them in. "You may come too, Vi."

The temple inside was divided into small subchambers with cots and beds. Flint passed a sister applying a plaster cast to a broken wrist, and a weeping couple being comforted by two more. The temple echoed with cries of pain and sorrow as the sisters plied their trade. At the rear of the chamber, Corvaria led them through a doorway into the sisters' living space, and then her own chamber. It was plain, spartan even, save one wall lined from corner to corner with leatherbound books, scrolls, and texts. "Ask your question, Daughter of Felix."

Kiara looked to Flint, who exhaled deeply before starting. "Mother, the Garda have been seizing dogs and other animals— mostly dogs—off the streets Downtown for as long as anyone can remember. They killed my Mutt in front of me not two weeks ago."

Vi and the Raveness exchanged a knowing glance at that admission but didn't interrupt.

"Last night, we heard rumor that the animals are being harvested for magical purposes. But that didn't make sense, because we know magic is tied to the soul's energy, and an animal has a spirit, which means they cannot cast. Does any of that make sense to you?"

"Ah." Corvaria smiled a brittle, knowing smile, and nodded in understanding. "True. A soul and a spirit are similar, in the sense that a plum and an apple are similar, but each distinct in its own way." She retrieved a scroll from her shelf and unrolled it. "Can you read? No? No matter. Kiara can, that I know. Flint, my office—the office of the Raveness—is most concerned with ensuring that when a being passes, their soul truly does *pass*. Their soul is sent for judgement, and their earthly remains must return to the ashes and dust from whence we all came. Thus do we deny necromancers, reavers, and soul-binders the essentials they need to ply their foul trades. Ashes to ashes, dust to dust is not just a pithy phrase, young man, but the proper end of all things."

"What's a soul-binder?" Flint asked.

"Someone who practices human sacrifice to animate their spells and artifacts. Potent magic, the kind that could bind a soul into a magical blade such that it could cut through anything, or an invulnerable suit of armor. The histories claim the reason the Alfar seized control of Westlocke was because it had become a haven for such wretched practices, and it took old magic to defeat the soul-binders who'd appointed themselves the rulers."

"So it follows, then, that a lesser creature, one with a mere spirit instead of a soul, could be spirit-bound into an artifact? Like, for example, the flowstones that cleanse the streets? Or the evertorches?"

Mother Corvaria's eyes widened. "That follows," she admitted. She stood and paced the room silently for a minute. Flint dared not interrupt. "It pains me to admit I had not considered this before. It seemed plain that the flowstones were some kind of Alfar magic, distinct from soul-binding, or the kind that uses a *tryllestav*, or a *taikakalu*, for that matter. All the histories made such heresy out to be cataclysmic power, not something innocuous like an evertorch. I had not considered it could simply be a lesser form of blasphemy."

"Mother?" Vi said. "When I took Mister Valens' remains to the crematorium, Tiber was at the door, just leaving. 'Not tonight, Vi,' he said. 'Come back tomorrow.' I saw a squad of Garda just past him, with two wheelbarrows filled with dead animals. Goats and dogs, mostly."

"I think we need to speak to this Tiber next," Flint said. "Perhaps there's more truth to this rumor than we'd like to believe."

"And then what?" Corvaria asked. "Will you send my brethren Uptown more business? More bruises? More broken bones to heal, and more bodies to burn?"

Blood rushed in Flint's ears, and he felt as though he'd stood up too fast. "Mother Corvaria, I—"

"—have no idea what I'm referring to?" Corvaria interrupted. "Flint, is it? Flint, the whole of Westlocke has been in an uproar since your Mutt died. Garda, killed in the streets. An *assault* on the gaol to free the prisoners inside. A successful one, no less! Some madwoman—no one here knows who she was—reaved not one, not two, but *three* Garda in the streets outside Stormford, and went out in a fireball that took a dozen more Garda with her. The fire was so fierce, there was no need to cremate the remains. Ash to ash, indeed.

"And then the backlash. Although you townies may scrape by on what food the brothers can provide, *all* that food is grown by the farmers here in Midtown, and if you think the Garda haven't taken out their fears and frustrations on them, too, you're even more young and naïve than you appear."

A silence descended on the Raveness' chambers for an infinite moment.

"I just want them to stop," Flint declared, "and I don't much care if it makes a few Mids uncomfortable. Mutt was the best, the *only* friend I'd had. They grabbed him and made me take them to Felix's clinic. Then, when they had Felix in manacles, they killed Mutt out of spite, and it spiraled out of control pretty quickly after that. Maybe trying to stop them is foolish. After all, what's a little blasphemy between friends? So a few townies get dragged, so what? So a few townies' dogs get *harvested* so there's clean water for the Mids to wipe their arses. All for the greater good, innit? Maybe they'll nab me on my way out the door, and I'll be dead before tomorrow, I've no idea. If not for Kiara, the last beating they laid on me might've. Only takes one rib in a lung before you're off to the burn pile.

"What I do know is, Ceres died to save Felix, Kiara, and me, and I'd do the same for them. The Mids? The Mids don't give two rabbit pellets about us townies. Scum, the lot of us, good for nothing but gutting fish on the docks, breathing fresh coaldust, and dancing on the row to remind the Mids who's in charge. Tell you what, you get back to me when you and yours are riding the ragged edge of starving and getting beaten a couple times a month. Let me know when your finery is little more than rags that reek of fish oil and piss. Let me know when the Mids get uncomfortable enough that maybe they start to see the shite that goes on Downtown *every single cursed day*, and decide that today's the day to do something about it. To the nine hells with the Mids. I don't owe them more than a swift kick in the arse."

"Gods and Demons, Flint," Kiara gasped, horrified. "You can't just talk to the Raveness like that!"

Mother Corvaria stared back at Flint, mute, for another moment. Then, shockingly, she burst into laughter. "Well, he did, can't take it back now. But please, don't hold back, Flint; tell us how you really feel."

"The Mids are *sheep*, Raveness. Content to work the field while getting fleeced, season after season. They're frightened of the wolf, but it's the farmer who serves them up as mutton for dinner. A weasel might be small, but at least it has teeth."

Flint left.

* * *

Kiara found Flint in Central Park an hour or more later, sitting under a tree. It was his fourth. Garda Wardens had urged him to move on three times already. This one had the added bonus of being within shouting distance of the massive, charred circle burnt into the park grass. One of the Warden's Overseers worked on the patch with a life magic wand topped with an emerald, but got nowhere. The patch where Ceres died was as lifeless as stone now.

"So how much trouble am I in?" Flint asked as Kiara got within earshot.

Kiara shook her head in exasperation. "None, believe it or not. If anything, you might have scored some points with her. Seems it's been a while since anyone was that brutally blunt with her, and she found it refreshing."

Flint opened his mouth to reply, but Kiara shushed him. "Having said that, don't go thinking you've got a free pass to be 'That Raging Townie Arsehole,' neither. She didn't know it was Ceres who died there, and she didn't know the gaolbreak was to rescue Father, either. Ceres was her first teacher at the Respitoreum as an aspirant. That Ceres judged the matter worth dying over went a long way toward getting her to bend, where she might have been rigid."

"Seems she's been a bit too flexible on the whole spirit-binding thing in the first place," Flint grumbled. "You can't convince me she didn't at least suspect."

"And that was her big concession. Even though animals have spirits, and not souls, whatever the hal'far are doing is the closest thing to soul-binding she's seen, and she won't ignore it anymore. Some of the other sisters confirmed they've occasionally seen Tiber removed from his own crematorium so the Garda can dispose of the dead dogs in batches. If the pattern holds, they ought to be there tonight, tomorrow, or the next. Now let's get back to Shara's, stay out of sight until the sun's set, and we can work in peace and quiet."

* * *

A bleak drizzle rolled in that afternoon, heralding the coming of winter rains, and banished everyone with good sense indoors.

Flint didn't particularly count himself among that group, since he'd laid on his belly on the only flat stone roof with a view of the crematorium in all of Downtown that night, and the next, and again now for the third. He shivered under his cloak as the water beaded off it, dripped down onto the slate, and soaked into his tunic from underneath. The tunic had been warmed by the fire during the day, but was still damp when he'd put it back on.

He hated winter. It was chill, damp, and miserable, but he and misery were long acquainted. He'd be glad to take his misery out on the dog-murdering, spirit-binding Garda thugs if given half a chance, and it looked like he'd get that chance tonight, since a hand of figures had just arrived at the crematorium door, hauling carts.

He slipped off the roof and splashed down into the mud. He worried about the noise, but the rain hid the sound well. He and Kiara had scouted the area around the crematorium, and he knew where she'd be hidden, curled up in a recessed doorway along one of the only two pathways that was even enough for a handcart. Nero and Wen watched the other. He slipped through the rear of the doorless hovel, padded through the main room in the house, and stood at the doorway. He kept his voice low. "It's me."

Kiara moved slowly, stiffened by the cold, and unused to curling up on bare stone as she was. "They didn't come this way. You're sure?"

"I am." He offered her a hand, and she staggered to her feet.

Despite being sheltered in the doorway, her fiery, curly hair was bedraggled, stringy, and dark. She pulled at a strand in her face. "I'm going to be a frizzy disaster tomorrow."

"Stop it, you're going to be spectacular as always. Nero and Wen were the lucky ones to spot them coming. Let's go."

This time, he led the way, and a few short minutes later he slipped into a low-fenced yard that reeked of goat. The goats had had the sense to huddle inside their shelter, as Nero crouched in the shadows behind it. "Wen's gone on ahead to intercept Tiber and bring him back here," Nero said. "I'd like a word with him."

As though summoned, the Incendiarian emerged from the drizzle, followed by a hulking form Flint took to be Wen.

He'd never met Wen before, but Nero had described him as a big man. Nero had been understating. He was twice as broad and half again as tall as Flint, with a beard to his collarbone, and arms as thick as Flint's legs. Nero rippled as he willed his appearance into his "old man" guise and emerged from his goat pen, with Flint and Kiara close behind. Nero wrapped an arm around Wen's charge and escorted him down a side path to interrogate him, leaving the other three alone.

"How long you figure we've got?" Kiara asked.

"It'll be a while," Wen said. "They had three carts, and the ovens were cold."

"Lovely," Flint said. "Couldn't have happened on a nicer evening."

When Nero returned, he was alone. "Tiber will be back in the morning. The squaddies tend to wait until a miserable night like this to minimize the chances of someone seeing them coming or noticing the smoke. Wen, I'll want you at the base of the switchback. If they're going to notice anyone trailing them, it'll be you. Kiara, you and Flint will wait here. I'll be by the Perch. If they pass, great; I'll parallel you. If not, one of you can come find me, and we'll adjust. We've been assuming they came down the Blackwood switchback, but there's no guarantee that's the case."

Wen and Nero moved off, leaving Kiara and Flint alone again. They sat in a doorway opposite Nero's goat pen. When the others were well gone, Kiara turned to face Flint. "You think I'm 'spectacular?'" Kiara asked quietly.

"I, uh, well—yes?" Flint stuttered. "I mean, obviously. You're smart, fierce, and brave, talented with magic, and a brilliant healer, but you're also the most beautiful girl in Downtown. Anyone who doesn't see that is an idiot. Despite all recent evidence to the contrary, I'm not an idiot."

"Thanks," Kiara said and allowed an awkward little smile to cross her face. "I think that's the nicest thing anyone's ever said to me."

Flint stared. "You're joking. I'd have thought the townies would be throwing themselves at you."

"Oh, they do," she said, "with monotonous regularity, accompanied by crude remarks, indecent proposals, and more attention paid to my bosom than my brains."

"To be fair, it's a very nice—" Kiara whipped her head around to glare at him, and Flint paused. "Brain. I was going to say brain. You're scary smart. It's obvious you know more about healing than anyone I've ever met. When you fixed my ribs, and everything else, that was perhaps one of the most intimate experiences of my life, and when the pain was gone, I felt better, healthier, than I have my entire life. And still did, right up until this accursed rain arrived."

"Oh!" Kiara said. "Here." She drew her fire wand and concentrated. The air around Flint warmed dramatically, and he shook his head free of rain, like Mutt used to after a bath. Upon closer inspection, he realized Kiara didn't look nearly as damp or miserable as he was, and it wasn't just because he'd been on a rain-swept roof the previous two nights.

"I have got to get me one of those," Flint said. "Um, awkward question, but I've only known you for a fortnight, and it's been pretty intense. What do you do for fun?"

"For fun?" Kiara repeated. "I don't know. Pretend to be drunk and knife an unwitting Garda in the ribs?"

"You, too? Phew, that's good to hear," Flint said with a grin that nearly glowed in the drizzly darkness. "Maybe we could do that again some time."

"I'd like that," Kiara said. She got to her feet and pulled Flint up after her. "Here they come."

She leaned in to embrace him. Flint was stunned at first, as her arms encircled his waist, but as her lips came to his ear, she whispered, "Don't get handsy, we're not there yet. This just keeps our faces hidden."

Flint pulled her close, but kept his eyes firmly on the pathway outside. He didn't know how she did it, but even in the middle of the night, in the middle of a frigid, misty autumn rain, she smelled of vanilla and cinnamon. It was *intoxicating.*

The Dog Squaddies grumbled and squelched their way past, and Flint let go as soon as they were away. He rather regretted they wouldn't likely need that particular ruse again soon. He led the way, moving from fencepost to support beam to darkened doorway. When it became clear they were indeed headed for the switchbacks, Flint gave Kiara a quick nod and broke off to splash ahead on a parallel street the carts would struggle to navigate.

At the late Ceres Decarius' home, Flint found Nero and gave him the update. Nero was already moving by the time Flint finished. "Wen and I will meet you at the top, then. Good work." And then Nero was gone, still wearing his illusory old man's face. Flint didn't know how he maintained the concentration necessary to hold the illusion. It must have been exhausting.

Flint returned to the main path and strode purposefully through the shanties until he found Kiara again. He got back just in time and caught sight of the squaddie's heels as they made the first turn up the switchback. Kiara held Flint back for a moment. "I don't see Wen anywhere; did you find Nero?"

"I did. He was going to find Wen and get up to Midtown before the squaddies, so they'd be in wait."

"Let's go, then."

They'd only rounded the second switchback when Flint's heart leaped into his throat. "*Where'd they go?*"

This third stretch of hill passed directly by Shara's cavehome; Flint had walked the path nearly every day for the last two weeks. It was the longest, straightest part of the road; there was nowhere the Garda could have hidden unless they'd somehow sprinted on ahead to round the next bend. Their three wooden carts made that unlikely.

"Demons, Flint, you don't think they rumbled us, do you?"

"I don't see how they could have, and even if they had, where would they go? I'll run on ahead, you tuck in at Shara's doorway, and I'll be back. If you hear me screaming, I'd appreciate another rescue."

"I'll do what I can, you know that. Worse comes to worst, act drunk, flirt, and stab them in the heart."

Flint grinned. "I'll keep that in mind." Then he was off to the end of the switchback, slowing as he reached the point where he could see the next stretch of path, but it too was empty of pedestrians, half-elf or otherwise. Panic threatened to overwhelm him. *Where could they have gone?* Two more bends, and he reached the top. Midtown. He cast his eyes about furiously, searching the shadows of Central Park.

Nero emerged, to Flint's relief, but his words doubled Flint's fears instantly. "Where are they? Did you lose them?"

"They didn't reach the top?" Flint asked, but he knew the answer. Nero couldn't have missed them any more than Flint could have. "We saw them as far as Shara's, or closest thing to hers. Where did they go?"

"I've no idea," Nero replied. "Back down we go. I don't want to wait another fortnight before we get another chance at them."

He beckoned for Wen, who lumbered out from behind an enormous tree trunk, and Flint retraced his steps. He described the point where he'd last seen them.

Nero cursed. "I can't imagine their Overseer is powerful enough to render them all invisible in the middle of a rainstorm." He stroked his chin in wonder. "Then again, all illusions are tied to elemental water in the first place. Be interesting to experiment."

Kiara wasn't in Shara's doorway when they turned the corner. She'd moved up the street and beckoned for them to hurry. "I think they went in here," she whispered when they caught up.

"You can't be serious," Nero gasped. They were at the door to the cavehome directly adjacent to Shara's. The door was wide enough for the carts, Flint had to admit, and when he knelt at the doorway, the sill beneath gleamed with moisture. Nero looked *offended*. "And we've *also* been hiding in a magically excavated cave for how long?" he wondered aloud. "There's no new games, just new players."

"One way to find out," Wen rumbled. "Shall we?"

He tried the knob, but it was locked. Flint knelt and eyed the lock, and produced his force wand. One of the first tasks Nero'd had him work on was turning a key in a lock, under Kiara's supervision. He'd had an idea, though, that he could maybe use the same force energy to turn the lock itself, without the key, if he could just envision the key right. In his mind's eye, he imagined the key sliding into place, and he twisted his fingers as though turning it. Like his club, his wand manifested a small translucent key, and Flint slotted it.

The lock resisted, but the keyhole looked no different than the one on Shara's front door, and he'd seen her with that exact key. He shifted the teeth on the key and tried again.

Click.

"Will wonders never cease," Nero murmured. "Well done."

Flint stood back, and Wen eased the door open. "I'd say you guessed right, Miss," the big man said. Flint could make out the cart tracks inside easily, with freshly muddy bootprints between the wheels. The interior was mostly bare and looked unlived in, aside from some clay jars on a shelf, and a ratty, bare bookshelf. The tracks disappeared beneath the bookshelf in a way that reminded Flint of Shara's armoire.

"How did we miss this?" Flint hissed, and Nero let a flash of anger cross his features.

"I don't make a habit of patrolling the switchbacks on nights with shite weather, boy. Now shut it, there's likely five, maybe more squaddies in here, and we still need to find the artifact itself."

Nero led the way. His keen eyes spotted a tension line hooked to a nail on top of the bookshelf that would have yanked the jars onto the floor. When Flint took them down, he was surprised to find them full of *something*. Something acrid.

"Lovely," Nero said. "Blaze cloves, demoncurry, ground galafiend, and soukuria. If those jars had shattered, the dust would have had us all crying our eyes out and coughing up our lungs. Put them over there." He pointed to a corner of the otherwise empty room where they'd be out of the way, then paused. "On second thought, one jar each. Maybe we do unto the squaddies, since they didn't do unto us."

Wen took the galafiend, Nero took the curry, and Flint had just handed the jar identified as the blaze cloves off to Kiara, when the bookshelf swung open. A trio of squaddies drew up short, surprise written across their faces. "Shite!" Flint yelped and heaved the jar of sokouria at them.

The jar struck the passageway wall just behind them and shattered, spilling a pale-yellow dust into the air. Thus inspired, Kiara did likewise, covering them in a light brown dust as well. They fell to the ground, gasping, coughing, hacking, and writhing around like pithed snakes. Nero pulled his cloak around his face to protect his lungs and pounced on the nearest one. He drew the hal'far's rapier in a flash and ran each one through with it. They stilled, and his eyes wept when he crawled out of the passageway.

"Gods'n Demons, that's appalling," he gasped. He leaned against the wall, spent. His eyes were reddened, his voice was hoarse, and mucus dripped from his nostrils. "Take notes, you three. No new games, just new players. We can source hot peppers and spice from the market the same as these arseholes."

"Oi!" came a voice from deeper down the passageway. "Did you idiots knock the pots over? What's that stench?"

Flint stepped up to the passageway, wand now in hand, and envisioned an enormous fan projecting from it. Sweat beaded on his forehead as his will took translucent shape. He beat the air with it, pushing as much of the choking powder down the passage as he could. A bit of the cloves got in his eyes, and they started watering, but he kept fanning the caustic cloud as hard as he could. The cursing voice turned to coughing, and Flint pushed on.

A hand gripped his left hand, and from it, a warmth flowed into him that beat the debilitating effects of the powders back into submission. Kiara bled from a new cut on her forearm, just below the earlier one from Shara's, and she buried her face in Flint's cloak to minimize the effects on herself.

Flint had to keep going, or he'd waste her effort.

The passageway opened up into a large chamber with dog pens, currently empty, along one wall. Along the other was a strange torture-device looking mechanism, and on the floor, crying their eyes out, were the last two Garda troops.

"Damn you, townies," the Overseer gasped, and pointed a wand up at them. A bolt of flame lanced up from it, and Flint instinctively used his "fan" to swat it away. He hadn't known he could do that. The impact felt like it had singed his hand, though—and then the healing energy from Kiara flowed into him, and his hand felt instantly better. Flint kicked the Overseer's wand away and brought the thin edge of his fan down on the Overseer's throat. He felt a *crunch,* and the hal'far's eyes bulged as he tried to breathe through a crushed windpipe.

BOOM!

The last squaddie held his pistol outstretched, smoke rising from the barrel, and Kiara was falling.

"NO!" Flint screamed. He dove for her. She clutched her side, where a fist-sized chunk of meat was missing, and the coppery scent of blood mixed with shit. She'd been gutshot. Her eyes were scrunched shut, and she let out an ear-piercing shriek.

"Gods, Kiara, no, you've got to be okay, hold on, just hold on!" Flint had seen this once before, and he knew what to do. He surged to his feet and manifested his club again. With a two-handed swing, he shattered the squaddie's knee, and brought the club down in an overhead smash on the squaddie's hand.

The half-elf screamed as fingers broke, but Flint paid him no mind. He threw the pistol aside, then his blade, put a knee to the back of the man's elbow, and heaved. The man howled in pain as his elbow cracked. "You'll not shoot nor stab anything again, bastard," Flint snarled.

He dragged the thoroughly crippled hal'far over to Kiara, whose eyes were going glassy. "You can do it," Flint said, "just like Ceres did. Just like how she saved your father."

"S'not that easy," Kiara whispered. "Healing yerself—even harder." She spat blood, which dribbled down her chin and stained her shirt.

"You're smarter and tougher than any woman I've ever met, damn you," Flint said. "Don't you give up on me now!"

He drew Kiara's dagger, the one she'd opened her arm with to heal him, and wrapped her fingers around it. Then, with his fingers around hers, he plunged the blade into the crippled hal'far's back. He stabbed again, and on the third strike, found the squaddie's heart.

Kiara gasped, and her eyes shone with gold as the energy flowed. "I can feel—" she gasped. With her other hand, she probed her wound. "Help me," she groaned.

"What can I do?"

"Hold this." She groaned as she pulled out a length of her own intestine and put it in his hand. It had been totally severed. Bloody fingers returned to her wound and passed the other end to Flint as well. *"This is going to hurt,"* she said, and then her eyes erupted with dazzling golden light that washed over the two halves of her guts. She shrieked. When she fell back against the wall, the loop of her guts was intact, as though it hadn't been hurt at all. Flint stuffed the rubbery thing back into the hole.

"So much damage," Kiara whispered. "Not enough power." Her eyes closed, but her lids still glowed from within.

"Demons, Flint, what in the nine hells happened?" Wen asked from the doorway.

"He shot her!" Flint shouted. "The Overseer got a bolt off, and while I was handling him, he shot her."

"And now she's reaving him to repair the wound," Nero said. He knelt next to her and examined the wound. "Demons, that's a bad one."

"It was worse a few seconds ago," Flint said. "That thing on the table must be the spirit-binder." He pointed to the torture rack. "I'm busy here."

The glow had faded from Kiara's eyes. She looked up at Flint. "That's a lot of it. Thank you. I'm sorry, but it's not enough."

"It has to be enough," Flint pleaded. "What's still wrong?"

"I burned up the last of the energy cleansing my insides," she gasped. "If I didn't, I'd die of fever, but now I don't have enough to close the wound itself."

Flint stared down at her injury. It bled less now than it had. The missing flesh was still missing, a fist's worth, and that wouldn't get better on its own. He glared back down the hallway, where the first three Garda cooled. If Nero hadn't slain them so quickly, she could have used their energy, too.

Unless—

When she'd healed him at Shara's, she'd cut herself for the blood sacrifice.

When she'd countered the effects of the choking powder, she'd cut herself again.

She'd used the outside of her forearm, because it could be hidden beneath a gauntlet and wasn't as dangerous to cut.

But she and Ceres had both shown they could use another's blood for the sacrifice, too. The blood provided the energy, and the dagger linked the energy to the user.

He took her hand, the one with the blade in it, in his again. "Do you trust me?" he asked.

"Wha?" Kiara said dumbly. She'd lost a lot of blood. If she lost consciousness, it was over. He pinched her on her left tricep. "Ow!" she snapped, but it brought her around again. "Yes, of course," she slurred.

"Good. For once in your life, don't argue," he urged, and she nodded. With her dagger, he opened his own forearm from elbow nearly to wrist. Blood wept, he hissed in pain, and her eyes shot open. "Use it!"

Kiara's mouth dropped open, and her eyes regained their previous glow, but muted. She clamped her hand over the injury, kicked her heels, and bit back a scream, but then it was done, and her bloodied hand came away from her belly, now unblemished. Flint let out a gasp of relief.

"Thank the Gods," he said, and with his knife, he cut away a strip of the dead hal'far's uniform for a makeshift bandage. He pulled her to her feet, and although wobbly, they joined Nero at the device.

If anything, it resembled a trebuchet in miniature mounted to a table. There were attachment points for locking in the dog's collar, and chains and manacles for the dog's legs. The victim would lay on its side on the table, with the trebuchet's arm mounted above it. At the very tip of the arm was something that looked like a parrying dagger, locked in place with straps, and a peculiar hollow where the pommel should have been. The blade was hollow along its length, and the tip was razor sharp.

Flint pulled one of the table drawers open, and it rattled with the stones contained within. Blue, green, red, gray, and silver stones, of all shapes and sizes, organized by color, and in a small compartment, a tin of beeswax.

"The stone goes in the hilt, and the wax holds the stone in place," Flint reasoned. "The blade comes down, pierces poor Mutt through the heart, and the dagger channels the spirit into the stone."

"That easy," Nero breathed.

Kiara snarled, "All you have to do is be willing to murder poor, defenseless animals so the hal'far don't have to light new torches every night."

"What do we do with it?" Wen asked. "Heave it into the bay?

"We hadn't really planned this far ahead, but that sounds as likely as any."

Nero shook his head. "That may have been the plan once," he said slowly, "but I think we need to reconsider."

"What?" Kiara gasped. "You want to keep it?"

"Absolutely not," Flint added. "We didn't do all this just to *steal* the accursed thing!"

"Maybe yes, maybe no," Nero said. "Consider what we could do with such a thing. Healing charms for the Respitoreum. Sharper knives, stronger tools. Permanent illusions, the better to hide us from them when they come storming through, and weapons that spit fire on command, no training needed. We needn't sacrifice dogs to make this work, we could use other creatures instead, those destined for the slaughterhouses anyway. Goats. Cattle. Sheep, or fish."

"You're talking about spirit-binding, Nero," Kiara objected.

"Says the woman who just reaved her first hal'far," Nero said. "Desperate times and all that. Don't tell me you'd give this kind of power up to save a few goats?"

"You've been thinking about this a long time," Flint said, shaking his head sadly, "haven't you?"

"Every damned day," Nero replied sharply. "Every time I pass one of the evertorches. Every time I wash my face in a flowstone trough. Did you know the farmers here have *four* harvests a year, thanks to the garden charms, where we'd normally only have *one*? I've wondered what I could accomplish if I could unlock the mystery, and here we are. Now quit whinging like children, and collect up these stones. It doesn't look like we need the apparatus itself, just the dagger, the gems, and the wax."

He loosened the clamp holding the dagger in place on the armature and slid the sacrificial blade free. "Now hurry up, we've wasted far too much time already, and someone will come to check on them once they're overdue back at the barracks."

Wen dutifully opened a pouch on his belt and shoveled handfuls of gems inside. Flint glared at them as if they were somehow responsible for how the night had gone, then opened his own pouch to help. Kiara refused. "If you misuse this, Nero—if you hurt anyone or, Gods forbid, soul-bind someone? I'll kill you myself."

"On that day, you'll be welcome to try," Nero replied and eyed the half-elf's body on the floor. "Hazards of the job, I suppose. Blood sacrifice is always most attractive when it's someone else's blood, isn't it?"

* * * * *

Jamie Ibson Bio

Jamie Ibson is from the frozen wastelands of Canuckistan, where moose, bears, and geese battle for domination among the hockey rinks, igloos, and Tim Hortons. After joining the Canadian army reserves in high school, he spent half of 2001 in Bosnia as a peacekeeper, and came home shortly after 9/11 with a deep sense of foreboding. After graduating college, he landed a job in law enforcement, and was posted to the left coast from 2007 to 2021. He retired from law enforcement in early 2021 and moved clear across the country to write full time in the Maritimes.

Jamie's website can be found at ibsonwrites.ca, where he has free short stories available for download. To find out when he releases something new, follow him on Bookbub at bookbub.com/profile/jamie-ibson. He's also on Facebook, and runs The Frozen Hoser's Winter Wasteland on Discord.

He's married to the lovely Michelle, and they have cats.

* * * * *

Blood of Dragons
by Sam Witt

An Eldros Legacy Story

The first bloody rays of dawn clawed their way over the horizon as Kor clambered up the eastern side of a brambly hill to survey the land ahead. He and Tallis had left Alura Kenai with little more than the clothes on their backs, but the hunter had his eyes on a prize that could make both their lives much more comfortable.

If he survived to claim it.

"What is that?" Tallis asked, as she joined him. The former tavern owner jabbed a finger toward a blob of shadow moving through the darkness between the sun's rays. The object of her attention was still a few miles off, but even at this range, it was sinister.

Kor rolled his shoulders and shook the tension out of his scarred and tattooed arms. The message the Sainted Order had sent to him through his dreams had given him the rough location of a significant deposit of dragon blood crystals. That was a prize that would change his life for the better.

But the Order's dreamspeakers had also warned the hunter that he wasn't the only one in search of this treasure. He'd hoped they were wrong, but that ominous shadow, slowly resolving into individual figures bearing massive, red-streaked banners, dashed his dreams of an easy score.

"Shindoran Hellwalkers," he said with a sigh and motioned for Tallis to follow him back down the hill, out of sight. "They'll want the blood crystals."

Tallis frowned at the hunter's words. "I thought only the Sainted Order of Hunters knew how to use the crystals."

"We're the only ones who can use them *safely*," Kor clarified. "The Shindorans don't give a plague rat's shit about safety."

"What will they do with the crystals?" Tallis knew Kor didn't like answering questions, but she needed to learn as much about his world as she could. For too long, her mind had been focused on ale and sausages, right up until the moment she'd nearly lost her life to an ancient, vampiric Giant.

She wouldn't make *that* mistake again, even if it meant annoying the hunter who'd saved her from that horrible fate. Knowledge was the only kind of power she could claim, and in a world filled with monsters, Tallis needed every scrap of power she could snatch.

"They'll eat them," Kor said, amusement and anger warring in his words. "The Shindorans believe killing themselves with dark ichor removes evil from the world and helps them ascend to the next higher cycle of reincarnation."

"Does it?"

"Dead is dead," Kor said. "No one gets a do-over."

Not that Kor blamed people for clinging to whatever beliefs got them through the cold, dangerous nights they faced.

Unfortunately, the cultists' beliefs put them on a collision course with Kor. It was hard enough to raid an ancient dragon's tomb without a pack of assholes baying at his heels the whole way. Their arrival added problems to his life he didn't need.

What he needed were the dragon blood crystals. They were pure, crystallized dark ichor. With that power, he could augment his Hunter's Curse and heal the old wounds the power had inflicted on him over the years. It would extend his life by a decade and make his job slaying monsters much simpler. Armed with that power, he could do a lot more good before the grave claimed him.

"Couldn't we just split the crystals with the Shindorans?" Tallis asked. "We'd all come out ahead."

Kor peered through a gap between a pair of hills. The cultists weren't headed in his direction, which was a relief—and a worry. He was relieved that he was unlikely to run into them head-on, but worried they were now marching toward the mountain he believed held his treasure.

"They won't share," Kor said. "They believe they're the keepers of a sacred truth. They think hunters are monsters who defile the world by harnessing the dark ichor. They're as like to kill me as talk to me."

The Shindorans weren't the only ones who felt that way about hunters. Kor and his fellows had long ago learned that the people who hired them to kill monsters were happy to have them around until the precise moment the monster was dead. Then the people with money realized if someone could *kill* a monster, maybe that someone was a real threat to their power.

Men and women who fought the worst the world had to offer never came away from those battles unscarred. They wore the evidence of their victories where anyone could see them.

And people did not like what they saw.

Too late, the hunter realized something had changed while he was lost in thought. The desert crickets, usually so loud at this time of day, had gone silent.

Kor held up a hand to bring Tallis to a halt. "Something's wrong," he whispered. "Be ready to run—"

"There's nowhere to run to," a woman's husky voice rang out as its owner crested the hill ahead of Kor and Tallis. Thick bands of lightning-blue dye stood out in stark contrast to her deeply tanned face. She held a heavy scimitar in her right hand and a small round buckler in her left.

Kor looked around and cursed under his breath. More rough and ready figures surrounded the hunter and Tallis. He should have been more careful. He should have spent more effort listening for trouble than answering his companion's questions. But what was the point of traveling with someone if you didn't talk?

The hunter sighed and raised his hands. "Take me to your leader."

* * *

The Shindoran scouts treated Kor and Tallis with respect, but kept their weapons ready. If Kor even looked like he was about to manifest his Hunter's Curse, the scouts would turn him into a pincushion.

Kor wrestled with that choice as the scouts herded them toward the other cultists. He doubted the archers could kill him before the Curse flared to life. His ability would protect him from their arrows and blades, at least until he'd broken free of their circle. He could probably outrun them after that. With luck, he'd find the dragon blood crystals before the Shindorans caught up to him. And with those crystals in hand, it would be no fight at all.

Kor would slaughter every one of the scouts, and anyone they brought along to the party.

But taking that route meant leaving Tallis behind. The Shindorans would kill her outright or use her as a hostage to trap him.

"Hunters walk alone," his old teacher Roxilus had warned him. "There is no room on our narrow path for another at our side. Companionship breeds weakness."

Kor had taken those words to heart for many years since he'd first heard them. But Tallis had offered him comfort in a world that had grown cold and dark, and the time they'd spent together had changed him. Her questions were annoying, but her company was welcome. And unlike what Roxilus had threatened, Kor felt stronger with Tallis than he had alone.

He would never abandon the woman. He would just have to find another way to win his freedom.

The scouts didn't say another word until they'd come within spitting distance of the main Shindoran force. Then their leader stopped in front of Kor and stared into the hunter's eyes for a long, tense moment. Her hand tightened around the scimitar hilt on her hip before she found whatever she was looking for in his gaze and relaxed.

Just a little.

"Our graveseeker has met your kind in the past," she said, her voice so low Kor could barely hear the words. "It didn't go well for them, or for her. If you wish to survive this meeting, temper your words and treat her with the respect she deserves."

"I was minding my own business before you showed up," Kor said. "Cut us loose, and we can go our separate ways."

"That's not an option," the scout said. "The graveseeker sent us to find you. She *knew* you'd be out here. She'd skin me alive if I came back without her prize."

"Great," Kor said. "Let's get this over with. I don't plan on picking a fight with your leader, but I won't go meekly to the slaughter, either."

The scout nodded and thrust her hand out to Kor. "I am Miyka. Let's hope we don't cross swords."

Kor shook her hand and his head. These cultists weren't what he'd expected, but he wasn't fool enough to believe they were friends.

The Shindoran force was still on the move, so the scouts had to pick up the pace to reach the front of the long train. Kor guessed there were two hundred or so men and women in the group, though not a child in sight. That, at least, was a relief. The hunter had a soft spot for kids, mostly because he'd never have any of his own, and worrying about their safety would slow him down in a fight. Their absence gave him freedom.

What the Shindorans did have was a diverse group of adults. Elves, Delvers, even Gnomes mingled with the Humans, all of them wearing dark robes that covered their torsos and legs while leaving their heads and arms bare. Their uncovered skin was dotted and striped with the same electric blue dye that adorned the scouts. The designs were all unique and reminded Kor of the sigils and runes etched into his own skin. They weren't the same, but there were uncomfortable similarities that led his thoughts down heretical paths.

Maybe the Sainted Order wasn't so different from the cultists after all.

Or maybe one was just the bastard reflection of the other.

Kor wasn't really sure which he hoped was true.

The cultists watched Kor and Tallis with open curiosity as they passed by. There was some hostility in their intense stares—clannish groups weren't welcoming to outsiders as a rule—but no one spat on them or hissed curses in their direction. Mostly what Kor saw in their eyes was curiosity, and he imagined they saw the same in his appraising gaze. They'd never seen a hunter, and he'd never seen a Shindoran.

Both sides of this coin had a lot to learn about the other.

"Here we are," Miyka said. "Watch your tongue."

"I will if she does," Kor promised.

"Kor," Tallis whispered, "don't get us killed."

They reached a large palanquin carried by six cultists, their backs bowed beneath the heavy bloodwood poles that held the vehicle. Obsidian posts rose from the litter's bed to support a raw silk canopy decorated with designs that Kor almost recognized. They were uncomfortably close copies of the runes that defined the Sainted Order of Hunters: Honor, Duty, Sacrifice.

Surely, these insane cultists couldn't hold to the same code the Hunters had followed for so many centuries.

Surely not.

A wizened creature sat on a mound of pillows in the center of the shaded interior. Her face was puckered into a toothless mass of wrinkles, the only sign of life the jade glint of her cataract-clouded eyes. She extended a limb tipped with an appendage that looked more like a raptor's talon than a flesh-and-blood hand toward Kor.

"Come closer, thief," she said. The words were no louder than a whisper, but they commanded the hunter's attention far beyond the power of the insult they carried.

The Hunter's Curse roused but didn't quite ignite. A tingle of power raced along the tattoos, telling Kor that the creature on the palanquin had directed some arcane force in his direction. Were it not for the dozen armed men and women within striking distance, the hunter wouldn't have allowed *that* insult to stand.

He had no interest in dying, though, and wouldn't allow his actions to endanger Tallis. He held his tongue and did as his host demanded. Kor stopped just short of the palanquin and raised both hands to show he meant no harm. "I'm no thief," he said. "I'm wandering in search of my next job."

Which, while not exactly the truth, was close enough to it that Kor didn't care. He didn't owe these people any explanation, and telling them he'd come to take the dragon blood crystals would only antagonize them.

"My eyes may not show me your face so clear, hunter, but my vision has shown me your path," the graveseeker's words fell out of her mouth with the rattle of pebbles tossed down a well. "You have come to this place in search of the blood of dragons, as have I. But you would twist it to serve you, where I seek only to free this mortal world from its toxic evil."

"I have no desire to cross you or your people," Kor said, "but you have no hope of retrieving those crystals without my help. They will be guarded by dangers you cannot comprehend."

Dragon blood crystals were only found in the corpses of dragons who'd died of natural causes. It was rare for intelligent dragons to pass on peacefully. Those who did were entombed by their followers, and those elaborate graves were as deadly as their inhabitants had been in life. Few could survive a trek into their depths, and fewer still would live to see the surface again.

"I have brought fine warriors with me," the crone said. "They are not abominations like you, but their skill and strength are without peer. And if they were adept enough to capture you, mighty hunter, surely they can succeed in this mission."

Kor's pulse quickened at the graveseeker's words. She was willing to throw away the lives of her people to secure those crystals. She'd have no qualms about killing him.

Or Tallis.

The hunter's mind raced to find a way out of this disaster. His knowledge of the Shindorans came mostly from anecdotes he'd heard from others in the Sainted Order. The graveseekers were the oldest and most experienced of the cultists. They believed it was the cult's destiny to purify deposits of dark ichor through their deaths, removing its evil from the world of mortals. If that was the case, then...

"I would not deprive you of your ascension," Kor said to the ancient woman. "Let me help your people retrieve the blood of dragons. My companion and I will leave you in peace, and you can join the next cycle of reincarnation."

The graveseeker looked up at the mountain peak. The milky layers that covered her eyes blinded the crone, but Kor knew she hadn't lied when she said her vision was clear. Whatever she saw gave her pause enough to consider the hunter's offer.

"I have been told not to trust your kind," she said quietly.

"And I've been told your kind are dangerous and mad," Kor said with a shrug. "But if you can do what you say, then I'll help you get the crystals."

"Why?" the crone asked.

"Because it's better than dying," the hunter replied. "Do we have a deal?"

The crone leaned back on her pile of pillows and gestured toward Miyka.

"We do," the Shindoran scout said. "Gods help us, we do."

* * *

Kor admired the way the scouts moved. Their keen eyes picked out the easiest path up the mountain's slope, and their bodies followed it without hesitation. It was the kind of efficiency and ruthless determination many strove for, but very few achieved. Keeping up with them was a struggle, but he did his best to learn from their performance, and encouraged Tallis to do the same.

"Follow in their footsteps," he said. "You'll learn a lot."

"They didn't kill us," his companion said, marveling at their survival.

"They've got more to gain by keeping us alive," Kor said, "for the moment. It'll get dangerous when we reach the crystals, though. We have to be ready to fight."

Miyka didn't treat Kor like a prisoner. His hands weren't bound, and she'd returned his weapons. That, more than anything, told the hunter she didn't consider him a threat. Maybe she was right. Outnumbered, far from civilization, Kor and Tallis were at the mercy of the Shindorans. Running or fighting would be pointless.

The scouts had ranged ahead of their new allies, and Kor spent the next hour working to make up the lost ground. Tallis had an even harder time keeping the pace. Her fingertips were bloody where she'd torn them on the mountain's sharp flanks, but she didn't complain. She was determined to prove herself to Kor and these strange new acquaintances.

She also worried about what they'd find in this dark crypt. During their journey, Kor had explained that dragon tombs were far more dangerous than anything she could imagine.

That didn't stop her mind from spinning dark visions in its corners. Dragon zombies rising up from moldering tombs with fangs dripping rot. Immortal servants drawing blades carved from ribs and bows shaped from femurs. Deep pits filled with gurgling orange lava that sent noxious fumes into the darkest corners of her thoughts.

Kor would fight any dangers that threatened them, she knew. He'd killed the Master, after all. And yet, she wondered whether he was up to this task. During their time on the road, she'd heard him coughing in his sleep, and she knew old wounds pained him during their walk. He *needed* these crystals, but the Shindorans wouldn't let him have them.

If she got a chance, Tallis silently promised the man who'd saved her life, she'd steal crystals for him.

It was the least she could do.

* * *

They spent the day hiking up the ancient mountain's slope. The terrain was treacherous, with washed-out gullies that could break an ankle hidden beneath the branches of low-lying shrubs and enough loose scree to make every step a gamble, but Kor was thankful they didn't have to climb.

As it was, the difficult terrain had them all grunting and gasping for air, and by the time the sun disappeared behind the mountain's bald peak, the Shindorans called for a break. Tough as they were, even they had limits.

Unfortunately, Kor couldn't let them give in to those limits.

"Can't stop here," he said, knuckling his lower back to see if he could get the angry muscles there to loosen up. "Too dangerous."

A young Delver, one eye closed by a puckered scar, scratched his bushy beard and shook his head. "You don't call the shots here,

Hunter. Miyka, tell this filth-eater we're stopped for the night. Someone will snap a leg trying to hike up this mountain in the dark."

The scouts' leader nodded her agreement. "Baz is right," she said. "It's too dangerous to go on."

The rest of the Shindorans nodded their agreement, but Kor wasn't about to give up so easily.

"Night will bring a lot of trouble the day has held at bay," he said. "Things can sense the treasure we're after. Dark things. They'll gather near the dragon's tomb. You really don't want them to find us sleeping."

Miyka strode up to Kor, only stopping when their chests bumped each other. This close, the hunter saw the fierce determination in her eyes and smelled the fire on her breath. "You don't make decisions for my people."

"Fine," Kor said, refusing to give an inch, "but you can't ask me to lay down on this little plateau and wait for death. Because that's what you're doing if we make camp here."

Miyka's nostrils flared at the challenge in the hunter's voice. She wasn't used to taking orders from anyone but the graveseeker who led her sect. Out here, her authority was second to none. Kor knew he might have to fight the woman and all her jumpy pals, but he didn't care. Stopping for the night would end with him and Tallis both dead.

"How do I know what you say is true?" she asked him.

"You don't," Kor said with a rueful grin, "but you know I'm a hunter well into his middle years. Think about what that means."

The scout grunted, then walked away from him. She paced back and forth away from the rest of her people and looked out at the coming night. Kor felt her indecision. She knew he was right—or should if she had a lick of sense in her head—but she'd also taken a stand against him. If she followed through on her orders to camp here, she'd lose some of her men to monsters, but if she gave in to the hunter, she might lose all of them to doubt regarding her ability to lead. It was a tough place for any commander to be in.

The hunter let his senses spread out around him, drawing information from his surroundings. He saw deep pockets of shadow beneath rocky outcroppings, smelled the too-sweet odor of rotting scraps of meat. There was a sound, too, faint, but still audible to one who knew how to listen. His years in the wilderness had taught Kor what all those meant. Maybe he could make Miyka's choice easier.

He moved in a blur, knowing his gambit could have dire consequences. His hand fell on the head of his axe, and he ripped it free of the loop on his belt. The haft fell into his hand, and he lunged forward, whipping his arm out ahead of him.

Two of the Shindorans saw him move, but they weren't fast enough to stop him. A third could only stare in wild-eyed horror as the hand axe tumbled end over end on a collision course with his head.

Before the Elf could react, the hand axe swept past their ear and vanished into the darkness of a boulder's shadow up the slope.

And then every weapon on that hill was aimed at Kor's head.

"What in the burning hell was that?" Miyka asked, her eyes blazing.

"A demonstration," Kor said, his eyes alive with dark humor. "Let me show you."

Miyka nodded, but none of the other scouts lowered their weapons. Kor had raised their hackles, and they weren't about to let him get away with another stunt like that. He kept his hands raised, showing them he meant no harm, as he retrieved his weapon from the darkness. A long, sinuous form emerged from the shadow along with the hand axe, which was buried in the creature's wide head. Kor held the legless lizard aloft, showing the others its spatulate head and heavily-scaled body.

"This is a rotdigger," he said. "It feeds on the things bigger monsters leave behind. It's here because the night-hunting beasts will come soon. It couldn't pass up a good meal."

Miyka narrowed her eyes with suspicion. Baz spoke before she could, though, just as Kor had hoped.

"I've never heard of a rotdigger," the grizzled Delver said, and spat on the ground at Kor's feet.

"Nor I," the Elf said.

"Kor's right," Miyka said, her mouth twisted into a moue of disgust. "We can't stay here."

The other Shindorans grumbled at that, but saw the logic in their leader's stance. They shouldered their packs again and followed her up the hill.

"I've never heard of a rotdigger, either," Tallis whispered as they brought up the rear.

"No one has," Kor said with a low chuckle.

From the darkness ahead of him, he imagined he saw Miyka turn back and offer him a grateful nod.

* * *

The early morning sun found the group paused before a narrow crack in the side of the mountain. Mounds of heavy stone lay on either side of it, and a boulder partially obscured the crevice.

"This can't be it," Miyka said. This time she'd decided to question Kor away from the other Shindorans. The hunter was grateful he didn't have to make up another excuse for her to back down when he proved her wrong.

It was easier for them both that way.

"It is," Kor insisted. "I can smell the dark ichor from here."

"You mean the dragon blood crystals," she corrected him.

"Whatever," Kor said. "It doesn't matter what we call them, they're in here."

"Doesn't look like a tomb," Miyka said.

"It looks like a very *old* tomb. Millennia of storms, snow, and sun have done their work."

"Why should I trust you?"

Kor didn't have a good answer for that. They weren't friends, they were borderline enemies. But there was one thing she knew to be true.

"If I'm lying, you'll kill me," the hunter said, "or at least try. And that will hurt my feelings."

He expected her to threaten him again or give him a snide comeback. Instead, her eyes softened, and Miyka met his steely gaze with eyes filled with compassion. "You've been doing this a very long time. It's taken a toll on your body, but more than that, your spirit is battered. There's a place for you with us when this is over. Find the dragon blood crystals, and the graveseeker will adopt you and Tallis."

"I doubt that very much," Kor said. "Our philosophies are like oil and water. Sooner or later, that mess will boil over, and we'll all be burned."

"Do you think I'm a fool?" she asked.

"If I did, I'd have tried escaping before now," Kor answered honestly.

"Then you should treat my words with more respect than to toss them into the dirt," Miyka replied. "Do you ever wonder what your life would be like if you fought *for* something, instead of always searching for the next creature to fight *against*?"

The words struck Kor in a vulnerable spot. He was so tired, they almost made sense, but they were heresy. His purpose was to find monsters and kill them, again and again and again, until his road ended.

"Think on it," Miyka said, "while you're leading us into this dragon's tomb."

* * *

"This place is impossible," Tallis said a half hour later. They'd made their way past the crumbling entrance of the dragon's tomb and found a place of wonders. The walls and ceiling were smoothly polished stone engraved with intricate designs that shed a flickering, fiery light. It was impossible to look too long at the engravings without becoming dizzy and losing all sense of time and place. More than once, Tallis and Kor had snapped each other back to their senses.

In stark contrast to the tomb's decorations, its architecture was simple and brutally straightforward. The entrance tunnel widened until ten men could walk abreast, then met a wide staircase that descended beneath the domed vault of a ceiling hidden in shadows. The stairs ended at a sheer cliff overlooking a bubbling sea of magma a hundred yards below.

A matching set of stairs climbed up from another cliff face five hundred yards away. The only path between them was a narrow obsidian bridge with no handrails. Kor's stomach did a slow roll at the sight of the path.

"Why did we stop?" Miyka asked as the Shindorans caught up to Kor. They'd let him roam farther ahead to check for traps, and he'd found a doozy.

"This is a good way to die," he said. "This is obviously a trap. We should take some time to find another way to the tomb."

"Can you sense the crystals?" Miyka asked.

"Yes," Kor admitted. "They're somewhere on the other side of this sea of fire, into which this bridge will dump us when we're halfway across."

Miyka chuckled and shook her head. "This is the way," she said. "The universe wants us to cleanse the stain of these crystals from its face. Have faith!"

And with that, she strode past him and onto the bridge. Baz hurried after her, and Kor found himself walking out onto the obsidian strand with Tallis on his heels.

"These people are insane," the former tavern owner grumbled. "By the bloody eyes, this is madness."

Kor wanted to agree, but found he couldn't say the words. The hunter had never had much use for the pretty sermons that spilled from the mouths of preachers. They were just words, most of them aimed at keeping the average peasant cowed and controlled by their churches.

But in the short time he'd spent with the Shindorans, he'd seen just the opposite. Miyka *believed* in her cult. She had real faith demonstrated through actions. Yes, they seemed insane, but he'd seen into the woman's eyes. She wasn't crazy.

She *believed*.

Must be nice, Kor thought to himself.

Baz called out for them to stop a few minutes after they began their crossing. An unpleasant odor, sharp and irritating to the nostrils, had spread its wings around them.

"Dragon's breath," Baz said. "A single spark will set it off."

"And then what happens?" Kor asked.

"You'll be dead before you see the light of its fire." Baz chuckled. "Look down there. See those black spots in the magma? Those are gas vents. Pass the word that as long as we can see them or smell the gas, no weapons."

An ugly predator's shriek echoed through the cavern a moment later. All eyes shot toward the ceiling, the clear source of that terrifying sound. Shadows, long and sinuous, writhed above them.

"Dragons," Miyka said, her voice tight.

Kor didn't want to believe her, but he'd come to the same conclusion.

"We can still go back," he said, though he knew it was a longshot. If the dragons decided to attack, they'd have to fight. Fighting would mean sparks. That would be the end of all of them.

"No we can't," Baz said. "Run!"

The vibrations from the group's stomping feet dislodged chips of stone from the edges of the bridge. Ominous creaking and grinding noises echoed from the cavern all around Kor's party. They heard the danger, but also knew they couldn't escape it. They couldn't stop until they reached the other side. The dragons could dive down from the ceiling at any moment.

Kor couldn't get his head around how dragons could have survived down here. They were far too large to fit through the crumbling passage he'd found. There had to be another way out, unless these creatures were fed through some magical means. And if that were the case, this tomb belonged to a dragon far more powerful than he could imagine.

He didn't have to worry about that long, though, before something more pressing made its way into his thoughts.

Shadows fell from the ceiling, and as they plummeted into the dome of light cast by the boiling earth beneath the bridge, they morphed into sleek, deadly shapes. Great, leathery wings battered the air, maws filled with ivory fangs the size of daggers yawned wide, and scaled tails cracked the air like whips.

The dragons were coming.

* * *

Kor, Tallis, and the Shindorans reached the far side of the lava sea mere heartbeats ahead of the bestial dragons. A low-ceilinged, narrower passage lay at the center of the heavily-engraved wall ahead of it. Massive black circles marred the pattern of runes and glyphs on the wall, raising a puzzle that Kor had no time to solve. He put all his effort into reaching the opening. If the group reached it before the dragons tore them apart, Kor was confident they could hold the flying beasts at bay.

It was their only chance at surviving this mess.

An ear-piercing scream from one of the pursuing dragons deafened Kor. The smell of its breath, hot and bloody as a steak fresh carved from a steer, made the hunter's heart skip a beat. The flyers were too fast. The runners would never reach the safety of the passage ahead before talons and fangs ripped them to shreds.

Wind from the dragon's beating wings blasted past Kor, and Tallis took a stumbling step ahead of him. Her feet skidded in opposite directions, the soles of her boots losing traction as her center of balance shifted forward. The dark-haired woman tried to lunge toward the passage—it was tantalizingly close—but slipped instead.

Kor's throat closed around a knot of worry. He couldn't breathe, he couldn't think of anything but getting Tallis back on her feet. He reached out to grab the back of her shirt. His fingers closed around the fabric, and he heaved.

Only to have something slam into his back. The unexpected blow sent Kor tumbling forward. He caught himself with one hand on the floor, and something hit him again, spinning him across the smooth stone like a rock skipped across a still lake.

He rolled back onto his feet as Tallis slid next to him and drew his hand axe. He spun to face his enemy.

The hunter cursed at what he saw. Two of the Shindorans had stopped to hold off the dragons, while two more of their number raced to reach the passage. Even as the last of Miyka's people reached the safety of the passage, the spearmen cried out.

The dragons tossed their bodies about like cats playing with mice. The screams of the dying rivaled the dragons' piercing shrieks.

"Do not let their sacrifice be in vain," Miyka said.

"Why did they throw their lives away?" Kor asked.

"For something greater than themselves," Miyka replied. "The graveseeker believed you were important to this mission. All of us would do the same if we must."

And with that, the Shindoran leader turned away and walked deeper into the tomb.

* * *

The smell of dark ichor clawed its way into Kor's thoughts. It was far more intense than any trace he'd ever caught wind of before, and it shook him to his bones. This much of the foul stuff could only have come from an enormously powerful dragon. One who had lived so long that the evil power within it had crystallized within its veins and organs as it died.

This was a treasure beyond imagining. He'd be a legend if he claimed it for the Sainted Order of Hunters.

But something about all this didn't seem right. The dragons who guarded the trove were young, hardly a hundred years old, judging by their size. They couldn't be the only defenses the dragon's followers had left to deal with intruders. There was something else waiting for them.

Kor knew it. And when they reached the golden doors that barred the passage ahead of them, he warned Miyka.

"There's something far more dangerous than young dragons behind that door," he said. "Let me go in first. The Curse will protect me."

Baz snorted a laugh at that. "You just want to get your hands on the crystals before us. Then you'll use your powers to tear us apart."

"Miyka," Kor said, "your people saved my life back there because your graveseeker knew I was important to this mission. Let me do this. Let me save you more grief."

The scouts' leader bowed her head, eyes closed. Kor heard the faint whispers of her prayers and turned away. Nothing he said would convince Miyka more than the guidance of her faith.

"I'm sorry," she said after long moments of introspection, "but I can't endanger our mission. It's too important for the graveseeker."

Kor raised his hands and stepped back. "I'll watch for any of those dragons squeezing their way down the passage."

Someone *did* need to watch for danger, but he honestly didn't want to see what would happen to Miyka when she opened those doors. And there was the dark ichor to consider. The smell had already driven him to distraction.

If he saw a pile of crystallized ichor...

Some temptations were too great, even for a hunter.

"You deserve those crystals," Tallis whispered to Kor, "at least some of them."

"Maybe," Kor said, "but we don't always get what we deserve."

A moment later, the heavy golden doors swung open with a sound like the grating of broken bones.

* * *

Curiosity got the better of Kor. The Shindorans sounded too damned excited for him not to look into the tomb.

He was shocked at the chamber's glorious excess. A massive golden throne, easily thirty feet high from the clawed feet at its base to the crown of daggers at its head, rested on a twenty-foot-high and hundred-foot-wide obsidian slab. Silken tapestries, their woven threads glimmering with ancient magic, cascaded from golden posts in the ceiling. Kor couldn't understand the glyphs stitched into their surfaces, but he felt their power just the same.

Power that belonged to the hulking skeleton seated upon the throne. The dragon whose tomb this was glowered down at the Shindorans who'd invaded its home, eye sockets like caverns in its polished skull. Heaps of treasure surrounded the dead thing, gold and silver coins, gemstones the size of apples, and, of course, a mound of dragon blood crystals as high as Kor was tall in its lap.

Two of the Shindorans had already clambered up into the dragon's bony lap to fill their packs with fistfuls of crystallized dark ichor. The purple-black glow of evil energy cast their faces in deep shadows.

"There's so much," Tallis said with a sigh. "They could share."

Kor agreed with his companion, but he knew the cultists wouldn't. The crystals represented much more than power to them. They were the graveseeker's salvation.

Maybe they were right to hoard the stones.

Maybe.

You know better than that, Hunter.

Kor's blood ran cold at the words that had invaded his thoughts. They echoed through his mind, rough-edged and ancient, and the hunter knew their source.

The skeletal dragon might not be as dead as they'd thought.

Or maybe he was just exhausted and giving in to the inner demons that haunted all men of violence.

A strange grinding noise reverberated through the tomb. It raised Kor's hackles and sent his hand reaching for his hand axe. He looked overhead, fully expecting to see the stone ceiling coming apart.

But what he'd heard wasn't stones.

It was *bones.*

The Shindorans were so excited to gather the hoard of crystals, they hadn't even noticed the bony wings flexing above them, or the dragon's fingers squeezing the arms of its golden throne.

Watch them die, Hunter. You're next.

"Miyka! Get out of there!" Kor shouted. He cursed to himself, knowing he should have been the one to go in there. He would have noticed the skeletal dragon before it was too late. He wouldn't have been blinded by zealous beliefs in something bigger than himself.

Greed blinds, too, the ancient voice taunted the hunter.

The scout's head whipped around at the alarm in the hunter's voice. Her arms were filled with jagged crystals, their unwholesome light filling her eyes and open mouth with deep, eerie shadows. "Not yet," she said, stuffing more of the precious material into her pack. "We need more for the graveseeker's ascendance."

"The skeleton!" Kor shouted. "Get out of there before it kills you all!"

The sounds of leathery wings slapping against the dark air sent prickles of dread running down Kor's back. The angry scream of a young dragon kicked his instincts into gear, and the hunter whirled to face the threat approaching from the lake of magma. To his shock, Kor saw that the stones of the tomb *were* shifting. The tunnel's ceiling had risen, and the walls expanded. Coruscating arcs of dark magic flashed through the air, reshaping the tomb to allow the dragons to reach its invaders.

This was bad. The hunter had no illusions about their ability to fight off the monstrous pile of bones at the tomb's heart. Adding what sounded like at least a half-dozen more dragons, even young ones, to the mix didn't improve their odds.

"Time's up," Kor shouted to the Shindorans. "We have to get out of here, now!"

"We can't leave this behind!" Miyka shouted back at him.

"It will do you no good if you're buried with it!" Kor hollered, angered at the Shindoran's lack of sense. He wanted the crystals, too—gods, how he wanted them—but there was no time to gather more. The only hope the Shindorans had, a slim hope at that, was to flee this place with whatever they carried.

But the hunter knew they wouldn't. They were zealots who believed their religion was more important than their lives. They'd sacrifice themselves to give their graveseeker her chance to ascend.

"They're here," Tallis said, her voice calm and steady.

The tunnel was wide enough for one of the dragons to make its way toward them, its wings folded flat along its back, its head lowered. Sparks of fire danced in the beast's gullet, but it wasn't old enough to bathe them all in gouts of fire. Kor was thankful for that small miracle, but he doubted it would be enough to tilt the odds in his favor.

"I'll hold them," the hunter said, unlimbering his short sword and hefting his hand axe. "Get those fool Shindorans out of that tomb before it's too late."

Tallis nodded, but Kor didn't have time to see if she'd follow his orders. He reached down into the darkest part of himself and activated the Hunter's Curse. The power raced along his tattoos, making his hair stand on end as Life and Line magic surrounded him. His skin hardened like iron, and his heart pounded with vitality that throbbed in his veins.

It was time to kill, or die trying.

Time slowed and lurched forward in erratic bursts as Kor's mind fell into the almost trance-like flow of battle. Conscious thought vanished beneath a red wave, his mind and body merging into the relentless killing machine that years of hunting monsters had created. He charged at the approaching dragon, weapons at the ready.

The beast, larger than its siblings and covered in midnight-black scales, roared a challenge. Its claw lashed out to tear Kor's guts from his body, but the hunter dodged to the side and countered with a brutal chop from his hand axe. The weapon's heavy head bit into the dragon's scales just above its wrist, fracturing the bone, and unleashing a sticky gout of scalding red blood.

The hunter followed his attack with a brutal thrust from his short sword. That weapon's broad blade slipped through the gap opened by his hand axe and found a cluster of nerves and blood vessels. With a savage twist of the blade, Kor ruptured the joint and crippled the beast's claw.

The dragon's head came around with a savage cry of pain and rage. Its moist breath blasted Kor, filling his head with the smell of the thing's last bloody meal. The hunter caught a glimpse of fabric caught between the dragon's teeth.

One of the Shindorans' cloaks.

A scream came from the tomb's innermost chamber, breaking the hunter's concentration. It was the sound of a man breathing his last, a warning that the ugly fight was about to get a lot worse.

A hellish roar followed the scream, a sound no living throat could make. The skeletal dragon was on the move.

Kor's wounded foe ducked its head and retreated, as if even its dumb mind understood the approaching danger.

But Kor wasn't done with the fight. He lunged forward and slammed his hand axe into the monster's face, splitting its snout and shattering a handful of teeth. Wounded and shocked by the attack, the dragon sprayed the hunter with a bloody roar and backed away as fast as it could on three good legs. The hunter wanted to pursue it, to end its life, but he knew it was pointless. The young dragon gushed blood, not dark ichor. Chasing it would only weaken Kor further. He had to turn his thoughts to escape.

And he believed he knew how they could all get out of there.

"Tallis! Miyka!" he bellowed. "To me. Now!"

The Shindorans emerged from the tomb, weighted down with packs heavy with crystals. There were only four of them now, each one covered in thick smears of gore. Kor couldn't tell who all that muck belonged to, and he didn't care. The cultists had known the dangers of coming to this place, and none of them had complained about the risk. Now they knew Kor hadn't been exaggerating.

The hunter stood beneath one of the black circles he'd spotted earlier. The tomb's twisting architecture had moved it into the tunnel, and he could now see that it wasn't just a disk of darkness. It was a hole.

He formed a saddle with his hands and nodded to Tallis. "Get up in that hole, girl, and crawl for all you're worth."

The former innkeeper nodded and put her foot in the hunter's hands. "It's awful dark. What if we get lost?"

"Keep climbing up," Kor said. "You should be a lot more frightened of the big fucker headed this way than the dark."

Tallis brushed the hunter's lips with hers, then let him hoist her into the darkness of the tunnel.

"Your turn, Miyka," he said.

"No," she said, her voice flat and emotionless. "Gondree, go."

Gondree, a tall man with a wicked rope of scar twisting the left side of his face into a perpetual sneer, hesitated for a moment. "You should—"

A long blade of bone lashed out of the darkness and silenced the man's protest forever. The dragon lich had emerged from its tomb, empty sockets burning with unearthly hatred of all things still living. Crystals rained from its yawning jaws, the last remnants of the blood that had once filled its enormous skull, feeding a brain that schemed greater evils than any man had ever imagined.

Kor wanted to slide under the thing's clashing fangs and snatch those crystals up. There were enough of them to make him one of the world's most powerful hunters. His name would live on in legend. His legacy would be complete.

But he knew that was a fool's thought. The skeletal dragon's massive talons would tear him to shreds and feed him to its younger kin. Treasure was no good if you weren't alive to put it to use.

"Fucking *go*"!" Kor shouted so loud his throat ached.

Miyka didn't hesitate this time. She hoisted the pack over her shoulders and jumped up, her foot landing easily in Kor's hands. The hunter thrust her up toward the hole with a grunt.

She was suddenly very, very light.

And the world had turned very, very red.

Miyka grunted with pain as she landed on her back, blood gushing from the stumps of her legs.

Too slow, Hunter. Your blood will slake my thirst when I have finished with these morsels.

The dragon's clawed wing had missed Kor's head by inches. "Shit," he cursed, falling to one knee to survey the damage, even though his instincts told him the Shindoran scout was dead, even if she didn't know it yet.

"Take it and go," she said, wrestling out of the pack and thrusting it toward the hunter.

Kor grabbed it, his eyes widening slightly at the extravagant gift. "Thank you."

"Swear you'll get it to the graveseeker," she panted through gritted teeth, face gone as pale as the dragon's bone that had done her in.

"Gods damn it," Kor grunted. "Fucking Shindorans."

The hunter wrenched the bag out of her hands and leaped up at the hole in the wall. He looked back once at Miyka, who'd levered herself up into a sitting position and drawn her bow horizontally in front of her. It was an awkward, stupid way to fight, but Kor knew the scout didn't hope to win. The last of her followers took up positions beside her, faces set into grim masks of determination. The Shindorans were buying him time to escape with the crystals for their graveseeker.

Then the hunter flung the bag up into the hole and scrambled up after it.

Seconds later, the screams of Shindorans and dragons mingled, and Kor told himself he couldn't hear the awful crunching and tearing as the beasts fed on Miyka.

It was a lie he would never quite believe.

* * *

The hunter climbed through the darkness for long minutes and caught a swift kick in the face for his troubles.

"Kor?" Tallis asked from a few feet ahead of him.

"I think so," the hunter replied. "Hard to tell with my brain bouncing around inside my skull."

"Sorry, I thought you were something else," Tallis whispered.

"You thought I was a dragon?" Kor asked. "That's a high compliment."

"No," Tallis said. "That's not—"

"It doesn't matter," Kor said. "Keep climbing. Those dragons will be after us soon."

"Did Miyka make it?" Tallis asked.

"No," the hunter answered in a voice as cold as the grave.

* * *

Light slowly infiltrated the winding tube of stone. The smooth-walled passage was big enough for Kor to crawl along it with Miyka's pack on his back, but he couldn't see much past Tallis. His back ached, and something inside him felt too warm and loose. The Curse's price had been paid, and it had been steep this time.

The thought of all those crystals poking him through the pack's thick canvas made his mouth water. He hadn't sworn to Miyka's ridiculous request. His honor would be clean, even if he stopped right there and gorged himself on the dark ichor the crystals contained. He needed to be healed. Surely he deserved that much after all he'd been through.

But that would mean stopping for the long minutes it would take for him to maneuver the pack off his shoulders, select a crystal, and break it down into ichor. There'd be time enough for that when they got to the surface. No need to endanger their whole trip by giving into gluttony here.

And was that the sound of claws against stone headed this way?

It certainly sounded like it.

"Faster," he croaked, throat dry. "The dragons are coming."

"Shit," Tallis said.

"Not right now, I'm behind you," Kor begged.

"This is not the time for jokes, you old goat," Tallis said, scrambling forward on her hands and knees.

"It wasn't a joke," he said, then coughed on the inhale.

There was a foul smell in the air.

Dragon's breath.

This day just kept getting better.

The light, Kor realized, came through narrow cracks in the tunnel's belly. Years of erosion and the traffic of dragon bodies had played havoc with the floor of the passage. As thin lines opened in the stone, light from the pool of lava far below made its way into the feeding tunnel. And with that light came deadly flammable gas.

If the dragons caught them in this tunnel, they were dead, either from tooth and claw, or from a desperate weapon strike kicking up sparks. The dragon's breath was so dense, it made Kor's head swim. It took all his concentration to keep moving, and his burning lungs screamed for him to stop.

Tallis was having much the same trouble, he realized. The young woman's pace had slowed, and he saw her long hair drooping alongside her sinking head.

"Move," he commanded, slapping her thigh hard enough to draw a yelp of pain.

"I *am*," she said.

"Then move faster," Kor said.

It took minutes for the gas to fade, and the dragons had fallen behind. He heard them back there, bickering amongst themselves like wolves arguing over a kill.

The light had faded, as well, and Kor realized the cracks in the floor had vanished. Clean, icy air had replaced it. They were close to the surface, but the lack of sunlight told Kor their salvation was far from assured.

He had to stop the dragons.

An idea flickered to life, and he grabbed Tallis by the belt.

"Oil," he said. "You said you've got lantern oil?"

"In my pack," she gasped and fumbled around with her gear to retrieve what Kor wanted. "Here."

She passed the ceramic bottle back between her legs, along with a flint and steel. "Thanks," Kor said.

"Don't kill us," she said, too exhausted to even laugh.

"No promises," the hunter replied.

He tore out the cork with his teeth and upended the heavy flask. Its contents gushed out with liquid gurgles, and Kor listened to it flow down the slope behind them.

His eyes burned as he struck sparks in the darkness. The flashes of light showed him the black trail of oil he'd poured out.

The oil caught on the third splash of light from the steel striking the flint. A tongue of flame raced away from Kor, a mesmerizing yellow-orange will o' wisp of doom.

"Go," Kor rasped, dropping the flint and steel to race after Tallis.

They hadn't gone far when the flame met the gas.

As they rounded a sharp corner and clambered up a natural stone chimney into the midday air, a fist of flame squeezed Kor's lungs. He smelled burning hair and pushed Tallis up and out of the tunnel, then scrambled after her. His skin felt too tight against his bones, and wisps of smoke rose before his eyes.

This isn't over, Hunter. My people will make you pay for what you've stolen.

* * *

"Where's my flint and steel?" Tallis asked.

Kor could barely hear her over the horrid ringing in his ears. He opened his eyes, then immediately closed them against the blinding sun. "Are we dead?"

"You wish," Tallis said. "I should kill you for losing my supplies. The Shindorans didn't make it?"

"They didn't," Kor confirmed. He sat up, squinted against the light, and surveyed his surroundings.

They were on the side of the great mountain, not quite halfway up its side. The hole they'd emerged from was shielded by a shadow from the massive rock outcropping above it. What wasn't hidden by the shadow was the black marks that radiated from the hole like long, ugly scars on the mountain's south face.

"Then you get the crystals," Tallis said.

"Not yet," Kor said. "We have some walking to do."

"No rest for the wicked," Tallis grumbled.

"Who say's I'm wicked?" Kor shouldered his pack and began walking.

"Wasn't talking about you," his companion added.

They both chuckled at that and made their way down the mountain, which began a very unpleasant rumbling before they reached its base. Sinkholes opened behind them, and the pair had to dodge more tumbling boulders than they liked. By the time they reached the mountain's base, long after dawn the next day, they were exhausted.

Not that the Shindorans who met them cared. They escorted Kor and Tallis to their leader, weapons held at the ready.

"You have the crystals?" The graveseeker asked the question without so much as a polite inquiry about the missing scouts.

"Your people paid a high price for these," Kor said, shrugging out of Miyka's pack.

"And it was worth ten times what it cost," the graveseeker said, her milky green eyes fixed on Kor's despite the fact that there was no possible way she could where he was looking.

"I doubt that," Kor shot back, too tired to give a single rat's ass about being polite. "Miyka was worth more than a bag of stones."

That brought a rumble of warning from the heavily-armed and -armored guards watching over the proceedings.

Kor knew they could ram those big, ugly spears right through his back before he could make a move. The Curse's price had left him without the strength for a serious fight.

But he just couldn't care. The hunter was sick of the rich and powerful ordering their people into hopeless situations.

The world had evolved to serve the whims of predators.

No, that wasn't the right word.

Parasites.

"They would disagree with you," the graveseeker said, sounding every bit as tired as Kor felt. "Miyka died doing what she'd sworn to do. Returning these crystals to me, that I might use them to cleanse evil from this world."

"You'll crush them up, then snort them up your nose," Kor said, nodding his head at the bag on the palanquin's foot. "Then you'll die. At least if I used them, I'd go on to fight monsters with my new strength. *That* would at least be useful."

"Ah, yes," the graveseeker said, "the mighty hunter. You know nothing."

"Then explain yourself."

Kor thought that might have been too much. He felt the spear tips press against his back. Then the graveseeker spoke.

"Imagine the evil in this world flows from its source like a river," she explained. "You stand on the river's banks, plucking leaves and twigs from the turbulent waters, and say that you are cleaning it. But most of the filth passes by your grasping hands. Insidious poisons find their way through your fingers to wipe out whole towns downstream."

"You don't know what you're talking about," he shot back. "I've saved more lives than you can count."

"You aren't listening." The graveseeker clucked her tongue. "Yes, these crystals would make your life easier—for a time. With them, you can find and kill bigger, deadlier monsters. You would save lives, yes. But for me, these crystals are tools to build, not destroy."

"You're not making any sense," Kor said.

"With these crystals, I will build a dam across the river of evil. When my work is complete, an entire stream of darkness will cease to be. You would stop a few leaks. I would empty the reservoir."

The hunter didn't believe a word the graveseeker said, but he didn't have to. Miyka had saved his life. He could honor her memory, even if it cost him.

"Take the fucking crystals," Kor said, and tossed the bloody pack onto the palanquin. "Do what you want with it."

The grave seeker ignored the outburst and gave Kor a deep smile. "Miyka died with a name on her lips."

"Yours, I'm sure."

"No," the graveseeker said. "Yours. She knew you would do the right thing. We both knew from the moment we saw you. You've done a hard thing today, Sainted Hunter Kor, and I will carry that knowledge with me into the next cycle. You will be rewarded for your valor in the life to come."

"Fuck off," Kor spat and left the Shindorans to their foolishness.

* * *

"What the hell was that?" Tallis asked.

"Duty," Kor said. "Honor."

"You didn't want to stick around and see if the graveseeker would ascend?" Tallis asked.

"No."

"But why?"

"By the Giants, you ask a lot of questions," Kor grumbled. "And the why is that it doesn't matter."

Tallis hurried to catch up to his longer strides. "It would be very nice to tell her corpse you told her so if she failed."

Kor sighed and draped his arm across Tallis' shoulders. "I've got nothing to gain by seeing her fail. Or succeed. My quest remains. My duty never ends. Their superstitions and foolish rituals can't change what I am, or what I do."

Tallis watched Kor from the side of her eye. He talked a big game about not caring about the Shindorans, but she'd seen the look on his face before. It was the grim countenance of a man wrestling with a simple question: What if my life is a lie?

"I have a surprise for you," she said in a conspiratorial whisper.

"Good," Kor said. "Today's my birthday."

"Is it?" she asked, surprised.

"I have no idea," Kor said. "It might be."

Tallis pulled a blue-back crystal from her pouch. "This fell out of your pack."

Kor chuckled. "I should bring this to the—"

"Happy birthday, Kor," she said, rolling her eyes. "Just take the fucking thing. You've earned it."

* * * * *

Sam Witt Bio

Sam Witt is an avid gamer, RPG designer, and author of horror and fantasy. When not adding tales to the *Eldros Legacy*, he spends way too much time attempting to smoke the perfect brisket.

* * * * *

Of Claws and Men
by Mel Todd
A Small Magics Universe Story

"I'm sorry. What did you say?" I looked at the phone, sure I must have misunderstood. Karen Bigsby was the local vet, pretty enough to be way out of my league, but I'd been trying to work up the courage to ask her out. In theory, a Beast Whisperer and a veterinarian should be the perfect team.

My life rarely worked as theory said it should.

"I need you. Can you get to my office in the next ten minutes?"

My mind blanked, then raced into unrealistic trains of thought. I had to pinch myself to stop the daydreams and let reality in. There was a possibility I'd been single too long.

"Sure. I'll head over right now."

"Thanks, Jonah." She hung up, and I sat there, dead air in my ear, until I put the phone back in its cradle.

I gazed out the frosted glass of my door, trying to think of why she might need me. To my dismay, all the reasons were obvious, mundane, and would in no way create the possibility of a date to come. Odds were, she needed me to talk to an animal that was in pain. Snorting to myself about my own stupidity, I grabbed my keys and headed out. If she wanted me there in ten minutes, I needed to get moving.

My trusty Mercury Bobcat waited for me. While it would never win any style awards, the Champagne Sparkle finish made me smile every time. I jumped in, slipped in my favorite cassette—Queen—and drove toward the clinic. The news had been playing in my office—you never knew when you'd get a tidbit about a job—and it had been chattering about a small Airstream that had been wrecked, possibly in a bear attack. Which meant I might get called to find the bear. Anyone who kept food in a camper they left near the woods got what they deserved, as far as I was concerned. Though I would have loved to own one of those rich-people Airstreams.

But for now, I needed a mind cleanser, and Queen did that wonderfully.

It took me eight minutes to get to the other side of town and pull into the parking lot of Animals First vet clinic. I climbed out of my car, patting my Bobcat on her hood, and walked inside.

The receptionist, a teenager who looked vaguely familiar—when you grew up in a small town, everyone was someone's kid—nodded at me. "Mr. Moby, Dr. Bigsby is waiting for you. Straight back and you'll see her office." She waved down the hall, and I nodded, following her guidance.

It had been a long time since I'd been here. Oddly, I didn't have pets. I like animals, obviously, but I'd learned that being able to hear a dog talk was exhausting. Other types weren't much better; reptiles complained about the temperature nonstop, cats were mercurial in their temperament switches, and birds were vainer than beauty queens. It was easier not to have one. A pet rock was pretty nice, though.

I could hear the chatter of animals around me, mostly variations of "I wanna go home" and "Ow, ow, ow." I'd grown tense by the time I reached Karen's office. The door was slightly ajar, and I knocked gently.

"It's open," she snapped.

That got a raised eyebrow as I pushed it open. She lifted her head to look at me and blushed. "Sorry. It's been a day. Come in and tell me what you think of this. I have no idea what to do with it, or what I *should* do with it."

I took a minute to enjoy the flush on her face. Her dirty blonde hair was up in a ponytail, and she looked even prettier than the last time I'd seen her. I really needed to learn how to ask women out, but my track record sucked. My ex-wife was proof of that. My eyes followed her hand gesture to the object on the desk, the one she'd been studying when I stepped in.

It took me a minute to realize what I was seeing. It was shiny black, almost like obsidian, curved and coming to a point like any raptor's claws. There was a jagged, flat edge at the end where it had obviously been broken off, but the size of it made it almost impossible for me to verify what I was seeing. One of the largest birds on earth, a Roc, might have a talon as big as my hand—maybe. This was the size of my *forearm*, and about as thick.

"Huh. A dragon claw." The words came out of my mouth, and Karen stared at me.

"Dragons are real?"

I started to say no, then stopped, staring at the claw. "I guess so?" It came out as a question, and I prodded at my mind and magic, confused.

"Wait, if you don't know dragons are real, how do you know this is a dragon claw?"

I rubbed the back of my neck. "It's part of my magic. I know what type of animal it is. It has to do with knowing how to talk to them." I looked up to see her eyes light up, and I held up my hand. "Stop, before you get too excited. It means I can look at fur and tell you wolf, boxer, or even Lab, but I can't tell you which animal, or if it's a purebred. Sometimes my answer is just dog. And it has to be enough hair, or something recognizable. A bone won't do it; a skull will. It's a weird balance between what magic will tell me and what it won't. But apparently that was enough to tell me dragon."

"Oh." She sagged a little. "I got excited there for a minute. But still, dragon? That's incredible." There was the same excitement in her eyes horse girls got when you talked about horses. I'd had a lot of girls pay me to come out to talk to their horses over the years, and they all had the same look in their eyes: hope, excitement, and elation at getting to hear what their best friend thought.

They were *always* disappointed.

"I wouldn't get excited quite yet," I cautioned, my eyes locked on the base of the claw. Or was it a talon? I wasn't sure about dragon anatomy.

"Why not? This is huge. People have been searching for proof of dragons for years." She looked like she wanted to jump up and go dragon seeking this very minute. It was cute.

"True, which is why I'd either get rid of or hide that talon," I said.

She all but hugged it to her chest. "What? Why?" A flicker of betrayal flashed across her features as she gazed at proof of living dragons.

The beginnings of a headache pounded at the back of my skull, and I really wanted a hot shower to beat away the tightness that formed from the domino effects I could see coming. "One, per myth and legend, dragons are intelligent, vicious, and more than a bit cranky and territorial. They treat people as walking snacks."

Karen waved that away. "So are tigers and barghests. They still don't eat people."

"On a regular basis," I countered. "Neither of them are the size of a house, nor do they have the ability to read, and they aren't known for collecting treasure." I held up my hand before she could protest, and she sighed, waiting for the rest. "And this particular dragon is freshly missing a claw, and is likely to be enraged, hurting, and more than a bit snappish. I don't know about you, but finding out exactly what a dragon in a snappish mood is like doesn't sound good for my continued health."

Karen glanced down at the weapon on her desk. Tied to a wooden handle, it could have been a very effective melee weapon. I reached over and gently lifted it. It had to weight about five pounds.

"I think the average reptile has claws weighing what, maybe 1/500th of its body weight?" I'd spent way too much time watching Mutual of Omaha's Wild Kingdom specials.

She shrugged. "I guess. Not sure I've ever weighed one and done the calculations."

"Let's assume I'm correct. This weighs about five pounds. That means the dragon itself could weigh…" I floundered, trying to do the math in my head, but the answer popped up. "It would be about 2,500 pounds," I said, and Karen gaped at me. "What? I'm pretty sure the math is right."

Karen frowned, then nodded. "Yeah. Um. Any chance this is a hoax?"

I shrugged. "You're the vet. Is that fresh blood on the base? Does it look real? I can't swear it isn't a dragon claw from long ago. My magic doesn't work like that." I didn't mention that I doubted it was a hoax. My magic didn't hit as strongly with fossils, at least not normally. "Besides, would you have called me out here for a hoax?"

She frowned. "I don't know whether I wanted you to tell me it was a hoax or not. Maybe I wanted to lie to myself." She started to say something else when a tech knocked on the door.

"Doc? Your patient has been waiting for five minutes."

Karen shot a look at the clock, then growled. "We've been talking longer than I thought. Tell Mrs. Simpson I'll be there in a minute, please?" The tech nodded and left, shutting the door behind her.

I didn't want to stop talking to her, but I understood work and prior commitments. I stood as she did. "Let me know if there's anything else I can do to help."

"Thanks. Right now, any clue what I should do with it?" We both stopped to look at the item on the desk, all but glowing with mystery.

"How did you get it?" Somehow, I didn't think she'd found it laying outside.

She groaned a bit. "That's a long story. Levi Joseph, outside of town. He's got that herd of goats, does the artisan goat cheese?"

I nodded. It was good goat cheese, if not something I wanted daily.

"He said two of his goats had broken out and gotten hurt. Slashes on their backs. I stopped by to take a look, but they weren't too bad. He showed me the fence, muttering about the goats. I found it over near the broken fence. But I didn't have time to do much besides verify the goats would be fine before I had to be here."

I tried to think of where Levi had his farm, but I couldn't place it. I'd have to go look at the territory, maybe talk to the goats. But if the goats said dragon, it would become a lot more serious.

"I wouldn't talk about it, but you know it'll get out." Rubbing the back of my neck, I blurted, "If you tell me where it was found, I could go take a look around. See if any of the animals saw anything."

"Ooh!" Her eyes lit up again, and I fought back a smile. Horse girls were crazy. They might always be disappointed, but their passion could never be denied. Looked like Karen was a dragon girl. "You free tomorrow? Then we could both go? That way maybe I could watch you work?"

I shrugged, trying not to dance with excitement in the office. It wasn't a date, but if you squinted hard and I didn't screw up, maybe it could become one.

"Sure. I don't have any jobs tomorrow. But watching me work is like watching me talk to an animal." That was another issue, but work had been better since Sheriff McAlister had mentioned my assistance to a few people. Even Karen had used me once or twice, but really, no one wants to know what a parrot's thinking. Trust me on that.

"Excellent. Meet me here at ten tomorrow? Wear hiking clothes."

I nodded agreeably. Hiking clothes I had. If she'd said a suit, there might have been a major issue.

I said my goodbyes and headed back to my house. The answering machine could catch any calls. I needed to research dragons and maybe call a few other Whisperers.

* * *

I met her at nine AM the next morning, my convenience store coffee in hand, and an extra one on the seat in case she needed it. I pulled my Bobcat into the parking lot with a purr, and I narrowed my eyes. Either my carburetor was having issues, or the car was developing a personality. Either would be problematic.

None of the two Whisperers who'd answered the phone had anything to say on dragons. The one I really wanted to talk to, a guy named Doolittle, didn't take calls from random Whisperers. And I still say he changed his name to Doolittle. No one gets that lucky with their magic type.

Karen stood outside, leaning against her Datsun Maxima, wrapped in a puffy pink jacket. I tilted my head, getting out, looking at it. Karen didn't strike me as the pink type.

"Don't ask. It's my sister's. She left it, and unfortunately, it's warmer than most of my other stuff. Plus, it seems to be impervious to anything and everything."

"Ah." That seemed a safe answer. "Coffee?"

She wrinkled her nose, and a pang of betrayal flashed through me. "Nope. I'm a morning tea person. But I'm good. We taking your car or mine?"

I tried to look on the bright side. She might not drink coffee, but that meant I had two cups for me. Her Datsun glowed bright orange in the morning light. "Your call."

She cast an evil eye at the coffee I protectively held. "Mine. I've got vet stuff in the back. Might come in useful. And I grabbed this." She turned and picked the claw up from her front seat. It glittered in the morning light, like an omen of things to come. I wasn't sure if they were good or bad things though.

"Sure." I locked up the Bobcat, grabbed both cups of coffee and my backpack, and headed to the passenger side of her car. I slipped in and buckled up. You never could tell how wild a driver someone was. Her car was neat, if worn, and the faintest hint of iodine tickled my nostrils.

She smiled a bit at my buckling up, but I focused on my coffee. The Datsun started right up, and a minute later, we were pulling out of the lot and headed to the foothills.

I watched the scenery go by. It had been a while since I'd been a passenger out this direction, and it was nice to get a chance to pay attention to what had changed.

"You like talking to animals?"

I turned to look at her, jarred from my quiet, contemplative state. "Like? Do you *like* healing them with your own magic?"

She pondered the question, then nodded slowly. "I do. I still had to go to school for it, but it does make it easier. I still need to do surgeries and give vaccines, but small things like cuts and broken bones are much more easily dealt with. Cancer or diseases, my gift doesn't help as much." She didn't look at me as she said that, but I understood.

In the world of magic, everything was judged by how others saw your magic. Mine was treated as useless by most big companies and the government, so it was a "small" magic. In common parlance, magic was small if it couldn't create or change. My ex could change metal, multiple types, and therefore she had "big" magic. My magic just let me talk to animals, it didn't "*do*" anything—hence, small magic.

Karen was a healer—always big magic, even if limited to animals—but if she could only do physical wounds, not cure cancers or infections, the demand for her would be lower. Healers who could do that had multi-million-dollar practices or worked with horse racing teams. But still, anyone with a healing skill was usually prized.

"Still, healers are rare. Why are you out here in the middle of BFE?"

She gave a quick chuckle at my acronym for bum-effing nowhere, but didn't answer my question. The car slowed and turned onto a gravel road I barely recognized. The sign at the entrance declaring "Joseph's Ranch of Many Goats" solidified the memory.

"Oh, yeah, he paints their coats on Easter, doesn't he?" A vague image of goats in pink, blue, and green swirls pranced through my mind.

"That would be him. I called him. He said it's fine for us to explore, just don't upset the goats. There are a few that are heavy milk producers."

I quirked a look at that, but she didn't elaborate. She brought the Datsun to a stop near one of the larger barns. "We need to hike around it and up the hill a bit."

I swapped to my fresh cup of coffee, glad of the heat. Late September mornings could be downright brisk. Karen set off at a steady pace, and I mourned the loss of the opportunity to ogle, as the pink monstrosity covered her almost to her knees. I pushed away my baser desires and paid attention to where she led me. The barn was actually a very large shed more so than a barn. It stood only a single story, and I suspected it provided shelter and food for the goats. The larger building looked more like where the cheese business was done.

Levi had a good portion of his land fenced in, and it took us five minutes to walk up to where the fence had been repaired. The shine of the metal and unweathered wood told me it was new.

"I found it here." She pointed to two rocks. "It was jammed in, but fell out when I looked at it closer and tugged. Which, now that I think about it, makes no sense."

I went over to look at the rocks. Two pieces of granite rooted up through the mountains towering over us with a crevasse between them. I could see scratch marks in the granite. But Karen was right. Anything strong enough to rip the claw off a dragon should have made it like Excalibur for the unworthy when it was pulled out.

I fought a smile at the image of Karen lifting the claw into the sky and declaring herself vet to the dragons.

"What?" I looked up to see Karen staring at me, her brows pinched together.

"Nothing. You're right, this wouldn't have been tight enough to break off a claw that size. At least, I'm assuming it would be about as hard as tearing a nail off of my hand." I diverted her train of thought. I didn't know yet if she would find the image amusing. Another thing to figure out.

"Harder, actually. They have more tendons in that area than we have holding our nails to our fingers." She looked at her hands while she spoke—short nails, clean, good hands. "Yeah, it would take a really hard jerk to break that off. And before it did, it would hurt like the dickens."

I looked back at the fence, and there was a line of goats, all staring at us. As far as I could remember, I'd never talked to a goat. First time for everything, I guess. I braced myself on the fence, peering over at the goats, mostly white with spots of brown or black.

"Did you see anything when your herd was attacked?" They flicked ears at me and moved closer.

Whisperer.

The lead one spoke. Horizontal pupils stared at me as the head tilted. I waited. Every animal reacted differently, and intelligence varied. I still thought it was part of my magic that gave them anything approaching words, but small magic wasn't worth researching.

Healer. Good healer. Saw. Wings, claws, hunger, pain. Clumsy kid, deadly kid.

I leaned back, translating that in my head. "The thing that attacked you was already hurt?"

Wounded. Pain. Hunger. Saw herd food. Food?

"Sorry. I don't have anything, but I'll ask Levi for some treats. Was it a dragon?"

Treats. Treats.

The five that had been watching me turned and trotted back to the barn, leaving us standing there.

"Well? Did they see a dragon?"

"Don't know. They saw something with wings and claws that was already hurt." I puzzled over the words. "I think it was young, or acted young. They called it a 'kid.' That's a baby goat, right?"

"Yes. Huh. Interesting." She turned and looked up the mountain. "Want to go exploring?"

I followed her gaze up the Cascades. The foothills here were covered with trees and shrubs, with granite boulders everywhere. But as you moved higher, the trees and shrubs faded quickly, leaving spires of unforgiving granite.

"Fine, but we only look for three hours, and then head back. If we do anything more than that, we need proper supplies, and to let people know where we're going up."

Karen nodded. Only idiots just wandered out into the mountains. "I've got basic supplies back in the car. Enough for a few hours."

Part of me relaxed. Looking for dragons was one thing; hiking up here without proper supplies was something else. "I've got some basics in my pack, too, though I'd like more. At least some water and food before we set out," I cautioned. Maybe it was that I'd talked to way too many animals that had snacked on dead humans. I'd rather be safe than sorry.

She flashed me smile. "Great minds think alike. Let's go talk to Levi."

"Absolutely. See what we have, and then if we need anything extra, we can ask him."

We headed back down and spent an hour talking to Levi. He hadn't seen or heard anything. He'd just found the wounded goats and the torn-up fence. When we were done, we dug canteens out of her trunk and filled them. He gave us a few apples and said he'd raise the alarm if we didn't come back before dark.

Karen had some jerky and granola bars stashed in her trunk, as well as medical supplies, a rope, backpack, and more stuff than I had in my garage.

"Is this normal?" I stared at her trunk, a bit in awe, a bit perplexed.

"For a vet in the country, yeah. I really need a truck with a good toolbox, but honestly, my trunk holds more, is better organized, and doesn't get wet." She shrugged and handed me stuff.

"I get the canteens. Why the granola?"

"Some calls are long, and if I'm starving, I get a bit snappish," Karen admitted, not looking at me.

"Noted. You start chewing on me, I feed you."

Her laughter lit up her face as she finished putting stuff in the backpack. "That would be wise. I think we're ready." She put the claw in her backpack. Just in case.

Levi waved as we headed out, the goats surrounding him, eating the treats I'd promised. He'd offered us a rifle, but while I could use it, hunting was too hard for me. I ate meat, but I preferred to let someone else deal with the killing. Karen just shook her head at the offer.

We didn't talk much once we reached the fence. The repair work was obviously a stopgap until he could get the supplies up there. The walk quickly turned into a hike, and we stayed quiet, partially because I really needed to exercise more, but mostly to listen to the environment. I didn't want to ignore any warnings that might be available from the animals.

It was a beautiful late fall day. The crunch of our feet through needles and leaves made it sound like a herd of second graders were tramping along with us.

"Jonah, look at this." Karen motioned me over to some rocks jutting out of ground, remnants from the last ice age. There on one of the outcroppings were scratches and a streak of dried blood.

"Goat got hurt two days ago?"

Karen nodded, staring at the markings. "You really think it's a dragon?"

I wanted to respond again that dragons weren't real, but that claw, talon, whatever, had screamed dragon to my magic. I had a sudden desire to go to the museum of natural history and see if any bones were mislabeled.

"No clue. Maybe my imagination is affecting my magic?" I brushed off the idea and kept walking. We'd gone about another half hour, the trees becoming scragglier and rocks more common, when I stopped, holding my hand up to stop Karen.

"What is it?"

I held my finger up to my lips and turned in a slow circle. The animals around us had gone silent. Unless I paid attention, animals were background music, birds tweeting, "like me, like me," or "food,

food, food." I ignored it ninety percent of the time. But the noise from the various animals had vanished.

Karen gazed at me as I pivoted, looking for something, anything, that would freak all the animals out enough they were silent. In my experience, animals were only silent when they were scared or killing mad.

Rocks, mountains, bush, tent, trees, bare dirt, met my eyes as I scanned. Then I jerked my attention back to the tent. I'd cataloged it as a dome pup tent, but it moved, and I realized the green of the tent was wrong. Those looked like scales.

My throat went dry as I realized we were about thirty yards from something large and scaly. I still struggled with the reality of a dragon, though. I raised my hand and pointed at the body. Karen followed where I pointed and gasped.

"Holy moly." Her voice was a reverent whisper.

We stood there staring at the rising and falling green scales.

"So, is it a dragon?" Karen whispered to me as we stood there, frozen.

I opened my mouth to ask how I was supposed to know, but the answer popped out. "Yep, it's a dragon."

"So cool." She was almost giddy. "A dragon!"

The reality of it finally began to seep into my brain. "Maybe we should leave. We found the dragon. I'm not sure we're prepared to deal with a dragon."

Her face sagged along with her shoulders. "Why are you always so logical?"

"Sheer terror and very little faith that anything that big won't think we're food." Though if what we were seeing was the back of the dragon, it might only be the size of a large elephant, maybe not even that big. My mind spun, trying to deal with the reality of a dragon as we backed up. A resounding *crack* shattered our fraught silence.

I jerked my head to stare at Karen, who stared at the stick that had snapped under her feet with a look of sheer betrayal. "Stupid branches."

A low groan filled the air, and my eyes locked on the hump of scales and skin as it rippled, then moved. My heart leapt as I stared, unsure if it was excitement or fear, as a long, snake-like neck rose above the boulders, stared at the two of us, and burped.

I gagged as a wave of foul-smelling air wafted our direction, and the creature whined.

My stomach hurts. Make it stop.

It came out as hissing and whining, but I had no problem understanding it.

Karen looked at me, her face pale. Apparently the dragon fever had worn off. "Do we need to run?"

"No. I think it's hurt or sick," I said, moving a bit closer to look at it. The dragon groaned and dropped its head back on the ground.

"Hurt?" she asked, the reverence gone from her voice. "Where?"

"Stomach. Sounds bad." Even *I* knew if a predator didn't react, it was really sick.

Before I could say anything else, she'd raced forward and was scrambling over the rocks.

"Karen!" My heart lodged in my throat as I stared at her.

"Get over here. I need you to help me figure out what's wrong," she snapped out in a brisk command, then her voice completely changed. Rather than the drill sergeant it had been, it was calming, almost hypnotic. "It's okay. I'm here to help. Relax. I know it hurts, but I need to figure out where."

I scrambled over the rocks toward her and skidded to a stop as I took in the sight. I'd been right about the elephant size; African, not Indian. It lay on its side, belly oddly swollen.

"Does it hurt when I press here?" She continued talking in that same soothing voice as she cocked her head at me, jerking it toward the dragon.

"Healer. Will help. Tell her where." I moved closer to the dragon, though still hopefully out of the range of its teeth.

Healer?

The dragon lifted his head, snarling. I jerked back, ready to grab her, then I realized he was moaning.

Hurts. There. Swollen. Hurts.

Karen carefully manipulated his belly. "Did you eat something? When's the last time you... pooped?"

I shot her a funny look, and she made a face at me. "I don't know what dragons call going to the bathroom; do you?"

"Never thought about it before," I muttered back, though now I couldn't stop wondering what different animals called poop.

Days since scat. Hurts. Ate the wrong thing. Shiny thing, not good.

The moans were clear even as the dragon lay there, almost panting.

"Oh, this isn't good. There's a laceration in the lower intestine." She had her hand over his lower body, eyes closed. "If dragon anatomy follows most mammals—and yes, I think it's a mammal the same way a platypus is—it's near the sphincter. I think the blockage is at the point where the wound is, too. I can heal it, but not until I make sure there isn't anything in the wound." She chewed on her lip as she used her magic on the dragon.

It was adorable.

"Blockages in animals are dangerous. If we don't help him, it could kill him." Karen had a frantic but determined look about her, and there was a small part of me—the part that had been so relieved when Elizabeth had divorced me—that wanted to run. But the rest of me wanted to see what she would do.

"Okay. How do we help?"

She stood looking around. "Dang it. I don't have my full kit with me. Which means I don't have access to anything that would let me look and see where the injury is. I guess I'm going to do this the *very* hard way." Karen set her lips and looked unaccountably grim. "But first I need to see if I can verify where and what the blockage is. If we're lucky, it is just a clump of shit. If we aren't... well." She shrugged.

A pang of worry flashed through me. "What does that mean? You aren't going to operate or anything, are you?"

"Out here? I mean, if it had been a broken bone or wound, maybe, but this? No, this is going to be the *hard* way. And I'm really hoping a dragon's intestinal system is relatively standard. At least at the back end. But until I figure it out..." She shrugged.

I blinked. "'Back end?' What are you planning on doing?"

Karen rummaged in her backpack and pulling on a pair of gloves as she shucked off the pink puffy jacket. "I can tell the wound is about ten inches in. I should be able to reach in and feel it. If it's a simple cut or tear, I can heal it. But I suspect whatever's piercing his intestines is causing the blockage. If I remove the item, it should break the blockage. Since it's relatively close to the sphincter, a bit of water and prodding should loosen it up."

It took me a minute to process that. "Wait. You're going to stick your *hand* up a dragon's *ass*?"

Dying, so much pain.

"That's generally where shit comes out, so yes." She seemed so matter-of-fact about it. I cast my mind back to diaper changing days with my son and took a deep breath. If I managed to deal with shit coming out of a tiny human body when Paul was a baby, surely I could deal with it coming out of a dragon.

"How can I help?" The words weren't even forced, which vaguely surprised me.

In response, Karen handed me gloves. "Just in case. You keep talking to him, tell him what we're doing, and for god's sake, let me know if he's about to bite our heads off. This will hurt, but if I don't do it, he'll probably die."

"He?" I asked, glancing at her, as I didn't see any obvious evidence.

Karen gave me a grin. "Only a man would be complaining this much."

I mock flinched at the blow and went over to help her. She started talking, and I translated as we went.

"The healer says you have a wound and blockage where you go poop. She's going to try to loosen it up so you can relieve the pressure. It might feel uncomfortable. Can you let us do that?"

Yes. It hurts. Won't hurt healer. Hurts so bad. Dying. She can kill me. Pain will stop.

"You're not dying. She'll make you better." I really hoped the "won't hurt healer" included me.

The dragon just moaned again, a sound that vibrated through my bones. Meanwhile, Karen had stripped just to her undershirt and was digging through her bag. "Do you have any oil or lotion?"

"Umm…" I pulled open my bag and looked. "All I have is some petroleum jelly. I keep it in there for various reasons." It was a standard for wounds and chapped lips, but you never knew when you could use it.

"Perfect." She grabbed it and pulled off her shirt, leaving her standing there in just her white bra. I forced myself not to stare as she slathered it up her arm, using the majority of it. "You'll need more. Sorry."

I nodded, keeping my mouth shut. "Now what?"

"Now I stick my hand up his butt and see if I can find out what's going on."

My breath shuddered out, but I kept my voice even as I spoke to the dragon. "Healer is going to help. She is going to have to go up your... umm... your butt to help you." Never in my life had I thought I'd be telling anyone a woman was about to stick her arm up their rectum, much less a dragon.

There was no response, just a moan. I looked at Karen and shrugged. "He's as ready as he's going to get, I think."

She took a deep breath. "Come over here and hold the tail out of the way." I followed her instructions and watched in awe as Karen slid her hand up into the dragon, keeping up a steady patter that I translated.

As the dragon was laying down, it wasn't a struggle for her arm to fit, even if it was more than a bit gross. "Okay, the wound should be right here," she said, her eyes closed as she concentrated. "What in the world?"

"What? What's wrong?" I looked anxiously at the dragon, who was moaning more now, the tail thrashing a little, but luckily not toward us, yet.

"I found something stuck—a knife, maybe? Tell him this is going to hurt for just a minute, but I'll heal it."

I translated that, but the dragon just whined in response. "Go for it. No promises."

She glanced at me, and her body moved. The dragon screamed, a loud, long sound that threatened to shatter eardrums and cause heart attacks. My heart thumped so hard I couldn't breathe.

"It's okay. I got it. It's all over. It's healed. Let me pull it out." She slid her arm out, brown and red goo coating it. As her hand cleared his body, I focused on the butcher knife in her hand.

"What in the world?" I moved my attention to the dragon. "Dragon, what did you eat?"

Shiny. Smelled good. Crunchy. Upset my stomach.

It took me a minute. "I think he ate a camper."

"What?"

"That Airstream that was destroyed. I think he ate it." We both looked at the knife in her hand.

"That might explain this. I'm going back in. I need to see if I can dislodge the rest of it." She laid her hand on the dragon and closed her eyes. "I don't sense any other wounds, internal or otherwise. Hopefully it's just impacted at this point and needs to be broken up." Karen flashed me a smile. "Once more into the breech."

I let the dragon know as Karen slid her arm back in. "Got it. Breaking it apart now."

"You'll feel better in a bit."

Dying. I know it. Hurts so bad.

"Just a few minutes," I said, hoping I wasn't lying. From what I remembered, Paul had always felt better immediately after filling his diaper.

Not dying?

"Not dying," I reassured him.

"Got it. It's solid, but dry. Let me break it up, then we need to get some water into him. I don't suppose you have any booze with you?"

"That's not one of my normal supplies, no. Just the water and Tang."

"Predator. Not sure Tang would be up his alley." As we talked, she pulled out handful after handful of clumped matter. It had little bits of silver sparkling out of it.

"I think that's it," she said. "Now he just needs to push. I'm going to dump the water down his throat. Can you ask him to try to go? If he pushes and it comes out, it shouldn't hurt anymore." Karen had pulled her arm out and wiped it off with a handful of pine needles.

"Will do. I have a spare t-shirt in my bag; you can use that with some of the extra water to clean your arm off a bit more." That t-shirt I would then toss in the trash. Who would want something covered with dragon shit?

"Let's get him taken care of first. Then I'll do that." She looked at her arm and torso. "Though I'm not sure how I'm going to get clean without a shower." Shaking her head, she moved up to the front of the dragon, grabbing the canteen. "Let him know."

"Healer needs you to drink water. Then try to poop."

Poop? Water?

I peered around and saw Karen dumping the water down the dragons throat.

"Yes, try hard to poop," I told him.

"Jonah, you still back there?" she asked.

"Yeah, I don't see any blood or anything." I figured she was worried about that; there'd been blood mixed with the stuff on her arms. I'd be worried if there was blood leaking out of my butt.

Dragons looked odd from this angle. I guess, like many reptiles, all their sex bits were tucked up inside. That meant you had a tail, an asshole, and then smooth skin. It was oddly creepy.

"Oh, good. But you might want to move out of the way." I could hear her, but couldn't see her. Did she need me up there?

"Huh?"

Pushing.

There was an odd, rumbly sound, and a rush of gas that made me gag. I bent over, coughing, ready to move out of range of the toxic fumes. I stood up, taking a gas-free breath. I gasped in the fresh air, my eyes watering and nose running.

Oh, it moved.

I heard the sounds and translated them into words just as a wall of hot, wet, putrid shit hit me full on. My feet slipped out from under me as the flood just kept coming. I tucked my head into my arms, trying to protect my mouth and nose, and held my breath. Laying on the ground, I curled into a fetal position as the shit covered me. Air was becoming a problem, but I waited. The idea of breathing that in sounded worse than dying, though drowning in it sounded really awful, too.

Oh, feels so good. Pressure gone.

My lungs burned, and I lifted my head. I was still surrounded by fecal matter. I crouched on all fours and forced myself to stand. The crap fell from me in clumps and globs, the sound of wet splats all around as I stood and gasped for air. I choked and gagged, as I hadn't remembered to wipe my face clean first.

Unable to stop myself, I threw up my coffee and biscuit from earlier that morning, the taste and smell of regurgitated coffee a *heavenly* aroma compared to what surrounded me.

"Jonah?"

I looked up to see Karen staring at me, her eyes wide and hand covering her mouth.

Oh, thank you. I'm not dying. I feel wonderful. No more silver crunchy things for me.

The dragon rose up on all fours and shook like a wet dog, farting a bit more as he did so. I gagged again, but at this point, I didn't think my nose would ever recover.

Thank you, Healer, Whisperer. I feel much better.

The dragon turned to look at us, still a bit wobbly. The extra height the head gave it made me swallow nervously, then gag. I still had shit in my mouth.

"Um, does he want his claw?" Karen pulled it out of her backpack. I translated slowly, still trying to move out of the pile of dung.

Keep. Earned. Will grow new one. Here.

It spat, and a tooth fell out.

Hurt eating shiny thing. No more shiny. Stick with deer. Thank you.

He launched into the sky, the powerful downdrafts pulling up dirt and needles and coating me with them. A moment later he was above the trees, and he just vanished. I blinked, narrowed my eyes, and peered. The dragon was gone, but I could see a few treetops buffeting in a way that implied wind blowing down on top of them.

"It can turn invisible," I muttered as I looked down at myself. I'd started out the morning in hiking boots, good wool socks, jeans, undershirt, a Henley, a flannel overshirt, and my jacket. Every one of them was ending up in the trash. There wasn't enough soap or bleach to ever make them wearable again.

"Are you okay?" she asked, her hand still over her mouth.

I took stock of myself. I was covered in shit, yes, but other than the abuse to my nose and wallet, I didn't seem to be hurt.

"Yeah." I looked around, and slowly moved out of the pile of crap, and the breeze off the mountains turned the sodden, wet clothes into ice cubes weighing me down. I scraped off what I could and sighed. Today officially was the worst day ever. Nothing else could make it worse.

"Karen?"

She'd dropped her hand, and her lips were pursed tight. I realized she was trying very hard not to burst out in laughter at me.

That just proved I had nothing left to lose. Even almost dying would have been less embarrassing. Why not cap off the day?

"Yes?" she responded, swallowing hard.

"Would you like to go out to dinner sometime? On a date?"

Karen blinked at me. Her eyes did a slow down and up over my shit-covered being.

"I'd love to. But you aren't getting in my car until *after* you've showered."

I glanced down and sighed. "Valid. Wait, yes? You would?"

"You found me a dragon. How could I say no?"

"Point. But I get to keep the claw. I think I've earned it at this point."

She nodded, still trying very hard not to laugh. "Agreed." Karen bent over, picking up the tooth, her eyes wide with delight. "But I'm keeping the tooth. This is amazing."

"You won't tell anyone?" I waved around me. "About this, I mean. I don't care about the dragon."

She shot me an incredulous look. "Are you kidding? I'm telling *everyone*. This is going to be my top ten story for *decades*. Unless hanging around with you gets me a better one."

We started the slow hike back, her carrying both bags, and I tried to decide if that last comment was a compliment or an insult. In the end, it didn't matter; she'd said yes.

I had a date with Dr. Karen Bigsby. Maybe today hadn't been all that bad. After all, we'd gotten to talk to a dragon, and you know, sometimes shit happens.

* * * * *

Mel Todd Bio

Mel Todd has over 27 titles out, including her urban science fiction Kaylid Chronicles, the Blood War series, and the urban fantasy Twisted Luck series, with short stories in various anthologies and magazines. She hopes to keep writing tales that will capture your heart and imagination. With one co-author, and more books in the works, her stories can be found currently on Amazon.

Follow her on Facebook at: facebook.com/badashbooks/.

You can also sign up for her newsletter and follow her blog at: badashpublishing.com.

* * * * *

Fluffers
by C.M. DeMott
A House of Drimmett Tale

*D*amn dog. Thaddeus Ozymandias Andrew Drimmett III
stared at the tattered ruin of his best cloak. The
journey back to the Appletor Academy of Magical
Arts hadn't improved what his mother's beloved Somerese lapdog
had done to it. *She just laughed and told me it'd be easy to fix. A mere trifle.*

He sighed and laid the abused garment back on his bed. *I'm her
eldest son, sired by one of the strongest mages in the land, with a grandfather
legendary for his skills. A third year student at the best, most exclusive mage
school in Malusaria, and the blasted fuzzball that did this brings more credit to
her lineage than I do to mine.*

"Hey, Andy." His sister Julianna swept through the door, her
red-gold hair escaping its braid in joyous strands. "Wow. Fluffers
really did a job on your cloak." She poked at an exceptionally ragged
tear. It grew another inch. "Oops. Sorry."

"Not a problem. I should put it out of its misery and have done."

"But Mother said—"

"That I could repair it just like that." He snapped his fingers.
"Unfortunately, we both know I can't. You could, and you're a year
behind me. Our little brother could without even breaking a sweat."

"I'm sorry, Andy. You know I'd help."

"Yeah, but Mother would know. It's got to be me."

"You'll do it. You're good at enchanting fabrics."

"Precious little else."

"Jules, come on!" Their younger brother Willy came to a halt at the door. "We don't want to be late for dinner. They're serving roast aurochs tonight!" He saw the cloak. "Boy, Toad, that's a real mess. Good luck fixing it."

Jules frowned. "Don't call Andy that."

"Why not? The rest of the school does."

His sister narrowed her eyes, and he spoke before she could. "We're coming, Willy. Why don't you go on ahead?"

"See you there!"

They heard him running down the hall. Jules turned her frown on Andy. "Why do you let him call you that?"

"Because he's right. Ever since Marc Willis noticed what my initials spell, everyone here does but you. Now, let's go eat."

"But—"

"I'll work on the cloak later. We've only just gotten back. I promise I'll do it as soon as we've settled in."

"All right. I still think you should say something to him."

"Wouldn't help. He's not going to risk a fight with his friends over me."

"Still, Andy." She flashed him a smile. "Grandfather and Father both rose above those initials, and you will, too. Can you imagine what'd happen to someone if they called Grandfather that?"

Andy smiled in spite of himself. He *could* imagine it. The fool who did would be lucky to die. Grandfather wasn't called "Soulreaper" for compliments' sake.

* * *

Andy's classes this year included controlling power, transformations, illusions, and the crafting of philters and ointments, as well as a couple of languages he'd thought useful. Though he'd told Jules he couldn't enchant much more than fabrics, his knack for that was the one thing his classmates didn't question.

Appletor allowed its students to sell the magical items they made, and prided itself on the quality of those goods. So what if occasionally one of his anti-theft pouches was reluctant to open, even for its owner, or a garment made to repel water had to be cleaned with sand. Master Edmund'd told him it was just a matter of focus and control. "You get frustrated and put too much power into what you're doing. Use those meditation exercises I gave you. They'll help."

Well, they aren't helping tonight. Andy glared at his cloak. He'd found wool that was a close match for that particular shade of gray, but it wouldn't fill the holes properly. He concentrated, and his latest attempt undid itself. The hole got bigger. *I still can't get all that damn dog's hair off it. Never mind the spit.* He rubbed at yet another stain. "Ouch!"

He sucked his injured thumb and examined the spot more closely. Careful rubbing revealed a tooth. Andy picked it loose. *Great. Hair, spit, blood, AND teeth. At least she's too well housebroken to mess on it.*

His thumb continued to bleed. *I've been at this for two hours, and all I've got to show for it is a cloak no self-respecting* beggar *would touch, and a bloody thumb.* Grabbing the mess, he wadded it up and threw it at the wall as hard as he could. "Damn it, Fluffers!"

If I had half the power the rest of my family does, I'd not only restore this thing, but make it better. Protection from the elements. That's easy. Protection from people. That'd be good. And protection from that miserable fluffball. Perfect. That's what I need, and that's what I'm going to get.

Taking all his frustration, anger, and shame, he focused on the pile. *I will* make this work. *I will!* He lashed out. The cloak leaped into the air, throwing off sparks as it spun. He continued sending power into it, envisioning what he wanted. The cloak became a blur. "Fluffers! Da—" Before he could finish, the cloak threw itself at him. The last thing he saw was a wave of gray.

* * *

Someone was patting his face. *Feels* like *they've been doing that for a while.* He tried to move away, and the headache waiting for him pounced.

"Oooooooh." He tried again, and only succeeded in rolling onto his side. The patting continued, becoming more insistent. He waved feebly at the source. "Stop. If you want to help, get me some water."

It ceased. Andy covered his eyes with a hand. *Overuse headache. Lost my temper and used too much magic. Good thing they shield all the students' rooms, or I'd be in trouble on top of dealing with the pain.* "Oooooh."

Something bumped his hand: a mug, cool and wet.

"Thanks," he managed. Eyes squinted shut, he grabbed it and took a drink. The cool pushed back the pain. Another drink, and he was able to sit up. Blinking, he looked for his companion and saw... no one. He sipped again, looking around slowly. He was alone.

"Where are you?"

No answer. He finished the water, setting the mug down beside the gray pile of cloth next to him. *Must be more tired than I thought.* He rubbed his forehead. The headache gleefully thumped on. *No help for it. I've got to get up.*

Through an effort of will, he staggered to his feet and over to his bed. Working his way to his nightstand, he got the drawer open, and removed a squat, brown bottle and a spoon. With shaking hands, he carefully poured some of the thick, purple liquid it held into the spoon, raised that to his mouth, and swallowed.

"Gaaack!" He carefully replaced the stopper and put bottle and spoon back where they'd come from. "Wish I had more water. Yeeech."

He sat holding his head with both hands as he waited for the medicine to take effect. *Worst overuse headache I've had in a while. Haven't missed them a bit.*

Something bumped his right arm. He opened his eyes. The mug was back, refilled. Holding it up for him was his cloak. He froze. The mug bumped his arm again. He slowly reached out a hand and took it. The cloak stayed where it was. He drank, staring at it. "Thank you... I think."

The cloak quivered, rubbing a fold gently along his arm. He emptied the mug and set it on his nightstand.

"You can't really be doing this. You're a cloak." The fabric withdrew and somehow managed to look offended. "Okay, okay. Have it your way." The cloak relaxed. *I'm apologizing to a pile of fabric. Maybe I should go to the infirmary and get checked out. Nah. Too many stairs.*

He lay down. *I was trying to repair my cloak and make it something to be proud of. Something that'd protect me against the elements and people. And Fluffers.* He reached a hand over the side of the bed. The cloak pushed a fold into it. *Light above, did I make a Named Object? If so, what did I name it?* He thought back to the last thing he'd said before blacking out. *Oh, no. Not that. Anything but that.*

"Fluffers?" he whispered. The cloak surged up onto the bed and snuggled against him. Andy closed his eyes. *I've made an Item of Power and named it after my mother's dog. I will never, ever live this down.*

* * *

Getting dressed the next morning was... interesting. Fluffers kept trying to help. When it leaped up onto his shoulders and arranged itself in proper cloak fashion, he tried to take it off—to no avail. "Okay. Stay there, but stay still. Pretend you're a normal cloak." He swore he heard a huff of indignation. He hesitated, then gave it a tentative pat. "Good Fluffers. Stay."

Jules and Willy were halfway through their meal when he got there. He slipped into the chair next to his sister and wolfed down a sweetroll. "What took you so long?" she asked.

"Just tired. Stayed up too late, working on my cloak."

She looked it over. "Nice repair. I like the mix of tan and gray. Subtle, but it does look good."

"Thanks." He pushed down a fold that was aiming for her arm and hoped she hadn't noticed.

Willy glanced up from his eggs. "Yeah. I was wondering when you'd do it." He gulped down another mouthful. "Or if."

"Well, I got it done." This time he was ready for the fold headed for his brother and turned his grab into a smoothing gesture. "All nice and ready for winter." He was spared any more comments by the bell tolling for their first morning class. "Got to go." He grabbed his last roll and headed out at a run.

Sliding into his desk in Illusions, he ran a hand down his cloak. "Stay still, Fluffers. I'll be okay," he whispered. A quick glance showed no one was looking at him. He pulled out his book and turned to the spell assigned as homework. He was concentrating on the description of gestures needed when he felt a tap on his arm and looked up. Master Percy was taking his place at the front. He patted his cloak gently and whispered, "Thanks."

Master Percy stared at them over his glasses. "The best illusions are more than merely visual. You need them to seem *real*. That means sound, scent, texture, and/or taste when appropriate. Now, using the assigned spell, I want each of you to demonstrate the illusion you've prepared when called upon. Benjamin Archer, you may begin."

Andy watched as his classmate sent a mouse running across his desk. It looked good, but the sound wasn't consistent. He turned back to his book. *Damn cloak. Spent so much time on it, I didn't work on this.*

"Annalee Benton." A small tree grew from her desk. It produced yellow flowers that smelled vaguely of lemons. *So, no trees, no mice. What to do?*

He licked the last trace of sweetroll from his fingers. *Cinnamon, sugar, bread. Maybe a hint of butter? Worth a try.* He gathered power for the attempt, concentrating on the spell and what he'd have to do. "Andrew Drimmett."

Focusing on what he wanted, he moved his hands carefully through the required gestures. *A little more emphasis on the finger twist to bring out the cinnamon. A slowing of the wrist here to make the icing ooze down the sides. There.*

Master Percy came over to his desk. He inhaled, then touched a finger to Andy's creation. "Not bad. Need to work on the temperature a bit more." He licked his finger. "Ptah! And on the flavor. I don't think 'old shoe' is what you were after."

"Understood, sir." Andy let the illusion fade, ignoring the amused coughs of several classmates. Master Percy moved on to the next student. Andy thought over what he'd done and tried to figure out where he'd gone wrong. His cloak gave him a reassuring pat. It was oddly comforting.

His next class was Tradespeech, the language used by merchants throughout the Nine Kingdoms. Given his skill with magical cloth goods, it was bound to be useful. Happily, it was something he had a knack for. Where others struggled, he saw connections and patterns. It was the same with Ogrimal, the much more difficult language spoken by the nomadic Ograna tribes to the north. He found he enjoyed its complexity. It was a welcome relief from the problems he had with some of his other classes.

He made it to lunch without further interference from the cloak. Once he'd settled down with his food, he took out a book on Ogrimal and flipped to the section on tenses.

Willy plopped down next to him a few minutes later and glanced at what he was reading. "I still don't know why you're wasting time on that. When'll you ever be able to use it? Ogre'll take your head off before you get one word out. "

"They're called 'Ograna,' and they trade with us. It'll be useful then."

Willy swallowed what he was chewing. "Only when they can't steal it. King's had to send troops out twice this year to head off raiding parties."

"Only twice. It's mostly young warriors out to impress the ladies."

His brother snorted. "You make those green freaks sound harmless. You think Father bothered to *talk* the last time the clans rose? Hardly. They understood what a wall of fire meant just fine."

Jules joined them at the table. "Who did?"

"Our dear brother thinks he'll be able to talk the next Ogre raiding party into leaving us alone."

Andy sighed. "I didn't say that. I like learning languages, and they do trade with us at times."

"Trade what they've stolen," Willy said. "What will you offer back? A patched cloak?" He grabbed a fold of Andy's. The fabric wrapped itself around his hand and squeezed, shaking what it held. "Hey! That hurts!"

"Fluffers! No! Bad cloak! Drop it!"

The cloak let go, grumbling as it did so. A fold remained poised to strike. Andy stroked it gently. "Good Fluffers. Let him be." The fold relaxed.

Willy rubbed his wrist. "Did you just call that thing 'Fluffers?'"

"Well—"

"Oh, Andy," Jules said. "You didn't."

Willy burst out laughing. Andy put a restraining hand on his cloak. "It just happened."

"How? You were trying to patch your cloak and turned it into a Named Object in the process?" She rolled her eyes. "Only you, brother."

"Oh, this is just too good. Wait'll I tell Marc and the rest of the gang." Willy shoved the last of his sandwich in his mouth, chewed quickly, and washed it down with cider. "Thanks, Toad. You really made my day." He grabbed his tray and left.

Jules watched as a fold of gray patted Andy on the leg, then raised to "peer" at his face. "It even acts like her. That's just what the real Fluffers does when Mother's upset."

Andy stroked the raised bit and sighed. "I know. Guess I need to train this one. That'll be easier than explaining to our parents why it strangled Willy."

* * *

After his Philters and Ointments class, he turned down the hall that led to Master Edmund's office. The door was open when he got there. Peering in, he could see the master pouring over a manuscript at his desk, his gray-streaked brown hair as unruly as ever.

Andy hesitated. *Maybe this isn't the best time.* Before he could leave, Master Edmund looked up. "Come in, Andrew. Something I can help you with?"

Andy came in. "I had a little problem with a spell last night."

"Ah. I thought as much." He waved a hand at the seat across from the desk. "Sit down."

Andy sat. "How did you know, sir?"

"That was a lot of power you used. The healer on duty contacted me about it but didn't think you'd need attention. "

"Oh?"

"So, what spell was it? I can't think of any power management homework I've set you that'd require that much, and I doubt any of your other masters did."

"I was repairing my cloak."

"Your cloak? The one you're wearing?"

"Yes, sir."

"Lose your temper?"

Andy sighed. "Yes, sir."

Master Edmund shook his head. "Well, let's see it."

Andy undid the clasp and slipped the cloak from his shoulders. He went to pass it across the desk. It promptly wrapped itself around his arm and refused to go.

Master Edmund raised an eyebrow.

Andy rose and gently unwound it from his arm. "Come on, Fluffers. He just wants to see you." The cloak obediently went limp.

His master came over and looked without touching. "Nicely done. I caught a glimpse of it the day you came back. You named it 'Fluffers?'"

"My mother's dog, the one who damaged it in the first place, her real name is Sandridge Fluffy Delight. Fluffers is a nickname."

He went on to tell the tale. Master Edmund shook his head when he was done. "That's one of the reasons I gave you those exercises. You've more power than you give yourself credit for. You're lucky you weren't seriously injured, or worse." He extended his hand toward the cloak. "May I touch you, Fluffers?"

The cloak twisted to "stare" at Andy. He nodded. "It's all right."

Fluffers extended a fold toward Master Edmund. He ran his hands lightly over the fabric. When he was finished, he patted the cloak and let it go. It slipped up Andy's arms and settled back around his shoulders. The master smiled. "Congratulations. Creation of a Named Object is a fourth-year spell, and an advanced one, at that." He took his seat again. "What problem did you wish to discuss?"

* * *

Andy sat down in Illusions, Fluffers lying quiet on his shoulders. *Took me all winter and a bit of spring, but I trained you.* Following Master Edmund's suggestions, he now had a cloak that would act like a cloak—most of the time. If he got excited or felt threatened, Fluffers would take the initiative and do something about it. Such things usually made it worse. As a consequence, Andy was doing much better with his meditation exercises.

Andy patted the cloak and turned back to his lesson. He could now do a complete tray of fresh sweetrolls at the proper temperature and flavor. He watched as the pony he'd created for today's exercise left a steaming pile of manure beside a less-friendly classmate's desk and hid a smile.

Jules had advanced to third level early and was now in his Philters and Ointments class. He nodded to her as he came in and took his seat. "Any problems with that wound balm?"

"No, it was easy. I thought of a way to make it spread better, too." She passed a small white jar over to him.

He opened it and took a sniff. "Lavender?"

She nodded. "Like it?"

"Yes. Mother would love it." He closed it and passed it back. Mistress Katarina came in before she could answer, and they turned to listen.

* * *

Willy joined them for lunch after class. "Hear the news?"

"What news?" Jules said as she buttered a roll.

"Rumor has it there's an Ogre raiding party gathering. A big one."

Andy reached for a slice of ham. "The king'll take care of it."

"He'll have to find it first." Willy paused for a gulp of cider. "It's supposed to include more than one clan, and there's several villages that could be in danger."

Andy stopped in mid chew. "How do you lose something that big?"

"Shamans."

"Shamans?" Jules snorted. "They've never been a threat before."

Willy laughed. "Apparently, Ogres *can* learn if you beat them enough."

Jules frowned. "Think Father will have to go?"

"I don't know. We're a lot closer to the area involved than he is." Willy finished his pie. "Marc overheard a couple of the masters talking about it in the hall. Said they were planning to discuss it, then call us together and tell us what they've decided."

Andy put his bread down. "Which villages are in danger?"

"Greenridge, Cutter's Hollow, and Ladysmith. Marc didn't hear the other names."

"Those are all to our north and west, within a couple days' ride."

"You don't think they'd come here, do you?" Jules asked.

"They wouldn't dare," Willy answered. He drained his mug and rose. "We won't even see a flash of spellfyre in the distance."

Andy wasn't so sure. He finished his meal in silence.

"Do you think he's right?" Jules asked as they left the dining hall.

"He probably is. The defenses here are legendary."

"But you're not sure."

"They teach some Ograna culture in my Ogrimal class. This is unusual. It feels like a test for something more serious than a raid."

"Another war?"

"Hope not." He saw her worried look and forced a smile. "That's just me being me. Willy's probably right. He's got more sources than I'll ever have."

They walked down the hall, turned right at the intersection, and continued on. "Some here have family in Ladysmith," Jules said. "It's not that far from here."

"The army and the masters here will do their best to keep us all safe. In any case, we can't do anything until we get more information." They came to another intersection and stopped. "You go on to your Herbs class. See you at dinner."

"Okay." She turned down the left hand passage. He continued on. His Ogrimal language class was next. If he were lucky, Master Roland would be willing to answer more questions about the last Ograna war.

* * *

Sitting beside his sister with the other third year students in the Great Hall, Andy thought over what he'd learned. Signs pointed to growing unrest among the Ograna clans. With their few crops damaged by storms, and the flooding of some of their hunting ranges during the spring thaw, they had no choice but raiding if they didn't want to starve. This area of Malusaria hadn't been hit as badly in the last war, so the pickings'd be good, and they knew it.

The low murmur of others talking filled the hall as the last of the students filed in. He watched his brother and friends take their seats with the first years. *Wish I had his skill at making friends. Having a group of people my own age to share studies and just hang out with, even a smaller group like my sister's, would be good.*

I just don't have people skills. Never have. Mother says I'm like Grandfather that way. He shuddered at the thought. *Hope that's the only social trait we share. I think he actively discourages people from getting close. Wonder what Grandmother Elsie saw in him?*

A sharp rap from the podium caught his attention. The talking stopped as all present focused on Headmistress Isabeau. "By now, you've heard the rumors. Some of the Ograna clans are rising to our north. The king's sending reinforcements, but they'll be delayed, due to damaged roads. We've been asked to send some of our older students to help scout the Ograna positions and guide those forces to them."

She rapped again to silence the murmur that rose. "Volunteers only. You won't be expected to fight, but there will be risk. Those remaining will be assigned tasks to help with the defenses here. Those wishing to volunteer, stay. The rest of you, go back to your rooms and your studies."

Andy watched as his sister and her friends rose and left, talking amongst themselves. He remained seated as more students filed past him. *I might be able to help. I do know Ogrimal and something of their culture. I'm quiet, and I can perform decent illusions. I'd rather do something than stay here waiting. Ah, well. They can only say no.*

The crowd flowed out, leaving only a handful of students, a few senior instructors, and the headmistress. Andy got up and walked forward. When he reached the front, he glanced at the others who'd stayed: six fourth years, two other third years, a second year, and four first years. Andy suppressed a sigh. The firsts were Willy and three of his friends.

Isabeau looked them over, then focused on the younger group. "I called for older students only. Do you have any special skills?"

The second year raised her hand. "Laurel Greenridge, ma'am. I was born in Greenridge, and I know every inch of the land around it. Figured that would help with scouting."

The headmistress nodded. "Useful, indeed. Point made." She turned to Willy's group. "And you?"

"I'm good at getting into places without being seen," Willy said, "and I have a knack for Spellfyre."

"Also good at not being seen, and quick on my feet," Marc added.

"We're fast and sneaky," Rob and Jon Mellwood said together.

Isabeau frowned. "We'll see."

The fourth years, four boys and two girls, were all good at illusions and combat magic, as well as having some experience navigating the outdoors. Anna, the third year girl, was skilled at herb gathering, while Bert was an excellent rider. The headmistress turned to Andy. "You're the one with the Named cloak?"

"I am, ma'am. I also speak Ogrimal."

"Hmm." She widened her focus back to the group. "Sign Master Edmund's list and return to your quarters. The assignments will be posted here in the morning."

She turned to talk to the other instructors. One by one, the volunteers signed the list and left.

Andy signed and waited for his brother. "Are you out of your mind? Spellfyre or not, you don't stand a chance against an Ograna warrior."

Willy raised an eyebrow. "And you do? I'm at least decent in archery. Do you even know which end of a sword to hold?"

"Yes. I'll be getting more practice in after dinner."

Willy's friends came up. "Toad bothering you, Willy D?" Marc said.

"Just the usual croaking about my age."

The Mellwood twins laughed. Willy grinned. "See you, brother. My friends and I have plans to make. If you have to worry, better think about how you're going to get yourself out of this. We'll be just fine."

Andy watched them go down the hall. The worst of it was, Willy was right. He sighed and went to do some badly needed sword practice.

* * *

Dinner tasted like sawdust and stale ditch water. Andy kept to himself, running over what he knew of the Ograna clans and what he'd take if he did go scouting. He also thought of what he'd tell his parents if anything happened to Willy. Jules was too busy talking to her friends to notice him. He didn't think she knew Willy'd volunteered, and he didn't want to worry her more than she already was.

The headmistress won't allow him to go out. She said she only wanted older students. Right. You know he'll probably be better at this than you will. Talking to Ograna traders is one thing. If I have to say anything to a warrior, it'll likely be the last thing I ever do.

He forced himself to finish his meal and trudge back to his room. Once there, he readied his knife and sword, and made a list of everything else that might be useful. He stared at it, realized he'd need a pack mule to carry it all, and started over. It was nearly midnight when his cloak started tugging him toward the bed. He sighed. "All right, Fluffers."

He laid the cloak on his bed and got ready to join it. When he slipped under the covers, the cloak came up to wrap around him. It gave him a hug and snuggled in. "Thanks, Fluffers." He closed his eyes and drifted off in spite of himself.

* * *

Andy stared at the trail leading down from the hills toward Cutter's Hollow. Willy was three trees over, doing the same. They'd been sent by the mayor to watch this road, with orders to come back quickly if they saw any trouble.

Three days of this. They're supposed to put supplies at the broken oak tomorrow. A light wind stirred the leaves, followed by the patter of a steady rain. Fluffers settled around him, hood perfectly positioned to keep water out of his eyes. Willy muttered a curse and pulled his own cloak tighter. Andy smiled.

The rain and wind continued all day. The sound was soothing, but made it hard to hear anything else. As the shadows deepened, they ate some bread and dried meat, washing it down with water.

"You take the second watch," Willy whispered. "I'm too damp to sleep."

"All right."

Andy got into a more comfortable position and closed his eyes. He managed a light doze 'til something wet hit his face, covering his mouth to stifle noise. He came fully awake to find a fold of his cloak there, and the rain over. There was a slight sucking noise, repeated just when he thought he'd imagined it. A muffled clink of metal. The breeze brought the odor of wet, smoky leather.

Ograna. They're coming toward the town. Andy eased himself up and touched the peg he'd stuck in the tree to point the way to his brother. He strengthened his personal sound-muting spell, then counted the few steps to the next tree. Willy met him at the second and whispered, "Ograna."

"Yeah. Need to get back."

Willy made a few gestures. "Got the guide up. Follow."

Together, they slipped back down the trail. The guide spell acted like a series of tiny markers that could be felt by those who'd cast it, allowing them to move without using a light. Andy had no idea how the Ograna were managing, even with their better night vision. From the faint sounds and occasional muffled grunts he heard, they were moving slowly, and were still some distance away.

He followed his brother, every nerve straining to stay quiet and avoid detection. *If they find us, we're dead, and Cutter's Hollow with us.* He paused, listening. The sounds behind them continued. *Are they closer?*

He picked up the pace as much as he dared. The silencing spell cloaked what noise he made. His brother's wasn't as good. He heard the muffled *crack* as Willy stepped on a stick and froze again. *Maybe they'll think they made it. Maybe—*

There was a thump, followed by a deep grunt. Willy yelped. Andy saw his brother's face in the quick flash of Spellfyre sent at a much too close Ograna. Then a louder thump, and the smell of scorched flesh. Andy leaped forward into the darkness, only to stumble over the warrior's body. Willy grabbed his arm. "Run!"

Faint lights appeared. They could hear cries from the warriors behind and to both sides. Only the way back to town was open.

They ran. For a brief moment, they widened their lead. Then the lights began to come nearer, drawing in on both sides.

We're *not going to make it, but one of us might.*

Andy yelled at his brother, "Go on. Get word to the town. I'll delay them."

Willy glanced sideways at him. "But—"

"I'll use illusions and slip away. GO!"

Willy raced off. Andy made a quick gesture, causing some low branches to bend down into the path behind him. He repeated it a few strides farther, conscious of the lights. He sent a streak of mist that gasped and smelled of blood off to one side, and was rewarded by seeing some of the lights follow. He sent off a couple more, each angling away.

Willy's guide spell was fading. *Good. Willy's getting away. If I can keep them here a little longer...*

He sensed an opening and dodged off the path, leaving a last, stumbling wraith behind him. He went as far as he dared, then stopped by a large tree. Leaning against it, he tried to catch his breath without gasping. Fluffers arranged itself around him with irregular bits poking out to conceal his shape. He could hear the muttered curses of those hunting them. None of the lights he could see were moving townward.

Andy continued to breathe, conscious of the faint trembling in his hands. *I used a lot of power. Now, to stay out of their way, and hope Willy gets through.* The nearest lights came together. He couldn't make out more than a word or two, but it was enough to hope they were turning back. *Nothing here but trees. The town's been warned. Please, please, go.*

He wove an illusion around himself, careful to keep his hands concealed. *I'm just another tree. A little one.* The group of lights moved toward him. Then the first was passing, held by a tall Ograna warrior. The scowl on his green-skinned face was enough to curdle milk. Two others followed, then a fourth. The fifth was younger, stalking forward with barely suppressed rage. As he came even with Andy, he lashed out with his sword at the undergrowth. Fluffers lunged up to block the blow. It bound the edge, but the force threw Andy into the tree behind him. His head struck the trunk, and everything exploded into darkness.

* * *

The world was moving, shaking pain through every part of his body, especially his head. A sudden wave of nausea rose. He vomited. Coughing, he gagged, then threw up again. There was a curse. A blow fell across his shoulders. "Worthless lump! Stop that!"

Andy swallowed hard. Beneath him, he felt his cloak shift to pad his belly. Looking down, he saw hooves. He tried to pull back, only to come up against the ropes holding him there. He closed his eyes. *Ogrimal. They're speaking Ogrimal, and I'm tied to a horse. Hope Willy made it.* He took a deep breath, then began one of his meditation exercises as he tried to forget where he was.

* * *

A hard two days later, Andy sat where he'd been dumped near the other prisoner, an angry young man in farmer's clothes who ignored him to glare at their captors and grumble curses. His sword and knife were gone. His hands were tied, his feet hobbled. Fluffers snuggled around him, with only the occasional quiver to let him know it was still there. Andy's headache was mostly gone, replaced by a cold feeling in the pit of his stomach. *They're going to kill us. The only questions are how and how long it'll take.*

He raised his head, looking at the camp around him. He was at the edge of a circular area with a fire pit at its center and tents along it. A twist of his head showed more tents. He turned back toward the clearing. There was a hide-covered seat on the other side. An antlered stag skull topped a pole holding a black and white horsehide banner next to it.

Utala clan. Not the worst, but not the best, either. They'll have no fond memories of Father. As for Grandfather… He shuddered. *Best hope they don't realize what family I come from.*

A young boy came by with a bucket and threw a dipperful of water in his face. Fluffers caught it in a fold. As the boy turned to do the same to the farmer, Andy lowered his head and drank, hoping no one saw him.

The other prisoner yelled and lunged for his tormenter, only to fall when he lost his balance. The boy laughed and ran on.

Fluffers patted his face and slipped down again. Andy continued to watch. *We're at the center of camp. When they're ready, they'll stoke the fire and deal with us. A bit of entertainment before dinner.*

From the looks and comments of those who passed, that time would be soon. There'd be no rescue. The king's forces were probably too far out, and their priority was protecting towns, not one unlucky student wizard, no matter how important his family. *At least I can feel my hands. Probably have Fluffers to thank for that.*

A young warrior came over to him. Andy thought he was the one who'd captured him. He stared up into his enemy's angry yellow eyes. "This knife. Yours?" The words were in his own Malusarian. Andy looked at the knife the other thrust toward his face and swallowed hard. The leather sheath was carved with a wyvern in flight, wings spread and spitting fire. *Oh, yes. That's mine. The one Father gave me for my last birthday with the family crest on it.*

There was no point in denying it, and Andy found he didn't want to. He looked back at the warrior. "Yes."

The other clenched his fist around the sheath and shook it. This time he spoke Ogrimal to someone behind him. "Ayee! It is as you thought, Mag Eskeh! He is the son of the Flamelord!"

A much older Ograna came forward. His dark brown hair was streaked with gray, and his face creased with wrinkles, reminding Andy of an old, mossy tree. He wore a necklace of carved red and green stones, and bracelets of the same. Andy could feel the magic in them. "You do not deny this?" the shaman asked in Malusarian.

"No." He felt the other touch him with a thread of power.

"He speaks truth."

The warrior grinned savagely and turned to Andy. "Son of Flamelord, will he come?"

"No."

The grin grew broader. "Must fear Reaper of Souls? Will come for you?"

"No." Andy switched to Ogrimal. "And if you fear *him*, think what it's like to *live* with him."

The warrior's eyes widened. Andy heard muffled laughter from some of those watching. The warrior heard them, too. "You joke now. You will watch what we do to ordinary prisoners first. For *you*, there will be something special."

He left. The shaman stared at him a moment longer. Andy stared back. To his surprise, the shaman inclined his head to him slightly before going.

Andy shivered. He'd heard tales of what the Ograna did to "special" prisoners. Overheard more when his father and mother were talking and didn't realize he was there. *They'll take my hands so I can't work magic. My eyes, and any other bits they think I can live without. Death would be kinder. That's exactly what the prisoner father found chose: death by fire, so his family wouldn't have to see what he'd become.*

* * *

Three hours later, the fire was burning, and the area around the circle was full of Ograna of all ages. Two warriors stood on the other side of it, dressed for combat, with faces painted in yellow and red.

The younger bared his teeth at Andy in a parody of a smile. A drum started up; slow, measured beats like a heart. A powerful Ograna warrior wearing an antlered black and white headband strode to the opposite side of the circle, followed by a proud young warrior, and two Ograna maidens. They remained standing as the chief sat on the seat prepared for him. Mag Eskeh took a place nearby.

Andy and his fellow prisoner were dragged to their feet and brought into the circle. Andy's companion yelled, "My people will come! They won't leave me here! They'll cut yours down like the savages you are! They—" A cuff across his face silenced him. The drum stopped.

The chief narrowed his eyes. "They will not come. I, Chief Otogeh of the Utala clan, hold your fate in my hands. Beg for mercy on your knees, and your death will be swift."

The one he addressed tried to spit at him, but missed.

Otogeh smiled and pointed at Andy. "Put this one where he can watch what comes. Prepare the other for battle."

Andy let his guards move him to one side. The farmer was taken closer to the fire, where his ropes were cut. "You will be given a sword." Otogeh said. "If you can kill the one who captured you, you can go."

The older warrior stepped forward. One of those holding the prisoner laid a sword on the ground, then both left. The farmer grabbed the weapon and came up in a crouch, facing his opponent. The other closed slowly, stopping a short distance away. The young man screamed a curse and leapt toward him, swinging wildly. The warrior dodged, slicing him as he passed. The man screamed again and turned.

Andy forced himself to watch as the farmer continued to charge blindly at his foe. If he'd had more than rudimentary training, it didn't show. The Ograna continued the macabre dance, never taking a single blow himself. When the prisoner finally fell, too weak and broken to continue, the warrior turned to his chief.

"Finish him as he deserves," Otogeh said.

The warrior saluted him with his sword, then turned toward the fire. He took three pieces of unburnt wood, placing one under his unresisting victim's neck, and one under each wrist. His sword came up. The first cut laid the man's belly open from ribs to groin. As the screams faded into moans, the second and third blows took his hands. The last took his head. The warrior wiped his sword off on his victim's clothes, saluted his chief again, and left the circle. Two others came in and dragged what was left away. Then it was Andy's turn.

For my family. Andy took a breath and walked with his guards to the center of the circle. The young warrior who'd captured him stepped forward as the crowd jeered. All save the chief's younger daughter, who stared at him with sorrow. *Why should she be sad? Can't be for me.*

Still, he kept looking at her, if only to ignore the catcalls of the rest. The chief rose, and he met his eyes, waiting to hear his fate. This time, the chief spoke Ogrimal. "A most important prisoner. What is your name, son of the Flamelord?"

"My name is Thaddeus Ozymandias Andrew Drimmett the Third. I am called Andrew."

"So, Andrew. Will you beg for mercy now, after what you have seen?"

"No. There is no point."

The chief nodded. "Wise for one so young."

He looked at those holding Andy.

Fluffers quivered as they cut his hobbles. He tapped a warning to his cloak. It stayed quiet, letting them cut his arms free without protest. Andy shrugged his shoulders, trying to loosen them. He noticed two more shamans were now at the edge of the circle. *So, no Spellfyre, even if I was fast enough to use it.*

They laid his sword on the ground. He saw the young maiden watching him still and gave her a sad smile. Pretending she cared stilled the trembling in his knees as he focused on his opponent. Taking three steps forward, he picked up his weapon and came on guard. Fluffers tensed on his shoulders.

The warrior stalked closer to stand just out of reach. Andy didn't move. He watched the other's eyes as he'd been taught.

The first strike was a feint. Andy twitched, but kept his blade in line. A second feint.

He saw the warrior's eyes narrow and managed to block the strike aimed for his legs. Fluffers swirled out, giving him room to move away. His opponent followed with a flurry of blows. Andy blocked as best he could, leaving Fluffers to deal with the rest. When it was over, Andy was bleeding from a deep cut in his right leg and a gash to his left arm.

The Ograna growled and circled him, moving to put stress on his wounded leg. Andy matched him, keeping his sword up. When the next attack came, he took another cut to the same leg. Fluffers blocked a second strike as he danced back. He landed on a piece of wood left from the previous fight, tripped, and fell into the fire.

Fluffers wrapped around him. Andy rolled out of the flames and was forced to block another strike as his cloak patted out the sparks in his clothes. The next strike came for his shoulders. He got his sword up in time to block, but was knocked off balance. As he stepped back, his wounded leg buckled. He lost his weapon when he landed. Rolling over, he saw his foe grin as his sword came down.

Fluffers released his shoulders and threw itself into the path of the blade. With a high-pitched snarl, it wrapped itself around his foe, binding his arms to his sides as it slapped him repeatedly across the face.

Andy scrambled away on hands and knees to grab his sword. The warrior got a hand free and tore the cloak loose, tossing it back at Andy. Andy tripped over it as he staggered forward. He landed on his face, losing his sword again.

He rolled as the warrior's blade struck, narrowly missing his fingers as he tried for his own weapon. Fluffers dodged between his enemy's legs, bringing him down. Sliding up, it wrapped itself around the Ograna's blade. Andy threw himself on top of the warrior. Grabbing him by the hair, he managed to bounce his head on the ground twice before he was thrown off.

The warrior rose. Fluffers snarled again and slid further up his body, wrapping around his face. He dropped his sword, trying to tear the smothering folds away.

Andy got up just as he succeeded. The warrior threw the cloak to one side and lunged after him. With no time to grab a weapon, Andy ran, favoring his wounded leg. The warrior gave chase, Fluffers gamely following and trying to wrap around his legs.

Andy made it completely around the fire as the crowd yelled encouragement, some of it even for him. His breath came in gasps, as much from pain as exertion. Someone on the sidelines tried to trip him. He managed to dodge and stumbled on. The warrior grabbed for his shoulder, only to fall as Fluffers tied his legs together.

More running. He passed his sword, but couldn't stop.

As Andy came toward the chief, a small boy stuck a stick between his legs. He crashed down, sliding to a halt at the young maiden's feet. Her eyes were wide as they met his. He tried to rise, but simply couldn't find the strength. *That's it, then.* He gave her another sad smile and lay still.

Her mouth twitched. She looked past him and started laughing. Andy followed her gaze, to see Fluffers slapping the warrior as he attempted to reach him. The snarling turned into an even higher yipping noise as it lunged and lashed at any part of the Ograna it could reach. As he danced to avoid the angry cloak, the maiden laughed even louder.

The chief stood. "Hold!"

The warrior froze. Fluffers gave a yip of triumph and lunged for his throat.

"Fluffers! No! Drop that!" yelled Andy.

The cloak released the gasping warrior and slid back over to Andy. It reared up to growl at the chief, then settled protectively against him. Otogeh looked at his still laughing daughter.

He shrugged and turned back to Andy. "You," he said, "are a problem."

* * *

Andy leaned against a cushion, his wounded leg stretched out in front of him. He'd been taken to this tent, had his wounds treated by a grumbling old woman, and been allowed to clean up. Fluffers lay protectively around his shoulders, as clean as he'd been able to make it. He took another drink of water and sighed. *I've no idea why they didn't kill me. Don't really care.*

He bit into a piece of bread. Whatever she'd given him to dull the pain was working. He felt fuzzy, and simply glad to be alive. He gave his cloak a pat. "Thanks, Fluffers."

He'd finished eating when the tent flap opened. The young maiden and a much older Ograna woman came in. He started to rise. "No. Don't," the maiden said. "You'll hurt yourself."

Andy settled back. She sat on the stool the healer'd left, her hands folded in her lap. Her companion sniffed and remained standing by the door.

"I believe I owe you my life," he said. "I don't know why, but thank you..."

"Tsileawa."

"Thank you, Tsileawa, Chief's Daughter."

She nodded. "You truly don't know?"

"Why you saved me? No. Not that I'm complaining."

"I have sorrowed deeply since my mother's death three years ago. My father grew concerned. He vowed last year that I'd wed the one who could bring laughter to my lips again. So he let you live."

"Wed? As in marry you?" He drew away, eyes wide. "But—"

She stared back, then dropped her face into her hands and began to cry. "You find me ugly."

Ignoring the glare of her companion, Andy pushed himself up to lay a hand on hers. "No! No! It's not you, it's me!"

"W-what?"

She looked up, tears flowing down her cheeks. Fluffers made a soft noise and began to dry them. "It's me," Andy repeated. "I'm terrible with a sword. I'm an embarrassment to my family. Even my brother calls me 'Toad.' Surely you can find someone better?"

"Toad? You mean the Ugkunk? But they are powerful shapechangers. Their singing brings rain. It is a fortunate name!"

Andy managed a wry smile. "Not among my folk. To them, they're brown, warty things that live in mud and eat bugs."

Her tears stopped. Fluffers slid down to lie between them. "Why does he call you that?"

"My brother? Because that's what my initials spell: Toad. And my hair is the color of one."

"Oh." She took his hand. "My name doesn't fit, either."

"It means 'Singing Bird,' doesn't it?"

"Yes, but I can't sing. Not like my mother or my sister. Even my brother sings better than I do."

"I can't sing, either."

Fluffers patted her hand. She looked down at the cloak. "May I pet it?"

"Yes. I don't think Fluffers'll mind."

"Fluffers? You named your cloak?"

"My mother has a little dog she calls that. Her dog tore my cloak up, and I had to fix it." He watched as she gently ran a hand over the fabric. Fluffers leaned into it. "I got angry when I couldn't do it easily and used too much magic." He patted his cloak. "So, now I have a protective cloak named after my mother's dog."

"Oh. I wish I had a cloak like this."

Andy swallowed. *I'll miss Fluffers, but I owe her. Marriage just won't work, so...* "Fluffers, would you like to be Tsileawa's?"

His cloak gave a strangled yip and leaped back to wrap itself around him. Tsileawa sighed. "It doesn't look like it."

"Okay, Fluffers." He gave it a reassuring pat. The cloak loosened its hold and settled over his shoulders. *Could I make her one? Maybe.*

"If you can bring me a cloak, I can try to make you one like Fluffers. No guarantees, but I can at least make it better protection against the elements."

She clapped her hands. "I'd like that." She turned to the woman. "Bring me my brown wool cloak."

The woman frowned but went to the door. She called another woman to watch them as she went for the cloak. When she returned, she handed the cloak to Tsileawa and went back to her place by the door, still glaring.

Tsileawa passed it over. "What else will you need?"

Andy thought. "Some hair, spit, and blood from a favorite animal. And a tooth, if you can, though I can skip that if it means pulling it. I'll also need a few drops of your blood just before the final part to bind the cloak to you."

"When can you start?"

"Give me a few days to get my strength back. I'll need permission from your head shaman, too."

She squeezed his hands and rose with the cloak. "I'll get it."

She left with the other women. Andy looked at Fluffers. *Hope I can do it. I don't want to let her down. Never mind what her father will do to me if I make her sad again.*

* * *

Tsileawa came back three days later. She'd let her palomino mare chew on her cloak, rubbed her down with it afterward, and soaked up blood from a couple of fly bites in the process. She'd also brought one of the mare's baby teeth and some of her tail hair for good measure.

Mag Eskeh warded the tent. Andy sat quietly at the center, gathering strength. When the shaman was finished, Tsileawa gave Andy what she'd brought. Ignoring her still angry chaperone and the stern gaze of the shaman, he smiled at her. "Stand over by that cushion. I'm going to prepare the cloak. When it's ready, I'll need a few drops of your blood to set the spell."

She went to the cushion. "Call it 'KeKe.'"

He nodded. "Whatever happens, stay there. I don't want you to get hurt."

He took the cloak and the horsehair and went to work. Since this cloak was whole, he wove the horsehair strands into the fabric to make a dancing pony on the back. He took the rest, and added a second wavy band to the bottom, just above the white one that already ran around the edge. Then he took the tooth and wove it into the center of the wavy band.

Holding what he'd made, he turned to Tsileawa. "I need the blood now."

She came over. Taking her knife out, she pricked a finger, then squeezed a few drops of her blood onto the tooth and surrounding area before going back to wait.

Gathering power, he focused on the cloak and what it had to become. *Protection from the elements. Protection from people who'd harm you. And protection from the mare you chose to link this to, just to be certain.*

He called his emotions. Summoning his fear of failure, his anger at not being a better wizard, and the shame he'd feel if he couldn't keep his word to her, he wadded the cloak into a ball and threw it into the air. Then he lashed out with the power he'd gathered. The cloak hung, spinning. Sparks flew. He envisioned all it had to be and pushed more power into it. As it became a brown, sparkling blur, he yelled, "KeeeeKeeee!"

The cloak dove for him. He threw his arms up to protect his face. Fluffers growled and lunged between them. The brown cloak swooped upward, slapping him as it passed, and headed toward

Tsileawa. He heard a surprised "Oh!" as it reached her. He managed a smile before he passed out.

* * *

Murmurs. Something cool on his forehead. Something soft under his head. Then, pain. *Damn. Overdid it again.* He groaned.

"I don't know what you see in him."

"He's kind, Akkitsina. He makes me laugh."

"Ha. He's a worthless human, and ugly, all maggoty-white."

"He is *not,* Akki! And he gave me a wonderful cloak."

A derisive snort. "Tsileawa! He took your cloak, played with it, and gave it back! That's *not* a true gift!"

He groaned again.

"It is for me! Now go! He wakes."

Andy opened his eyes. Tsileawa was holding a wet cloth to his forehead. "Have any water?" he asked.

She put the cloth down and reached for a mug. He dragged himself into a sitting position. Once steady, he took it and drank. "Thanks."

He finished the drink. She used cushions to prop him up. He rubbed his forehead.

"You hurt?"

"Overuse headache. Was expecting it. Just need to sleep for a while." He looked over at her cloak. "Did it work?"

In answer, her cloak slid over and "peered" at his face. Fluffers put a protective fold between them. "It's okay, Fluffers." He looked at the other cloak. "Keke?" It nodded and went to Tsileawa.

"Good." He lay fully back, closed his eyes, and let exhaustion take him into darkness.

* * *

A week later, he was sitting at a small table in his room at Appletor. There was a knock. Willy and Jules came in without waiting for his answer. "Andy!" Jules swept toward him. "Don't rise." She hugged him tightly. "Didn't think we'd ever see you again."

Andy looked over at his brother. "Congrats, Willy! Heard you saved the town."

Willy held back. "I left you to die. Didn't think you'd want to see me again, but—"

"You left because I *told* you to. You saved the town. I'm back. Now get over here, so I don't have to keep twisting my neck to see you!"

Willy came to him in a rush and hugged him. He and Jules sat. "Mother and Father will be here tomorrow," Jules said as she poured them cider. "So, brother, did you really steal a horse and escape like they've been saying?"

Andy took a drink. "Not exactly."

"So, what happened?" Willy asked. "You show up alone on an Ograna horse more than two weeks after you vanish. Come on. Tell us."

"Please, Andy," Jules added. "We've been reading about the Ogres since you went missing. It... wasn't good."

Andy sighed. "All right."

He took up the tale where Willy'd left him, trying to stick with the facts and keep the memories it dragged up out of it. When he finished, he took another drink. "So that's it. I made her a Named Cloak. When I'd recovered, she gave me this." He held up the green stone bird that hung around his neck on a leather thong. "Her father gave me a horse and an escort to get me out of Ograna lands. After that, I came here. I'm supposed to go back this fall and discuss things. Trade, I think."

Willy and Jules looked at each other.

She asked, "Do you know anything about Ograna marriage customs?"

"No. I've been concentrating on trade and war. Why?"

"What we read about what they did to prisoners was... pretty grim, so we read each other interesting bits of their customs," Jules said. "It's traditional for the suitor to give his intended a cloak. If she likes it, she gives him a gift back."

Andy choked on his cider. "What? Can't be. I gave her the cloak because she saved my life."

"And the chief pledged her hand to whoever could make her laugh. You did. Then you made her a magic cloak, and she gave you that bird," Willy said.

"But—"

"No buts about it, brother." Willy grinned. "Congratulations on your engagement!"

* * * * *

C.M. DeMott Bio

C. M. DeMott is a small animal veterinarian living in southwest Virginia. Since discovering the Society for Creative Anachronism in 1976, she has been writing and performing original ballads based on legend, faery tales, and myths under the name Morgan Wolfsinger. She currently has seven CDs out, and is working on an eighth. "Choices" in *Talons and Talismans II* was her first published story. "Fluffers" in *The Keen Edge of Valor* is her second. You can find her music at morganwolfsinger.bandcamp.com.

* * * * *

Nostalgia
by Mark Wandrey
A Traveling Gods Story

Denver

"Elanor?"

"Yeah, Mom?"

"We expect you to act like an adult while we're gone."

Elanor sighed and rolled her eyes. Her father narrowed his. She glanced out the vast window facing west, where the sun was sinking toward the Rockies' front range.

Her father pursed his lips. "Maybe we should ask Wilma to look in on her?"

Wilma, her busybody neighbor, was the last person Elanor wanted to stick her nose in every fifteen minutes. Her parents going to Saint Petersburg for two weeks in early March was a dream come true. She'd only gotten her driver's license in September, but had driven to work and with her friends since then without incident. Regardless, it had taken weeks of unrelenting pestering to convince them she was ready for the responsibility of being alone in their Denver home.

"Dad, I'll be responsible and take care of everything, I promise."

He looked at her mom, and she knew she'd closed the deal. A few minutes later, they were hugging. Her parents went through security and out of view.

Elanor walked back to the garage and her car, practically skipping. She'd already planned for her friends to come over that night and have a little party. Just some girls playing videos and drinking sodas. More than a few, and one of the neighbors would rat her out anyway.

She drove from the garage, using voice-mode to compose a group message to her friends. As she turned onto the expressway passing the airport, her mother texted her.

Just taking off, see you soon.

Elanor looked at the airport, and as luck would have it, the green and white livery of a Western Airlines 737 was just climbing into the sky. They were a small airline, and only flew out of Denver once in the morning, and once in the late afternoon. It had to be their flight. She ordered the phone to compose a response just as it happened.

Pain. Pain beyond tolerance. A white-hot rod had been inserted into her brain and was being wiggled around. Elanor screamed in agony. Then, as fast as it came, the pain was gone. The only thing remaining was the memory, sharp as a knife, and just as real.

She looked around. The car was dead. The motor 'hadn't stopped, *everything* had stopped. The display that showed all the car's functions was dead. The pain had only lasted a couple seconds, and the car was still rolling along, slowing. Her phone clipped to the docking station on the console was dead as well. She tried turning the car toward the side of the road, but it didn't respond to the wheel. "Oh, shit," she said.

In a near panic, she looked around at the other cars, afraid she was about to get hit by a truck, but every other car was, just like hers, slowing to a stop. Somewhere nearby, Elanor heard the unmistakable sound of crunching steel. However, it wasn't near her.

"How can *all* the cars just stop?" she wondered aloud.

Without the sound of the car's sound system and all the other cars' wheels and motors, the tortured report of a plane hitting the airport perimeter fence was incredibly loud. The planes were all stopping, too. Horrified, she searched the sky and found her parent's plane just as it bellyflopped to the ground and was engulfed in a massive fireball.

East of Rawlins

Elanor sat up with a start. The ancient bus rocked as the wind howled through long shattered windows. It took her a moment of looking around to remember where she was, and that she'd been reliving the moment of her life change, five years gone. She'd stopped to eat some jerky and drink some water, hoping the wind would let up. It hadn't, and she'd drifted off.

"Stupid," she said as she closed her pack and slung it once more. "What if someone came up while I was napping like an idiot?" In another minute, she was up and moving. She'd run out of her ADD/ADHD medicine years ago. Sometimes her mind drifted off. Lately, it had gotten worse.

The wind was terrible. Elanor remembered, when she was a little girl, it would blow so hard that semis on the freeway would tip over. She massaged her temples, the memory of the pain echoing in her mind.

"Freeway," she said, the whipping winds tearing the words from her mouth so they never reached her ears. "Trucks and cars," she spoke into the maelstrom, then laughed. In the near distance, she could just make out the road sign.

Salt Lake City	295
Rock Springs	112
Rawlins	5

Did we really drive across states in hours, or even days?

A gust hit her—had to be more than fifty miles per hour—and she barely stayed on her feet. After the last years, the theory of cars and cities making the weather worse had gone from science and fear to a joke around the campfires. The fall winds in Wyoming had become worse—much, much worse. The winters were colder, and the summers hotter, too. The only things missing were the scientists and politicians looking for something to blame it on.

Maybe that was all magic, too, she thought with a mental laugh. Her last words had rewarded her with a mouthful of dust, so she thought it. *Five miles to go, and I don't even know what to expect.*

Something moving off to the left caught her attention, and she froze. The sun was well up behind her, and she still couldn't see more than a hundred yards in any direction. Swirling dust and a vague impression of stunted trees was about it. Her sling was in her left hand before she consciously thought about it. There were four-legged predators in this region, but the two legged ones were more common, and more deadly.

There it was; another flash of movement. Elanor fished a ball bearing out of her belt pouch and moved in a crouch back the way she'd come toward the rusted ruins of a FedEx van. There was no true cover inside it, just some metal concealment between her and whatever it was. When she reached the relative safety of rusted metal and decaying plastic, she breathed again.

The sling hung down from her left hand, a bearing in her right fingertips. You didn't load a sling until you were ready to fire. Centrifugal force made it highly difficult to alter your point of aim more than a dozen degrees, and if you turned suddenly with a bullet resting in the sling, it could fall out before you started. Better to wait until you were sure of your target before loading and starting your swing.

She strained her eyes, looking for the movement. When it came, she almost laughed. A trio of tumbleweeds was being propelled across the overgrown and rock-strewn interstate. Then she did laugh, despite dust getting into her mouth. In spite of what she'd just seen,

Elanor waited in the lee of the FedEx truck, out of the worst of the raging wind.

The truck rocked as a powerful gust hit. She took a long minute to look in the direction the tumbleweeds had come from. You didn't survive in the wilds if you refused to adapt or develop a healthy degree of paranoia.

Finally, when she was certain there was nothing out there except tumbleweeds and dust, she got back to her feet. She couldn't see the sun through the haze, so she checked the old Seiko windup watch on her left wrist.

"Five miles," she mumbled under her breath, and settled her pack once again. The sun was certainly below its zenith; she needed to make progress or risk getting caught out on the highway after nightfall.

It was difficult to make good time with the wind gusting as bad as it was. She needed to make certain of her footing with each step, which reduced her to a slow walk, she guessed less than two miles per hour. As the sun continued toward the west, two hours after the tumbleweed incident, it began getting dark.

"The front range is just west and south of me," she said to the wind. A dim shape ahead to her right, nothing more than a shadow, began to resolve. She hoped she knew what it was long before she could see for sure. As the sunlight quickly diminished, the form became apparent; two badly sandblasted and rusted columns supporting a sign that read "I-80 Travel Plaza." An empty frame above it had once held an advertisement for Sinclair, a company with a dinosaur on it selling gasoline.

"I made it," she breathed and hurried her pace a little in anticipation. A short time later, she heard the challenge.

"Who's out there?"

Elanor stopped immediately. "My name is Elanor," she called out, having to shout over the din. "I'd like to spend the night?"

"You that skinny, little black-haired girl?" a man replied in a native Wyoming accent, pulling out the end of the word "skinny" and making the G in girl harder than other places.

"Yes, that's me. I've been through before."

Up ahead, she heard a mechanical scraping sound, and light suddenly grew. A man stepped forward holding a lantern. It wasn't an artifact, it had been made after the breaking, and by a skilled metalworker, it appeared. It had a nicely shaped glass lens, and a shroud protected the flame from the wind. By the looks of the flame, it was burning kerosene, something she knew the Travel Plaza had for trade.

"Hands up, please," the man said. He had a faded red bandanna over his face, with weather-beaten plastic goggles over his eyes, and a cowboy hat held with a strap against the wind. He looked as weather worn as she felt. Her own eye protection was more elaborate, what had once been expensive, synthetic polycarbonate shooters glasses that wrapped around her eyes to give nearly full protection. Now they were just another artifact of a dead world.

She complied, of course. The man with the lantern had a sword sheathed on his belt, the two who stayed back both held bows, and she could make out arrows nocked and ready. They didn't play games with people; too many out there existed to steal and kill.

The man with the lantern walked around her slowly, using the beam of light to examine her top to bottom. He paused for a moment at her sling looped over her belt, then at the long knife she wore, finally settling on her backpack. "Let's see inside the bag," he said.

"You didn't search my bag last time," she complained.

"There've been some changes," he said.

She hesitated, unwilling to do as he'd requested. "What if I say no?" she asked.

"Then you can turn around and go back the way you came. You know we patrol all around Rawlins, so don't think you can just sneak in; we'll find you."

What he said was true, of course. Rawlins had done well after the breaking, hundreds in the surrounding countryside banding together to create a new community, scraping an existence from the town once perched on lush rangeland and rugged Rockies foothills. One of the ways they survived was by keeping a careful track of who came through or stayed, even for a short time.

She wondered what might have happened as she carefully slid her backpack off her shoulders after releasing the hip strap. Placing it on the dusty ground and using herself as a windbreak to keep it from filling with sand and dust, she opened it for him.

"Step back."

"I won't," she said, finally drawing a line.

His hand fell to his sword hilt, a seemingly casual gesture.

"I have stuff in there I don't want covered in sand, guardsman." She pulled the string to open it as far as it could go. "Aside from trade items and some food, I don't know what I could hide. A bomb, maybe?"

The old man grunted, sharing the joke, and angled the lantern down to peer inside. "Is that a gun?"

"Belonged to my dad," she said as he looked. Having her things examined made her brain itch.

"Gotta weigh a couple pounds in that case. Why keep it?"

"Why wear that watch?" she asked, having noticed the long dead digital watch he wore on her first visit over a year ago.

He gave a grunt, half laugh, half acknowledgement of a point made. "Watch weighs a lot less than the gun. Besides, maybe it'll come back on one day."

"Better to hope the moon and sun cease chasing themselves across the sky," she replied.

He stood and called to his fellows. "She's fine." The other men removed arrows from strings and returned them to quivers.

"You going to tell me what you were looking for?"

"No," he replied and held out a necklace. Made from simple leather cord, it had a half-dollar hanging from it. A 1968 half-dollar, to be precise. A nod to the city's founding in 1868. The old coin was rare, though not impossible to find. The guards changed the leather cords regularly. This week it was stained green. "You know the rules?"

"Have they changed?"

"No." He looked at her expectantly through his aged goggles. "Don't cause trouble," he added before returning to his comrades, all three fading into the swirling dust like post-apocalyptic warriors, which she supposed they were, of a sort. She was alone in moments.

Reclosing the backpack, she slung it over one shoulder instead settling it in place and locking the buckles. Rawlins proper was still almost a mile down Interstate 80; the Travel Plaza was a truck stop near the small town of Sinclair. It had once been a rail stop, home to a maintenance depot and many oil tanks. It also had a hundred or so houses for the little town's very poor people. Rawlins had turned it into traveler's housing, anyone who wished was welcome to stay and rest, as long as it wasn't too long, and they followed the rules.

Leaving 80, she walked along Highway 76 as it led past the Travel Plaza. A few lanterns were visible inside. With dark following, there wouldn't be any trading, so she went into Sinclair. As the road proceeded, it descended away from the crumbling interstate. The low ridge the freeway had been constructed on provided some shelter from the wind, which she was extremely grateful for. She pulled down the handkerchief covering her mouth and breathed relatively dust-free air for the first time in days.

Once across the rusting railroad tracks, the road turned to parallel the interstate just a few hundred yards to her left. A lot of abandoned, rusted cars fell behind her, then the shadows of hulking pipes and tanks; the oil refinery. The ground fell away quickly now that she no longer had to tread so carefully. Even so, the cracked and pitted concrete had sand drifts as high as her knees. She could only imagine what it was like in the winter.

Eventually she passed a couple businesses—a restaurant and a shoe store. Both were intact, and she remembered they were working. The restaurant served good steaks, if you could afford them, and the shoe store dealt in artifact footwear and other clothing, salvaged from cities, or even the odd unlooted train or truck. There'd been a new cobbler, a shoemaker in Rawlins, if it was still in business.

Passing the businesses and what had once been the town square, now decayed and abandoned, she finally reached the residential area. A hand painted sign declared the rules she already knew.

1) You can stay in any unoccupied house.

2) If you burn the house down, best to start running.

3) Once you pick a house, stake out the sign tied to the porch.

4) Don't get comfortable; one week maximum stay.

5) Any fightin gets you the road, too.

Simple enough. She turned down the second road and walked a block, looking for a little salt-shack-style home. It was there, and no sign in the yard. She smiled as she climbed the creaky steps. The sign was there, and she quickly sank it into the sandy soil by the sidewalk before going inside. There was no lock on the door. Inside, some trash was scattered, empty snack bags and drink cans. Someone had stayed here since her last visit, which made sense. From somewhere came the odor of urine, a sign of visitors not interested in being courteous.

Elanor got out her own little lantern, an artifact made to use purified petroleum lamp oil, not forced to run on kerosene. It gave off a sickly yellow light, and she had to spin the little built in lighter half a dozen times before it caught. Now with light, she was able to see just how trashed the place was.

She almost left and found another. Eventually, she gave up with a sigh, dug a garbage bag out of her pack, and set about cleaning. Luckily, someone had only pissed on the back porch, and she didn't find piles of human excrement. The house was too small for more than a solo or a small family. Those types didn't stay anywhere for long. By the time it was completely dark outside, she had her sleeping bag set up in the far back corner of the living room. An ideal location, with no way for someone to come at her from behind.

She spent a few minutes in her calming ritual, taking out items from her past life and looking at them. Her old cellphone, a necklace her mom had given her, her dad's gun, a green rock she'd found. Her breathing became regular, and she sighed.

The last thing she did before climbing into the bag was to remove her tiny strings of jingle bells and hang one from each of the house's two exterior doors. Gratefully, she let the bag's insulation warm her as the wind roared through the old house's loosening shingles. Putting out the lantern, Elanor was asleep in minutes.

Denver

Elanor sat in her car for hours, crying and in shock, her grief battling the memory of the pain, before someone rapped on her window and yelled, "You okay?"

Dumbly, she nodded. "Did you feel that stabbing pain, too?"

The man nodded back and wandered on.

She got out, slowly realizing whatever had happened wasn't just a local event. It was full dark now, and the sky was alive with stars, more than she'd ever seen in her life. The airport was miles east of Denver, but even so, the massive city resting at the foothills of the mountains lit up the countryside for fifty miles. There was no light at all. Only a few people even had flashlights that worked.

Returning to her car, she reached in to get her phone, planning on calling... someone? The phone wouldn't work, and it took her a moment to remember she'd tried earlier. It was as dead as the car, and everything else. She got a flashlight from the glove compartment. Her father had given it to her when he'd bought the car. More tears came as she flipped it on and off. It didn't work. She screamed and threw it into the dark as far as she could.

"What the fuck is happening?" she cried at the sky. Nobody answered, not even the other people she could dimly see messing with their cars or walking along the freeway.

After a time, Elanor walked around her car to see if there was anything she could do. Of course, there wasn't. She realized she was getting cold. Pressing the trunk release on the fob didn't do anything, so she used the key to manually open the trunk and retrieve the cold weather bag her father had insisted she carry. Traffic and weather could strand you, and the winter could be deadly.

She stood, holding the bag, and cried some more. There was still some light, the fire of her parents' plane still burning. There were no firetrucks to put it out. Slowly, without really thinking it through, she started walking home.

It took two days to walk the thirty miles back home to northwest Denver, close to Boulder. She slept under a bridge when she couldn't go any further. The emergency blanket in the pack kept her warm, and a friendly old couple gave her a bag of potato chips. That, along with the jerky in the bag and a bottle of water she found, was her only food.

She'd hiked a lot in previous years. Despite that, she was almost stumbling as she entered their development. In two days, Elanor had seen exactly two working vehicles, both ancient, smoking behemoths she thought had once been Army trucks.

As she entered her subdivision, Elanor was less in shock at her loss, and more tired, cold, and hungry. She'd been wearing the emergency silver mylar blanket like a wind breaker, as the temperatures stayed low, and a drizzle began. Almost walking in a fog, passing houses she'd grown up next to, not realizing their state until she got to her own.

The front door had been kicked in, almost shattered in the frame. Elanor stopped and stared, not understanding what she was seeing, like a person who'd parked their car to go have lunch, only to return and find the car wrecked. She stood there in confusion, her world altered.

She'd eventually found an old flashlight in the garage that worked. Elanor wouldn't understand for quite some time that it was because semiconductors no longer functioned, but old-fashioned incandescent did. The house was trashed, everything of value taken. However, food and their camping gear was left. She'd waited there a week, hoping for things to return to normal. It never did, and eventually gangs started looting again, and she was forced to pack out.

Just as she was about to leave, she took one more walk through the house, not sure why she bothered. Everything of any use had been packed up already. As she was going through her parents' closet, the floor gave a little. Elanor got down with the flashlight, its batteries almost dead, and found a hidden compartment in the floor. Inside was the case with her father's pistol.

Who Runs Bartertown?

Elanor woke up with a sigh. She didn't know why she was reliving five years ago *now*, of all times. Maybe because it was fall and getting close to the anniversary? She did her best to put it out of her mind as she got out the little Emberlit stove and put it together.

Made of titanium, weighing less than a pound, and folding flat, you could burn anything in it, from leaves to wood pellets. She used some deadfall wood from the backyard and soon had water boiling for tea.

Breakfast was instant eggs and a very stale granola bar. About par for course, after she'd left the plains behind at the end of summer. She already missed the family she'd been working for on their farm, but it had been clear from the beginning it was just for the summer.

Her meager breakfast finished, Elanor put the tea in her vacuum thermos and repacked her gear. Even if she returned here, she'd leave nothing behind while gone. She made sure she had the half-dollar with its green cord over her head and headed out the door into the chill morning air.

Now that it was daytime, and the worst of the windstorm was over—though not gone, as it seldom was on the high plains since the breaking—people were out and about. A trio of women were slowly pushing a massive, homemade cart down the road, piled high with salvaged furniture. As they all wore green-corded half-dollars, she knew it was unlikely it was salvaged from Sinclair. As proof, a trio of guardsman rode just a block behind them on horseback.

She would have liked to get a horse. Who wouldn't? Her problem was simple; she was allergic to the animals. Well, that and they were horribly expensive up north. With the end of mechanical irrigation and diesel trucks transporting hay, it became difficult to raise large animals without grazing over massive acreage. She'd stuck with shank's mare.

The women scarcely gave her a look as she took the sign and put it back on the porch. The three guardsmen did, one of them a little too appraising for her liking. She glared back, and he whispered to his two fellows, causing them all to laugh. She ground her teeth and walked on.

Elanor's first stop was back to the Travel Center. It didn't look any better in the daylight. Only a few people were selling, and the group operating the place claimed they were almost out of kerosene. Last year, when she came through on the way to Colorado for the winter, one of the traders had said they had thousands of gallons left. It wasn't in high demand, because few kerosene stoves remained that worked without power. She couldn't see how it could all be just *"gone."*

The rest of the meager offerings were things like dried apples, sad looking potatoes, and collections of salvage, most likely from the same cars she'd passed in the long miles between Cheyenne and there. Her normal route was to turn south on Highway 289, but she was wondering if she should've headed south on 130 by Walcott. It was a lot tougher route because of the meandering road and climbs, but Rawlins was suddenly giving her the chills.

She needed to do some trading for food. Buried in her bag were valuables, the results of her summer's work on the farm. But if Rawlins was as bad as Sinclair… maybe she should reconsider.

In the end, she decided to move on to Rawlins. This time of year, their bazaar should be doing serious business. Lots of wanderers like her would be moving through to wintering locations, some probably to the same area she was heading to. Reluctantly, she picked up Interstate 80 and backtracked east, passing Sinclair to her right, this time from above on the freeway.

The walk to the Rawlins exit was only another mile. Long hours walking and the lower winds allowed her to eat up the distance quickly. In half an hour, she reached the checkpoint. Unlike the one by Sinclair, Rawlins' guardsmen manned a permanent defense point on the freeway in addition to roving patrols. A jumble of rusting cars were lashed together to make passage on the road impossible, where they'd been for years.

As she approached, Elanor could see the gradual improvements. A bus turned into a shelter. A shed for horses in bad weather. A semi-trailer with arrow slits cut in the side. A flatbed truck in the center, where several men could stand to examine anyone who approached. And finally, a tower made from repurposed scaffolding, which provided a considerable watch tower. *Post-apocalyptic fort,* she thought as one of the men on the flatbed waved her to stop.

"I came into Sinclair last night," she said, and held up her half-dollar, the green cord easily visible.

"Billy, check her out," an older man with a big, bushy white beard said.

"You bet, Captain."

Elanor looked at the bearded man. She'd met the captain of the guardsmen last year. The man had been no more than forty and was clean shaven. This was someone new, and it furthered her feeling that something had changed.

The younger man named Billy jumped down and approached her. He seemed at ease, though Elanor could see hints of movement behind the arrow slits, and a man in the tower nocked an arrow to his compound bow, an artifact model with machined wheels. Those were getting hard to find.

"Can I see inside your bag?" Billy asked after he'd walked around her slowly.

"I guess," she said, doffing the pack and opening it. "I went through this yesterday in Sinclair."

"Just procedure," Billy said, leaning over and looking inside. Just like the previous day, he only seemed to glance.

What could they be looking for with such a cursory examination? "What's all this about?" she asked, her curiosity finally getting the better of her.

"We had some trouble," Billy said. "A couple—"

"That's enough, lad," the captain said gruffly. "Anything?"

"No, just trade stuff," Billy replied.

With a grinding of rusty metal, a doorway opened in the side of a panel van. Brown paint was flaking off. She only noticed as she was climbing through the door that there were extensive barricades leading away from the guard post. It wasn't just a simple checkpoint anymore; they'd built a wall around Rawlins! How much effort had it taken to move hundreds of ruined trailers, train cars, and piles of debris to create the wall? She hadn't seen any sort of work of this degree since the breaking.

"Seriously," she said on the other side of the barrier, gesturing at the long line of stuff used to build a wall. "What the heck?"

"Just move along," the captain said, gesturing down the freeway off-ramp into east Rawlins.

She really wanted to ask more questions, then decided against it. The guardsmen in Rawlins had always been a sorta laid back crowd. None of the big rover gangs or salvagers bothered coming through. No big cities or large populations to mess with. *Yeah, something's changed, and the locals are being very tight-lipped about it.*

Elanor continued away from the checkpoint and down the ramp, glancing back once or twice. None of the guardsmen were giving her a second glance; all eyes were directed outward.

Rawlins had possessed three freeway exits, back when they were used for cars. Going west, the first was what they called a business loop, taking you through the center of the city's business districts. Not far off the exit was a Walmart, which was where they'd situated the bazaar once the city got organized. All the houses in Rawlins were either occupied or sealed. Squatters weren't welcome, and regular patrols of the guardsmen ensured that didn't happen.

She was relieved to see dozens of traders set up in the expansive Walmart parking lot. The interior of the building, looted five years ago, wasn't the indoor part of the bazaar. These spaces were owned by mostly locals and a few well connected traders. The network of people moving from region to region, carrying goods from other parts of the country, was growing quickly. Just before leaving the farm, she'd heard (second hand) of someone bringing coffee beans up from South America! That seemed a stretch, but there was fresh tobacco available, grown in Tennessee and carried north.

There was a fence around the Walmart and its parking lot, a layer of security that had been there for years. They were constructed of premade fence panels chained together, with barbwire on top. A dozen guards patrolled the fence from the inside. Crime was rare at a bazaar, but not unheard of.

She presented herself at the checkpoint to enter, and allowed her bag to be more thoroughly searched. You could trade *almost* anything in the bazaar, but not drugs. It was Wyoming, after all. There were tables set up to allow her to carefully put everything out to be examined.

"That a gun case?" a young man asked. "Why do you carry that?"

"It belonged to my dad."

"Heavy, for nostalgia," he said. She stared him down, and he shrugged as they went over her stuff.

"This pot?" a woman asked about a ziplock bag.

"Tobacco," she said.

She opened the bag and sniffed. "Wow, this is fresh!" Several other traders waiting to go in were looking curiously. "Where'd you get it?"

"None of your concern," Elanor replied.

The woman scowled, but carefully resealed the bag. She looked to be in her forties, and Elanor would bet she used to smoke. Despite being stale, packaged cigarettes were still valuable. Maybe not as much as sealed pipe or rolling tobacco, which was packaged in nitrogen and would stay fresh for decades, but still valuable. However, paper was also getting hard to find. She understood a cigarette rolled with printer paper was not a fun smoke. She also had a dozen hand-carved pipes in her gear. An older man on the farm had traded her for them.

Judging by the looks she was getting, trading for the tobacco and pipes before leaving the farm was a win. She'd always had good luck when trading, as evidenced by her continued survival. The shoulders of the nation's interstates were littered with millions of corpses, most from the first six months after the breaking. Not all, though. Every time she moved, she found fresh bodies, some still being pecked at by ravens and other scavengers.

"Okay?" she finally asked as one of the security guards was looking at her small collection of knives for the third time.

"Yeah," the woman said, obviously the one in charge. "Take your shit."

Elanor sniffed. *If it's shit, why were you so curious?* Of course, they didn't help her pack it up. That sort of treatment was common. Locals didn't like wanderers like her; they took away valuable materials believed to belong where they were. She didn't complain as she reloaded her pack, taking care to place each item where she wanted it. The person waiting behind her made impatient noises, which she ignored as she went into the bazaar.

At least inside it was the same as last time. She wandered for a few minutes, looking at what others had for trade, seeing how her stuff rated against theirs. On second thought, things looked pretty lean. *What's going on?* she wondered.

Procedures didn't look any different. She found an empty table and set up. Tobacco, pipes, a nice selection of disposable cigarette lighters. Four Zippo-style lighters, including one new in the box. She had a handful of flint dispensers, little plastic wheels holding flints for Zippos. If you were careful, you could use them on disposables, too. Even two 4-ounce containers of lighter fluid for the Zippos. Sure, you could use gasoline or kerosene, but lighter fluid worked so much better.

Elanor rounded out her table with her stash of chewing gum and other, mostly nonperishable candies. She had a talent for ferreting out little items like that in places that had been picked over a dozen times before. Most of her stuff usually wasn't valuable enough to get her in trouble. The tobacco, however, was a prime trade item.

"No shit, tobacco?" A gray-haired man using a cane was hobbling quickly toward her table.

"Yes, sir," she said, smiling.

He leaned over and looked at the baggies. Elanor had traded for four pounds and divided it into eight half-pound ziplock bags. In addition, she had an ounce in a smaller, "snack-sized" ziplock. She held it out. "Take a sniff."

The old guy grinned from ear to ear and opened the bag. When he smelled the contents, his eyes practically rolled back in his head. "We get people with tobacco, usually taken from cigarettes. Every once in a while, in sealed bags. But this?"

Elanor smiled. He bought one of her bags, a pipe, and a disposable lighter for a two-pound bag of rice, beans, and two cans of tomato sauce. Several others were right behind him. Two hours later, the tobacco and her pipes were gone, as were her Zippos, flints, lighter fluid, and all but one disposable lighter. Her candy hadn't proved as popular this time.

The only problem was her pack. The tobacco and other items she'd traded were compact. The amount of dried foods she'd traded for were bulkier. She had an extra shoulder bag, and it too was now stuffed. While she was repacking her bag, she put her dad's gun in its case on the table for a moment.

"That an old 1911?" an old man asked.

"Yeah, it was my dad's."

He nodded. "Can I look at it?"

She froze for a second, fighting her compulsive disorder to let anyone else touch her personal things. After a moment, she took a deep breath. "Sure." He seemed like a nice guy. He opened the box and whistled.

"It's in perfect shape!"

"I've taken care of it."

"Did you use it, before?"

"Yeah, I learned to shoot with it." In her mind's eye, she clearly remembered her father standing behind her, holding her hands, and shepherding her through the gun's recoil. At 10-years old, he'd seemed enormous.

The gray-haired man gently put a finger on the gun's walnut grip, closing his eyes, then looked at her. She gave a little shiver. It felt like he was looking *through* her. "I mean, after the pain?"

Everyone called it something else. "I only had six bullets," she said. "Ammo was impossible to find, until..."

He nodded in understanding. There were no bullets in the box. She'd used them all. Four for food, two to save her life. Then, months after the breaking, guns stopped working, too.

"I couldn't just throw it away."

He nodded again and closed the case, walking briskly away. In a minute, he returned and set a bag on her table.

"What's that?" she asked. He gestured at it with his head, so she investigated. Inside was a box of .45ACP ammo, Federal hollow point. In pretty good shape, too, though the box was a little rat chewed. "Why do you have ammo?"

"I used to have a gun shop," he said. "Believe it or not, some people still trade for ammo. I have no idea why."

"What do you want for it?"

He looked over her remaining goods and picked up two packs of chewing gum and a pack of Tic-Tacs, lifting an eyebrow.

"Done," she said.

He pocketed the candy and gave her a strange, lopsided grin. "Walk with the travelers," he said and strolled away.

The travelers? she wondered. *What the heck is going on here?*

She looked at the bullets and her gun. It had been a stupid trade; the box of ammo was several pounds. Mumbling to herself about impulsiveness, she opened the box and reloaded all three magazines in the box. She did it under the table, so nobody noticed. When she was done, she loaded one into the gun and, without conscious thought, racked the slide and set the safety—the way her father had taught her was the correct way to carry a .45—and then slid the gun into an outside pocket of her backpack.

Another hour, and she only sold a pack of candy, so Elanor called it a day. She had more than enough food now to make it to her winter home. Her last few items packed up, she put on her backpack, slung the additional duffel bag, and wandered around. There might be something interesting or worth her while to trade for. She'd found some good stuff, trading in the past.

The more she looked, the more she was certain things had changed in Rawlins. Most of the other traders looked despondent, watching her with suspicious sideways glances. Very few would meet her gaze. She'd about decided she was done with the place when a commotion caught her attention.

A group of six people, four men and two women whom she'd thought were wanderers like her, were having a loud argument with a woman and her preteen child. The woman was yelling something about "not wanting your type here." One of the female wanderers held out something toward the yelling woman, who responded by screaming and slapping the device out of her hand.

The angle was just right. It soared directly at Elanor, who simply reached out her hand and caught it like a line drive. She'd played baseball before high school, and had been a decent shortstop.

She looked down at what she'd caught. At first, she figured it was a big compass, but that wasn't exactly right. More like a plastic makeup case with a clear glass top. Someone had stuck a paper backing on the inside bottom on which were a concentric ring of compass directions with letters for the cardinal points. Instead of a needle, there was a plastic bead or a ball bearing.

Meanwhile, the woman who'd had the compass thing slapped out of her hand instantly punched the slapping woman in the face. Not a casual pop you'd give to someone 'who was annoying you, a full on fist to the face. Elanor stared in surprise. You saw enough violence on the road, but not often between women.

The four men watched the fight for a moment before moving in, laughing and pulling the women apart. Elanor looked around for someone to help. The guardsmen kept a tight rein on the bazaar. Fights like this could ruin a town's reputation as a barter town. She found an entire squad, six men armed with bows and long-bladed knives, just standing and watching the show.

Who's running this place? she silently wondered.

"Where'd it go?" the woman who'd started the fight asked, looking toward Elanor.

Elanor made the compass disappear. She wasn't a thief—far from it. However, it was a finders-keepers world she lived in. Making something disappear before someone else could claim it was a valuable life skill. The whole group started looking for their device. Elanor just stood there looking indifferent. If she'd tried to walk off, they'd have immediately suspected her. The woman who'd started the fight glared at Elanor for a long moment. Elanor returned the glare, and the other women moved on. *Then* Elanor went to make her exit.

She reached the exit and noticed the guardsmen were finally involved, only in detaining the woman and her child. The six scavengers were yelling at the guardsmen to tie up the woman, and they were doing as they were told.

Elanor paused. She couldn't get involved, she *couldn't!* These places didn't have jails or anything like that. If you got in trouble with their version of the law, you were screwed. What she'd been sensing was clear now; some group had control, or at least heavy sway with those in charge. She needed to get out now. *Then why am I just standing here?*

She started to take a step toward the screaming woman and her child when it happened. A strange tingle preceded the entire world exploding in brilliant light. For a split second, Elanor was afraid it was another breaking. But there was no pain, just all-consuming light. She tried turning away from it, but there was no source. It was as if it originated in her brain. Someone screamed, and others yelled as well. And then it was over. The light was gone as quickly as it had appeared, and so were the woman and her child.

Elanor left as quickly as she could. She might not have seen evidence of it more than a couple times in the last five years, but she knew magic when it happened. *Knew it.* Sometimes, on those rare occasions when a few wanderers would get together without killing each other around a campfire, they'd talk. Talk about the breaking, talk about how tenuous life was now, even about magic, in hushed tones. Rumors of wizards, of vampires, and even of demons talking in the dark of night.

Unlike all the campfire talk, she knew magic existed. She'd watched a woman in Chugwater four years ago kill a chicken, then make it get up and walk around like nothing had happened—for half an hour. As horrific as it was, the macabre display had been accompanied by the same tingle she'd just felt.

The magic display couldn't have had a greater effect on the crowd in the bazaar if someone had produced a working computer. Panic as people ran for the exits, shouts of outrage, cries of fear, and through it all, the six wanderers searching for the woman and her child, almost desperately.

Elanor didn't wait any longer to see where they'd gone. She'd seen enough to know *someone* was hunting people with magic. Deep in her guts, that scared the shit out of her, and she wasn't sure why. Plenty of people hunted other people, to steal their stuff, or worse. As a girl, she was always conscious of being alone with even one man, especially a fellow wanderer. She didn't know why someone hunting magic bothered her so much.

"Hey!"

She didn't turn around, she just kept walking. The voice was that of the woman who'd started the fight.

"You, I'm talking to you."

She was going to keep walking until a hand grabbed her roughly and tried to spin her around. Elanor dropped her shoulder and spun in the opposite direction, snaking a hand under her jacket and loosening her main blade. It had been ground down from a machete not long after she'd become a wanderer at the cost of a carton of cigarettes.

"Back off," Elanor growled. It was just the woman and one of the guys. The woman looked furious; the man looked amused.

"You were involved with that satanic episode," the woman said.

Elanor blinked, trying to understand. "You mean magic?" The woman snarled, and the man's amusement turned dark in an instant. "Somebody used magic; wasn't me."

"You need to come with us," the man said and moved forward.

Elanor backed away, fast. Her hand moved from the knife handle to snag her sling. Unlike the previous day, she immediately loaded it and swung up in less than a second. When eating depended on being able to grab a rabbit on the run, you got good at loading your weapon of choice. The sling cup with its 15mm stainless steel ball bearing made a *Vup-vup-vup* sound as it spun over her head. "One more step," she growled.

"Just grab the sinner," the woman snarled. But the man eyed the sling dubiously. He was apparently smart enough to realize how dangerous a piece of steel hurled at high speed could be. He moved his hand toward the box slung cross-body, and Elanor increased the speed of her sling rotation. One end was wrapped around her palm, the other pinched by her index finger. She could loose with a simple relaxing of her finger.

"What's going on here?" a guardsman demanded, striding toward them.

"This person is threatening us," the man said.

"Seems to me you tried grabbing *her*," the guardsman replied. He turned to glance at Elanor. "Could you stow that weapon?"

She lowered the sling and deftly caught the pocket, retrieving the ball bearing. She also heaved a little sigh of relief. The guardsman was Billy, the one she'd met earlier when coming into town.

"She's a satanic follower," the woman spat.

"Naturally, you have proof of that?" Billy asked.

"There was some sort of spell used against us in the bazaar," the man said.

"I saw nothing of what happened, only you trying to grab this woman.

"But—"

"That's enough," Billy said and came closer to Elanor, speaking softly, "I warned you things have changed. Do you have all your trade goods?"

"Yes," she replied sotto voce.

"Then I'd get out of Rawlins, now."

Elanor glanced up at the sun, well past its zenith. She didn't like the idea of being caught out on the road at night, though she liked being accosted by these crazy people even less. "Say no more," she said, and turned to quickly walk away.

"Your mayor said we had free rein against these sinners," the man said.

"That doesn't include grabbing anyone you want."

"We'll see about that," the woman said.

Elanor didn't glance back until she was turning a corner. The pair was watching her go and talking between them. Once out of view, Elanor ran.

United We Stand

There was the same sort of security west of Rawlins as she'd gone through east. Luckily, they didn't care about anyone leaving, as long as you had a visitor coin and turned it in on the way out. Several of the guardsmen eyed her extra large bag curiously, as if they'd like an excuse to search her. None of them bothered, and she was back on the highway.

The first thing she did was get off the old interstate. There were a myriad of small roads, typically dirt, and now mostly in terrible shape. She took the first one she came to, which went north of an old Flying J truck stop, its sign now empty, and the main building burned. That had happened shortly after the breaking. Even so, the area always smelled of diesel and burned plastic.

The problem with getting off the road was, none of them paralleled the interstate for long. The land around Rawlins was full of sharp, rocky hills, so she was forced to cut across old farmland constantly. That worked okay, because she was able to use her small binoculars to spy on the interstate for signs of pursuit. The wind was gusting around 25 mph, almost a calm day for the area. She just needed to get twenty miles or so away from the town before nightfall and any hopes of those people catching up with her would be nearly zero.

The sun dropped below the mountains to the southwest without sign of pursuit, and Elanor breathed a sigh of relief. She moved back to the small country road she'd been following—a rusted sign declared it was Knobs Road—and looked for an out of view place to camp. It was then she heard the sound. A woman crying.

It was a harsh world, and it had made her a harsh person. She'd passed people in desperate straits. Anyone still alive had. No matter how much you had, you couldn't feed everyone. You couldn't save everyone. Some didn't want to be saved, or were looking to take advantage of someone who had a kind heart. You got hard, or you got dead. Even so, it gave her pause.

What are you doing? she asked herself as she slowly traced the sounds. In the back of her mind, she thought she knew what she'd find. Concern mixed with fear and apprehension as she moved. Shortly, she was close enough to hear voices. A young girl saying she was hungry, and an adult woman crying. Elanor had heard the sound of despair before.

She moved a little closer then called quietly. "Hello?"

The woman screamed, and Elanor heard her pull the child behind her. "Who's there?"

Elanor moved forward. There was almost no light remaining. It was enough to recognize the woman, including the dark bruises on her face from her brief battle in the bazaar. "It's okay; I'm not with those people."

"W-what do you want?" the other woman asked.

Elanor paused for a moment before speaking. "I want to help," she said, finally. "I'm Elanor; what's your name?"

"Mary," the other woman replied. The preteen eyed the scene with eyes huge from fear.

"I'm Cynthia," the young girl said. "Do you have any food?"

"Cynthia," Mary hissed.

"It's okay," Elanor said, just managing to suppress a sigh. That was why she'd come down to them, after all. She dug out her little titanium stove and set it up. Using scattered pieces of deadfall twigs to get it going, she used one of her Zippos, filled with lighter fluid, to start the fire. The pair looked at her with eagerness tempered by the sort of pessimism everyone who survived the breaking possessed.

She took in the pair's condition. Their worn shoes, modern before the breaking, now had soles that were almost walked off. They looked as if they hadn't bathed in days, and smelled like possibly longer. Mary's cheeks were hollowed by hunger. While her daughter wasn't as starved, she clearly hadn't eaten well, either. She dug out some instant rice and a can of chicken with rice soup. Not a lot of protein, but it would be filling.

They watched her cook with eager eyes, and when she got out her plates and utensils, it seemed all Cynthia could do to not jump and snatch it from Elanor's hands. She barely had enough bowls and spoons for all of them, and ended up eating her own share from the cook pan, and used the big spoon as well. Mary had to keep Cynthia from wolfing it down. For herself, she ate slowly and carefully, further confirming Elanor's suspicion of how often Mary had been near starvation. You learned to eat slowly, or risk puking it up.

Before long, the food was gone. Water wasn't a problem, so she shared a canteen freely. As the two other women calmed, thanks largely to the food in their bellies, Elanor took stock of their condition. Mary had a simple backpack which seemed to contain little. A single large sleeping bag—not one made for real cold weather—a shovel, a small knife, an empty water bag, a badly worn disposable lighter, and an empty water bottle was the sum of their possessions.

"What happened?" she asked finally, gesturing to their meager possessions with her head.

"We were at a farming community," Mary explained, "near Hastings."

"I know the one. Haven't been there in a while."

"Well," she looked at Cynthia who was lying on the sleeping bag, her eyes almost closed, "there was an incident, and they chased us out."

"Magic?" Elanor asked.

Mary jerked, her eyes instantly afraid.

"It's okay," Elanor insisted. "I told you, I'm not one of them." She took the compass thing from her pocket. "How does this factor in?"

"I thought you caught it," Mary said. "Have you tried to use it?"

"For what? How does it work?"

"Swirl it around, then level it."

Curious, Elanor did as requested. There was a little light from the camp stove, and the moon was rising, too. She could see the little ball inside as she spun it in circles, then stopped. To her amazement, the ball seemed to unfold, and she realized it was a bug of some kind. Only, no bug she knew of had glowing antennae and tiny claws. Elanor almost dropped it in surprise. "What is it?"

"I don't know. But watch."

Elanor looked back down to see the bug-thing scurry to the outer-most compass ring, run along the edge, and stop, waving its antenna, reaching with tiny claws. She looked up and saw it was "pointing" at Cynthia. "Is it detecting..."

"Yes, magic. Or people who have it."

"Where did it come from?"

"I don't know," Mary said and sighed. "I saw the first one just after leaving Hastings. A group of fanatics like those back in Rawlins had one, and they were tracking another man. He must have had more magic, or whatever, because they didn't notice Cynthia."

"What can Cynthia do?"

"A few things. She can make little fires, but not reliably. A light that floats, she can do that whenever she wants. But the flash earlier, that was the first time I've seen that. It's like she's getting more powerful."

"I don't want to believe it's real," Elanor admitted. She gave the compass-thing a shake. The bug turned into a ball and rolled for a moment. When it stopped, it unrolled, walking around the edge of the compass. "But I don't believe in magic."

"No," Cynthia said, her eyes shining in the moonlight and looking at Elanor. She blinked at the strange way the girl was looking at her.

"I don't know how to thank you," Mary said, reaching over to smooth her daughter's hair.

"You don't have to," Elanor said. The bug had walked until it was facing her, waving its antenna almost hesitantly. "Wait, what—" Elanor stopped in mid-sentence, certain she'd heard something. She never saw what hit her in the head, only heard the scream of alarm from Mary. Too late... too late. Darkness engulfed her.

To Believe

Elanor forced her eyes open, the echo of a memory with her father running through her head. "A gun is just a tool, but a very dangerous tool. Like any tool, if you take care of it, it will take care of you. But you *must* respect it."

"Yes, Daddy," she mumbled.

"The bitch who stole the detector is awake," someone said.

Elanor blinked from the light. Had she been asleep all night? The light was wrong, yellow in color, and moving around. Slowly, too slowly, the memory of the night came back to her. The fanatics from the bazaar had snuck up on them. She'd been too busy chatting it up with Mary to even notice. *You deserve to die,* she thought. *Or worse.*

With fingers that didn't want to respond to her commands, she felt herself. They'd taken everything off her, sling, knife, even the multitool she kept in a pocket. She was lying, shivering in the cold, in only her underwear. *God, they're going to rape me,* she thought. Her fingers probed her head, and she hissed as she found a growing lump, and sticky, drying blood.

"You aren't the only one who can use a sling," someone said, a woman.

The one who fought with Mary?

"Are you in league with this devil?" another asked, this one male.

Elanor heard Cynthia crying, and Mary saying soothing words.

"I don't know what you're talking about," she said, her tongue thick. Her mind was clearing slowly, though the pain wasn't deceasing. The light was from the torches three of them carried. Off to the side, one was going through her pack.

"She has a lot of good stuff," the man said. "She won't need it."

"What are we doing with them?" the other woman asked.

"These two have to go back and be burned at the stake." Mary's crying and Cynthia's near hysterical screaming escalated. "That one, we can hang."

Elanor knew, if she got the chance, she could lose these people. Sure, they'd snuck up on her, but that was her mistake. She wouldn't make it again. She was lean and strong, and she could lose them in the dark. Two problems, though. She'd lose everything, and be in her underwear on a Wyoming fall evening, and it meant abandoning Mary and Cynthia. She couldn't let that happen. A plan formed, albeit crazy and desperate. She just needed a weapon.

Elanor struggled to her feet. It was a sign of their contempt for her that they hadn't bothered restraining her in any way. The man nearest her narrowed his eyes. "You mean to hang me, then get on with it. I'm cold."

The man digging through her pack stopped his pillaging and stared at her in surprise. Elanor pounced, diving at the man. One of the other men intercepted her trajectory with a foot to her midriff. She cried out and crashed into her pack instead of the man. *That was a stupid idea,* she realized as she missed her target and crashed into her pack instead.

It was mostly empty, so it didn't provide a very soft landing. More like faceplanting into a bag of groceries. Her gear was scattered in every direction, and she painfully rolled across it, watching all her worldly possessions scatter like chaff.

Elanor came to a stop with something digging painfully into her stomach. As the cretins laughed, she moved her left hand down and found the butt of her dad's pistol. She'd put it in a side pouch of the backpack, and her impact had knocked it loose.

"You know," the woman said, "I don't think I want to waste the time hauling those two back; we might as well hang all three right now."

"Get your skinny ass up, scavenger," the one who'd kicked her snarled.

Elanor rolled over, the gun in her hand. The guy stopped, aiming the lantern at her, then saw the gun and laughed.

"Will ya look at this?" he said, pointing. "Seems the scavenger missed the last four years. Whatcha draggin' that stupid thing around for?"

Elanor backed away, scooting over the hard scrabble on her behind, hissing at the pain in her side where she'd been kicked, and the throbbing in her head from the slingshot. The man had an evil grin on his face as he produced a knife, snapping it open with a flick of his wrist and advancing on her.

The gun in her hands brought a cascade of memories. Elanor as a young child, giddy with excitement as her dad took her on her first trip to the range. A few years later on a camping trip in the Rockies, Mom and Dad at a secluded gun range, having a fun day of shooting. Elanor firing hundreds of rounds through the venerable old gun, her dad's quiet nods of approval as she went from proficient to expert in the weapon. "It'll never let you down," her dad telling her.

Her mind fuzzy from the head trauma, she felt her attention do that thing it used to before the ADHD medicine had helped her learn to control better. All of her being seemed to center on the gun sights. She raised the weapon, aiming at the knife-wielding man, who roared with laughter. "It'll never let you down," her dad's voice said, as if he were leaning over her.

"That's enough, I'm gonna stick her."

"Poke her eyes out," the other woman said—not the leader.

Elanor swept the thumb safety off and put her finger on the trigger. "I love you, Dad," she said, and she could feel his strong hands on her shoulder as she squeezed.

BOOM! The gun rocked in her hands, familiar as her father's kisses on her cheek.

The man dropped the knife and looked down. There was a hole in his jacket, right over his sternum. A little curl of smoke rose from it. He turned and looked at the woman leading their group. "What?" he asked, and his knees gave out. He fell like a puppet with its strings cut.

"Hey!" one of the other men yelled. She turned. It was the guy with the sling, and it was already spinning up.

Instincts acquired after hundreds of hours kicked in. Elanor raised a knee, rested the gun butt on the knee, brought her other hand up to a two-handed grip, and fired again, all in less than a second. A tiny hole appeared in the sling-wielding guy's forehead, and an explosion of brains out the back. He dropped as well.

Two of the other men rushed her. *Boom, Boom.* Both went down, one like the sling man, the other through the gut. He hit the ground screaming. The remaining man ran, leaving both women standing in confusion. Elanor rose to her feet; a sound almost like a song seemed to link her to the gun. She pointed at the woman leader, who was holding a knife. "Drop it."

She did, instantly, but the other woman screamed and ran. Elanor could hear her yelling "Impossible" over and over into the night.

"How?" the leader asked.

Elanor gave a little laugh. "I have no idea."

Mary had sat through it all, holding her daughter. Cynthia seemed the least surprised. She kept looking at Elanor with a knowing expression. For her part, Elanor addressed Mary. "There was some duct tape in my bag; can you find it and tie her up?" Mary nodded and retrieved one of the fallen lanterns to search.

Elanor flicked the safety back on the 1911 and looked at the weapon. Guns hadn't worked in almost five years, yet she'd *known* it would a minute ago when she'd picked it up. She remembered the roly-poly bug waving its tentacles at her, just like it had at Cynthia.

The girl was on her feet, standing next to Elanor, and smiling. She held out a hand, and a tiny but brilliant blue flame appeared in it. She pointed at the gun with her other hand. "Now do you believe?"

"I guess I do." Slowly, she considered the possibilities.

* * * * *

Mark Wandrey Bio

International bestselling author of military sci-fi, space opera, and zombie apocalypse, Mark Wandrey is also the only four-time DragonCon Dragon Award finalist! Military Sci-fi has always been his favorite genre, however, he's recently begun diverging into urban fantasy with his upcoming Traveling Gods series, a dark take on the genre. Living the full-time RV lifestyle as a modern-day nomad, Mark Wandrey has been writing science fiction since he was in grade school. He launched his professional career in 2004 with the release of Earth Song—Overture. Now, 15 years later, he has more than 25 books out, including many bestsellers, and dozens of short stories.

* * * * *

The End of the Story
by D.J. Butler
A Tales of Indrajit & Fix Story

"**A**s you have surmised, it is I who was purchasing information from the Lord Archer's Fanchee administrators about the kelp farms they run." Grit Wopal nodded as if in salute to his own cleverness, his dirty yellow turban bobbing neatly. "On behalf of the Lord Chamberlain, of course, as the head of the Lord Chamberlain's Ears."

Wopal stood in a sparsely-furnished room in the palace of Lord Chamberlain Orem Thrust. Indrajit Twang and Fix sat on a low sofa; sitting, they were nearly as tall as the Yifft spymaster. The Yifft's famous third eye was closed and invisible.

"We did surmise that," Indrajit agreed, "but not until we almost got killed by a Yeziot, a Chark, *and* an angry Fanchee."

"I wouldn't think a single Fanchee would be much of a threat to you two. They're kelp farmers, not renowned for their martial prowess."

"This one was really angry," Indrajit said. "The point is, you could have told us more up front."

"I could have." Wopal smiled. "I didn't want to."

Indrajit ground his teeth. "Do you know what I'm remembering, and with pleasure?"

"Punching me in my third eye?" Wopal suggested. "Twice?"

Indrajit nodded.

"Savor the memory. I know I think of it often."

"You didn't want to reveal to any unnecessary person anything about your information-gathering operation," Fix said. "We understand. But now we've recovered the stolen information, so that's it. That's the end of the story."

"The stolen information, please." Wopal held out a hand, palm up.

Indrajit extracted four knotted leather straps from his kilt pocket. Apparently, they were written documents containing information about the Lord Archer's kelp farms. Grit Wopal had bought the information from the Lord Archer's Fanchee kelp farmers. It had been intercepted by the poetess Oritria and her accomplices, and the Protagonists—Indrajit and Fix—had recovered it. In the process, they'd learned that the conspiracy of kelp-farm information sharers gave their strings to one of the Trivials of Salish-Bozar the White, a small man named Meroit. Meroit passed the information on to other agents of the Lord Chamberlain by painting it in symbolic form in pictures of buildings.

Indrajit handed over the documents.

"It's not quite the end of the story," Grit Wopal said.

"The girl," Indrajit guessed. "The poetess Oritria."

"She stole the information from her father, who was your spy," Fix said. "You want to know who hired her."

"Of course," Wopal said. "The Lord Chamberlain trades in the stolen information. If there is some third party availing itself of the same data, he could get fleeced. And what if the poetess' employer was a hostile foreign power?"

"Maybe it's better if someone else handles this job," Fix said.

"As you pointed out, I strongly prefer not to spread knowledge of these activities any farther than is absolutely necessary."

"Then just send me. Indrajit has feelings for Oritria."

"I do not," Indrajit said. "And besides, you have feelings for all written texts, and that didn't stop you from going after the kelp strap writings with me."

Fix sighed and shook his head.

"You two," Wopal said. "Both of you. That's who's going to track Oritria and find out who employed her."

"Her and the Yeziot Squite," Fix said.

"And Chark," Indrajit pointed out. "Big, scaly guy, four arms, nasty claws? Remember him?"

"The Yeziot is dead," Grit Wopal said.

"Are we certain Chark is in league with Oritria?" Fix asked. "Perhaps it was the confusion belowdecks on the *Duke's Mistress*, but I thought maybe Chark and Squite were battling."

"They were." Indrajit shrugged. "But she knew his name, and they seemed to me to be disagreeing over tactics rather than fighting as enemies. Then Chark destroyed our chambers."

"If Chark isn't in league with Oritria," Wopal said, "then I want to know who employs him, as well."

"Who do you *think* employs them?" Fix asked. "Shouldn't you be testing hypotheses?"

"Indeed, but I don't plan to share them with *you*."

"You think you know," Indrajit said, interpreting the conversation for himself, "but you're not going to tell us. Even though knowing what you think you know might help us prove whether what you think you know is right or not."

"Look at you, Recital Thane," Fix said. "You're fit for the Hall of Guesses now."

Wopal nodded.

"Ah, good," Indrajit said. "Blind and ignorant, that's how I'm most comfortable. If someone actually told me what was going on for once, I'd feel downright out of sorts."

"Like a fish out of water?" Fix suggested.

Indrajit ignored his partner. "How do you know the Yeziot is dead?"

Wopal nodded. "His body is on display at the Blind Surgeon."

"Something about that bothers me," Indrajit said.

"Perhaps that you owed the Blind Surgeon's publican, Anaximander Skink, a prodigious debt before entering the Lord Chamberlain's service?" Grit Wopal suggested.

"No."

"Perhaps that you were humiliated in hand-to-hand combat at the Surgeon's, first by Skink's bouncers, and then by Yashta Hossarian, a jobber in the employ of Holy-Pot Diaphernes?"

Indrajit shuddered at the memory of the bird-legged man. "No, but I feel we're getting closer."

"The four-armed, scaly fellow," Fix said. "Chark. He mentioned the Blind Surgeon."

"That's it." Indrajit closed his eyes and could visualize the encounter, complete with Chark's sibilant hiss and his disdain for the Blaatshi Epic. "He knew I'd once been a regular there. And, ah, some unflattering financial details."

"Welcome to Kish," Fix said. "It's a small town when you need a big one."

"And a maze when you need a crossroads." Indrajit sighed.

* * *

Indrajit inhaled damp sea air as he and Fix strolled down the ramp from the Spill onto the West Flats. The air reeked of the exhalations, bodily odors, and effluvia of all the thousand races of man, but the cool salt of the sea on the breeze gave it a bracing metallic edge. They passed two carts, creaking with the day's pungent catch, and pushed away a troop of men with shaven heads and yellow-green robes who were chanting a song about how the wind heard all the words ever spoken.

"What are the odds," he asked Fix, "that Grit Wopal is withholding information you and I would actually like to know?"

"One hundred percent," Fix said. "Perhaps that's because you and I are unusually curious fellows."

Indrajit bobbed his head from side to side. "In this profession... you make a good point."

"But I doubt he'd get nearly as much value out of men who were less curious."

"Another good point," Indrajit said. "When I compose epic epithets for you, one of them shall certainly reference your curiosity."

"I'm disappointed to hear the epithets do not already exist," Fix said, "but pleased that they will be plural."

"Multiple," Indrajit said. "Many. And mostly not overlapping with my own."

Fix slowed his step as they neared the end of the ramp. "Anaximander Skink doesn't know me. We should go in separately. Would you feel safer if I went in first, so you're not in there without backup?"

"Safer?" Indrajit snorted. "A hero is safe at all times. If you enter first and unnoticed, though, perhaps you'll be able to identify possible sources of trouble before I even arrive. You can wait, armed and unnoticed, to leap like a bolt of lightning into the fray when needed."

Fix nodded. At the foot of the ramp, Indrajit turned right and slowed his pace. He drifted down to the sea, where he stood, listening to the cries of the gulls, the slap of the waves, and the whistles of the fishermen plying the trade that sustained the East Flats, the West Flats, and the Shelf alike. From this angle, he saw that the northern rim of the Blind Surgeon squatted over a narrow canal that connected directly with the sea; a long wooden boat lay there, tied to a post. The tide was going out, and the boat bobbed steadily lower as he watched it.

He gave Fix five minutes, a time he could accurately estimate because it was the length of time it took him to recite a dry account, with no embellishments or physical articulation, of the Taking of the Bone Tower. When he reached the line in which clever Gondahar, long of thew, took the Mistress of the Keys astride his dolphin mount, he stopped.

Then he turned back, climbed up the pebbly beach, littered with refuse and scarred by the hulls of boats, and went into the Blind Surgeon.

The corpse of the Yeziot Squite hung from ropes, lashing it to the ceiling. Strictly speaking, Indrajit had no idea whether it was in fact Squite, as opposed to some other Yeziot; all he could really tell was that it looked like a heaped mass of mildewed rope, each strand joining in a central clump that was accented with eyestalks and split by a gaping mouth filled with multiple rows of teeth. But since Squite was the only Yeziot Indrajit had ever seen, it seemed likely the living man and the corpse were the same. Customers of the public house yanked on the Yeziot's tentacles and touched the sharp tips of its teeth with cautious fingers.

"Indrajit Twang!" Anaximander Skink howled. The barkeep and owner of the Blind Surgeon was a Wixit, a furry, bipedal race of man with a muzzle like a little wild dog's. On the ground, he would only have come to Indrajit's knee, so he stood on a rough catwalk nailed to the backside of the bar.

"Don't let him recite!" a customer bellowed. Indrajit glared back at the man, a fur-wrapped Yuchak with three axes hanging from a broad belt.

"Now, now." Skink made a clicking noise with his tongue. "That's no way to treat an old friend. Besides, Twang's credit is good now. Old Bird Legs wiped it clean, didn't he?"

"I don't need credit." Indrajit smiled. "I have cash now."

"Ah, good." The Wixit pointed at the dead Yeziot. "Because that's two bits already. Price of admission to see the dead monster."

The crowd inside the Blind Surgeon jeered. A dozen of the races of man thrust their faces in Indrajit's direction to hiss and boo. A Zalapting made obscene gestures in the direction of the Yeziot.

Indrajit didn't see Fix. His partner would have his face down on a table somewhere, or would be lurking behind some burly patron of the bar to remain unseen until he was needed. Indrajit didn't look too hard; no sense finding his partner, only to give him away.

Indrajit strode up to the bar. "Wine. And none of that Ylakka piss you like to pass off as beer, either. Give me the good stuff."

The Wixit hauled on a short rope to pull a bottle from beneath the counter, sloshing dark red liquor into a stone cup.

Then Indrajit realized that Fix had the money. This was at Fix's insistence; his partner swore Indrajit had no sense of economy or fiscal prudence, and should only be allowed to touch coin as a last resort.

"Actually," he murmured to Skink, "I seem to have left my purse at home."

"Your credit's good here now," the Wixit growled. "Just don't try to pay me back in poetry."

"I wouldn't dream of it." Indrajit took the stone cup and sipped; the wine was sour, but he liked the aftertaste, and he found himself thirsty. He drained the cup and beckoned for more, which the Wixit promptly poured. "Who sold you the Yeziot?"

"No one *sold* it to me." Skink sniffed. "He was a customer with a large tab. He died before I could collect, so I claimed the body."

"Died in the common room, did he?" Indrajit asked. "Or did you drag him here from the Shelf all on your own?"

"What do you think you know, Twang?"

Indrajit took another sip. "The Yeziot was named Squite."

The Wixit sneered. "Next you're going to tell me about his starving wife and pups."

"I killed him." Indrajit pointed at the visible scorch marks around Squite's mouth and eyes. "Lit him on fire."

"Smork droppings," Skink said.

"Ah, yes. I remember this about you."

"My tough-minded, skeptical approach to life?"

"Your obsession with Smork feces. Shall I recite to you the tale of my battle with the Yeziot?"

"Kill me first."

"I'll tell you how you got the Yeziot's corpse," Indrajit said. He finished the cup of wine again. Was it a Wixit-sized cup, that he was draining it so easily? "You just fill in the blanks, and I'll pay you for it."

"On credit?"

"Yes."

Skink frowned. "Okay. Tell me how I got the Yeziot's corpse."

"A Fanchee woman," Indrajit said. "Green, with face tentacles. Quite pretty. You might have noticed her carrying a wax writing tablet, and you might have heard her using the name 'Oritria.'"

"Go on." Anaximander Skink's eyes narrowed.

"She ran up quite a bill here," Indrajit suggested. "Maybe you rented a room to her, or to her Yeziot pal, or both. Or you sold them a horse. Maybe a Yeziot drinks a lot of wine."

"Raki," Skink said. "A Yeziot puts away a lot of raki, it turns out."

"Expensive."

"And a room," Skink added. "They both slept in my supply room downstairs."

Indrajit nodded.

"That much information was free," Skink said. "The next thing I tell you costs you money."

"She came to you last night. She needed something, or she would have just run away. What did she need?"

"Two bits," Skink said.

"Agreed."

"She needed a place to stay. Said her business in Kish wasn't done yet."

"And she offered you the Yeziot's body to pay off her bill."

"Two bits."

"Agreed."

"Yes, she offered me the body."

Indrajit growled, leaning over the bar to look menacing.

"Okay, okay, yeah, she gave me the body. She needed a place to stay for a couple more nights, and I told her if the Yeziot brought in enough cash, she could stick around here."

Indrajit frowned. "And enough of your patrons are willing to pay two bits for a glimpse of a dead Yeziot to pay off a big raki tab?"

Anaximander Skink shrugged. "For a full Imperial, I let people cut off one of the limbs and take it with them. No one's paid the two Imperials for a tooth yet, but at this rate, I'll be burning the thing's head by morning, with a coin-fat purse to hide away."

"That *thing* is a man," Indrajit muttered.

"That you killed." Skink shrugged. "Smork droppings now. I might as well make a few coins."

Indrajit swallowed a long diatribe studded with reproach and condemnation. "And where is she now? The Fanchee woman?"

"That's a full Imperial," Skink said.

"Making the total…"

"Call it an even two Imperials."

Indrajit wished he'd started by simply asking where Oritria was, but maybe his indirect approach had help open the Wixit up. "Two Imperials it is."

"She's in my supply room downstairs," Skink said.

"I'm not going to ask you how to get there," Indrajit said in his most commanding Recital Thane tones. "I've paid you enough; now you're just going to tell me."

"Back around in the kitchen," Skink said. "There's a trap door and a ladder."

"Lead me."

Indrajit followed the Wixit behind the bar and under a rotting brick arch into the kitchen. A pot of something meaty bubbled over a fire in one corner of the room; tottering stacks of shelves held pots, kegs, bottles, barrels, and eating utensils over most of the floor.

Another Wixit crouched over a heap of dirty mugs and plates, wiping the food and drink from them with a greasy cloth.

"What possessed you to dig a hole under this place?" Indrajit asked.

"We didn't dig anything. Neither did the fellow who sold me the Blind Surgeon; he built over a natural cave."

"Just a cave?"

"Nothing strange down there. No walking dead or Druvash mutants or anything." Skink held a finger in front of his muzzle to call for silence, and Indrajit held his tongue. With careful motions, the Wixit rolled a threadbare square of carpet away from the floor, revealing a rectangular trap door underneath.

"Give me a taper," Skink whispered to the other Wixit. She set down a gravy-smeared bowl, tossing her wiping rag on top of it, and lit a short, fat taper.

"Is she alone down there?" Indrajit felt a little slow; perhaps he'd had a bit too much wine, but he wasn't worried about facing Oritria alone.

Skink took the taper and nodded. "I'm to awaken her at nightfall. Let me go first; if she sleeps still, I'll signal you. And if she's awake, I'll maneuver her so her back is to the ladder."

"You're cunning, Skink. I shall have to be more careful of you in the future." Indrajit drew his heroic sword, Vacho, and steeled himself. Should he call for Fix? Fix hadn't seen fit to make himself visible, so perhaps he was watching other dangers. Perhaps he'd found the four-armed, red-scaled man Chark and was tailing him. All in all, he decided to leave Fix hidden.

Skink crouched beside the trap door as the other Wixit retreated across the room. "If you lift the door, I'll descend."

The trap door had an iron ring for a handle, sunk into a circular groove cut into wood polished smooth by years of hands. Indrajit spread his legs wide to lower his body. Holding his sword up and to one side, and breathing in a calm, controlled fashion to avoid accidental grunting, he hoisted the trap door.

Below, darkness, and the soft lapping sound of water.

Two enormous hands seized Indrajit by the right wrist. He spun, twisting his arm and torso to try to claw his arm free, but in vain.

The hands that gripped him were at the end of two enormous, muscular right arms. They were covered with red scales, patched here and there with brown fur, and they corresponded to two left arms attached to the same huge torso.

Indrajit stumbled and lost his balance. Chark, the four-armed, scaly accomplice of the poetess Oritria, hurled Indrajit down into the darkness.

He wasn't sure what part of his body hit the floor first, but he survived. Pain exploded across multiple points in his chest, back, and ribs. But the loud metallic clanging told him Vacho had fallen into the pit with him. Lying on stone, hearing the ring, he groped in darkness toward the sound and found his weapon's hilt.

Lifting it was an effort that caused his breath to come short, but the sword felt the right weight; it hadn't snapped in two, at least.

Was this, after all, a storeroom? Or did Anaximander Skink's public house conceal some sort of dungeon, or murder hole?

"Fear to come at me, fell monsters," he grunted. "I'm armed."

"I'm not," Fix said in the darkness. "On the other hand, I don't think there are monsters down here."

"Frozen hells. What happened?"

"I was grabbed from behind. Outnumbered. They disarmed me and threw me down in this hole."

"What's down here?" Indrajit knew Fix would have begun exploring the moment he was conscious.

"Boxes," Fix said. "I haven't finished poking around."

"Did you find the canal?" Indrajit asked. "There should be a water channel. A sluice of water runs right up to the building."

"I hear the water, but I haven't found it yet."

"You hear it slapping?" Indrajit said. "That's the action of the tides. It means the water in this room connects to the sea."

Fix cursed mildly.

Indrajit patted around on hands and knees, and had just found the lip of the channel, when the tide suddenly dropped enough to admit light through the groove. It was the pale northern light of an autumn afternoon, but after a couple of minutes of darkness, it nearly blinded Indrajit.

And then it was gone as the water returned.

"We'll get more of that," Indrajit said. "Let me get down in the water and see if there's a way out of here. You dig around in the boxes. Look for raki. It's a very hard liquor, double-distilled grape."

"I know what raki is. I assume you don't just want to get drunk."

"Wine won't burn. Raki will."

He lowered himself into the cold water, feeling the push as a long wave came in, then the pull as it dragged out. The water dragged him forward with it, but then he abruptly stopped; the channel was blocked off by an iron grate beneath the wall of the Blind Surgeon.

He took a breath and dove.

The iron bars descended all the way to the stone floor of the channel, and from wall to wall, completely blocking off the passage. When the tide reached its ebb point, he got several seconds of light, and could see both the boat bobbing just on the other side, and the heavy iron lock on the bars.

"It's locked," he told Fix. "Can you pick locks?"

"No. You?"

Indrajit climbed out of the channel, sloshing water on the stone floor. In the few seconds of light, he could see they were indeed in a natural cave, with rough walls and a floor of cold, hard-packed, pebbly dirt.

"Picking locks is one of the few skills not illuminated in the Blaatshi Epic," Indrajit said.

"Seems like an oversight now," Fix said. "Perhaps you should compose a few verses."

"If we escape by picking the lock," Indrajit said, "I will. But I intend to get out of here by lighting a fire."

"Burning us to death," Fix guessed.

"We'll crouch in the channel while the water's still high."

"If the Blind Surgeon collapses, we'll still be killed."

"I don't think Anaximander Skink will allow the Surgeon to collapse. I also don't think Oritria will allow me to be killed."

"You romanticize a spy who probably murdered her father."

"She told Chark she needed me, and not to kill me," Indrajit said, "back on the *Duke's Mistress*. And indeed, today, when Chark could easily have murdered me, he knocked me into this hole instead."

"It seems a thin reed," Fix said, "but I see no other."

Working in spurts as they had light, they broke down a crate of raki. The straw inside, and the board of the crate, they piled against a stack of other crates containing various dried goods—beans and rice and tamarind. They shattered several bottles of raki, soaking all the crates and the tinder.

Then Indrajit struck the hilt of Vacho against a rock until he produced a spark.

Blue flame leaped up, engulfing the heap of crates.

"Truly, Vacho is the hidden lightning." Fix lowered himself into the watery slot, arms at the lip so as to be able to quickly emerge.

"The Voice of Lightning," Indrajit said, "which is to say, thunder. And this is an abuse I have heaped upon Vacho. I shall have to make up for it by plying him with raki later."

"You will drink it for him, of course."

"I will do him this service." Indrajit lowered himself into the channel with his partner. He laid Vacho on the cave floor, in easy reach, so he could leap out of the canal, instantly armed for the fray. "For being the Voice of Lightning, he's surprisingly not possessed of a mouth."

With the stack of crates in flames, Indrajit now saw a pile of lumber behind it, and a rolled bundle of cloth—an unused curtain, or blankets?—on wooden shelves. He considered climbing out again to push other flammable material into the fire, but the flames leapt well enough on their own so that in moments, the cave was a burning hell.

"My head might bake," Fix complained.

"Keep dunking yourself," Indrajit suggested.

"I also might suffocate."

"We knew there were risks."

Indrajit heard stampeding feet overhead. The ladder out of the cave, visible now in the firelight, was a series of iron rungs bolted into stone leading up to the underside of the trap door. The trap door opened to the sound of several voices yelling. Anaximander Skink lowered a foot to climb down the ladder, and then immediately pulled it back with a pained shriek.

"The ladder is hot!"

"I didn't think about that one," Indrajit said.

"You morons!" Anaximander Skink squealed.

"Come on," Fix suggested, "let's grab that curtain."

They snaked between two burning columns of wood to seize the rolled-up cloth. It smoldered, so they tossed it into the channel and jumped in with it. The water was now only waist-high and dropping at the height of the tide, but they trampled the fabric deep into the water to thoroughly soak and chill it.

Then they threw the wet curtain over the iron rungs of the ladder and climbed.

Indrajit went first, climbing with one hand and pushing ahead of him with Vacho to clear the path. He dragged himself through the trap door into a kitchen filled with smoke. Chark lunged for him with his falchion, but it was a half-hearted attack, and Indrajit drove him away with the sharp tip of the leaf-bladed sword, and then gave Fix a hand.

Oritria stood in the door, a short, thin blade in her hand.

Skink was yelling something so shrill and wild that Indrajit couldn't make out the words. "Listen, you should go around," he told the Wixit. "Unlock the canal gate, then slosh water onto the flames."

"I've already lost a fortune in wine and raki!" the Wixit wailed.

"You're losing more fortune by the minute," Fix pointed out.

The Wixit skittered away, leaving the Protagonists standing with Oritria and Chark. Without any spoken agreement to hold off hostilities, they all stumbled out onto the street. Fire raced up several walls. The Yeziot had been stripped of limbs and sagged like a bushel of teeth from the ceiling of the Blind Surgeon, which was aflame.

The tavern's customers had evaporated, other than the handful who were trying to help fishermen sling water onto the burning building.

Indrajit kept a tight grip on his sword. Chark had a leather bag slung over his shoulder and stood crouched, as if prepared to spring into battle.

"If you want the leather straps," Indrajit said, "they're gone."

"Our patron will be displeased," Chark growled.

"I don't know whether I should care about that or not," Indrajit said. "Here's what I'm prepared to offer. You tell us who your patron is, and in exchange, I'll listen to you explain what it is you need from me."

"I need nothing from you," Chark said.

"Her." Indrajit pointed at Oritria with his sword. "What *she* needs from me."

Chark snarled.

Oritria turned to Fix. "I will offer *you* a trade. Give us the Blaatshi, and we will tell you the identity of our employer and give you your weapons back."

Fix addressed Chark. "Give us the girl, and we'll let you go."

Chark laughed, a sound like metal being folded. "I have all your weapons, you impudent sack of meat."

"I see we are at an impasse," Indrajit said.

"I want to be your apprentice," Oritria said.

Indrajit stared.

"Nonsense," Chark rumbled.

"Terrible idea," Fix said.

Indrajit raised a hand. "Wait a minute."

"You can't be serious," Fix said.

"You want to learn the Epic," Indrajit said to the poetess. She already composed like a Recital Thane. She'd sung to him perfectly-composed lines about his own death as she'd attacked him.

"I want to finish learning it," she said. "My grandmother sang many songs to me from the Epic. I would learn the rest."

Indrajit's head swam. "Why?"

"Because it is beautiful. Because it is the truest thing known to all the races of man."

"Oh, no," Fix muttered.

"Was your grandmother Blaatshi?" Indrajit stumbled at the idea. "I don't understand."

"She loved a wandering Blaatshi singer," Oritria said. "He'd been apprenticed to become Recital Thane, but had fled the responsibility. But he carried the Epic with him. He couldn't escape it, and neither could she. And neither can I."

"And neither can I," Indrajit murmured.

"When you say *loved*," Fix said. "Do you mean… *loved*?"

"I am full-blooded Fanchee," Oritria said. "My grandmother wed my grandfather, but she cherished the secret of her youthful love and passed it on to me."

Indrajit heard his own heart pounding in his ears. He felt as if he were living an episode of the Epic.

"Are you aware of this runaway apprentice Recital Thane character?" Fix asked.

"No," Indrajit said. "This is a tale of the generations it will be my privilege to add to the Epic. The goddess has brought this girl to me."

"She tried to choke you. And stab you. She imprisoned you in a basement."

"What was the apprentice Recital Thane's name?" Indrajit asked.

"Rupavar," she said.

"I do not care to be gutted by the Lord Archer for this nonsense!" Chark roared.

The Lord Archer.

Indrajit shook his head. "Arda Ne'eku? That's your employer?"

"It seems reasonable," Fix murmured. "Plugging the leak in his own organization. I wonder if that's one of Wopal's hypotheses."

"What does the Lord Archer want?" Indrajit asked.

"The four texts you stole from us," Chark roared.

"We can't get them," Indrajit said.

"Unless..." Fix frowned.

Was Fix contemplating assaulting Orem Thrust's palace to take the strings back? But why would he do that when there were authentic knotted cord-messages to be had elsewhere? "Frozen hells," Indrajit said. "I believe I'm going to do something impious."

"Poor Meroit," Fix said.

"He's faking, anyway," Indrajit pointed out. "He knows the strings contain information. He reads them."

"What are you talking about?" Oritria asked.

Indrajit sheathed his sword. "We'll get you back the four strings. Then you'll be in the good graces of the Lord Archer, right? And Chark, you can go on your way, eating babies, or whatever it is you do normally. And Oritria, you can get paid, and will be freed to study the Epic with me. Right?"

Fix grumbled without words. Chark nodded hesitantly, and Oritria sprang to Indrajit, kissing him on the cheek.

"Where shall we bring you the strings?" Indrajit asked.

Oritria hesitated.

"Do you know Salt Alley?" Fix asked.

"In the Dregs?" Chark growled.

"There's a well on Salt Alley," Fix said. "Can you meet us there at moonrise?"

"That's about six hours." Indrajit nodded. "It should be enough time."

"We'll be there," Oritria said. Chark pulled Fix's weapons from his bag and handed them over, and then he and Oritria disappeared into the shacks of the West Flats.

The fire at the Blind Surgeon was nearly out. "I owe Anaximander Skink two Imperials," Indrajit said.

"After what he attempted?" Fix snorted, and they headed back up toward the Spill.

"Why Salt Alley?" Indrajit asked.

"I don't trust them." Fix shrugged. "I didn't want them to choose the location, and Salt Alley is... well, it's a place I know from my youth. We'll get there early, and we'll watch."

Indrajit had difficulty focusing on his steps. Was he, after all and in spite of his efforts, about to find the apprentice Recital Thane he'd come to Kish seeking? But their relationship had had such an inauspicious beginning—she'd stolen documents from her father, and Indrajit had been hired to recover them.

And she *had* attacked him, at one point.

They hiked up into the Spill and quickly to the ashrama of Salish-Bozar. A row of Trivials in white tunics filled the street in front of the rectangular building, stopping passersby to talk.

A woman with chalky white skin and four stubby horns on her forehead gripped Indrajit gently by the wrist. "Have you ever felt exploited?" she asked, her voice gravelly and seductive.

"Sometimes." Indrajit shrugged. "Mostly, I feel ignored."

The chalk-colored woman opened her mouth to say more, but Indrajit and Fix pushed on into the ashrama. They found Meroit in his cell underground, sitting at a small easel, and painting a large building. He swiveled his yellow, root-like head to look at them as they approached.

"Look." He pointed at the painting.

"The Palace of Shadow and Joy." Indrajit shut the door behind himself.

"You know it?" the Trivial asked.

"The opera house," Fix said. "We've been there."

"Think of all the drama that happens inside." Meroit sighed.

"Quite boring, really," Fix said.

"Listen, Meroit," Indrajit said. "We're going to take four of your strings."

"What?" Meroit's skin was normally the color of a rotting potato, but it grew white. "No. No, you said you were going to give me four more. The four you had, you were going to give them to me."

"We're going to do this one way or the other," Indrajit said. "Are you going to force me to brutally rip away your disguise?"

"I don't know what you're talking about."

"Brutal it is," Fix said.

Indrajit pointed at the painting. "This painting right here. You're recording in it the data you read on the string we brought in here, the one we let you touch. The one you *read*."

Meroit's mouth fell open.

"The information on the strings isn't useless, and you know it. It contains data about the kelp farms of the Lord Archer, smuggled out by Fanchee double agents. And you know that, too."

"You don't have to tell anyone," Meroit said.

"The god would know," Fix said.

"But the Selfless wouldn't! And it would be all the same; I could finally become one of the Selfless! You know what a worthy goal that is, Fix. Remember when you were one of us, a Trivial like me!"

"You would cheat the god." Fix stared, as if by gaze alone he could drill holes into Meroit's forehead.

"I don't know what the information is!" Meroit squeaked. "Yes, I know it comes from the kelp farms, but I don't know what it says! Yield, plantings, territory covered, price, strains, pests, labor, I have no idea! The patterns are abstract to me; they might as well be useless information!" Sweat poured down the conical head of the little Trivial.

"How do you get paid, Meroit?" Indrajit asked.

Meroit shut up again.

"Is coin slipped to you by the Hierophant Selfless?" Fix's voice was bitter. "Or are your paintings purchased for surprisingly large sums of money by strangers, who then transmit the information onward!"

"I sell the paintings!" Meroit squeaked. "And half of the proceeds go to the ashrama!"

"And the other half on wine, women, and song?" Indrajit guessed.

"Caveat number one." Fix's voice was flat and hard. "No information that can be sold for money is useless."

Indrajit drew his sword. Meroit scooted away from his easel, pressing his back against the far wall.

"You wouldn't take the easy way," Indrajit said. "The easy way would have been for you to pretend to be innocent, but let us take four of your strings. Now you have to choose between the hard way and the *really* hard way. I've drawn my sword in case you choose the really hard way."

Meroit plucked four strings from his collection and handed them over. Fix took them and tucked them into his kilt pocket.

"Will you return them?" the Trivial asked.

"Probably not," Indrajit said.

"Will you tell anyone?" Meroit pressed.

"As of now, I think it's in all our interests that this whole episode stays quiet." The hardness in Fix's voice and stance had softened. "If you recorded the knot sequence, or can reconstruct it, you may be able to talk the Selfless Bonk into letting you include these in your ten thousand useless pieces of information."

Meroit said nothing, and his lower lip trembled.

Indrajit and Fix left.

"I don't feel very good about that," Indrajit said, "if you're wondering."

"I don't feel so bad," Fix said. "If you're going to go around professing a god, eating at that god's table, sleeping in his ashrama, and seeking the company and praise of his devotees, you should live your life accordingly. You should at least *try*."

"You'd have been a good priest, Fix. Ironically." They emerged into a street full of cold rain, and Indrajit took a deep breath. "Well, I *did* try to do it the easy way."

They crossed the Crooked Mile and took the street heading into the Dregs. Indrajit didn't recognize the jobbers on guard at the gate, but he thought they nodded at him with deference.

The Dregs was smaller than the Spill by quite a bit, but it had far more alleys. Every block seemed to have a single stone or brick building at its heart, five hovels of wood or clay nailed to its sides, and seven alleyways cutting through and around it on all sides. Salt Alley turned out to be a winding path that ran along the wall of a large brothel, between a gambling den and an ironmonger, past a small square surrounded on three sides by cramped temples to foreign gods, and then into the courtyard of a hostler's.

The well was in the plaza surrounded by temples.

"Who are these gods?" Indrajit asked.

"The one on the left is Aileric. Technically, he's a saint, not a god, so that means he isn't worshipped, he's revered. Or maybe contemplated."

"Karthing?"

"Ildarian. That's him, distributing food to the poor in that painting. You can tell he's a saint by the horns on his head."

"Ah, I assumed that was one of the races of man I didn't recognize. I know the Ildarians; they're practically neighbors."

"The one in the middle is Tlacepetl," Fix said.

"Xiba'albi," Indrajit said.

"Is he in the Epic?"

"He's a sorcerer who sends dead men marching over the mountains against his enemies."

"And, in fact, he's the Guide. Here in the Dregs, he leads the unfortunate through the mazes of their lives, but he also blazes the trail for the dead through the multiple underworlds. And sometimes, he brings them back."

"The one on the right is gruesome. Her face is a skull, and her hair is snakes."

"Sharazat the Kind."

"What does she do?"

"She kills you."

"How is that kind?"

"She kills you when your life can never get better, at the moment your life takes a permanent turn for the worse. Her priestesses visit the sick to dispense the blessings of the goddess, but the goddess herself distributes death much more widely."

"The gods of mankind are many and strange," Indrajit said.

"Men are many and strange," Fix answered. "Where shall we hide?"

"The hostler's," Indrajit said. "I don't want to get in Aileric's way, and the other two frighten me. Let's see if we can get up on that wall."

They passed through the hostler's gate and pulled up short at the sight of a powder priest of Thûl, pointing his musket at Indrajit's face. Except that, looking at the way the loose robes and scarves hung over the priest's frame, Indrajit was pretty certain she was a woman.

And she wore a tunic marking her as one of Gannon's Handlers, a rival jobber company.

As did the three Yuchaks with scimitars and shields who crowded in on Indrajit and Fix's sides.

"Don't move," the Thûlian said, "and I won't shoot."

"I thought we were friends," Fix said, "or basically even."

"At least at peace," Indrajit suggested.

One of the Yuchaks raised a horn and blew it; it was a wild sound, a noise that would have been at home on the steppes, but it rang false and alien within the walls of the decadent old city.

Indrajit looked uneasily over his shoulder and saw the doors of all three temples open. Gannon's Handlers slowly came out: the Zalaptings, the Luzzazza with only three arms, the Sword Brother, others he didn't know.

Not the Grokonk, because Indrajit and Fix had killed them.

And there was Tall Gannon himself, the Ildarian-looking man who was the public face of the jobber company's true leader, a one-cubit tall green midget.

"We're friends, Fix," Gannon said. "You're going to want to come into this stable now and meet with some other friends."

"Most of my friends don't point muskets and swords at me," Fix said.

"You're right, it's time to end the misunderstandings." Gannon waved a hand, and the powder priest lowered her weapon. The Handlers moved across the square and blocked Indrajit and Fix from retreat, forcing them to follow Gannon into a stable to the right.

The stable had been emptied of horses, and mucked out, so it stank considerably less than stables usually did. Oritria waited there, fists clenched and eyes narrowed. She stood beside Chark, who scratched at the earth floor of the stable with the talons of his feet, and gnashed his teeth from time to time. There was a third person with them, too.

"My Lord Archer," Indrajit said.

Arda Ne'eku didn't look like an archer. He was imposing, a tall, broadly-built, violet-skinned man with a heavy jaw and a stubby nose. A bit like some artist had tried to render a Zalapting and had gotten every descriptor other than the color backward. He wore a wooden breastplate and a kilt of studded leather, both stained yellow.

"The Protagonists," the Lord Archer said. "Forgive me for forgetting your names."

"I'm Indrajit—"

Ne'eku raised a hand to stop him. "I don't care. This whole thing has gone far enough, and I've called this meeting to put an end to it."

"I thought we arranged this meeting," Fix protested.

"I know you did." Ne'eku grinned, all his teeth visible past thick, rubbery lips. "Let me tell you a story. I learned from a loyal Fanchee servant, who was willing to betray his own family, that information about my sea-farming enterprises was being recorded and transmitted to parties unknown. Certain purchases in the Paper Sook suggested to me that the buyer of the information might be the Lord Chamberlain, my colleague and rival. I decided to test the hypothesis."

"This again," Indrajit said.

"I was fortunate enough to know that among the Fanchee of my plantations was a lovelorn, idealistic, somewhat unhinged young poetess named Oritria, enamored of the idea of foreign travel, and song, and all the usual romantic nonsense. I knew of her infatuation with the Blaatshi Epic in particular. I also knew that Orem Thrust, the Lord Chamberlain, had a Blaatshi poet on his payroll, working in fact for his spymaster, head of the Lord Chamberlain's Ears. From there it was obvious and easy."

"You told her to steal the strands," Fix said, "and said it would bring the Recital Thane here, running."

"Which would prove my hypothesis that Orem Thrust was behind the espionage." Arda Ne'eku smiled.

"Why use the girl?" Indrajit asked. "Why not use, I don't know, Mote Gannon?"

"I didn't want to disturb the Fanchee," Ne'eku said. "I'd rather have them think there's a mad poetess running around, causing havoc, than know the truth. Those who are spying should continue to spy. Those who are loyal should stay blissfully unaware they're being spied on—unless I choose to inform them."

"And if someone other than us showed up to investigate the issue?" Indrajit asked.

The Lord Archer sighed. "Well, you see, it was always going to end the same way for Oritria, no matter how right or wrong my hypothesis turned out to be."

"Don't kill her," Indrajit said.

Oritria jerked, as if making a break toward the door, and Chark grabbed her with all four arms.

Ne'eku chuckled. "No, nothing like that. But she can't go home. That would rather undermine the point. Fortunately, she doesn't *want* to go back to the plantation."

"I hate farming," Oritria said. "I want the heroic life."

"Farming's not so bad," Indrajit said. "It's honest work."

"I'll send her to join the household of a Bonean noble family that's friendly to me," Ne'eku said. "Chark will accompany her. She'll study poetry and be treated well. Like a curiosity, and perhaps like a pet, but well."

"But she won't study the Blaatshi Epic," Indrajit pointed out. "She was going to be my apprentice."

"Ah, yes. Well, that was never going to work out, either." Ne'eku smiled. "She's a little mad, you see. Did you know she seduced the Yeziot Squite? Squite was a plantation worker. I have quite a few Yeziot who work for me. Their ability to breathe underwater is a real boon, not to mention their strong resemblance to the kelp itself. Good for hiding; they make excellent guards on a kelp plantation. I asked her to work with Chark; he's no jobber, he's on my permanent staff. She didn't quite trust him, so she seduced Squite."

"She does seem… very intense," Fix pointed out. "She tried to kill you. Her apprenticeship might have looked a lot like an imprisonment for you."

Indrajit shook his head. "But then I'm back where I started."

Ne'eku sighed. "Well, there was always only going to be one outcome for you, too."

Indrajit grabbed Vacho's hilt. "We've beaten the Handlers before."

In his peripheral vision, he saw Fix preparing to draw axe and falchion.

"We've never fought in a fair fight before," Tall Gannon growled. "Are you ready to try your luck now, fish-head?"

"No, no, no," the Lord Archer said. "Nothing like that. You Protagonists go home now."

"But… we caught you," Indrajit said.

"And *I* caught *you*," Ne'eku pointed out. "So you *will* tell Grit Wopal what you learned, and we will continue as before. Now Orem knows that I know he's spying, so maybe he'll be a little more circumspect. I'll be a little more careful when I have truly sensitive information, so Orem doesn't get it. I'll be aware that he's trading on knowledge about my farming. Maybe, at some point in the future, when Orem catches one of my agents with unauthorized fingers in one of the Lord Chamberlain's pastries, he'll remember this day, and the peace between us will continue."

"Frozen hells," Indrajit said, "the Yeziot died. He died so you could confirm what you were pretty sure you already knew."

"Don't forget," Fix threw in, "Grit Wopal *also* wanted to confirm what he thought he already knew."

"We broke a… a religious votary," Indrajit said. "He wasn't a very good one, but he was trying, in his way. We took away his dignity. Our chambers were turned upside down. A ship was burned to the waterline. A tavern… the Blind Surgeon mostly burned up, too, with a whole lot of raki and wine in its basement. Oritria's being exiled. All that, for… what? Nothing? Just to keep the city's great families comfortable in their usual corrupt competition? Just to maintain the status quo? The rich get rich, and the poor get crushed?"

Arda Ne'eku nodded as he strode toward the stable's exit. "Welcome to Kish."

* * * * *

D.J. Butler Bio

D.J. (Dave) Butler has been a lawyer, a consultant, an editor, a corporate trainer, and a registered investment banking representative. His novels published by Baen Books include the Witchy War series: *Witchy Eye*, *Witchy Winter*, *Witchy Kingdom*, and *Serpent Daughter*, and *In the Palace of Shadow and Joy*, as well as *The Cunning Man* and *The Jupiter Knife*, co-written with Aaron Michael Ritchey. He also writes for children: the steampunk fantasy adventure tales *The Kidnap Plot*, *The Giant's Seat*, and *The Library Machine* are published by Knopf. Other novels include *City of the Saints* from WordFire Press and *The Wilding Probate* from Immortal Works.

Dave also organizes writing retreats and anarcho-libertarian writers' events, and travels the country to sell books. He tells many stories as a gamemaster with a gaming group, some of whom he's been playing with since sixth grade. He plays guitar and banjo whenever he can, and likes to hang out in Utah with his wife, their children, and the family dog.

* * * * *

Leta of the Thousand Sorrows
by Glen Cook

or, The Triumph of Ruin
being a Chronicle of the Black Company
on the Long Run,
following the Unfortunate Events in
Chimney

Our days are blessed and cursed in equal measure.

We were slinking eastward and not covering ground nearly as fast as we old hands wanted. We had Taken hunting us, for the gods' sake!

Slowing us was a mob of new guys, lowlifes from Chimney and sailors from the ship that brought the Company to Chimney. None of them were people fit for a serious route march.

And we had animals and carts and wagons to slow us as we pushed through a forest without even a pretense of a road.

Me being me, I made one of my dumb choices. I just had to get up front with the pathfinders who were looking for the best way through the forest.

* * *

Nobody had much to say. We had bugs, heat, humidity by day, and freezing nights. Nobody went hungry, but salt pork and hardtack for every meal does get old.

Darling signed, "Do not be such a grouch."

Her smile helped, because I just might own the bleakest mood in the Company.

Why was Darling out front with us, when she would be more useful with the command staff if the Lady's enslaved sorcerers came for us?

Well, they were not eager to do so. Not right now. We'd killed one of them, filled him full of spears and burned him. Second Taken in two months. That left the others nervous and totally pissed off.

Darling was up front because Silent was the duty wizard with the pathfinders. He couldn't leave his special girl back with a mob of horny sailors and inbred delinquents not yet educated enough to know that "Hands off!" with Darling *really* means "Hands off, or you die! Quickly, only if you're exceptionally lucky."

You get hurt if you even try to flirt with the Company's most precious asset.

* * *

Elmo called a halt alongside a freshet of crystal spring water. Lunch time—for us and for the bugs.

I am used to fleas and lice and mosquitos. In those woods, you dealt with ticks and deer flies, too. Deer flies just zoom in and take a bite out of you.

Elmo settled beside me. "Why so sour today?"

I captured a tick scurrying north on my trouser leg. "I had one of these little shits on the head of my pecker last night."

"That might have been fun to see." The good sergeant had him a chuckle.

I said, "We been together for a while. How much woods have we ever had to deal with?" In our line, we go where the people are, either to protect them or to beat up on them. That's not in the woods.

Elmo was feeling philosophical. "It can't go on forever. If I recall my atlases, if we keep straight on, we'll find civilization again. So stay strong."

"Maybe we should've stood our ground."

"If we'd done that, you'd be under the ground."

Running might just be delaying the inevitable. We were leaving a pretty clear trail.

I grumbled, "And now the shit gets deeper."

Otto and Hagop, who'd been pathfinding for the pathfinders, crashed through the woods toward us.

Hagop said, "We run into something weird about a quarter mile ahead."

"It's a clearing," Otto said.

"A really creepy clearing," Hagop added.

Elmo called, "Silent! We need you."

Silent and Darling joined us. The wizard, as always when Darling was close by, wore a taut, stone cold expression. Those two made a seriously odd couple; him a wizard, and her a magical sink around whom no witchcraft or sorcery could work.

They can never really touch, but Darling is life itself to Silent.

There's a legend about lovers cursed to see one another only once a year. This situation might be worse.

Was Darling smelling danger already? Had Otto and Hagop brought something with them?

My default response was to look to the sky. When the Taken came, they would come from above.

Elmo told Silent to check out what Otto and Hagop had found.

Tall, lean Silent was not happy, but he joined Hagop and Otto, who were, reluctantly, ready to show what they'd found. Silent handed Darling off to me.

Darling sat down beside me. She signed, "Hello, Croaker." Teasing.

I signed back, "Hello, again. Do you smell trouble?"

She shrugged, pointed, signed, "Something that direction feels strange."

Elmo gave Silent and his companions ten minutes' head start. Then, "Saddle up, buckos. Time to move out."

Somebody declared, "It's just another glorious day in the Company."

* * *

This world is far older than most people suppose. Bad people, bad creatures, and bad things have been happening for ages. Good things, too, but we hardly ever remember those.

Dreadful, forgotten things lie sealed in a thousand places. Amongst those once was the ruling mistress of the monsters now hunting the Company, the Lady of the Tower at Charm.

The buried things lie ever restless.

What Otto and Hagop found could be such a place.

It was a treeless, brushless circle half a mile across, boasting not even one seedling tree. It was lumpy ground covered with pale, gray-green grass, every blade of which had a single sixteenth inch cream stripe on one side along its length. Nothing else grew out there except random wildflowers on top of the taller lumps.

The clearing felt totally creepy.

Darling did not like it at all.

It didn't like Darling, either. A dozen-yard semicircle of grass leaned away from her, lying down almost flat, when we stepped out of the woods.

The pathfinding crew stood around at the edge of the grass, grumbling and muttering.

Silent walked out into the clearing. He kicked things. Occasionally, he dropped to one knee and rested a hand on the ground.

He reported that there had been a city here, ages ago. Furious sorcery had destroyed it. Prodigious residual magical energies remained, but that wasn't deadly. We might have bad dreams but, otherwise, the clearing would be a safe place to camp.

I looked to the sky. Safe? Not from that direction.

If we camped where we could see the sky, the sky could see us, too.

I relayed Silent's report to Elmo as he made it. Elmo sent two Chimney recruits, Zeb and Dagoth, to let the Lieutenant know what we'd found.

The grass in the clearing might be good for our animals. They hadn't been feeding well since we entered the forest.

* * *

Two nights short of full, the moon rose as the embers of sunset burned out. The Annalist, having slunk back into the forest, wrapped himself in his blankets, intent on doing some master-class snoring. It had been a hard day.

The moon was bright overhead when my bladder wakened with a demand for relief. Which maneuver I executed with grace and style, then dove back into the sack.

What the hell?

Immediately, I found myself entangled with someone else—who, for sure, felt female. A female who was not Darling, because Darling was not so long and busty—and would never have gotten into such a situation with me.

But Darling was the only woman with the pioneers.

My companion shifted. More of her pressed against more of me now. She made sleepy girl noises and slipped a hand where no hand but my own had ventured for an age.

I was dreaming. Had to be. *Oh, man! My dreams are getting seriously realistic.*

That stopped nothing.

My companion was stronger than me. She forced me onto my back and climbed aboard.

Then, whatever this was, she was there only a moment more. Devil, succubus, forest-running amazon, my secret wishes made concrete, the woman faded away.

She was not my type, anyway. My type would be the Lady... Then, instead of mulling what really should have stricken me terrified, I laid me down and tried to recall what the Lady looked like, long ago, when I was her prisoner in the Tower.

I couldn't bring the woman fully into mind.

I spied a point of light just yards away, in the brush. A firefly, I first thought. I hoped. But, maybe, no. It wasn't firefly season.

Could *She* have been watching?

A whole new bucket of ill will might be about to get dumped on me.

Come morning, I was unsure that I hadn't dreamed the whole incident, including the firefly.

* * *

Everybody talked about ghosts. Everybody had had a creepy experience during the night, but nobody complained about horny lady spooks crawling all over them.

The rest of the Company didn't catch up that day. Us pioneers prepared for their arrival by gathering fuel and hunting. Otto and Hagop bagged a red deer stag.

I spent a lot of time watching the sky.

If that lightning bug was the Lady, and she told her Taken where to find me…

It's not comfortable, being scared all the time.

Being, in theory, the senior man on the scene, I could slack off some, which I did by strolling around the edge of the clearing, making occasional forays into the woods as I went. I didn't find much that was interesting. A spring that might be useful later. A tumble of dressed, rust-colored stone that had fallen a millennium or two ago.

Elmo asked, "See anything?"

I reported the spring.

"Ah. Still in the bleak mood. We need to get you laid."

I must have jumped a foot high, recalling my night.

"Hey! No worries. I'm not volunteering."

"Story of my life since I was about twelve."

"Sisters were faster than you, eh?"

"Older and meaner, too."

I *was* in a bleak mood. I didn't feel like playing the game. I didn't feel like doing much else, either—except feeling sorry for myself.

* * *

I found what I thought was a premium lay-up for the night. It had better leaf-fall for a mattress, with fewer sticks and stones in the mix.

I made one tactical error in the choosing.

The canopy overhead was thin. Night-flyers might be able to spot me.

Despite the talk about ghosts, everyone else spent the night in the clearing. The grass apparently made a comfortable bed.

Odd. The clearing had seemed so creepy at first, but now everyone else was comfortable with it.

Yes, that whatever-she-was found me again, soon after the moon rose. I wasn't yet entirely asleep. Suddenly, I was no longer alone, and this time I didn't get much sleep.

* * *

"Bad night? Nightmares?" Elmo asked over breakfast.

"Eh?"

"You look rough."

"I didn't get much sleep."

Darling stared daggers my way.

"What?"

She signed, "You know what."

I might have blushed. Me. Croaker. The man not fazed by anything, ever.

Elmo wanted to know, "What is this?"

Silent was interested, too.

Darling signed, "You, who survived the Tower, ought to know better. But you were first to surrender."

Two men eyed me intently, wondering what the hell?

I wanted to ask Darling how she knew about my insane night, but my lame response was, "You'll understand better someday, when you're older."

Which earned me: "You're not so young that you only think with your thing."

Darling has disabilities, but she isn't ignorant, nor is she stupid. She knows what goes on between men and women—and knows that stuff can destroy an otherwise exemplary life.

I was sure she'd suffered temptations of her own.

She was alive, and she was old enough.

Elmo remarked, "The vibe I'm getting is that Croaker got him some—for which, congrats, my brother—and everyone's sweetheart there is jealous. Not so? Whatever. So. Croaker. Where did you find a willing woman out here?"

He gave me no chance to answer. "Only, you break out in hives just thinking about playing with the other team. But the only female here is that frumpy, tangle-haired, flat-chested plain Jane who wants to cuss you out. So, what the hell? Talk to me, Croaker."

That all ripped out of Elmo in a high-speed yak.

Darling read Elmo's lips. She signed, "Talk to us, Croaker."

I manned up and told it.

Elmo blurted, "You spent the whole night plooking a *ghost*?"

"Ghost? No. She was pretty substantial. Maybe she's some crazy female hermit."

Not even I, desperate for weasel room, was ready to buy into that, though.

Darling signed, "She's more than a ghost. Maybe an *anima*. A small god. A spirit of the dead city underneath the clearing."

Our mascot and most precious resource owns a scary imagination.

Which is all a digression; Croaker ducking and dodging potential guilt.

But guilt? Why, that?

I latched onto something Darling had signed. "I'm the first? What do you mean?"

"I'm not sure. I think she'll keep taking more men as long as she can keep the Company here, and she'll become more incarnate each time."

Elmo betrayed a smirk. He was rehearsing some verbal jabs I had coming.

* * *

These facts obtain. This idiot, separated from Darling long enough to reflect and to begin to obsess—because he's a guy who obsesses about stuff that baffles his peers—majorly worried about that unseasonal firefly. Had it come round the next night?

Why, Croaker, do you feel guilty about having cheated on the Lady? Does that make any sense? Can you get any crazier than that?

* * *

Of a sudden, Darling was attached to me at the hip. I couldn't get five feet away. Did she think I'd contracted some sort of magical infection?

Meantime, Silent roamed the clearing constantly, poking, sometimes digging with a pointed stick, which he'd dipped in molten silver.

Elements of the Company proper began to arrive. Tents went up. Rude corrals were thrown together. The strange grass began its conversion into horse apples and ox pats.

Our commander, the Lieutenant—no other name—sent for Silent and me once his headquarters tent was up. Darling, of course, came along.

* * *

Darling was relentless. She was determined that I be totally forthright with the Lieutenant—or she would end me by poking me with a seriously pointy forefinger if I wandered far from the absolute, embarrassing truth.

I spent most of the meeting red of face.

The usual suspects basked in my discomfiture: the sorcerers One-Eye and Goblin; second-in-command Candy; Silent and Darling, of course; and several senior NCOs, including Elmo.

Darling offered her conviction that what had happened to me was going to happen to others, who would resist it no better than I had, even warned.

* * *

A Chimney lad called Jarhead wakened me and, in pidgin I could barely follow, told me the Lieutenant wanted me. Now!

The Lieutenant awaited me in his tent. Candy was with him, along with the usual crew.

Those two confessed that they'd endured a night of erotic excess identical to the one I'd reported. They agreed: the woman who'd visited them had to be the one that I'd known. Only... she was able to be with two men at the same time, in different places, all night long. While at the same time, snuggling up with me yet again. Just that. No hungry demands.

I am uncomfortable recording this stuff, but it was the burden we bore at the time. Still... my wondrous nights troubled me. *Leta... Leta? How do I know that name?*

There was something seriously not right going on here.

Candy and the Lieutenant agreed, with conviction.

We talked. We worried. We failed to make sense of the situation. One-Eye, Goblin, Silent, and Darling contributed nothing useful. Darling seemed drained, as though her null was under relentless, heavy pressure.

We came to no conclusions, but we agreed: we all knew the name Leta.

The Company didn't move on. I set my own tent up, and a rude sick bay, inside the clearing. Nobody bothered to watch the sky. Nobody cared about us having places to go and Taken to annoy.

Was this the final destination chosen for us by destiny?

The next night, another four men suffered the wicked woman's attentions—as did the veteran three. Elmo was one of the newbs.

Leta could overcome the proclivities of the he-man woman-hater Elmo had become? We might have us a serious problem.

Next afternoon, there I was, with an unhappy Darling practically hanging on to me while she tried to keep Leta's lovers inside her null.

Silent wandered the clearing, amongst the animals, studying the ground for the second or third time. Sometimes he poked a mound with his stick.

I signed to Darling, "What is he doing?"

"Killing the dead. He hopes."

Right. Ask a foolish question.

Then reality flashed negative.

The others experienced something weird, too, but no one as thoroughly as me.

Day inverted. It became darkness where it should have been light. What had been dark became ghostly radiant. The animals and Silent became amorphous, indeterminate, wobbly, pale shapes... apparently only in my eyes. Neither Silent nor the animals showed any reaction.

Silent stopped, looked around, shrugged, and went back to doing whatever he was doing.

His calm touched me. I stifled my panic. I made myself study my vision.

And I was amazed.

The clearing lumps... I'd assumed they marked chunks of fallen buildings, like sections of broken columns. Now I wasn't sure that was the case.

Almost every lump anchored white, ghostly threads, some only two or three threads, but others, dozens. Those threads writhed against the darkness. There were hundreds of them. Maybe thousands. Every thread had a slightly bulbous head, and right now, all of those were pounding at Darling's null.

The Lieutenant said, "We should have One-Eye and Goblin help Silent."

The two wizards had disappeared, possibly having smelled a risk of getting put to work.

Candy said, "Good luck with that, boss. You know those two got to be scheming how to get themselves a Leta of their own."

Something like that would be fermenting in One-Eye's melon, absolutely, but Goblin might do the right thing, because that would show up One-Eye.

I asked, "Anybody seeing what I'm seeing? Ghost threads trying to get at us?"

No. But they all knew something was happening. They were more scared than me because they couldn't see what I saw.

I described it the best I could.

Candy said, "I'll go round up Goblin and One-Eye again."

Darling signed, "Do not. There will be a reason the threads Croaker sees are trying to get to you men."

Whoa! Could that be? I figured they were aiming for her.

Candy said, "Seems to me like somebody ought to do something."

I said, "Oh, crap!"

* * *

Seven people stared at me. Six asked, "What?"

"The threads have stopped trying to get to us. They're twisting into one another now, like a bushel of snakes,… Well, damn!"

The Lieutenant suggested, "Talk to us, Croaker."

"They're knitting a woman. A Leta."

Candy said, "Oh, yeah! I can see it now. A ghost thing, but getting more real by the second."

The Lieutenant began to see it, too.

I glanced at Darling. She looked fierce. She could see the ghost woman developing, too, and she was not a fan.

Negative reality vanished. Normality returned, bringing color along with it. But I saw the ghost threads crocheting women. Now plural.

Silent drove his silver stick into a mound.

A few threads fell back as though being reeled in.

One ghost woman yelled. Everyone within a quarter mile heard her. Silent froze, stared. The rest of the Company closed in, all of them able to see the woman as clearly as I could. She was perfectly visible in broad daylight.

The threads let her go. Their work was done. They turned to us, briefly. Thwarted again, they began weaving another Leta.

Really.

Darling let me have it with her dagger finger, pointed. The first completed Leta was headed for Silent.

She wasn't moving fast. She had trouble keeping her feet on the ground. I said, "Guys, we need to get Silent before she does."

Darling bobbed her head, an emphatic, "Yes!"

Always the default assumption. Outsiders meant us harm.

The as yet unseduced gawked, probably thinking how sweet it would be if they could knit themselves their own hotty hot hotties.

Elmo observed, "That woman must have ice water for blood."

She wore just a short shift woven from white threads. As a red-blooded kind of guy, I have to admit, she wasn't hard on the eyes.

And here came One-Eye, back at last, having heard there were "nekkid wimmen" to be ogled. He'd probably offer to become the next Leta's pimp while drowning her in eye tracks.

Meantime, my mob was stumbling over each other in an effort to get to Silent before the Leta did, while staying inside Darling's protection.

I remained blind to what One-Eye was up to until, after a serious pile-up, those of us with Darling paused to get ourselves better organized. I then watched the smelly little wizard act entirely out of character.

He slashed at some ghostly threads with a borrowed sword.

He could see the threads? Oh, yes, he could! And he could *cut* them.

He was businesslike about it, which was not the One-Eye way, but then he turned bedrock One-Eye in a blink. Last I saw, before we moved on, was that little shit grinning huge as he collected his gorgeous prize, harvested seconds before she might have been invested with the wisdom to stay away from somebody like One-Eye.

We herded the original ghost woman using the null. She couldn't abide direct contact.

She yelled at us, probably using uncouth language. Interesting. I hadn't heard a word ever spoken by my night visitor.

Silent realized something was going on. He moved to put Darling at the mid-point of a line that ran from him to Leta. Then he entered the null.

Darling pointed to me, meaning that I should bring Silent up to date. I talked. Over Silent's shoulder, I watched the threads weave yet another Leta. A slavering Goblin stood by, sword in hand, awaiting his moment.

One-Eye had disappeared with his catch already.

Elmo broke a long silence. "If they work it right, our guys will be able to fix it so there's a girl toy for every boy who wants one."

Oh, did Darling lay a dirty look on him.

"Just saying," he told her. Grinning.

The Lieutenant is severely handicapped when it comes to a sense of humor. He began grumbling about how anyone who adopted a

Leta would need to feed and clothe her on his own. Which won him his own poisonous look from Darling.

Her ill regard didn't bother him. He winked at her.

Candy mused, "If they're really ghost women, maybe they don't need to eat. And the one I've seen don't seem to be much into clothes."

I suggested, "Maybe we shouldn't have so much fun with it before we know what we've actually wakened. Check it." Threads were reconnecting with the first Leta created.

Candy mused on, "If they're succubus ghosts, maybe they don't need any other kind of nourishment."

Elmo snapped, "You keep talking that shit, Darling will take you down and rip your noodle off."

Darling did look like she was in that kind of a mood.

Silent got my attention. He asked what I was seeing, because he didn't think he was seeing the same thing. I told him. Then he wanted me to step out of the null so I could show him where the threads were coming from.

I balked. Why sabotage Leta? No one had suffered any harm from her. Quite the opposite. Aside from Darling and Silent, everyone here had had a teen boy's midnight adventure. And that, somehow, had made it possible for Leta to duplicate herself so she could go out among us and duplicate herself with more of us, over and over. So it seemed.

My latent puritanical side insisted there would be a price to pay later.

A hint at the price? Nobody was talking travel plans. Three days and three nights on, and we remained rooted where we could be spotted easily from the sky.

Oh, yes. That was it. Leta might not be deadly in herself, but her appeal might be such that the Company would remain stalled until the Lady's hellhound hunters found us.

I decided to experiment. I left the null. I led Silent to a mound sprouting a bundle of threads. "Cut the threads, but don't bother what's in the mound."

Silent began cutting. Then we went to another mound. The cut threads regenerated behind us.

The first Leta woven seemed to understand what we were doing, and she accepted it. For the moment.

She was now as solid and real as me or Silent, and I was sure she wouldn't vanish like a night haunt Leta, unless... Unless what?

* * *

The Company's situation was unprecedented, insane, and unsustainable. We were the victims of a glamour that almost no one would recognize as such.

Leta wanted something. The ghosts had waited ages for this opportunity. But we, the living, as yet had no clue what that might be.

There was just one thing they knew how to do. And they did it with considerable enthusiasm.

Silent stopped cutting threads. The exercise was pointless. The threads just regenerated. (One-Eye might be in for a surprise.) And they kept spinning Letas.

* * *

Days passed. Vigorous nights passed. The woman came to me, every one. And then she stopped going away.

We, the Company, stopped doing much. Then, one cool afternoon, something sparked inside me. I snagged Silent's silver weapon, charged out into the clearing, and began slashing threads. If I couldn't stop it, someday there would be a thousand Letas. A thousand sorrows. And the Company would be no more.

Then Darling was there with me, pressed up beside me, showing me puppy dog eyes while signing, "Stop it! Please stop it!"

Paint my portrait confused. What was this attitude?

I asked.

She said she thought we'd jumped to a wrong assumption, back at the beginning, and the blame for our wrong thinking was all her fault.

I faced her squarely. She would have no trouble reading my lips. "So, sweet thing, what *should* we be doing? And why should we do it?" Beyond her, I could see four Letas being woven. There were at least forty of them now. Only the original seemed to be intelligent, curious, and inclined to communicate—and she was never far from me when the sun went down.

And here that Leta came, with hardly a glance for Darling. And, to our astonishment, she pushed into Darling's null, despite showing that the effort caused her severe discomfort.

Darling clung to me, suddenly frightened.

Leta stopped just inches from me. She rested her forearms on my shoulders, stared into my eyes, but did nothing more. Nor did Darling do anything but keep me anchored with her touch.

I got lost in Leta's hungry eyes. Those eyes desperately wanted to communicate something, but had no idea how.

* * *

Warning horns screamed.

Taken appeared over the clearing, high up, one, two, three of the Lady's sorcerer slaves, come to bring the fire, because a moral gag reflex had led us to leave her service.

After so much loafing, the response was lackadaisical—except in one unlikely quarter.

Goblin and One-Eye, wizard freaks and champion slackers, were good to go. They must already have slaked their perverted hungers. Old as they were, though, they probably only wanted their Letas for show. So, anyway, the two-man crazy wizard posse responded when the alert sounded—we thought.

I was unable to imagine how ground-squirrel level sorcerers like Goblin and One-Eye might engineer what happened. I guessed they'd been scheming since the day we disembarked for the *Cranky Bitch*. The Taken, including Whisper, who harbored a lethal grudge against us, came down at high speed... and slammed into totally unexpected resistance.

Goblin and One-Eye refused to explain what they did. They just preened.

I learned the truth by observing and eavesdropping.

Initially, I suspected they'd somehow suborned their Letas. From the start, there were hints that the Letas might be involved. Theirs and the rest, excepting maybe mine.

Mine? *My* Leta? What was this?

Step back, man. Reflect. So, yes. Take a look at everything, starting with that first night. And, oh, my! The Leta iteration with me now was the same one.

Amidst deadly chaos, I got it. Every Leta woven would take up with just one man and would stick with him till we got wherever they were going.

My Leta stuck with me and Darling as death hurtled down at us. It was too late to run.

The flying carpet of the lead attacker disassembled suddenly about three hundred feet above us.

Frame pieces scattered. Air resistance dragged the frame's cloth cover out from under the rider—who kept on coming, so fast that she had no chance to protect herself from impact.

The second Taken was Whisper. She came in equally hard a hundred yards back, but headed for a different target. For Darling and me.

Darling was a prime target because she was what she was. And Croaker had a special place in Whisper's black heart. It was him who put her into the situation where she could become Taken.

Whisper didn't suffer target tunnel vision. She managed to veer off.

But not fast enough.

Pieces began to come off her carpet underframe.

She made a hard landing at the far side of the clearing. She and her carpet wreckage tumbled on into the woods.

Some guys whose brains still functioned headed that way, hoping to end her threat forever. The Taken might be too broken to defend herself.

The third Taken managed to avoid disaster, but had no idea what to do next.

Modern Taken don't deal well with the unexpected.

The Lady doesn't choose them for flexibility or ingenuity.

The modern Annalist didn't deal well, either. He just stood there with his jaw slack, mouth-breathing, unable even to ask, "What the hell was that?"

* * *

The Lieutenant called a command staff meeting. The usual suspects assembled, along with my Leta, who was now attached to me, despite Darling's disapproval.

The lucky Taken remained on patrol, high above us.

White threads went right on weaving new Letas, not a one as bright as mine.

Most of the men just stood around now, less active than the Letas were. Their disinterest baffled me. But I didn't have ambition enough to pursue it.

The Lieutenant reported, "Whisper got away. They found pieces of her carpet and some blood where she crashed, but no body."

Candy said, "This is one of those times when I wish we had some dogs." Candy would be a cat kind of person.

Goblin and One-Eye said nothing. They were all puffed up and smirking.

Elmo announced, "The Taken is on the move."

Indeed. She or he was headed down and away from us, the direction Whisper was headed when she crashed.

Elmo said it. "Picking up the ugly witch."

Right. The carpet rose with two riders aboard. It strained and staggered as it claimed altitude.

"A new Taken," I guessed. "Not skilled at working a carpet yet."

Carpet and riders shuffled off westward.

Elmo said, "Poor Whisper. That's, what? Twenty times we've messed her up?"

He exaggerated. But we had embarrassed the woman several times.

Some people just will not leave us alone.

I said, "Guys, we have to get moving again. We can't just sit here, holding our peckers, until every swinging dick gets him a girlfriend."

"That isn't what's happening, Croaker," Candy said.

I knew that. The clearing was the problem. It stripped us all of ambition.

I couldn't work up ambition enough to figure out why it would do that.

Candy and the Lieutenant checked my Leta: how she was becoming increasingly attached to me. They probably wondered if their woven women were going to get more clingy, too.

The Lieutenant asked Goblin, "How did you guys do that?"

One-Eye launched a rambling proclamation of his own natural-born genius—without ever actually telling us anything useful.

Silent made a giant gesture that demanded attention, then signed, "They didn't do it. The Leta women did."

My Leta smiled and nodded.

Oh, boy. A clear facial expression and first evidence that she was getting a handle on what was being said around her, at least in sign.

Candy observed, "I guess it's Croaker's turn to take one for the team."

I got that. I'm the guy who learns languages fast, and I was the guy with the number one, best Leta.

Big bunch of smirks. Comments about how my main squeeze in the Tower might not be so happy. I offered no comebacks. I was obsessing about unseasonal fireflies already.

* * *

The meeting broke up. I put on my physician's hat and started the post-mortem on the Taken who'd been knocked down. Leta stuck with me, watching. Darling didn't. Silent had talked her into backing off. For now.

The Lieutenant watched, too. "She's just a kid."

Yeah. Younger than Darling. *Very* pretty. "Does she look familiar? I feel like I've seen her before."

Clearly, slow and mush-mouthed, Leta said, "Bad. Trouble. Coming."

"Eh?"

Carpet number three, without Whisper aboard, streaked in low above the treetops, lifted its nose suddenly and launched a salvo in a ballistic arc. It then rolled and raced away.

Four items came our way. Three were hardly big enough to make out, but the other one was a huge black barrel—headed straight toward me.

"Oh, shit! Run!" I grabbed Leta's hand and tried to pull her along.

She wouldn't move. She just stared at that barrel.

The Lieutenant hauled ass as fast as his bony legs would pump. He'd seen big black barrels before.

Peripherally, I noted that all the Letas remained in place, staring.

The barrel stopped falling.

It did explode.

Flaming oil sprayed everywhere, to broader effect than would have been the case had the explosion occurred on impact.

Raindrops of fire fell, including onto me. My clothing protected me.

Nobody died, but I stayed busy treating burns well into the night. My Leta stuck with me. After a while, she began helping. And she did quite well.

Goblin was my last patient. He was sullen, but didn't take it out on me. He had a curious observation to share. "None of the Letas got burned." Then, "I think that barrel was meant for the dead Taken, not you."

"Eh?"

"They must not want you getting a close look."

"That makes no sense."

"Not to you. But it doesn't have to make sense to you, does it? It only has to make sense to them."

I went back to the beautiful child Taken. I saw nothing obvious. But I was too exhausted to go on. "I'll finish up with her tomorrow."

* * *

Yet again, I didn't spend my night alone. But this time, Leta didn't make her starvation level demands. All she wanted was to keep warm. I snuggled. I needed some warmth, myself.

* * *

I never had a wife. Sisters, whores, the Lady of my imagination, those were the extent of my experience with women. Darling didn't count. Darling was my daughter by adoption, not a woman. The fallen Taken, though... she wakened in me so many uncommon emotions, and I had no clue as to why.

Yes, she was beautiful. Put a few years on her, and she would physically be the woman I would weave for myself, were I the master of the white threads.

Her passing left me feeling a bit like the gods themselves had robbed me of my chance to meet my soulmate woman.

The analytical side of me was baffled.

How the hell did any of that make any sense? I knew nothing about the girl. My bride? My daughter? That would be nothing but just plain crazy thinking.

Clearly, absolutely, those who had no love for the Company had found themselves a way to mindfuck the Company Annalist.

Leta leaned against me, holding my left arm. She made sounds probably meant to be comforting. She whispered, "Sorrow again. So sad."

I got no chance to ask what that meant. Warning horns screamed. There was a Taken inbound.

This attack was identical to the last. The target was the same.

This time, I focused on the little black balls that weren't the big black barrel. I didn't worry about that. Leta and her sisters would deal with it.

The barrel was a distraction instead of the main course.

What became of the first three balls? I knew nobody had collected them.

The attack wasn't successful. The barrel exploded much higher than before. The fuel inside scattered farther, broke up into smaller drops, and almost completely burned out before it got to the ground. Nobody got hurt.

That convinced me the minor projectiles were what the attacks were actually all about.

* * *

The usual suspects gathered. I was there with my Leta. Everybody had witnessed both attacks, so nobody called crazy on Croaker's paranoid calculation.

I'd hardly gotten started before the Lieutenant called for runners to carry messages.

My Leta now stayed in continuous physical contact while, apparently, being lost inside herself—like she had to have the contact to remain anchored in this world.

A hidden fraction of the Annalist was thrilled. He enjoyed his situation so much that he refused to think about it having to end.

He was almost entirely content to mark time and savor the moment.

Four of the six black balls turned up. Each was the size of a hen's egg. One-Eye, Goblin, and Silent took possession. They studied the things inside the protection of Darling's null and wasted no time concluding that my paranoia was justified.

Each egg contained complex spells meant to enslave anyone who opened it. They rattled when shaken. People would want to find out why.

They couldn't activate inside Darling's null. They could be disarmed there. My Leta found the process fascinating. She told me, "Two Taken are with us."

"Hey, shit!" One-Eye barked. "Your old lady just nailed it, Croaker. That's what these things are! Remote Taking traps."

Goblin and Silent were startled by the notion, but nodded agreement.

Goblin said, "Two of the things are missing. How do we identify their victims?"

I kind of figured that was his problem.

Leta indicated Darling, then made the signs for "walk" and "camp."

I got it. Whoever was infested would react to Darling's null.

Goblin said, "Croaker, your other wife is gonna be *totally* pissed."

Leta touched my sleeve. She wore an expression that said she comprehended what the toad man had said, and she wanted to know what he meant.

I thought about fireflies.

I led Leta to the tent we now shared. I tried to explain that, for years, guys like Goblin and One-Eye kept accusing me of being some kind of self-flagellating lover of the Lady because she'd once held me prisoner.

Leta didn't understand. Maybe most women wouldn't have.

Darling found the two Company Taken before supper. One was a dullard named Jago, and the other a camp follower who called herself Iris. No way could either have become a threat, but One-Eye exorcised them anyway, making as big a show as he could contrive.

* * *

I got up to use the latrine sometime after midnight. We had them now. In fact, we'd had them so long, the pits were nearly full, and I was going to have to have a new set dug. That, however, isn't relevant.

Relevant would be the threads. There had been changes.

Every Leta, including mine, was now connected to a thread that had gone pastel. Only one cluster of white threads remained. That one came down right outside the tent shared by Silent and Darling.

Really? So far, no Leta had gone after Silent. No Leta would have any chance of success. Silent could never see any woman but Darling. Silent would never have any woman but Darling, although he couldn't have that. And he was all right with that.

Bladder eased, I scuttled over to check out the creation of the latest Leta.

"Oh, shit! What the hell?"

This was not another Leta. This thing was male, and he was gorgeous. I thought about rousing Elmo... then I had a thought.

That does happen occasionally.

This thing was being built to target Darling. The something that had blessed us with the Letas now wanted to captivate a young woman in the same way it had captivated so many men.

"Not going to happen," I muttered, adoptive papa making a decision on her behalf with no consideration for Darling's own wishes. I stepped over to Silent's tent. There was moonlight enough that, when I flipped the flap back, I saw his silver-headed short spear right away. I glommed it and went to work cutting white threads. My hand slipped a couple of times. I cut some male Leta, accidentally.

My Leta showed up, looking horrified. "What are you doing?"

"No way this is going to happen. Not to Darling."

The threads kept trying to reconnect. I kept cutting. Had Leta not been there, I might have lopped off a few limbs not yet fully formed.

People came to see what the ruckus was about. Silent was among the earliest. He needed only a moment to figure it out. The look he gave my Leta was so ugly that she retreated a couple of steps.

Have you seen lightning jump from the earth to the sky? It does happen.

A brilliant lilac thread snaked from my Leta's head, wobbled across the night, and settled to earth at the heart of the clearing.

Silent relieved me of his instrument and took over cutting threads and skin.

I heard a hum from my Leta's new thread.

Her eyes rolled up. She collapsed. The threads to the male thing stopped regenerating. The homunculus folded into a bloody kowtow.

The Lieutenant arrived in time to keep Silent from butchering the thing. "That's enough. We owe them a few lives. Croaker. Talk to me."

I talked. He listened. He considered my sad Leta, now stirring, and he told me, "Work a little harder on communicating with your woman."

Really? Yes. Bizarre as that might be, me and my Leta were now a unit in everyone else's eyes.

As were quite a few other pairs. The Lieutenant had a Leta as his other half. One-Eye and Goblin did, too. Candy did. Even Elmo did. And all those Letas were connected to the clearing by one pastel thread.

Darling finally turned up. She considered the situation for some time.

My Leta stumbled over to me. I had to help her stay upright. Her breathing was shallow and erratic. Her heartrate was severely elevated. Once she was in my embrace, I realized she was trembling uncontrollably.

Darling came our way, venom in her eyes. I feared that she meant to smack Leta. And she might have wanted to do that, but she was Darling. However angry she might be, she couldn't hurt anyone as deeply in shock as Leta was.

The Lieutenant barked, "All right, folks, let's break it up. It's over." In a softer voice, he told a couple of grunts to scrape up the male Leta and stash him in the tent that served as the Company sickbay so Croaker could have a look.

Yay. Another post mortem. In the morning.

* * *

That night, Leta clung to me like she would be lost forever if she let go. She was shaky for a long time. But once she managed to rally, she insisted on getting what she wanted, like that was critical to her survival.

There was no body to examine when I when I went to do the post mortem. What the hell? Had somebody stolen it? Had it gotten up and walked away?

I asked questions. Only Leta had answers, seriously opaque, about him having "returned." To where or what, nothing further.

I began to get inquiries: what happened to the Letas last night? Huh?

Apparently, they all got smarter. Most guys with a Leta companion were content to have them be dimwitted alley cats who were ready for boom boom on demand, but were not that excited when their companions tried to engage.

Something else happened overnight. The Letas developed language skills equal to those of my Leta.

That morning I began trying to improve communications with my Leta. And she began sticking even closer. She was afraid of something. She wouldn't say what. But she seemed to think I could protect her.

* * *

Company status? In Limbo. For some Company brothers, because their companions were now smarter than they were, Purgatory.

There we sat, unmoving, gifted with ever more Letas eager to play games by night. Nobody talked about traveling on. Nobody worried about what the Lady and her Taken might do next.

The Letas were not only smarter than most of us, it seemed they could turn off our brains. Hardly anyone among us, man or woman, had what it took to reject a Leta when she zeroed in. Silent. Darling. A handful of others.

No more male Letas were woven.

At some point, though, the fog cleared. I took my hands off my Leta long enough to consider the Company's situation—which had become an adolescent's penile obsession in actuality, and cosmically large.

I could see this as the Company's end of days. Instead of some grand massacre, limbs and guts scattered everywhere on bloody mud, an apocalypse might consume us because we couldn't stop thinking with our dicks. We might go down into the darkness, grinning, because the Letas took us to the far shore of fantasy.

What *were* the Letas, anyway? Not succubi in the traditional sense, but just as definitely, sexual vampires of some kind.

While my brain functioned well enough to produce an original thought, it occurred to me to wonder how long it would be until we saw the natural consequence of such profligate shaggery. Not disease. No. Every Leta remained unfailingly monogamous.

However, by now, there ought to be scores of buns in the oven.

Panic! I was *not* prepared to become a father. And it had been ages since I'd delivered a baby.

Soon, I might be delivering them by the dozen.

I tried to recall how long we'd been stalled. I couldn't. Certainly, long enough for Leta to have had a full cycle. Which she hadn't, insofar as I knew

Oh, damn!

* * *

The Lieutenant asked, "Could this shit be something the Lady has slapped down on us?"

I said, "It isn't something she started. I think, after what happened when the Taken came, she decided to step back and let whatever happens happen. If things go on the way they have, we'll starve to death before we start moving again. If the vampires don't use us up."

"The Lady's just laying back, watching? Really?"

Chill down my spine. "That's my guess." But she would have back-up plans, and Whisper would have her own schemes for when she had the chance to be obnoxious again. She had a history of healing quickly.

The Lieutenant said, "I suggested you work on communicating with your woman."

"I did."

"And the communication is all one way. Right?"

"Pretty much. She wants to know everything about us, but won't give up much about herself."

"Apparently, when one Leta learns something new, the others all know it, too. Even the new ones communicate like yours. Meantime, we have no way to put together what our people have learned about them."

Our discussion, naturally, took place with Letas in touching distance. His wore an amused little smile. As did mine, until...

Her face turned bleak. "The danger has returned." She pointed. "There. In the woods."

The Lieutenant told me, "Your other wife, she's just laying back and watching, huh?"

My Leta said, "It is the one called Whisper. She is not alone."

The Lieutenant's Leta said, "There are four. Two have been watching for days."

The Lieutenant grumbled, "That would have been nice to know before now."

My Leta said, "Indeed. But we have not been looking outward."

His Leta said, "Now we are."

The Lieutenant and I exchanged looks and shrugs.

An indigo thread wriggled up from the heart of the clearing. It was thicker than any I'd seen before. It stretched in the direction my Leta had indicated.

The Letas all stopped moving. They faced in that direction. Their mates, although confused, stuck with them. I muttered something about how well-domesticated we had become.

That earned me a startled frown from my Leta. Then she said, "They are not speaking your language."

"Uhm?" At least four languages were used in our camp. "You can eavesdrop on them?"

Leta did not answer me.

I said, "There are a lot of languages out there." I did not recall which was Whisper's milk tongue. "I am able to understand many of them."

"You cannot hear them."

I think she meant that in the sense of "unable" rather than "not allowed."

The Lieutenant said, "Here's an ugly idea. If they've just been watching, it's because they're trying to figure out what's up with all the look-alike women. If I was Whisper, I'd try to catch one."

My Leta made a little grunting noise.

Letas everywhere began to move, leading their partners, the Lieutenant and I, too. Every couple headed into a tent.

* * *

Leta was brushing the tangles out of her hair. She said, "Thank you, Croaker." First time she ever addressed me by name. Turned me a little wary.

She sensed that. She smiled. "I cannot hurt you. I love you. I cannot do anything else. That is how I was made."

Something was up for sure.

Finished dressing, we left our tent. Everywhere, couples were coming out into the afternoon sunlight. Leta said, "They are waiting for night. But we are waiting for night, too. And now we are prepared."

The people in the woods would be prepared, too. They would've seen the surge into the tents, and the uniform re-emergence. Whisper sometimes let emotion make her do dumb stuff, but she wasn't stupid. She would understand that something significant had happened.

I mean, *I* figured it had. I just didn't know *what*.

Leta slid in under my arm. "Now we wait." Then, a bit later, "We could always kill some time by…"

My dream girl.

* * *

Night fell. The litany is as old as time. Darkness always comes.

The things out there, although we knew they were there, and knew they meant us no good, still took us by surprise.

The clowder of lovely lovers returned the favor.

Once true night clabbered, before a nail clipping of a moon rose, shit happened.

That's the best I can report. I witnessed only scattered incidents. I wasn't a direct participant, and I wasn't a target.

Why would the Taken not focus on me?

Right.

Anyway, some kind of shadowy commandos got into our camp, and were seen seldom, usually only as a dark flicker in the corner of the eye. There were apparently just two, but they caused a lot of casualties—but only where there were no Letas. Letas responded to their proximity with blasts of blinding light. We found no bodies later, but I heard the occasional cry of pain.

The raid lasted twenty minutes. Nobody died. That seemed rather odd. Then, as the raid faded, something big happened out in the woods.

Meantime, my Leta clung to me so resolutely that I expected to find bruises on my arm come daylight—assuming I lived to see the big eye come up again. Leta never stopped murmuring about how much she loved me and that she had to protect me from the evil that was determined to consume me.

Every man I talked to afterward, every man paired with a Leta, reported the same experience.

Cynical me, having seen that fat indigo rope probe the woods, I expected some serious thunder. Any buried power that could create fully functional women woven of mystical yarn ought to be able to spank a Taken or two. Unless building sex-hungry homunculi was the power's only talent.

Then whatever it was *did* bring the thunder. Literally. Without any lightning. Without any visible light at all. The rumble rolled across the world. The earth shook. I fell down.

As I regained my feet, my Leta kissed me hard on the mouth. Once again, she told me that she loved me, then she headed for the woods.

All the Letas did that, their partners trailing behind them. I stumbled after my Leta, tripping every few steps. It was *really* dark. The only light was a barely perceptible pale glow streaming from the women.

Leaves and small chunks of tree rained down, evidently having been hurled into the air by the boom. Most of the detritus was determined to slide down the back of my neck.

The other men had the trouble I had with the footing, too. The ladies had no problem. But they had trouble keeping their feet on the ground, sometimes.

The Letas entered the woods, and the uproar in the camp ended abruptly.

The thunder spoke again. The earth shook again. I fell down again.

And then there was light. Massive light, as thousands of threads arched up out of the woods to connect with the clearing, twisting around the indigo rope. The rope was now thicker than my arm.

Despite the ringing in my ears, I heard screaming from up ahead.

I tried to run. The Letas...!

And down I went, leading with my schnoz. Then I was up again and, bleeding lightly, advancing a tad more carefully.

* * *

I was one of the first men to arrive on scene.

The threads of light were almost blinding. But I made out two craters, ten feet deep and fifteen feet across. The trees and brush that were once there no longer existed. Around the craters were tangles of tree remnants, all fallen outward, and all thoroughly shredded. Part of a Taken's carpet dangled from a leafless, drunken-leaning grandfather of an oak well beyond the craters. There was no other sign of the people who'd been scheming here minutes ago.

Was it over? Were they all done?

No, though confirmation of that would be a while coming.

I considered the scene without conscious deliberation. My thoughts focused on my Leta.

There were Letas everywhere, all looking alike, but I had no trouble singling out mine.

Something weird had begun to happen.

Most of the Letas were losing definition. Some of the newbies were already transparent.

The thing under the clearing must be taking them back.

Had it achieved its purpose? How could that be? What could that have been, if that was the case?

From where the Annalist stood, nothing that had happened since we came to the clearing made much sense. However, the Annalist was whom it had happened to, not who'd made it happen.

Both the divine and the demonic mind necessarily must be alien to that of a self-absorbed, mortal, upright-walking ape.

I collected my Leta. "Are you all right?" Her breathing was fast and shallow, like a panting hound.

"Yes. I will be fine after all."

"Meaning?"

"Meaning I will not have to leave you."

That startled me. Random fears rattled off the walls of my skull. Was I stuck here for the rest of my days? Those might not be too many. The Lady knew where to find me now.

Leta latched onto my arm. She said, "Those entities escaped, all four of them. The Whisper one was hurt again."

Entities? I turned so I could look into Leta's eyes. "Are you still you?" She seemed somehow changed.

Almost flirtatiously, she told me, "I'm more me now than I ever was before."

A glance around. There were no more than twenty Letas in sight. Most of those had turned transparent. "What's happening?"

She considered briefly. "It's not important. You don't need to know."

"Damnit...!"

"All right. They were harvesters. The harvest is complete now. I am here now. I am free now. They are no longer needed. Let's go back to our tent and do what we do best."

We did, with me as Leta's zombie attendant. We slept, me like the dead. Then I awakened as the most hated man in the Company. I wakened as the only man who still had a Leta.

I enjoyed a tough day, patching up folks who'd had a hard night last night, most of them in bad need of an attitude adjustment.

I finally had enough. I told Candy, "I didn't do it! You want to piss and moan, take it up with that something that's buried out there!"

* * *

Sometimes there's no dramatic unity. Sometimes truth just won't show its real face, be it ugly or benign. Sometimes there's no understanding the truth, even if it stands there holding up a sign. And sometimes you just won't look it in the eye.

The disgruntlement with Croaker faded once it became apparent that the clearing no longer held us in thrall.

We were free to go.

And my Leta was free to come with me.

* * *

The Company started moving.

Four days passed. Then Darling caught me while Leta was off dealing with the physical consequences of having become corporeal. She signed, "You do know your current woman is not quite the one who first came to you?"

I admitted, "Actually, I do. But…"

She signed, "You've helped something ancient escape imprisonment."

I snapped, "I know. What I don't know is whether that's going to be a problem. Is Leta another Lady? Or, worse, another Dominator?" That olden times sorcerer-king had been the torment of the world in his day. He made the Lady seem almost benevolent. "Or maybe she's the opposite? Maybe she was imprisoned by somebody like the Dominator."

Darling signed, "I think she might be somebody someone like the Dominator wanted to suffer forever. Maybe someone who bruised his tender feelings."

That could be. Some of the ugliest, most powerful, most totally narcissistic people ever to exist could become unbelievably cruel over the least of slights from someone who failed to appreciate them at least as much as they appreciated themselves.

Our discussion ended. Leta was back. She eyed us speculatively.

I reckoned, ere long, for good or ill, we would meet the true Leta.

* * *

Another night. Another need to get up and take a leak. Been happening way too much lately. When I stumbled back from handling my business, I spied a barely detectable silver thread rising from Leta's forehead and passing through the canvas roof of our tent.

I ducked back outside. The thread was hard to make out, but I caught it, arcing up and away, stretching back the way we'd come.

"Shit!" Leta hadn't gotten away after all. She'd just gotten farther than any of her sisters.

I plunged inside and shook Leta. "Baby! Wake up! Come on! You've got to wake up and fight!"

She opened her eyes halfway, gave me a languid smile. In a voice barely above a whisper, she said, "I loved you so much. I tried… but I was not strong enough."

Her eyes closed. She said nothing more. I got no further response from her.

Not the manly thing to do, but I teared up. I took several gods' names in vain. I'd become attached to that woman, more than I'd suspected.

Then, through the tears, I spied what looked like a firefly hovering outside the entrance to our tent.

* * * * *

Glen Cook Bio

Glen Cook is the perpetrator of several story collections and more than 50 fantasy and SF novels. He is best known for his Black Company series, which has been continuously in print, in more than a dozen languages, for more than 30 years. Sometimes credited with being the godfather of the Grimdark sub-genre, he has been both Guest of Honor and Special Guest at The World Fantasy Convention. His most recent books are *Port of Shadows* for Tor and *The Best of Glen Cook* from Nightshade.

Glen was born in New York City in 1944, grew up in Northern California, served as Walt Disney's gopher at the 1960 Winter Olympics, joined the Navy after high school, then went to work for General Motors after discharge. Most of his earlier novels were written on the assembly line. In 1969 and 1970, he attended the Clarion Writers' Workshop, and it was there that he met his wife of 50 years, Carol Ann Fritz. He (and she) have three sons. The eldest, Christian, commands 2nd Battalion, 7th Cavalry (in the footsteps of G. A. Custer & G. S. Patton.) Second son Michael is an architect specializing in airport renovations. Third son Justin is just wrapping up his doctorate in music. Glen has a whole herd of grandchildren, almost all of them female. He hopes to live long enough to finish the thirty-some novels still racketing around inside his head.

* * * * *

About the Editors

Rob Howell Biography

Rob Howell is the publisher of New Mythology Press, the fantasy imprint of Chris Kennedy Publishing (chriskennedypublishing.com), a founder of the Eldros Legacy fantasy setting (eldroslegacy.com), and an author in the Four Horsemen Universe (mercenaryguild.org). He writes primarily epic fantasy, space opera, military science fiction, and alternate history.

He's a reformed medieval academic, a former IT professional, and a retired soda jerk.

His parents discovered quickly that books were the only way to keep Rob quiet. He latched onto the Hardy Boys series first, and then anything he could reach. Without books, it's unlikely all three would have survived.

You can find him online at:

- Website: robhowell.org
- Amazon Author Page: amazon.com/-/e/B00X95LBB0
- His Blog: robhowell.org/blog

* * *

Chris Kennedy Biography

A Webster Award winner and three-time Dragon Award finalist, Chris Kennedy is a Science Fiction/Fantasy author, speaker, and small-press publisher who has written over 30 books and published more than 200 others. Get his free book, "Shattered Crucible," at his website, chriskennedypublishing.com.

Called "fantastic" and "a great speaker," he has coached hundreds of beginning authors and budding novelists on how to self-publish their stories at a variety of conferences, conventions, and writing guild presentations. He is the author of the award-winning #1 bestseller, "Self-Publishing for Profit: How to Get Your Book Out of Your Head and Into the Stores."

Chris lives in Coinjock, North Carolina, with his wife, and is the holder of a doctorate in educational leadership and master's degrees in both business and public administration. Follow Chris on Facebook at facebook.com/ckpublishing/.

* * * * *

Excerpt from Khyven the Unkillable

Book One of Legacy of Shadows, An Eldros Legacy Novel

Todd Fahnestock

Available from New Mythology Press
eBook, Hardcover, and Paperback

Excerpt from *Khyven the Unkillable*:

Two knights threw open the door of the tavern, and the scent of last night's rain blew in with them. Khyven heard their boots thump on the rough planks, heard the creak of leather and clink of chainmail as they shifted. He sat with his back to them, but he didn't need to see them to know where they were.

The room went silent. This dockside drinking hole didn't see knights very often, and their appearance had rendered the entire place speechless. That was respect. That was what being a knight meant in the kingdom of Usara.

They paused just inside the threshold, perhaps hoping to spook the fearful, but Khyven wasn't a jumper. He had more in common with the newcomers than those who fled from them.

Ayla, the pretty barmaid sitting across from him, looked past Khyven, her eyes wide. She had been a lively conversationalist a moment ago and he'd been daydreaming about what it would be like to kiss those lips.

Now she looked like an alley cat who'd spotted an alley dog. Reflexively, she stood up, the wooden stool scraping loudly on the floor. She froze, perhaps realizing belatedly that when the powerful—the predators—were in the room, it was best not to draw attention to yourself.

Khyven heard the metallic rustle of the fighters' chain mail and Ayla's face drained of color. He envisioned the alley dogs turning at the sound, focusing on her.

She needn't have worried. They weren't here for her or any other patron of the Mariner's Rest. They were here for Khyven.

He had killed a man in the Night Ring two days ago, and not just any man—a duke's son. The entitled whelp had actually been a talented swordsman, but his ambition had outstripped his skill. And the Night Ring was an unforgiving place to discover such a weakness.

After Khyven had run the boy through, Duke Bericourt had sworn revenge. No doubt he had been waiting for an opportunity to find Khyven alone, vulnerable, to send in his butcher knights.

Men like these, sent to enforce a lord's will or show his displeasure, were called butcher knights. Usually of the lowest caste—Knights of the Steel—butcher knights didn't chase glory on the battlefield or renown in the Night Ring. They were sent to do bloody, back-alley work at their lord's bidding.

Khyven took a deep breath of the smoky air, sipped from the glass of Triadan whiskey, and enjoyed the fading burn down his throat.

The booted feet thumped to a stop next to his table.

"Khyven the Unkillable?" One of the men spoke, using Khyven's ringer name—the flamboyant moniker the crowd had laid upon him.

Khyven glanced over his shoulder. Indeed. He had guessed right. The pair were Knights of the Steel.

There were three castes of knights in Usara: Knights of the Sun, Knights of the Dark, and Knights of the Steel, which was the lowest caste and the only one available to most lords. The pair wore chainmail shirts instead of full plate, conical steel caps with nose guards instead of full helms, and leather greaves and bracers.

As predicted, they wore Duke Bericourt's crest on their left shoulders.

There was a code of honor among knights—even butcher knights. Except in cases of war, civility was required before gutting a man, especially when there were onlookers. Often a knight would give a flowery speech—including the offense he'd been sent to address—before drawing weapons. This was enough to justify murder.

Sometimes there was no flowery speech, but a knight would always at least say their victim's name. If the victim acknowledged their name, that was all it took to bring out the blades.

Khyven didn't give them the satisfaction. He took another sip of his whiskey and said nothing.

"Did you hear me?" the knight demanded, his hand touching his sword hilt.

If Khyven had been a normal ringer—a caged slave thrown into the Night Ring to slay or be slain for the sport of the crowd—these men would probably have forgone their code of honor and drawn their swords already.

But Khyven wasn't just any ringer. He was the Champion of the Night Ring, and the king had afforded him special privileges because of that fact, like a room at the palace. Khyven had survived forty-eight bouts, the longest string of victories since...

Well, since Vex the Victorious had claimed fifty, won a knighthood and become the king's personal bodyguard.

Steel scraped on steel, bringing Khyven back to the present. The second knight drew his dagger and placed it against Khyven's throat.

Ayla gasped and backed away.

"You think you're protected," the second knight growled in Khyven's ear. "You're not."

Of course, if Khyven didn't acknowledge his name, there were other ways for the butcher knights to start the fight. If Khyven attacked them, for example, they could retaliate. The powerful could always push a victim into a corner when they needed to. That's what the powerful did. Khyven had learned that long ago.

That was why, when Khyven had won his fortieth bout and his freedom from the Night Ring, he'd continued fighting, risking his life in every bloody bout. For the prize at the end of ten more bouts. For the power that would come with it.

When Khyven won his fiftieth bout, he would be elevated to the knighthood, just like Vex the Victorious. And no one would look at him as a victim again.

The blade broke the skin, just barely, and a bead of blood trickled down Khyven's neck. His pulse quickened. The familiar euphoria filled him, the rush of pleasure that came with the threat of death.

The euphoria brought vision, and Khyven saw with new eyes, his battle eyes. He saw his foe's strengths and weaknesses as a swirling, blue-colored wind.

"You are Khyven the Unkillable," the man breathed in his ear. Khyven chuckled.

The second knight's face turned red. He slashed—

But Khyven was already moving.

* * * * *

Get *Khyven the Unkillable* soon on Amazon

Find out more about Todd Fahnestock and the *Eldros Legacy* at: chriskennedypublishing.com.

* * * * *

Excerpt from A Reluctant Druid

Book One of The Milesian Accords

———————————

Jon R. Osborne

Now Available from New Mythology Press

eBook, Paperback, and Audio

Excerpt from *A Reluctant Druid*:

"**D**on't crank on it; you'll strip it."

Liam paused from trying to loosen the stubborn bolt holding the oil filter housing on his Yamaha motorcycle, looking for the source of the unsolicited advice. The voice was gruff, with an accent and cadence that made Liam think of the Swedish Chef from the Muppets. The garage door was open for air circulation, and two figures were standing in the driveway, illuminated by the setting sun. As they approached and stepped into the shadows of the house, Liam could see they were Pixel and a short, stout man with a graying beard that would do ZZ Top proud. The breeze blowing into the garage carried a hint of flowers.

Liam experienced a moment of double vision as he looked at the pair. Pixel's eyes took on the violet glow he thought he'd seen before, while her companion lost six inches in height, until he was only as tall as Pixel. What the short man lacked in height, he made up for in physique; he was built like a fireplug. He was packed into blue jeans and a biker's leather jacket, and goggles were perched over the bandana covering his salt and pepper hair. Leather biker boots crunched the gravel as he walked toward the garage. Pixel followed him, having traded her workout clothes for black jeans and a pink t-shirt that left her midriff exposed. A pair of sunglasses dangled from the neckline of her t-shirt.

"He's seeing through the glamour," the short, bearded man grumbled to Pixel, his bushy eyebrows furrowing.

"Well duh. We're on his home turf, and this is his place of power" Pixel replied nonchalantly. "He was pushing back against my glamour yesterday, and I'm not adding two hands to my height."

Liam set down the socket wrench and ran through the mental inventory of items in the garage that were weapons or could be used as them. The back half of the garage was a workshop, which included the results of his dabbling with blacksmithing and sword-crafting, so the list was considerable. But the most suitable were also the farthest away.

"Can I help you?" Liam stood and brushed off his jeans; a crowbar was three steps away. Where had they come from? Liam hadn't heard a car or motorcycle outside, and the house was a mile and a half outside of town.

"Ja, you can." The stout man stopped at the threshold of the garage. His steel-gray eyes flicked from Liam to the workbench and back. He held his hands out, palms down. The hands were larger than his and weren't strangers to hard work and possibly violence. "And there's no need to be unhospitable; we come as friends. My name is Einar, and you've already met Pixel."

"Hi, Liam." Pixel was as bubbly as yesterday. While she didn't seem to be making the same connection as Einar regarding the workbench, her eyes darted about the cluttered garage and the dim workshop behind it. "Wow, you have a lot of junk."

"What's this about?" Liam sidled a half step toward the workbench, regretting he hadn't kept up on his martial arts. He had three brown belts, a year of kendo, and some miscellaneous weapons training scattered over two decades but not much experience in the way of real fighting. He could probably hold his own in a brawl as long as his opponent didn't have serious skills. He suspected Einar was more than a Friday night brawler in the local watering hole. "Is she your daughter?"

Einar turned to the purple-haired girl, his caterpillar-like eyebrows gathering. "What did you do?"

"What? I only asked him a few questions and checked him out," Pixel protested, her hands going to her hips as she squared off with Einar. "It's not as if I tried to jump his bones right there in the store or something."

"Look mister, if you think something untoward happened between me and your daughter –" Liam began.

"She's not my pocking daughter, and I don't give a troll's ass if you diddled her," Einar interrupted, his accent thickening with his agitation. He took a deep breath, his barrel chest heaving. "Now, will you hear me out without you trying to brain me with that tire iron you've been eyeing?"

"You said diddle." Pixel giggled.

"Can you be serious for five minutes, you pocking faerie?" Einar glowered, his leather jacket creaking as he crossed his arms.

"Remember 'dwarf,' you're here as an 'advisor.'" Pixel included air quotes with the last word, her eyes turning magenta. "The Nine Realms are only involved out of politeness."

"Politeness! If you pocking Tuatha and Tylwyth Teg hadn't folded up when the Milesians came at you, maybe we wouldn't be here to begin with!" Spittle accompanied Einar's protest. "Tylwyth? More like Toothless!"

"Like your jarls didn't roll over and show their bellies when the Avramites showed up with their One God and their gold!" Pixel rose up on her toes. "Your people took their god and took their gold and then attacked our ancestral lands!"

"Guys!" Liam had stepped over to the workbench but hadn't picked up the crowbar. "Are you playing one of those live-action role playing games or something? Because if you are, I'm calling my garage out of bounds. Take your LARP somewhere else."

"We've come a long way to speak to you," Einar replied, looking away from Pixel. "I'm from Asgard."

"Asgard? You mean like Thor and Odin? What kind of game are you playing?" Liam hadn't moved from the workbench, but he'd mapped in his mind the steps he'd need to take to reach a stout pole which would serve as a staff while he back-pedaled to his workshop, where a half-dozen half-finished sword prototypes rested. From where he stood, though, he didn't feel as threatened. He knew a bit about gamers because there were a fair number of them among the pagan community, and he'd absorbed bits and pieces of it. Maybe someone had pointed Liam out to Pixel as research about druids for one of these games—an over-enthusiastic player who wanted to more convincingly roleplay one.

"Gods I hate those pocking things," Einar grumbled, rubbing his forehead while Pixel stifled another giggle. "Look, can we sit down and talk to you? This is much more serious than some pocking games you folk play with your costumes and your toy weapons."

"This isn't a game, and we aren't hippies with New Age books and a need for self-validation." Pixel added. Her eyes had faded to a lavender color. "Liam, we need your help."

* * * * *

Get "*A Reluctant Druid*" at amazon.com/dp/B07716V2RN.

Find out more about Jon R. Osborne and "A Reluctant Druid" at: chriskennedypublishing.com/imprints-authors/jon-r-osborne/

* * * * *